Rachel Hore worked in London publishing for many years before moving with her family to Norwich, where she taught publishing and creative writing at the University of East Anglia before becoming a full-time writer. She is married to the writer D. J. Taylor and they have three sons.

Praise for

RACHEL HORE

'Compelling, engrossing and moving'
Santa Montefiore

'A wonderfully moving tale of love and loss,
hope and eventual reconciliation'
Barbara Erskine

'An emotive and thought-provoking read'
Rosanna Ley

'A story that stirs the deepest emotions'
Woman & Home

'A poignant story, rich in period detail'
Sunday Mirror

'Her women are brave and good, and you
desperately want them to win'
Daily Mail

By the same author:

RACHEL HORE

A Place of Secrets

**SIMON &
SCHUSTER**

London · New York · Sydney · Toronto · New Delhi

First published in Great Britain by Simon & Schuster UK Ltd, 2010
This paperback edition published 2024

1 3 5 7 9 10 8 6 4 2

Simon & Schuster UK Ltd
1st Floor
222 Gray's Inn Road
London WC1X 8HB

Simon & Schuster: Celebrating 100 Years of Publishing in 2024

Simon & Schuster Australia, Sydney
Simon & Schuster India, New Delhi

www.simonandschuster.co.uk
www.simonandschuster.com.au
www.simonandschuster.co.in

A CIP catalogue record for this book
is available from the British Library

Paperback ISBN: 978-1-3985-3314-1
eBook ISBN: 978-1-84983-186-4

Typeset in Palatino by Hewer Text UK Ltd
Printed and Bound in the UK using 100% Renewable
Electricity at CPI Group (UK) Ltd

MIX
Paper | Supporting
responsible forestry
FSC
www.fsc.org
FSC® C171272

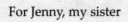
For Jenny, my sister

Look at the stars! Look, look up at the skies!
O look at all the fire-folk sitting in the air!
The bright boroughs, the circle citadels there!

'The Starlight Night'
by Gerald Manley Hopkins

If you are cheerful, and wish to remain so, leave the study of astronomy alone. Of all the sciences it alone deserves the character of the terrible . . . if on the other hand, you are restless and anxious about the future, study astronomy at once. Your troubles will be reduced amazingly. But your study will reduce them in a singular way, by reducing the importance of everything. So that the science is still terrible, even as a panacea . . . It is better – far better – for men to forget the universe than to bear it clearly in mind.

Two on a Tower by Thomas Hardy

The night before it all begins, Jude has the dream again.

She is stumbling through a dark forest, lost and crying for her mother. She always wakes before the end so she never knows whether she finds her, but it's very vivid. She feels the loamy earth, hears twigs crack under her feet and smells the rich woody fragrances that are always strongest at night, when the trees are breathing. It's chilly. Brambles catch at her hair. And the panic, the despair, they're real enough as she claws her way to consciousness; she scrabbles for the light switch and lies waiting for her sobbing breaths and racing heart to slow.

This is the nightmare she had when she was a child. What's brought it back now, she cannot say. She passed many terrible nights after losing Mark, but was never haunted by this particular dream. Just as she thinks she's regaining control of her life it scorns her feeble attempts and pulls her back into powerless infancy.

She once asked a school friend, who had an interest in dreams, what it could mean.

'A *dense* forest, was it? Mmm.' Sophie reached for a book from her shelf, flipped the pages till she found what she wanted and read out, ' "Loss in trade, unhappy home influences and quarrels among families." Ring any bells?' She looked at Jude hopefully.

'That sounds like a horoscope in a magazine,' Jude said. 'You can take it any number of ways. One, I was short-changed in the chemist today, and, two, my family is always bickering, like any other.'

'They are weird, though, your family,' Sophie said, closing the book.

'No weirder than yours,' Jude retorted.

But in the weeks that follow the return of her dream, she comes to realize that Sophie had a point.

Part I

Chapter 1

June 2008

How tiny and random are the events that shape our destiny.

By the time she left for the office the next morning, Jude had almost forgotten her dream. Waiting for the train at Greenwich station, the sudden wail of a toddler brought back fragments of her distress, but by the time she reached Bond Street these too were displaced by other, more mundane worries. She had no sense that something important was about to happen, something that on the face of it was quite insignificant.

It was Friday lunchtime in the Books and Manuscripts department of Beecham's Auctioneers in Mayfair. She'd been sitting at her computer screen all morning, cataloguing rare first editions of eighteenth-century poets for a forthcoming sale. A painstaking job, it meant describing the contents of each slim volume, noting its condition and recording any quirks or flourishes – a handwritten dedication, say, or scribbled annotations – that might tickle the interest of potential buyers. Annoying then, when anyone broke her concentration.

'Jude.' Inigo, who inhabited the next desk in their open-plan office, came over clasping a mess of paper festooned with multicoloured sticky-backed notes. 'Proofs of the September catalogue. Where do you want them?'

'Oh, thanks,' she murmured. 'Give 'em here.' She dumped the pile on the already overflowing tray beside her computer, then started to type another sentence. Inigo didn't take the hint.

'I really do think you should look at the Bloomsbury pages again,' he said in his most pompous tone. 'I jotted down a couple of points, if you'd like to . . . ?'

'Inigo –' she said, trying and failing to frame a polite way of saying 'mind your own business'. The Bloomsbury Group first editions were her responsibility and she didn't report to him in any way on them or on anything else. That never stopped him from interfering. 'Can we talk this afternoon? I *must* finish this.'

Inigo nodded and glided back to his desk where he started to get ready to go out. Jude couldn't stop herself watching, fascinated, as he slid his tweed jacket on over the matching waistcoat, tucked his fountain pen into the breast pocket, straightened his silk cravat and ran smoothing fingers across his schoolboy fair hair. It was a kind of ritual.

'Going somewhere important, Inigo?' she remarked.

Looking pleased that she'd asked, he whispered, 'I'm meeting Lord Madingsfield at Chez Gerard,' and tapped the side of his nose to indicate confidential business.

'Lord Madingsfield *again*?' she said, surprised. 'Well, have fun.' She turned back to her keyboard. Inigo had been toadying up to this wealthy collector for months now. In her private opinion the wily old aristocrat was stringing him along.

'We're in quite a delicate stage of negotiation, actually,' Inigo said and pursed his cherubic lips, as though the idea of having fun was beneath him.

Jude and Suri, the trainee cataloguer who sat at the desk opposite, exchanged mock-impressed glances. Suri looked back quickly at her work, but Jude could see her shoulders quivering with suppressed mirth. Inigo took everything in life too seriously, but most of all, his place in it. He locked the drawers of his desk, then, grasping his hand-tooled leather briefcase, he departed, pressing the release button of the door to the lobby with his usual little flourish. Through the glass, the women saw him jab at the lift button several times, his dapper figure fussy as a dog with a flea. Only when the lift arrived and swallowed him up did they give way to their laughter.

'I wonder what he'd say if he saw a video of himself,' Suri managed to say between giggles. She stood up to go out herself, adjusting the clasp in her glossy black hair and swinging her handbag onto her shoulder.

'He'd probably fall in love, poor boy,' Jude said as she typed. 'Enjoy your lunch.'

'Can I get you anything?' Suri said. 'I'm going past Clooney's if you want a sandwich.'

'Thanks, but I'll be OK,' replied Jude, smiling at her. 'I'll break the back of this copy, then maybe slip out myself.' When Suri had gone, she took a mouthful of mineral water from a bottle hidden under the desk. Lunch must be forgone. There was too much to do. Anyway, the waistband of her new trouser suit was too tight and she couldn't risk the buttons popping off at dinner tonight.

She picked up a musty volume from one pile, studied it quickly and laid it down on another. *Full calf* – she wrote – *rebacked with raised bands. Blind tooling to boards. A good clean copy of an important contemporary work.*

It was at that moment that the Hand of Destiny struck.

The phone on Inigo's desk began to shrill, piercing her concentration. Insistent, self-important, like its owner. She stared at it, willing it to stop. The caller would probably be a time-waster: a quavery old dear hoping to make a mint out of her dog-eared Agatha Christie collection, or a know-it-all antiquarian bookseller demanding a personal audience. But it would ring eight times, then transfer to Suri's phone and ring another eight before going to message ... Snatching up her own phone she pressed a button.

'Books and Manuscripts. Hello?'

'Inigo Selbourne, please,' came a plummy male voice.

'I'm afraid he's at lunch,' Jude said, and in case the caller assumed she was Inigo's secretary, which happened dispiritingly often, she added, 'I'm Jude Gower, another valuer. Can I give him a message?'

'If you would. My name's Wickham. I'm telephoning from Starbrough Hall in Norfolk.'

Jude felt a frisson of interest. Norfolk was home turf. Where on earth was Starbrough Hall, though? She leaned closer into the phone.

'I've a collection of eighteenth-century books I want him to look at,' Mr Wickham went on. 'I've been assured by a friend that they're likely to have significant value.'

Jude flipped to a fresh page on her notepad and wrote 'Starbrough Hall' at the top in neat capitals, then stared at the words, trying to understand why they tugged at her memory. She didn't think she'd ever been to Starbrough Hall, but for some reason a picture of her grandmother rose in her mind.

'Does Inigo have your number, Mr Wickham?'

'No.' When he recited it the local code was familiar. The same as her sister's, in fact. That was it. Starbrough Hall was part of the big estate where Gran had lived as a child. She wrote down the phone number and doodled a jagged star shape round it.

If she finished the call and passed the message on to Inigo, she'd have done her job. But the name Starbrough meant something to her, and she was intrigued. On the other hand, the material he wanted to sell might prove of little interest to Beecham's. 'Mr

Wickham,' she asked, 'what sort of books are they? It's only that the eighteenth century is my particular period.'

'Is it?' Wickham said. 'Well perhaps I should be dealing with you instead of Mr Selbourne.'

She opened her mouth to say that Inigo was perfectly competent to deal with the collection, and found she didn't want to. It was a conundrum. Robert Wickham had asked specifically for Inigo. Jude would be furious if Inigo took work from her – and Suri told her that he had done that once despite her name being recommended by another client. Still, she didn't want to sink to his level. It was ridiculous really, that they played this constant game of comeuppance. The head of department, Klaus Vanderbilt, was always banging on about how they should work together to wrest business from the other big auction houses. In fact she had a lot of respect for Inigo's professional abilities; it was his constant pushiness that irritated her. She could never quite relax with him in the office.

'Do you know Inigo Selbourne?' she asked Robert Wickham. 'I mean, was he recommended to you?'

'No, never heard of the man until a moment ago. Your switchboard suggested him.'

So she wasn't muscling in on something that was rightly Inigo's.

'Well in that case,' she told Wickham, with a shameful sense of triumph, 'I'll deal with the matter, if you like.'

'I'm happy with that. The collection belonged to an ancestor of mine, Anthony Wickham. He was something of an amateur stargazer, and most of the books relate to his hobby. I'd like you to value them with a view to possible placement for sale.'

'An astronomer, was he? That's interesting.' Jude was scribbling down details. Scientific tomes, particularly from the eighteenth century – the Age of Discovery – were a lively area at the moment. She could think of two or three dealers who would want to know more.

'There are several first editions among them, so I'm told. And I should mention the manuscripts,' Wickham went on. 'His charts and observation records. Can't make head or tail of them myself. My mother is more familiar with the material. Anyway, I expect you'll be able to tell straight away once you're down here.'

'How many books are we talking about? I don't suppose there's any chance you could bring them to the office?' she asked.

'Oh heavens, no. There are a couple of hundred or more. And the papers, well they're very delicate. Look, if it's a nuisance, I can always call Sotheby's. I was thinking of doing so anyway. It's just that my friend said to try you first.'

'No, don't worry, I'll come down,' she said hastily. 'I thought it worth asking, that's all.'

'We have some of his instruments, as well. Bits of telescope. And a whatnot . . . One of those spherical models of the solar system.'

'An orrery, you mean?' This whole thing was beginning to sound worth a journey. She shuffled books and papers with her free hand, looking for her desk diary.

'Orrery. That's it,' Robert Wickham continued. 'Shows the planets going round the sun. So you'd be prepared to make a visit?'

'Of course,' she replied. She caught sight of the diary in her in tray, under the mess of proofs Inigo had left. 'When would suit you?' She turned the pages. Could she get away next week? If Wickham was threatening to show other auction houses as well, she needed to be ahead of the game.

'I'm away now for a few days,' he said, 'so it'll have to be after that.' They agreed that she would visit Starbrough Hall on Friday, in a week's time. 'You'll be driving, will you? I'll email directions. It's too complicated for the phone. The nearest place of any size is Holt. And you can stay overnight if you like. Plenty of room here and my mother and I would be delighted to entertain you. My wife will be away with the children, so you'll have some peace and quiet.'

'That's very kind. I probably won't need to stay,' Jude said. 'I've got family in the area, you see.' She hadn't been home to Norfolk for ages. It would be a good opportunity. Perhaps her boyfriend, Caspar, would come, too.

After she put down the phone she prowled the department, unsettled. The Starbrough Hall collection was important, she was absolutely sure, though she couldn't put her finger on why she felt this. And if it was important and she could secure it for Beecham's it would look good. And looking good was important right now, because Klaus Vanderbilt was approaching retirement age and Beecham's would need a new head of department.

She was mulling over, as she often did, what her own chances of promotion were against Inigo's, when her eye fell on her notepad and the words 'Starbrough Hall'.

She still couldn't visualize the place. Going across to the department's reference shelves she extracted an outsize volume entitled *Great Houses of East Anglia* and laid it on Inigo's desk. When she turned to 'S' she found a grainy black and white photograph. Starbrough Hall was a graceful, if stark-looking Palladian villa with a gravel forecourt and a great featureless expanse of lawn. 'Two miles from the village of Starbrough. Built 1720,' said the short text, 'by Edward Wickham Esq. on the burned-out ruins of the old manor house of Starbrough.' Starbrough. That was very near Claire. She had certainly driven through Starbrough village at some point; she remembered the outsize church, a green with a pretty village sign and a bench girdling a mountainous oak tree. Gran's father had been gamekeeper on the Starbrough estate, she believed, but she didn't know where they'd lived.

She sat musing for a moment in the empty office, then reached for the phone to ring Gran.

The old lady drowsed in the afternoons now, especially when the sun played across the floor of her living room, filling it with warmth and flickering light. It being the last Friday in June, the coastal village of Blakeney was busy with holidaymakers, but if she removed her hearing aid the sounds of people and boat trailers passing her window, which looked out on the little Norfolk harbour, subsided to a soothing background murmur. In her drowsy state, pictures of the past seemed to dance across her eyelids. Half-deaf she might be now, but long-ago voices, skirls of happy laughter, bubbled up in her memory as fresh as spring water.

She was remembering being a child again, little Jessie, playing hide and seek at the edge of the forest. She'd been good at this game, could swarm up a tree in an instant and curl up in the crook of a branch, small and still as a little brown bird, so that the others never found her. But once she'd wandered too far, deep among the trees beyond the folly, where her father had told her never to go because little girls could get lost, or worse. It was that day that she first saw her – the wild girl. She sensed her before she saw her; she knew by a prickly feeling that she was being watched. Pausing, rigid, listening, her mind formed threatening shapes out of the shadows of the great trees and the flickering latticework of leaves and branches overhead. And all at once, something flashed silver among the lowest branches of a spreading oak. Jessie gasped, 'I can see you.' And after a moment the wood-creature slid down from its hiding place. It was a girl of about her own age, eight, and at first

Jessie was reminded of a picture in a story book at school. She looked like a flower fairy, this child, in a shabby brown tunic dress with leaves caught in her hair. 'Hello,' Jessie said, 'why were you watching me?' But the girl only shrugged. 'Can't you speak? Why can't you speak?' Jessie breathed. The child placed her fingers across her lips and said, 'Shh. It's a secret.' Then her eyes widened with merriment, and she beckoned. 'Where are we going?' Jessie asked, as the girl plunged deeper into the forest. 'I must go back. I'm not allowed . . .' The sprite shook her head and ducked down under a dead branch. And, following her, Jessie saw a crop of small pink flowers. 'Orchids!' She knew immediately, for her father had once brought home one he'd found while checking traps. The flower fairy stooped and plucked one and gave it to Jessie. 'Pretty!' Jessie said and she and the girl smiled at one another, complicit . . .

She drifted back to consciousness, dimly aware of a distant ringing, fumbling with her hearing aid as she made her way to the phone.

'Judith!' She would hesitate to say that Jude was her favourite grandchild, but she felt a closeness to her she never quite felt with Claire, dear cross little Claire.

'I'm going to Starbrough Hall next Friday, Gran. Can I stay with you on Thursday night?' Jude was saying. 'I'd love to ask you about the place.'

'Starbrough?' Jude heard Jessie's surprise, but all the old lady said next was, 'It would be lovely to see you, dear. Will you get here for tea?'

When she put down the phone, Jessie leaned against the sideboard, deluged by a flood of memories. Starbrough Hall. She'd thought about the wild girl a great deal recently; in fact her mind these days was like a reel of old film, playing random scenes from the distant past. And now her grandchild was going there. Why? She hadn't said. Starbrough. Perhaps the opportunity had come to make things right again.

Later in the afternoon, after an irritating couple of hours in which the phones didn't cease ringing, and a pedantic argument with Inigo over the Bloomsbury first editions, Jude finished writing her copy then took refuge in the storeroom next door to sort books into lots for auction. She always found it a soothing, absorbing task and it freed her mind. Musing about the Starbrough Hall collection she suddenly thought of her old friend Cecelia. They'd met at university, but whereas Jude had gone out into the Real World of work, Cecelia was still burrowing away in university libraries researching the scientific revolution of the late eighteenth century. When they'd last met, for a drink a year or so ago, she was sure Cecelia had said something to do with a book she was writing about astronomy of the period. She'd have to get in touch with her.

What seemed a very short time later, Suri put her head round the door. 'I'm off now, Jude. We're going straight down to my parents' in Chichester and the traffic will probably be awful. Have a lovely weekend.'

'Heck, it's nearly six. I mustn't be long either!' The storeroom had no windows, which could be disorientating.

'We're going to dinner with some friends of Caspar's tonight,' she told Suri, as they returned to the main office. 'Did I tell you, we're all going on holiday to France in a couple of weeks? I've only met them twice. Mad, aren't I?'

'It's brave, if you don't know them,' said Suri, looking unsure whether she was expected to agree. 'What happens if you don't get on?'

'I expect we will,' Jude said, trying to sound positive. 'They seem good fun. Anyway, lots of vino always oils the wheels.'

After Suri had left, Jude tidied her desk, returning books to shelves in swift deft movements and straightening the piles of paper. She wasn't sure she liked what she had seen in Suri's gaze – a kind of pity. At twenty-six and newly engaged to a boy she'd met at uni, Suri still saw life with a fresh innocence. Her world was wonderful, full of colour and hope and happiness, and Jude loved her for it. Even Inigo's patronizing comments rarely managed to cloud Suri's lovely glowing aura. *I was like that once*, she realized, with a little stab of self-pity.

Half-past six found her pushing her way through the aimless summer crowds choking the alley that ran alongside Charing Cross railway station down to Embankment tube.

Even if she hadn't known him, her eye would have been drawn to the figure leaning against a pillar, tapping something into his BlackBerry. Caspar was a powerfully built man in a navy designer suit and starched white shirt. Five years older than Jude's thirty-four, he was handsome and lively, with dark curly hair combed back into submission with the merest slick of gel. She'd met him a few months ago at a friend's drinks party. She, touching five feet ten, and voluptuous, was a good physical match for him. He was drawn by her soft dark eyes and the cloud of wavy strawberry-blonde hair, which she wore clasped at the nape of her neck. 'Quite a Madonna, you are. You looked sad, but then you smiled,' he said, when she once asked him teasingly why he'd been drawn to her that evening. 'So many people only smile with their mouths, but you smiled with your eyes like you cared. I liked that.'

She in turn had liked the way he moved fluidly amongst this sophisticated group of city-dwellers, so obviously enjoying himself, belonging. He'd never married, nor indeed had many of his large network of friends truly settled down. They were too busy working hard at careers they loved – Caspar and his friend Jack ran the New Media advertising consultancy – and playing hard, too. Even his married friends on the whole didn't have children. This was another thing that drew her to him, she knew, this living for the moment. They never talked about the future, but then the present was still all she could manage. When he asked her to come on holiday with some of his friends she hesitated, then thought, why not? 'It'll be a laugh,' he said. 'We have a great time.' She had every reason to believe him, but a worm of worry still wriggled inside her.

All her own friends, it seemed – the ones who witnessed her marriage to Mark six years before – were sending invitations to their own weddings, or announcements of the births of their children. As well as a niece, six-year-old Summer, she already had another godchild and was about to attend the christening of a third, Milo. Little Milo, aged eight months, the child of an ex-colleague, was a scrumptious wide-eyed bambino whom she had accompanied, with his mother, to London Zoo a few weeks back. She hardly saw three-year-old Jennifer, whose parents – Sophie was Jude's best friend from school – had moved to the States last year, but the photographs Sophie emailed Jude tugged unbearably at her heart.

'Hi. Sorry I'm late,' she said, her hand briefly resting on Caspar's tailored sleeve.

'You're not,' Caspar replied, pulling her to him for one of his quick but expert kisses. His dark eyes gleaming, his gaze flicked over her appreciatively, and she was glad she'd bought the trouser suit – and skipped lunch to fit it. 'Pretty earrings,' he commented, recognizing them, and she touched one of the elegant silver cube studs he'd given her for her birthday at Easter, soon after they'd first met. She was sure she had hinted that she usually wore gold, but she loved them anyway because they were his choice.

'Luke and Marney want us at eight,' he said. 'Let's go get a drink.' They found a wine bar nearby where Caspar magically secured the last table. After the first few mouthfuls of syrupy Burgundy on her empty stomach, Jude felt light-headed.

'How did your presentation go?' she asked him. He and Jack were pitching for a teenage sports fashion account.

'Good,' he replied. He'd drained his glass already and was pouring his next. 'They went crazy for the movie-clip idea. If we find the right kids for the shoot, it could be amazing. Jack's started going through the agencies. How's the dusty world of dead-tree technology?' He was always teasing her that her job involved handling old books when the future of modern media was online. The prices they sold at impressed him, though.

'Something quite beguiling has cropped up,' she told him. 'It's the collection of an eighteenth-century astronomer. I'm going up to Norfolk on Friday. It's funny really, it's just where Gran was brought up. Caspar, I wondered . . .' The alcohol gave her courage to ask. 'We weren't doing anything next weekend, were we, you and me? I'm staying with Gran on Thursday night and working on Friday, so I mean Friday and Saturday nights. I've got to go to Milo's christening on Sunday, but that's do-able. You could drive down and meet me in Norfolk on Friday evening. Or earlier, if you like. And come to the christening. I know Shirley and Martin would love to meet you.'

'Friday's the fourth, right? I think it's Tate and Yasmin's flat-warming – no, that's the Saturday.' He picked up his BlackBerry and started pressing keys. 'Yeah, but we don't have to do that.'

'Really? Only we could see my sister, Claire, and her little girl. You haven't met them, you see, and I thought . . . Their place is too tiny for both of us, but there's a bed and breakfast in the village or maybe we could go out to the coast. The countryside's beautiful; we could go walking . . .' She stopped, aware that he wasn't listening.

Caspar's eyes narrowed as he stared at his BlackBerry, the blue light from the screen flickering eerily across his face. He seemed tense, worried.

'Ah,' he said, suddenly cheered by something he'd found. 'I'm really sorry, Jude, but I'm due in Paris on the Sunday for a presentation on Monday. Jack and I'll need Saturday to prepare.'

'Oh, that's a shame. You haven't met my family. I particularly thought you'd like Claire.'

'She's . . . the disabled one?'

'She has a slight limp, that's all.' Disabled is not how Jude thought of her sister. Pretty, feisty, outspoken, an astute businesswoman, yes, but never disabled. She'd been born with one leg slightly shorter than the other; something that had meant a childhood punctuated by hospital operations. 'Her little girl's called Summer. I haven't seen them properly for weeks.'

'I thought you all met up at the airport last week.' They'd gone to see their mother off to Spain with her new husband, Douglas, who was renovating a villa in the hills behind Malaga.

'Stansted airport is hardly a relaxing place for a chat.'

'Well, I'll have to meet Claire and Summer – cute name – another time.'

Now he'd worked his way into the part he managed to look sincerely sorry, but Jude was disappointed. It wasn't the first opportunity he'd turned down of meeting her family, and it mattered to her. Come to think of it, she hadn't met any of his relations either. He was the only child of Polish parents, who lived in Sheffield, he'd told her that much. In all the time she'd known him, he'd never gone home to visit them and if they'd come down to London he hadn't told her. This hadn't struck her as odd before, but now it did.

One of the little earrings was hurting. She put a hand up and loosened it carefully. It came apart. She caught the bits just in time.

Chapter 2

Coming home to the white terraced house in Greenwich was always a pleasure. She elbowed the door shut and dumped her supermarket bags in the kitchen. She'd stayed at Caspar's in Islington the previous night, but, although today was Saturday, he had some things to sort out at the office, so she had travelled back into town with him on the Tube and they went their separate ways at King's Cross. They hadn't spoken much. He'd looked the worse for wear – he'd had far too much to drink the previous night, the dinner party having gone on until the small hours. If she was honest, Jude had enjoyed the evening even less than she'd feared. The six other people there, who encountered individually had seemed friendly and amusing, proved dreary en masse. Last night they talked about restaurants she hadn't been to, and designer names she didn't care about, and old university friends she'd never met and she'd quietly picked at her food, feeling excluded and mutinous. The thought of spending a fortnight in the Dordogne in their company was frankly depressing. When at one gap in the conversation she had asked about sightseeing near Brantôme, their hostess, languid Marney, had wrinkled her nose and said that they usually passed their days by the villa's pool, only emerging in the evening to find somewhere for dinner. 'It's usually too hot for walking around anyway,' she drawled.

'And let's face it,' broke in plump, giggly Paula, 'once you've seen one chateau you've seen the whole bloody lot.' Everybody laughed and Jude forced a polite smile.

Jude, whose pale English skin turned scarlet in the sun, hated lying around by pools. Her ideal holiday involved exploring tranquil towns and villages, and finding out about their histories, which were often surprisingly colourful and violent. It looked as if she'd be doing it on her own this time. She suspected from their conversation in the wine bar that Caspar didn't like walking and exploring either.

Safe back home now, she kicked off her shoes and went to fill the kettle, relaxed in her own company, though, in this pretty house, she never felt entirely alone. It was the home that she and Mark had chosen together when they got engaged, where they'd lived together for the three short years of their marriage, and she still felt a strong sense of him, as though he'd walk back in at any moment. During the last couple of years, various people – her mother, her sister, Mark's sister, Sophie – had begun to worry about this, suggesting she sell up, implying that it was unhealthy to surround herself with all these memories; but apart from letting them sort out his clothes she did nothing. It reassured her to be among Mark's things; it was part of her survival mechanism. The white-painted walls of the living room were still hung with the stunning photographs he'd taken – of the Patagonian wilderness, of Kilimanjaro and the Cairngorms – during climbing expeditions in the long holidays he'd enjoyed as a schoolteacher. Some of their modern furniture, like the wrought-iron bedstead and the bright-patterned sofa, they'd picked together, but the Victorian oval mirror and the William de Morgan tiles in the fireplace were Jude's choice. Mark liked new, Jude liked old. It was a joke between them. Whenever they went anywhere together – back home to Norfolk or for a day trip to the south coast – Jude would say 'I'm just popping in here' and disappear into some mysterious emporium filled with fascinating treasures, leaving Mark to check out modern gizmos in the camping shop or the chandler's. He'd laughed at some of her curios, particularly the small trio of Indian elephants, whose beady eyes had pleaded with her from a junk-shop window.

Drinking her coffee, she walked slowly around the living room, stopping to turn the small antique globe on the sideboard and to pick up one of the ebony elephants, loving the warmth of the wood in her hand. 'Elephants should always face the door or you'll get bad luck,' she'd told Mark.

'Why the door?' he'd drawled, crossing his arms, the signal that he was putting on his sceptical-scientist act. That was another difference between them. She loved old legends and superstitions; he was interested in debunking them. But they both enjoyed a lively discussion.

'It's something Dad used to say. Perhaps they need to get out easily if there's a fire or something.'

'I've never heard such a crazy idea,' Mark teased and they'd laughed.

They were so different from one another in so many ways, but they were meant to be together. She'd always felt it. Ever since the first time they met. So why had she been so cheated?

She dusted the little elephant and returned it carefully to its place.

The thought that today lay empty before her imparted a marvellous feeling. As she unpacked her shopping she considered what to do with the time. Walk up the hill to study the displays at the Royal Observatory, perhaps, and get herself into the mood for astronomy?

When she went to stow the milk in the fridge her eye fell on a photograph of her niece, fastened to the door. Summer.

The name suited the child's fine honey-coloured hair and blue eyes, her airy-fairy lightness. Extraordinary to think she'd be seven in August. It would be lovely if she could see her next weekend. She reached for the house phone and speed-dialled Claire's work number.

'Star Bureau,' came her sister's brisk voice. Claire ran a small shop with a friend in the Norfolk market town of Holt. It sold all sorts of gifts connected with stars and astrology. A nice sideline to this was a service enabling people to name a star, maybe after a loved one. For a modest sum, they received a certificate giving the location and official serial number of the star and a framed poem she'd written called 'Stardust', which Jude thought didn't quite scan in the third line, but knew her opinion on this, as on various other matters, would not be welcome.

'It's Jude. Are you madly busy?'

'Oh, it's you! Just a moment . . . Linda, I'll take this in the office . . . It's my sister,' Jude heard her tell her business partner. Then, 'I'd better be quick, Jude. The place is full of tourists. Hang on, move, cat.' Jude pictured Claire, small elfin face, whip-thin, shooing Pandora, the black and white cat that accompanied her to work some days. 'I was going to ring you, Jude. Would you like to come and stay sometime? Summer's been asking.' Summer, not Claire, Jude noted, then dismissed the thought as ungenerous.

'I was wondering about next weekend, actually. Are you likely to be around?'

'Now let's see. I'm in Dubai on Saturday with Piers and flying on to the Solomon Islands on Sunday with Rupert. Don't be silly, of course I'm around. When do I ever go anywhere? I can't afford it for a start.'

Jude recognized the old edge to her sister's voice, and her laugh was unconvincing. The Star Bureau struggled to make a modest profit, and much of Claire's share of that went on the mortgage for her cottage. Claire had never spoken of her jealousy of Jude's financial security, but the odd heavy hint made her feel guilty. And led her to post Claire a cheque occasionally, avoiding damage to her sister's pride by insisting the money was to buy something for Summer.

'Well, could I book myself in for Friday and Saturday nights? I'd have to leave early on Sunday.'

'Sure, it would be lovely to see you, if you don't mind going in with Summer.'

'I love sleeping in Summer's room. She doesn't snore like you. How is my darling niece, by the way?'

'She's all right.' Jude heard a slight catch in her sister's voice. 'She won a Magic Star for her reading last week.'

'A *magic* star?'

'It's when you get twenty-five ordinary stars.'

'Good old Summer.'

'Otherwise, oh, I don't know, I'm a bit worried about her.'

'Oh no, why?'

'She's not sleeping well. Keeps having bad dreams. I'm not sure you'll want to sleep in with her, come to think of it.'

'What are the dreams about?'

'I'm not sure. All she tells me is, "I couldn't see you, Mummy." '

A flash of childhood memory. *Where are you, Maman? I can't see you*. Waking in a small London bedroom, streetlight shining through pale curtains and an insect buzzing away at the inside of the window.

She wrenched her attention back to what Claire was saying. '. . . the doctor couldn't tell me. So I don't know what to do now.'

'Sorry, what did the doctor say?'

'Nothing,' said Claire irritably. 'He said there was nothing wrong that he could see.'

'You *are* worried, aren't you?'

'Wouldn't you be?'

'Well, yes, of course I would.' She was used to Claire's sharpness. There was no point taking offence. Claire was bringing up Summer on her own and sometimes the strain showed.

'Is she otherwise herself? She's not ill or pining or anything?'

'Not that I've noticed. She seems quite happy, in fact.'

'Perhaps it's the stress of school, then,' said Jude doubtfully, not really knowing about these things, but Claire seemed satisfied with this idea.

'Maybe you're right,' she agreed. 'There's an awful lot of tests and homework. And she's the youngest in her year.'

'There's so much pressure on them,' Jude added. 'I was reading about the Swedish system where they don't even start school until they're—'

'Jude, have you heard from Mum?'

'Not since she called last week to say they'd arrived in Malaga safely. You?'

'No,' said Claire bitterly, 'but she wouldn't ring me. I always have to ring her.'

'Don't be daft,' Jude said wearily. Reassuring Claire that she was loved was one of her roles in the family – it always had been.

'Well it's true. Look, I'd better go, there's a queue at the till.'

'Listen, quickly, how do you think Gran is? I'm going to stay with her on Thursday night.'

'Oh she'll love that.' Claire's voice softened. 'She's all right, Jude, a bit frail. Summer and I took her to buy shoes in Sheringham on Saturday. It was a bit of an ordeal because they didn't have her usual style but we found something in the end. What are you doing down here in the middle of the week, then?'

'I know it's a great coincidence, but I'm visiting Starbrough Hall to value some stuff.'

'Starbrough Hall? Really? Well Gran will fill you in about that. Look, I've got to go.'

Jude put down the phone with the deep unsettling sense that there was something off-kilter. It was partly the usual family tensions. Claire was wrong thinking their mother didn't care about her, completely wrong. Mum loved her elder daughter as much as she did Jude. Jude had never questioned her parents' love. Had just known it was there and accepted it.

I suppose Mum rings me more often because she relies on me, she thought as she stuffed dirty washing in the machine. Despite having Douglas, she misses Dad and I'm a bit like Dad – solid and reliable . . . Ugh, that sounds boring. Mum's relationship with Claire is more complicated. They strike sparks off one another. But that doesn't mean Mum doesn't love Claire, and, my goodness, she adores little Summer.

And there was Summer to worry about. She couldn't quite believe it yet, but she suspected her niece of having the same horrible dream that she had had as a child.

Chapter 3

'Gran! Gran!' Someone was knocking. Jessie opened her eyes, for a moment confused. There was a face at the window. Not the wild girl. Little Judith. Jude, her granddaughter. She hadn't been expecting her. 'Yes, you had, Jessie, you silly old fool,' she muttered as she pushed herself up out of her chair. Jude had telephoned, said she was coming to stay on Thursday. Today was Thursday and Mr Lewis had brought her round a nice bit of fish.

'Hello, I'm sorry to have woken you,' she said, when her grandmother opened the door. Peering through the window of the pretty flint cottage, she had worried for a moment seeing Gran slumped in a chair like that, mouth gaping in her wrinkled face, her thin hair coming down on all sides. She was thankful when the old lady finally stirred at her knocking.

Inside, she put down her bags and kissed her grandmother's paper-dry cheek. Jessie stood at a loss for a moment, looking her granddaughter up and down with an expression of delighted wonder.

'Oh you do look lovely, dear. Very elegant.'

'Thank you,' said Jude, who was still in the smart linen skirt and jacket she'd worn for a business lunch.

She followed her grandmother into the kitchen, dismayed to see how bent over she was getting. Jessie was eighty-five now – indeed the last time Jude had seen her was on her birthday in

May, when the four generations of women – Gran, her mother, Valerie, Jude, Claire and little Summer – had all crowded into the living room for sandwiches and a lopsided birthday cake that Summer had helped bake and decorated herself with jelly sweets. Later, Jessie had managed to hobble along the harbour on Jude's arm. Now, seeing her grandmother lean against the work surface for support as she fumbled with a battered tea caddy, she wondered for how much longer. Gran would be able to leave her house unaided. However would she reach the village shop or the doctor's surgery? Her mind raced ahead. Perhaps they needed to find somewhere more suitable for her to live. Gran would hate moving.

'Do let me help, Gran.'

Under Jessie's instructions she poured boiling water into the familiar metal teapot, laid out Great-Granny's porcelain teacups and carried the tray through to the living room. Jude loved visiting this little cottage by the sea, where her grand-parents had moved after her grandfather's retirement. She remembered starting to come here as a teenager when her father became ill with his heart and left full-time work, and they all moved to Norwich from London.

Jessie lowered herself into her easy chair with a little gasp. 'I can't get my breath sometimes,' she explained, seeing the concern in Jude's face. 'At least I'm not so dizzy today.'

'Dizzy? That doesn't sound good.'

'Dr Gable says it's one of these viruses. Pass me that cushion, will you? He gave me some pills but I won't take them.'

'Oh, Gran,' Jude chided as she helped her grandmother get comfortable.

'They make me feel all peculiar. Raw egg with a bit of brandy in it – now that's a good pick-me-up. Don't worry, Jude, I'm just old bones, and there's nothing can cure that. Now tell me all

Rachel Hore

about yourself, dear. Much more interesting. Help yourself to a fondant fancy, won't you? I know they're your favourites.'

'Thank you,' Jude said, anxiously watching Gran wield the teapot. She sipped her tea and dutifully peeled the paper off one of the gaudy cupcakes she'd loved when younger, but which as an adult she found sickly sweet. 'I'm sorry I don't get down here much. I'm crazily busy at work and then, well, the weekends fill themselves up. Seeing friends and so on,' she ended, feeling guilty.

'Anybody special?' Jessie looked shrewdly at her over the top of her teacup.

Jude hesitated, then smiled. 'There is a man on the scene, if that's what you're asking, Gran. It's not serious, so don't start hoping. I know what you and Mum are like.'

'Oh never mind us. Does he makes you happy, love?'

'I enjoy his company.'

'That's not the same thing at all,' she said severely. 'I worry about you, Jude.'

'I know you do, Gran. But you shouldn't. I'm over the worst now.'

Gran contemplated her thoughtfully then said, 'These things aren't easy to forget. Yet we must put them behind us and make the best of life. That's something I've learned the hard way.'

Her grandmother had a faraway look in her eyes, as though distracted by something beyond the confines of the room.

'Gran?'

'Sorry, love. I was thinking of something.'

'From the past?'

'Yes. From long, long ago when I was little. I suppose, looking at your old gran, you can't believe she was little once, hey?'

Jude, seeing her grandmother's wrinkled features transformed by a mischievous smile, said with spirit, 'I certainly can.'

Gran looked delighted.

'Was it something sad or happy you were thinking about?' Jude pursued.

'It was both. Well, since you ask, I was remembering someone I used to know. Oh, it was all a very, very long time ago. Have another of those cakes, dear. I won't eat them.'

'Maybe in a moment, Gran. But who was it you were thinking of?' Her grandmother rarely spoke about her childhood, and Jude so loved it when she did.

'You wouldn't know her, Jude. It wouldn't mean anything to you.'

'It would, you know. Gran, you are naughty, you know I'm fascinated by what it was like when you were growing up. Was this while you were living at Starbrough?'

'It was, yes. Once, when I was seven or eight, I met a girl in the forest near where I lived and we became friends.'

'Do tell me,' begged Jude.

'If you'll have another of those cakes,' her grandmother said, and Jude meekly took one and bit into it.

'I didn't know it then, but this girl was one of those travelling folk, a proper Romany gypsy, so that's why I'd see her for a few weeks or months and then not for a long while, a year maybe. Her name was Tamsin.'

She paused for breath and Jude said between mouthfuls, 'What happened to her?'

'I was coming to that. One day when I was nine or ten she turned up at school. I went to school in Starbrough village, you know. We were all sitting there doing our sums or whatever, and you could have blew me down when the door opened and the headmaster brought her in. Said she was a new pupil and, well, this was a red rag to a bull, he said she was a gypsy and we were to be kind to her.'

'Presumably you weren't.' Jude noticed Gran's country accent grew broader when she talked about the past.

'Some of them boys were the worst. It's no surprise she wasn't very happy at school. For a start she looked different with her jumble-sale clothes and her brown skin and gold earrings. She was behind with her work, was part of the trouble, and some of the other children thought her a fool. Called her names – said gypsies were thieves and the like. Got it from their parents probably, though I never heard that sort of nonsense at home. He had a word or two to say about poachers, my da', but he never blamed the gypsies more than any other. Anyway, I'm ashamed to say I was too frightened to be her friend at school. I thought I'd get picked on too, you know how children can be. But sometimes in the holidays if your great-uncle Charlie and great-aunt Sarah and me went up the folly I might see her and we often played together, happy as sandboys we'd be. It was like we had another sister. It didn't seem to matter to her that we ignored her at school. I've often thought how unhappy we must have made her.'

'Perhaps she understood that you were frightened,' Jude said, wondering where this rambling story was going. She was a little dismayed by how much this episode from long ago seemed to be bothering Gran.

'I hope so,' Gran said. 'At least I never joined in when they got at her in playtime. Some more tea, dear?'

'Thank you. What happened to Tamsin?' Jude asked her.

But Gran pressed her lips together. Finally, she shook her head sadly and said, 'We . . . her family moved away. I never saw her again. I always felt badly, mind. I didn't help her when she needed it, I couldn't help . . . And I took something from her, you see.'

'What?' but it was as though Jessie hadn't heard her. Jude was shocked by her grandmother's look of anguish.

'It's awful never to forgive or be forgiven,' the old lady said. 'It's always there – buried, yes, but you know it's there.'

Later that night, after they'd gone to bed, Jude could hear her grandmother moving about in the next room, the rumble of drawers opening and closing and Gran talking to herself. Just as she decided she'd go and see if anything was the matter, there came the creak of bedsprings, some coughing, then silence. Jude, who had to be up early, settled herself for sleep. If Gran needed her she'd probably call.

Sleep didn't come. She lay puzzling for a while over the story Gran had told her, about the gypsy girl in the forest at Starbrough. There was a folly. They'd played near the folly, she'd said. She'd have to look for that tomorrow.

Her mind drifted back to her own childhood. When they stayed here as teenagers, if it were a fine day, Granddad would take her and Claire out in his small fishing boat to see the seals basking on Blakeney Point. He'd been a gentle, quietly spoken man who had always lived in sight of the sea, a man one felt comfortable with just sitting together without much being said. He would listen when you wanted to talk, but didn't ask stupid questions all the time, about school and your favourite subject and what you wanted to be when you grew up, like some grown-ups talked to children.

Her grandmother by contrast was a practical, no-nonsense figure, always busy, organizing meals or sewing new curtains or, hands on hips, arguing with the milkman over his bill, putting the world to rights with the neighbours. Jude remembered how her mother always seemed like a cat on hot tiles when they visited Blakeney. It was unusual for the day to pass without Valerie and Jessie exchanging sharp words. They'd never got on well, Granddad explained once. It was funny how age had mellowed both of them. Funny, too, that Jessie, who rarely spoke of her childhood, had been so voluble tonight. This evening, it was as though the curtain separating the present from the past had briefly been twitched aside.

The past. Her past. She recalled what Gran had intimated, about Mark. That she had to let him go. It wasn't as easy as that. She was trying to with Caspar, trying desperately hard, hoping, by going through the motions of a steady relationship, that the dark stagnant pool in her mind would unblock and drain away, that love would flow again. Perhaps, like the earrings he gave her, forgetting what she'd told him she liked, Caspar was wrong for her. Or perhaps it was her fault and she wasn't letting him love her. He was the first man she'd been out with properly since Mark and she worried that she'd forgotten how to do it.

When the travel alarm woke her the next morning the house was still quiet. She washed and dressed herself in yesterday's suit with a fresh cami top, wanting to be smart to meet the master of Starbrough Hall. Down in the kitchen she scavenged for some Cornflakes then, as there was no movement from upstairs, wrote a thank-you note, propped it up against the toaster and let herself out.

Upstairs, Jessie stirred briefly then settled back into her dream. In it she was searching for something, something she urgently needed to find.

Chapter 4

Jude nearly missed the sign that said 'Starbrough Hall only. Private.' She followed the long, rutted drive across rough grassland, then past a lawn with a stone fountain to the sand-coloured Palladian house she recognized from the book in her office. She parked her shiny blue hatchback on the gravel forecourt next to a battered estate car. When she got out, a couple of large setter dogs in the other vehicle began to bark and jump about frantically. She ignored them, more interested in the house, which though still graceful was shabby, she thought. Some of the window frames appeared rotten and slabs of plaster were missing from the walls.

The BlackBerry in her pocket began to trill. Suri, she read on the screen as she pressed answer. It was nine o'clock. She couldn't escape the office for a moment.

'Suri, hi,' she said. 'You're early. I'd better not speak long. I've just arrived at the house. How are you?'

'Fine, thanks. I'm sorry to bother you now, Jude. I got in five minutes ago to find Klaus storming about – don't worry, I'm in the storeroom so he can't hear me. Finance brought down this month's figures and he's deeply not happy. There's a boardroom meeting you've got to go to at nine o'clock on Monday. He wants you in at half-eight.'

'Oh, marvellous. He's probably so antsy because the Americans are over. Tell him not to worry, I'll be there.'

'He wants you – you're going to hate me – to email him your projections for the next sale. And there's other stuff,' she ended vaguely. 'Inigo might ring.'

'I won't be able to do anything until this evening. Can't someone look up my projections? They're in the folder marked "September Auction". I can't remember the file name, I'm afraid.'

'I'll have a go.'

'Great, thanks. This place is an amazing pile. You should see it – like something out of *Pride and Prejudice*, but a bit more moth-eaten.'

'*Don't* think of me stuck here all day.' Suri sighed enviously before ringing off.

Jude stuffed the phone in her handbag and, taking her brief-case out of the boot, walked quickly past the barking hounds. A flight of crumbly shallow stone steps rose to the huge double front door, but, to the right, an arched gateway led, she presumed, round to the back of the house. She walked up the front steps and pressed the bell. After a minute or two, she heard footsteps and the door juddered open.

A fleshy man in his early forties, wearing knee-length shorts and an old rugby shirt, said, 'Ms Gower? Robert Wickham. Do come in.'

'It's Jude, short for Judith,' she said, shaking hands.

When he shut the door behind them the tiny lobby was plunged into gloom. 'I should have told you to come round the back,' said Mr Wickham, frowning. 'Under the arch, turn left. We don't often use this door.'

'You wanted me to come in through the tradesman's entrance?' she joked, as she followed him up a flight of marble steps.

'No, goodness, no, I don't mean to imply that you're a trades-man at all,' he blustered. 'It's merely that everybody finds all these steps a damned nuisance, especially with the children's whatnots.'

'Yes of course,' Jude said, thinking him nice but a bit humourless. 'I see what you mean.'

They had reached a circular, marbled atrium, where half a dozen classical stone busts frowned down from niches around the walls. An overflowing coat stand sheltered a collection of small brightly coloured wellingtons and toy umbrellas. A box of plastic cars, robots and dolls with grinning faces lay directly in the eye-line of a long-dead Caesar. The bust's outraged glare made her want to laugh again, but her host might be offended.

'May I take your jacket?' he asked.

'I'll hang on to it.' It was quite chilly. Must be all the marble, she thought. 'How many children do you have?'

'Three-year-old twins,' he replied, as if he didn't quite believe it. 'A boy and a girl. My wife's taken them to her parents in Yorkshire. It's been marvellously quiet here, I can tell you.' This time she saw with relief a twinkle in his eye. 'Though I do miss them. Come straight down.' He led the way down a long corridor to their left and opened a door to a room at the front of the house.

'Oh, how wonderful!' Jude exclaimed, as she walked into one of the most unexpected and loveliest libraries she'd ever seen. It was nearly oval, an effect created by the way the white-painted bookcases and cupboards filling the walls had been built in two sweeping curves, from door to window. Below the tall Georgian sash rested a huge old globe, slightly tilted, in a way that suggested it was about to rise into orbit. Nearby was the orrery Robert Wickham had mentioned on the phone, a spherical structure made up of interlocked wooden hoops to represent the different paths of the planets in the solar system. She moved closer to study it.

'Splendid, isn't it?' said Robert, stroking the outermost hoop. 'I was always fascinated by this as a child, not least because it didn't have all the planets we know now. When did they find Uranus, for instance?'

'William Herschel spotted it in the early seventeen-eighties, I think,' Jude said. She counted the planets. There were only six including Earth. He was right. No Uranus.

'I've no memory for dates.' Robert chuckled. 'Alexia is always complaining. Make yourself at home, Jude. I'll let my mother know you're here. You'd like some coffee, I daresay?'

'Coffee would be lovely,' she said. He left, closing the door behind him. She didn't mind him; he seemed pleasant enough, a country squire type, a bit nervy, but she'd had to deal with worse. She forgot about him, instead enjoying the peaceful gloom of the room, the comforting scents of wood and leather and old books, liking the sensitive visage of the young man in eighteenth-century dress in the portrait over the fireplace. The oval shape of the library gave her an odd sensation. It was like being cradled in a large egg, she decided, or maybe the belly of an old ship. There were a couple of sturdy leather armchairs and a sofa set round the marble fireplace that contributed to the air of masculine comfort. She leaned against one of the chairs and stared up at the painted ceiling. It represented an astrological chart of the night sky, the firmament coloured a midnight blue with images of the different star signs – the Water Carrier, the Twins, the Crab and the rest – painted in gold and carmine, silver and white. It was breathtakingly beautiful.

She left her briefcase by a big desk near the window and glanced out across the gravel forecourt to a lawn. Beyond this spread an expanse of scrubby, rough-cut grass then trees and a low flint wall that bordered the road. In the distance, hedges and fields rolled out to the horizon. She wondered where the gamekeeper's cottage might be, where her grandmother had lived, and the woodland folly she'd mentioned. To the right of the park a thick pelt of trees blanketed a low hill. The folly might be up there somewhere, she supposed, though she couldn't see any buildings.

She turned back to the room and began to wander around, idling over the bookshelves. Mostly there were works from the nineteenth and early twentieth centuries, fiction, out-of-date reference books, works of history and travel. Though evidence of a well-fed mind, none of these looked valuable. It was when she moved to the back of the room near the door that she found the books she'd come to see, behind locked glass doors. The key lay on a shelf nearby, but despite Robert Wickham's invitation to 'make herself at home' she felt it proper to wait for his return before investigating further. Through the glass she could make out some of the titles stamped in gold leaf on the leather bindings. *Compleat System of Opticks* by Robert Smith – if that was a first edition, she guessed someone might pay a couple of thousand for that alone. James Ferguson's *Astronomy Explained* was also possibly valuable, as was what looked like Flamsteed's famous *Atlas Coelestis* – translated literally as Atlas of the Heavens. Further up the bookcase she could glimpse volumes of what might be an early edition of Newton's *Principia* and felt a little rush of adrenalin. That would be incredibly rare. Suddenly she was glad she'd come.

She turned as the door opened and an elegantly dressed woman entered, followed by Robert with the coffee. 'Ms Gower – Jude,' he said, laying the tray on a table near the fireplace, 'this is my mother, Chantal Wickham.'

Mrs Wickham came to meet her, a graceful hand outstretched. 'Jude, if I may call you that, how lovely to meet you.' As they touched and their eyes met it was as though a current of calm, warm strength passed from the older lady through the younger, and Jude almost gasped.

Chantal Wickham had been beautiful – was still beautiful, Jude corrected herself. It was difficult to tell whether she was fifty-five or seventy. Almost as tall as Jude, straight-backed, with thick dark shoulder-length hair frosted with silver, and high cheekbones in a wide, intelligent, olive-skinned face, she possessed the kind of natural grace that a wardrobe-load of expensive designer clothes could never buy. Yet, though concealer did its best to disguise them, it was impossible to miss the great hollows beneath her chestnut-brown eyes. Here was a woman like herself who knew what it was to toss and turn at night, unvisited by sleep.

'You've come to inspect our treasures.' Even her voice was beautiful, husky, her diction formal and with a slight foreign lilt. 'I expect Robert will have explained how desperately sad we are to have to sell them. But apparently the house will fall down about our ears if we don't.' The distress behind her words was unmistakable.

'Mother, we mustn't start this all over again,' Robert said, looking up from pouring coffee.

Jude glanced uncertainly from mother to son with a sinking feeling. It was awkward when one of the parties didn't want to sell; it made her feel like a money-grabber, an asset-stripper, and, worse, if the squabble continued, it could mean she was wasting her time coming at all. Seeing her expression, Chantal Wickham immediately made amends. 'It's not your fault, of course, Jude. I'm sure that you will appreciate our collection. It must be wonderful, the job you do, handling these marvellous things.'

'I do love my work, yes,' said Jude, feeling she was walking a tightrope. 'Thank you.' She took the cup that Robert passed her.

'Jude,' Robert said, his eyes flicking to the wide world beyond the window, 'would it be all right if I left you with my mother this morning? She knows more about the collection than I do, and something urgent has cropped up. Mother, George Fenton phoned a moment ago. It seems the pheasant coops have been broken into during the night.'

'Oh no, Robert.'

Jude said, 'Of course you must go. I'm sure Mrs Wickham and I will get on fine by ourselves.'

Mrs Wickham gave her a complicit smile. 'Please call me Chantal,' she murmured, then told her son, 'I hope you find it's foxes, Rob. I don't like the idea of human thieves. George gets such bees buzzing in his bonnet about people and it leads to bad feeling locally.'

Robert nodded as he gulped down his coffee. Then with a 'See you both for lunch,' he hurried out of the room. A moment or two later the women watched the estate car lurch off down the drive, the dogs bounding about in the back.

'Dear Robert, he always has to be rushing about,' said Chantal. 'Come and sit down for a moment, Jude.' She patted the space on the sofa beside her. 'You must be tired after driving all this way.'

'Oh, I stayed in Blakeney with my gran last night.'

'So you know our part of the world, then?'

'Sort of. I lived in Norwich in my teens,' Jude explained. 'And some of my family are still here. Mum has a house outside Sheringham, but she's selling up and moving to Spain with my stepfather. My sister lives very close by – in Felbarton. Do you know a shop in Holt called the Star Bureau? She owns it with a friend.'

'Oh, the gift shop in the arcade? Such a pretty window display. All those starry lights and mobiles. I've always meant to go inside. I'll make sure I do now.'

'Yes, I think you'd love it. And, it's an amazing coincidence, but Gran used to live here on the Starbrough estate. She was the gamekeeper's daughter. Their name was Bennett – does that ring any bells? It was ages ago, though. She must have been born – oh, 1923 or so . . .'

Chantal shook her head. 'I'm afraid I don't remember any Bennetts,' she said. 'But then I didn't come to this country until 1959 and your grandmother had probably moved away by then.'

'Yes, she would have done. Her parents died in the mid fifties, I think. Where did you come from originally?'

'I was born in Paris, but I came here when I was twenty.' That made Chantal sixty-nine now, Jude calculated, so she was older than she looked. 'I always think of Starbrough Hall as home.' A deep sadness darkened her expression, but then she said in a low, passionate tone, 'I love this house. I married into it, but it's a part of me now. And Robert and Alexia have been so kind, letting me live here still.'

'They . . . moved in recently?' Jude guessed how Chantal would answer; knew, with a sudden rush of sympathy, why she felt such a strong connection to this woman.

'William, my husband, died two years ago, and the house became Robert's. The trouble is, as ever, filthy lucre. There is no capital, you see. My husband was forced to sell some of the estate before he died, then Robert had to pay dreadful death duties. And the repairs . . . oh, the paint's flaking off and the roof needs an overhaul, so Anthony Wickham's collection must go. It's so tragic. It is part of the house and its history. That's Anthony.' She indicated the portrait over the fireplace, which Jude looked at properly for the first time. Anthony Wickham had been a very slight young man with a small neat head and an owlish expression. A view of

Starbrough Hall appeared in the background to the painting, but the way he clutched the open book in his hand, as though the artist had interrupted his studies, indicated more strongly where his interests lay. There was a date painted in one corner: 1745.

'We think that was painted when he was twenty-two, a few years before his father died and he inherited the house. I cannot bear to think of his things being divided up among strangers, appreciated only for what they're worth financially. Robert means well, but I'm sure there must be some other way . . .' She looked suddenly guilty. 'Robert wouldn't be pleased. I've said far more to you than he would like. But you seem so . . . easy to talk to . . . *sympathique.*'

Jude listened to this speech with a swelling tenderness for Chantal. She was an outsider who had married into this family, and felt a part of it all, yet had no right to make decisions about her home. At the same time, remembering those rotting windowsills, it was possible that she and her husband had not been completely realistic about the costs of keeping up Starbrough Hall in the modern age.

'Please don't worry about what you've told me,' she said quietly. 'I understand, and I feel for you . . . I do this work because I'm fascinated by the books themselves, not just the words in them but as artefacts, the way they've been created and cared about. Of course, I have to decide what they are worth, because that's my job, but I'm like you. I love to know the stories of the people who owned them and read them and cherished them.' She was surprised at how passionate she felt. So much of the time her work was stressful, but sometimes she remembered why she loved it.

'So I was right to say these things to you. Thank you, dear. Now, let's look at the books.'

Jude draped her jacket over the back of a chair and followed Chantal to the glass-fronted cabinet. Chantal spread the doors wide and stood back so that Jude could see. With a practised eye, she took in the dozen or so shelves, twenty-odd books on each. Easily two hundred and fifty books. And then there would be the manuscripts and the instruments. This was indeed a day or two's work. She reached up and extracted a volume of the Isaac Newton, laid it down on a console table and examined the preliminary pages. She was right, she saw with a rush of pleasure, it was a third edition! She turned the pages carefully, marvelling at the good condition. There was some foxing – tiny brown spots – on some of the pages, but that was only to be expected for a book this age. 'Did you know that this is a very rare printing?' she asked Chantal.

'We had our suspicions,' Chantal replied. 'Robert's friend thought it might be valuable, but we'd never employed an expert before.'

'Not even for insurance purposes?' Jude felt rather shocked.

'I say with some embarrassment, no. My late husband, dear man though he was, did not share my interest in this library. Robert, too ... he's an outdoors kind of man. He sees this collection as ... dispensable.'

The phone in Jude's handbag began to ring. She retrieved it with foreboding. Yes, it was Inigo. She sent the call to message and turned off the phone.

Returning to the bookcase, she took down the other volumes of the Newton and inspected them. She could hardly believe it. They were a complete set, all in the same good condition. She fetched her briefcase, and while she waited for her laptop to start up she pulled a chair over to the table and started making notes on a pad.

Chantal asked, 'Shall I show you where everything else is first? Then I'll sit quietly out of your way and work my tapestry, but be ready to help if you need it.'

'Thank you,' Jude said.

'In this cupboard –' Chantal unlocked the pair of doors below the bookshelves and pulled them open – 'are the notebooks and charts. Robert must have told you about them. I'm afraid it's a bit of a jumble. Here . . .' She extracted a leather-bound foolscap tome from an untidy pile on the shelf and opened it at random. It was filled with dense handwriting in a neat, even script, the ink faded to sepia.

'What's this?' Jude said, taking it from her, fascinated.

'One of Anthony's observation journals. A year or two ago, when I found myself with time on my hands, I transcribed some of the first volume.' Her smile was regretful. 'It wasn't easy.' She showed Jude a school exercise book. 'I didn't copy the very technical material, the mathematics – that didn't interest me so much, only his commentary. My eyes aren't so good . . . I'm afraid I didn't get very far.'

'It was good to have started, though,' Jude murmured, turning the pages of the original. She was used to deciphering old handwriting. 'It'll be very useful, I'm sure.'

'And these scrolls are some of his charts. This one . . .' Chantal crouched down and eased out a roll of parchment. Jude put down the journal and they looked at it together. 'It plots some of the double stars he found,' Chantal explained.

'Those are pairs of stars, aren't they, that revolve round each other?'

'Yes. It was thought useful to monitor their movements. Somehow that helped them measure the distance of stars from Earth. They were becoming very interested in stars rather than just planets, because of the new telescopes.'

'Your son mentioned something about a telescope.'

'It's in here.' Chantal went over to a tall cupboard in the wall between some bookshelves and opened it to reveal a blackened wood and metal cylinder about three feet high, standing on the floor. 'Or rather, the bits of it are.' She tried to drag it out, but it was heavy and Jude had to help. 'Tilt it to the light, like this, then look down into it,' Chantal told her.

Jude did so, and gasped at a flash of light and then, all at once, her own faint image staring dimly back at her. 'Mirrors!' she said. 'Of course!'

She knew this was part of an early reflector telescope, which worked by mirrors collecting light from the sky and projecting it for viewing through a magnifying lens in the side of the telescope. They were better for studying faint objects than the original refractor telescopes. Refractors were longer and clumsier, and meant looking at objects directly through lenses, which often distorted the light.

'And this one belonged to Wickham?' Jude asked and picked up from a shelf what looked like an eyepiece.

'It seems likely, don't you think? These bits were found in one of the barns soon after I first came to Starbrough. Robert's father thought there had been more of it originally, but in the war odd bits of scrap were often sent off to make shells. This escaped somehow.' Jude helped her shut the heavy capsule back in the cupboard.

'This whole room,' she said, gazing round, 'is so wonderful, Chantal. Magical, really. Did Anthony Wickham make it?'

'We believe so, yes,' replied Chantal. 'We don't really know, you see. Most of the archives for that period were destroyed in an office fire in Victorian times. My husband's father was a great reader – a lot of these later books were his. For me, this room has often been a place of great solace. That's why I feel so upset that Robert . . . Oh, I shouldn't say this to you.'

For a moment her eyes were great pools of remembered pain. They were such expressive eyes, Jude thought.

'I'm sorry,' she said, 'about your husband. The same thing happened to me. My husband died four years ago.'

'Oh my dear,' Chantal said, touching her hand to her mouth. 'And you're so young.'

'I was thirty,' Jude said. It seemed like a lifetime ago; she'd been a different person then. 'It was a climbing accident.'

Even talking about it, all these years later, brought back the shock of that terrible moment. She'd been driving home, following a police car down their road. It stopped outside her house. She'd parked her car askew, walked up her garden path, legs trembling, to meet the young officer standing on her doorstep, the news naked in his face. She blinked the image away to see Chantal staring at her with a look of deep concern.

'An accident. That's terrible,' Chantal whispered. 'I'm so sorry.'

'Your husband . . .' Jude prompted, desperate to push away her own pain, the pain that could split her wide open so suddenly, even now.

Chantal said quietly, 'William was ill for several years. The cancer kept returning and,' she spread her hands in a hopeless gesture, 'eventually it won. We'd been married for more than forty-five years.' She shook her head. 'For many months I could do nothing. I would come here, into this room, and sit by myself, or with Miffy; she's my little dog; a great companion. I came to the idea of copying out Anthony Wickham's notebooks. It wasn't a task I had to think much about, you see. And it passed those great acres of time.'

'It must have helped having grandchildren.'

'Yes, it's marvellous watching them grow. Georgie, now, she reminds me very much of my William, a very sturdy little thing. You didn't have any children?'

'No,' said Jude slowly. 'It's something I regret.'

'I understand,' said Chantal. 'I expect your friends and family say this: you are young, there is plenty of time.'

'I wanted Mark's children,' Jude blurted out, her voice harsh in this peaceful room.

It had seemed as though there was all the time in the world when they were newly married. They'd both had jobs they loved; they took pleasure in one another's company. Babies had always been in the plan somewhere, but not yet. And then it was too late.

'It must be difficult to accept,' said Chantal, and Jude wondered at how she and this older woman, strangers, had volunteered such intimate information to one another.

She sat down at the desk where the pile of books awaited her attention, but felt suddenly at a loss about what to do next.

'I'll fetch some more coffee,' murmured Chantal.

She closed the door gently behind her and Jude sat for a moment with her face in her hands. Recovering, she got to work, opening a new file on her laptop and carefully listing all the books, describing their condition and publishing history, occasionally scribbling queries on her notepad. She was leafing through John Flamsteed's *Atlas Coelestis* with its beautifully drawn representations of the constellations, when she realized something. At the same moment, Chantal returned with coffee, a sewing bag, and an elderly King Charles spaniel in tow.

She helped Chantal with the tray then said, 'Look!' She showed her a picture of Gemini in the Flamsteed and pointed up at the ceiling.

'They're the same! I hadn't noticed before,' exclaimed Chantal. The Heavenly Twins from the Atlas were faithfully reproduced above their heads. 'What about Aquarius?'

Jude turned the pages of the book until she found the Water Carrier. Flamsteed had been the model for that part of the ceiling, too. She looked inside the front of the book to check the date. Anthony Wickham had been given the book by someone: in the flyleaf was written 'AW from SB, 1805'. Was SB the artist, perhaps?

'It's fascinating, isn't it? We often wonder who could have painted it.' And now Chantal left Jude in peace to work while she sat and worked a tapestry with a design of flowers and fruit. Miffy snored on the rug. It was companionable, and Jude found the time slipped quickly by.

At lunchtime, Robert returned and the cosy feeling evaporated. 'We ought to eat,' he said, and they repaired to a breakfast room next to the kitchen, where the daily woman had left plates of sandwiches on the big pine table.

'How have you got on this morning?' Robert asked Jude. 'Is the collection worth much?' He spoke casually, but there was expectation in his face. She'd seen that expression on clients' faces many a time.

'I haven't been through everything yet by any means,' she answered cautiously, 'but there are certainly some rare editions of important works. I was explaining to your mother about the Isaac Newton.'

'I thought that would interest you. You can't put a figure on them yet? Even a rough estimate?'

Sellers were all different. This one wanted instant answers. 'I'll give you a ballpark figure later today,' she said, 'but I must research one or two things further once I get back to the office.' She was thinking of the Newton and the observation journals. 'I need a specialist for the instruments.' She needed to put him off; she didn't like to raise people's hopes unrealistically, and hated it when people were impatient, as though her mere

appearance meant a cheque in the bank. She was always careful
to explain that although she could estimate what items might
fetch at auction, there was simply no guarantee. That was the
point of a reserve price – the safeguard level below which the
owner would not sell.

Then there was the system of taxes and commission that was
always disappointing for people new to the business to learn.
Illogical though it might be, she, as the bearer of bad news, usually
felt guilty. 'That's ridiculous,' Inigo had sneered once when she'd
foolishly confided in him about this. 'They have to learn that it's a
business, not a treasure hunt.' She remembered Inigo's call. She'd
have to get back to him when she had a moment.

'What did you discover about the pheasants, Robert?'
Chantal asked, moving from one difficult subject to another.

'Well, unless the local foxes have acquired wire-cutters
and heavy boots, it's the work of human thieves. Fenton, who
is, Jude, shall we say, traditional in his views, is sure it's the
gypsies. He was all for going up to the site to challenge them,
but I calmed him down and persuaded him that it was a job for
the police. We're meeting an officer at the pens in an hour, so
I'm afraid I'll be leaving you by yourselves again.'

'That's fine,' Jude said mildly, and she and Chantal smiled at
one another, comfortable in the shared knowledge that Robert
would not be restful company for the task in hand.

'There's trouble in the village over the travellers,' Chantal
explained on the way back to the library. 'They've always
come to a site nearby which used to be our land, but the new
landowner isn't happy about it. The council are trying to find
somewhere else for them but of course nobody wants them in
their back yard.'

The afternoon passed peacefully, Jude alone for some of it,
because Chantal liked to take an afternoon rest. She worked

her way through a couple of dozen more books, then, for variety, again picked up the first of Wickham's observation diaries. She loved the feel and the smell of the old leather binding, and the beautifully tooled spine. The script proved fairly easy to her practised eye, even without the help of Chantal's transcription. Each entry began with a general description of the sky before listing the detailed observations of each object viewed. The date of the first entry was 2 September 1760.

A clear night with no moon. The jewelled cloak of the Milky Way adorns the north to the south-west. Queen Cassiopeia rides the north-eastern sky, the constellation of her husband Cepheus nearby. To the east lies their daughter Andromeda, chained to her rock, and nearby her saviour Perseus, with Pegasus his winged horse. 'Tis a delight that the skies tell their story.

5 September
To the south lies the Great Square of Pegasus. The head of Pisces faint, but lonely Fomalhaut bright tonight.

9 September
New moon rising. Shreds of cloud. Camelopardalis shimmers just visible.

The entries continued much in this vein. As well as observing constellations, Wickham seemed interested in the planets, especially Mars, to which he referred as 'our nearest celestial brother'. Only rarely did his personality threaten to break through the dry objectivity of his notes: 'Moon too bright again. A night wasted.' Or 'Rings of Saturn wondrous bright, praise the hand of our Creator.'

There were seven or eight more notebooks like this, each covering two or three years, and she flipped through several of them, admiring the occasional small diagram plotting the position of a new-found star or the patterns on the face of the moon. Sometimes the entries were in a different handwriting and this new hand gradually became more frequent. Halfway through the last book, which covered 1777 and early 1778, the new handwriting prevailed. It was puzzling. The recordings were still in the same clipped tones, but they were definitely penned by someone else. Dictated by the original writer, perhaps. Curious. Jude considered the saleability of the journals. It was difficult to put a value on something like these without knowing more about their context. She would email her friend Cecelia tonight, to ask if she'd have a look. She opened the final volume again, at random, and read with a little jolt of surprise the following entry for 1 June 1777, written in the newer hand:

The new telescope installed at the folly. Some adjustment necessary. Twelve midnight. The stars in the long tail of Draco the Dragon immediately more clear. A crescent moon of ethereal beauty.

The folly. The same one Gran had mentioned, presumably. Jude put down the book and stepped over to the window to look out again at the distant line of trees. She couldn't see anything. Perhaps it was in the grounds at the back, where she hadn't been, but Gran had talked about it being in a forest.

'Chantal,' she asked, when she came in with a tea tray, Miffy shuffling behind. 'Is there still a folly on the estate? There's a mention of it in one of the journals, you see.'

'There's a tower, yes. You see where the trees begin? You can't usually see it from the house, but it's up on top of the hill there.'

So Jude was right. She stared at where the wood sloped gently upwards and scanned the skyline, but she still saw no tower.

'It's hardly visited now. I've only been up it once; it's considered dangerous and kept locked. Once, years ago, some hippies broke in and had a party, and someone had a dreadful accident. After that it was fenced off. It's a listed building, but we couldn't afford to repair it. William sold the forest where it stands a few years before he died. It seemed sensible and we knew the person we were selling it to. He looked after the woods properly. Unfortunately he died soon after William, and his widow sold the land on. We don't know yet what the new landowner plans – apart from not wanting the poor old gypsies.'

'Will he keep it as woodland?'

'I don't know, Jude, but wouldn't he have to if it's ancient forest? I hope so, anyway. There are so few really wild places left. There are deer there, and badgers, and rare birds, Robert says.'

'What about the gamekeeper's cottage?' Jude remembered. 'Where Gran was brought up. Is that still standing?'

'Yes, it's up the road to the right, but that too is no longer ours. It went with the farmland back in the sixties. We don't really know the man who lives there now.'

'Not your George Fenton?'

'No, no, he's not a real gamekeeper. George is more of an odd-job man and works for different people. He lives in the village.'

'It is *such* a coincidence for me to have family connections here.'

'Isn't it?' said Chantal, smiling. 'That Robert should have found you and invited you here is amazing.'

'He might have got my colleague Inigo,' Jude recalled. 'But it was me who answered the phone.'

'These things are meant to be,' Chantal said, turning up her palms. 'Perhaps there's some purpose in your visit we don't yet know about. I do believe in fate, destiny, whatever you like to call it. Don't you?'

Jude glanced up at the ceiling, at the zodiac signs. 'Standing under these, it's tempting to agree. My sister would; she's always reading horoscopes. I used to think that things were, as you say, meant to be.' She thought of Mark. 'But now it seems to me that they're chaotic, random. That's why I like fossicking about in the past, I suppose. You're safe with history. It's all happened and there waiting if you look for it.'

'But sometimes even the past has the power to surprise you,' Chantal said softly and Jude felt a feather's touch of fear.

At four o'clock, Robert reappeared. His presence in the oval library was irritating, for he wouldn't sit quietly and let Jude get on with the job in the way that his mother did. He paced up and down, looking over her shoulder and generally ruining her concentration.

'What makes a book valuable?' he asked at one point, and Jude patiently described matters of rarity and printing history, the condition of the volume and the realities of the market – whether collectors were currently interested in the author or the subject matter.

'And you think this collection really will be in demand?'

'I do. The history of science is a popular area at the moment, and you've some particularly well preserved examples of some quite rare—'

'But you can't put a price on them now?' he interrupted

'I'm getting there,' Jude said gently. 'It's—'

'Yes, of course, you've explained. It's impossible to tell what they'll actually fetch. But that ballpark figure . . . ?'

'Robert, stop bullying the poor girl,' Chantal ordered. 'She's worked so hard today—'

'I didn't say she hadn't,' Robert said quickly. 'You'll stay to dinner tonight, Jude, I hope? Would that be all right, Mother?'

'Actually, no, thank you anyway,' Jude broke in. 'I promised I'd eat at my sister's. In fact, if you don't mind, this seems a good point to finish for the day. I'll be back in the morning, of course.'

Leaving the formal confines of the house and getting into her car wrenched Jude back to the modern world. Turning on her BlackBerry and checking her messages underlined that. There were two missed calls and four emails from Inigo, each one terser than the last. The final email told her he was desperate to talk to her about something, would she please respond *asap*? She wondered why he sounded quite so cross. There were several other messages; she hoped there would be one from Caspar, but there wasn't. With a sigh she dialled Inigo's office number, praying that he wouldn't answer. He did, after the second ring.

'About time. I've been trying to get you all day,' he whined down the line. 'Lord Madingsfield's taken his collection to Sotheby's. It's a bloody disaster. Klaus thinks I wasn't proactive enough, but you know how long I've spent charming the old fox. You must speak to Klaus and remind him. He's furious. Oh and Suri can't find those blasted figures for Monday on your computer. Are you sure they're there?'

'Yes. The folder's clearly labelled and the file must be something like: "Valuations". I'm sorry about Lord Madingsfield, Inigo, and I'll certainly talk to Klaus on Monday, if you honestly think it would help.'

'It turns out Madingsfield has a cousin at Sotheby's, can you believe. He was obviously using us as a stalking horse all the time to up his cousin's offer.'

'Really? How can that be your fault? Have you explained to Klaus?'

'Yes, of course I have.'

'I expect he'll calm down once he's thought about it. It sounds like he's under pressure from upstairs. And on that subject, who else is going to be at this meeting on Monday?'

By the time Jude ended the call, the peace of her day was in shreds. Why did Inigo make everything so pressured and competitive? When she'd entered the world of antiquarian books ten years before, following her PhD, she'd believed it would be a quiet and civilized job, dealing with cultured, civilized people. But the atmosphere at Beecham's was anything but that. The senior management and the American owners, she'd long concluded, were a cut-throat crew with their eye on the bottom line. It was a business like any other, she supposed, stuffing the phone back into her bag and turning the key in the ignition.

Chapter 5

Instead of returning the way she'd come that morning, she turned right out of the park towards Felbarton – the village a couple of miles away, where Claire and Summer lived.

The calm beauty of the countryside, bathed in late-afternoon summer sunshine, eased her inner turmoil slightly. She kept half an eye out for the gamekeeper's cottage, but must have missed it, then the route took her on through a tunnel of trees, the beginning of the woodland she'd seen from the library window. She wondered now about the folly, where exactly it might be. She slowed a little, to peer through the dense foliage on the right as she went up the hill, but could see nothing that might be a building. As she rounded a bend, a large transit van swerved past her in the opposite direction, horn blaring and lights flashing. She realized with horror that she'd veered across the middle of the road. Shaky with shock, she stopped in a passing place to recover.

It was dark and cool under the trees; few rays of sunlight slanted down onto the narrow lane. Somewhere in the car from a previous visit, she might have a large-scale map. She got out and rummaged in the boot till she found it, but was disappointed to find it was a holiday map of Norfolk that concentrated on tourist attractions. Unfolding it, she found Starbrough village, but Starbrough Hall wasn't even labelled, and although the markings indicated forest, there was no sign of any building that might be the folly. She did notice a line suggesting a public footpath leading through the woods and it started from this road. If she walked up the hill a little further, she might find it.

She looked at her watch. Five o'clock. Claire wouldn't leave the shop before half-past, and then would need to collect Summer from a friend's house, so the earliest Jude need turn up at Blacksmith's Cottage was six. She dug a pair of trainers out of her weekend bag, pondered and rejected the embarrassing idea of struggling into her jeans by the roadside. She'd only be a moment. She hid her handbag under a seat and locked the car. Crossing the road to face any oncoming traffic, she set off up the lane, looking for the footpath. The woodland was so thick with ivy and brambles, it would be foolhardy to try to force another way through.

She almost missed the track when it came. It wasn't labelled as a public footpath. Instead there was a newish-looking sign that said 'Private Land' nailed to a tree. Well, it had looked like a public right of way on the admittedly sketchy map. She'd go a little distance along and see where it led.

The path, at first clear, soon became arduous and she wished she'd put on the jeans. Brambles snagged her tights, nettles stung her bare skin. She brandished a dead branch to forge her way through.

Just as she was ready to turn back the landscape began to change. The scrawny sycamore and hazel poking up from dense, scrubby undergrowth gave way to big, more widely spaced trees – beech and oak and sweet chestnut – whose thick canopy excluded much of the light so that beneath it little grew, save patches of ivy and bright dots of woodland flowers. The walking became easier.

Sometimes the trees petered out altogether into patches of grass, littered with brushwood. There was little sign of human influence on this wilderness. The air all around was alive with birdsong. Ahead, a grey squirrel leaped up a tree, clacking angrily at her approach. She was suddenly aware of the loneliness of this spot. Why had she come here? No one knew where she was. She could trip, break her ankle, and lie here all night until someone raised the alarm and then it might be hours before they found her car . . . Her thoughts ran on crazily.

Suddenly the world exploded with a series of loud cracks. Gunfire. And close by, too. Was she the target? She couldn't tell. She gazed round wildly. Run. She'd read that somewhere. She staggered into a trot, ahead, uphill, away from the sounds. But the shots seemed to be following her.

The path took her through denser woodland. She pushed and tripped her way, her breath came in heavy, sobbing pants. Finally, exhausted, she slumped against a tree. The shots were moving away now. Relief gave way to rage. How dare they? Didn't they know people might be there? She remembered the 'Private' sign. Still, children might wander in. She crouched in the loam, the smell of rotting leaves immediately overwhelming. She should go back, but she was fearful of walking into the gunfire again. She tried to think calmly.

It was then she saw it. The most horrible thing. A rotting tree trunk festooned with dead animals in varying degrees of decomposition: a fox cub; a couple of rats; a mess of black and white feathers, all that remained of a magpie. It must be a gamekeeper's gibbet, the corpses a warning to the scurrying scavengers of the forest: keep away or this will happen to you! She crept past the gibbet, her gorge rising, and hurried on.

Ahead through the trees streams of sunlight poured down on open ground. She should be near the top of the hill now, and it might be possible to get her bearings. She walked towards the light.

Emerging into the clearing, she blinked at the brightness. After a moment she saw the tower.

At first, dazzled and confused, she thought it the trunk of some huge tree, then she grasped that the column was made of brick. Shielding her eyes, she looked up to see it looming high above her, up in the forest canopy, as tall as the tallest tree. It was dizzying. She took a step towards it and felt something claw at her leg. She looked down, gasping with pain. The sun glinted off the coil of barbed wire digging into her flesh. She crouched to unhook it, then cried out as blood quickly surged from the cut.

Glancing around she saw the wire was part of a vicious-looking fence, but here it had been cut and bent back. There was another sign, like the one that said 'Private Land', hanging off a fence post. 'Keep Out, dangerous structure' this one read. Everywhere shouted 'Go away' at her. How horrible this place was. She fumbled a packet of tissues from her jacket pocket and clamped one over the wound, trying vaguely to remember the date of her last tetanus jab.

While she waited for the bleeding to stop she spotted some-thing caught in a coil of fence a few feet away. She hobbled over to look. It was an animal, a small deer, and it was dead. A baby perhaps, she thought, or one of those little muntjacs; yes, a muntjac, she decided, from the grey markings on its face, a young one at that. She'd seen a picture of one in a newspaper. It hadn't been dead for long, poor thing. Its eyes were just glazing over. She put out a finger and touched its shoulder – the body was still warm. When she brought her hand away it was sticky with blood. She wiped it off hastily on the grass and studied the corpse more closely. Its head hung at a strange angle and there was a gunshot wound in its side.

Anger surged through her – anger and fear and sadness. How could someone do this to such a fragile creature? Wound it so it fled, terrified and in pain, and caught itself on the wire, as she had.

A noise made her look up. From round the side of the tower came a man swinging a spade. She couldn't see his face against the light and suddenly she caught a remnant of the muntjac's terror.

He stopped when he saw her. 'What are you doing here?' he said roughly.

She got to her feet, her heart pounding, and all the rage and fear of the last few minutes rose in her like hot lava.

'Why the hell's it your business?' she cried. 'How could you do this to a defenceless animal? And I nearly got shot myself.'

'Oh, for goodness sake. What are you doing here when everything's marked private? You look old enough to know better.'

'I saw the signs, but I took what I thought was a public footpath. What if I'd been a child? Does a "Private" sign give you the right to be cruel? And that gibbet, it's . . . medieval.'

'Do you always shout at complete strangers?' he said. The man was monstrous. He ignored everything she said.

'I do when they shoot at people,' she cried. 'And animals. You did shoot this deer, didn't you?'

'No,' he said quietly. 'But I did put it out of its misery, poor bastard, and now I'm going to bury it.'

'How incredibly kind of you,' she sneered, still angry, 'when it was your barbed wire it was caught up in.'

'It isn't my barbed wire. You really are extraordinary,' he said, shaking his head. 'You're accusing me of all sorts of things I haven't done. I think you'd better go. No, not that way!' he cried, as she turned back the way she'd come. 'You'll get shot at again!'

'Don't you threaten me!'

'I wasn't. You've misunderstood.' His voice was gentle. 'Look, you have nothing to fear from me. But you really ought to go. Not least to get that cut dealt with.'

She examined the wound. It was an awful mess.

'What are you doing here, anyway, dressed up like a dinner?'

'Looking for this,' she replied, nodding at the tower, and starting to feel a little foolish.

'The folly?'

'Yes.'

'Why?'

'It interests me, that's all.'

'Because . . . ?'

'It's complicated.'

'OK, well you've found it now. And believe me when I tell you it would be sensible to go. I don't know who's been out shooting, but they might be along any moment.'

She really hadn't much choice and she didn't feel like exploring now anyway.

'Come on,' he said. 'I'll show you the quickest way back to the road. Do you have a vehicle?' She nodded. He set off across the clearing and she had to hurry to keep up, the throbbing pain in her leg only just bearable.

As they passed out of the dazzling light and under the trees at the other side of the tower, she was able to view her companion more clearly. He was big, powerfully built in a way that reminded her of Caspar, but his dark curly hair was longer, more unruly than Caspar's and where Caspar's skin was boardroom pale, his was tanned. He glanced back at her occasionally to make sure she was following and though he didn't smile his dark-fringed eyes were not unfriendly. Again, she was reminded of Caspar, which confused her. Both men had the same physical presence, a charisma. He wore a flannel shirt, the sleeves rolled up to show strong-muscled arms. His jeans were tucked into wellingtons. The spade swung lightly in his strong brown fingers. She imagined those fingers dispatching the wretched muntjac and shivered.

After two or three minutes they reached a wider path, marked with vehicle tracks.

'Walk down there, turn left at the T-junction and after a few hundred yards you'll be back where you started,' he said briskly. 'Are you all right with that cut? I can take you back to mine and—'

'I've got some plasters in the car,' she interrupted. 'Thanks,' she added grudgingly, and set off down the path. He called out something and she turned. 'What?'

'I said, come and find me another time and I'll show you the folly. You shouldn't go up it on your own.'

'What . . . ?' she said again, though she'd heard him that time, she was just surprised at the offer.

'I said it's not safe. The house at the bottom of the hill. That's where you'll find me.'

'All right,' she said. 'Maybe.'

The trudge down the slope jolted her weary body and she reached the car feeling terribly weak. She collapsed in the driver's seat for a few moments, then remembered there was a chocolate bar in the glove compartment. She dug it out from among the CD boxes and old biros, glad to find her small first-aid kit there, too. When she'd eaten the chocolate she peeled off her wrecked tights and cleaned up the wound. It didn't look very serious, though it still hurt.

Feeling better she drove up the hill, wondering about the house he mentioned. She must have passed it in the car earlier, further back towards Starbrough Hall. Noticing the junction with the lane where she'd parted from him, and wishing she'd found it rather than the overgrown footpath, she continued towards Felbarton.

Chapter 6

Jude closed the rickety garden gate of Blacksmith's Cottage and walked up the path. Then stopped, amused by the sight of a small girl periodically rising and falling above the level of the back-garden wall, to the rhythmic accompaniment of thuds and squeaks. Summer's eyes were closed as she bounced on her trampoline and her lips moved as though she were lost in some chanting song. How ethereal she seemed, Jude thought tenderly. In her pink capri pants and embroidered crop top, with her fine hair flying about her face, her niece was as light and supple as the swifts that dipped and soared in the evening air.

As though sensing she was watched, Summer's eyes flicked open. 'Auntie Jude,' she shouted. She launched herself off the trampoline and disappeared from sight, but Jude could hear her calling, 'Mummy, Mummy, Auntie Jude's here,' in the depths of the cottage.

As Jude waited for the front door to open, she admired the mass of white roses growing over the porch and the window boxes of geraniums and trailing lobelia. Her sister had a natural ability with these things. She remembered the solitary, straggling spider plant on her own kitchen windowsill in Greenwich.

'Well, aren't you coming in then?' Claire called from the doorway. Her abrupt manner was always a surprising contrast to her gracious ways with beautiful things. Only those, like Jude, who knew her well, saw beyond it to the warmth beneath. The brusque way of speaking had long been part of her armour against the world. 'What the hell have you done to yourself?' Claire cried.

Jude looked down at her crumpled jacket and skirt. Blood was seeping out from under the plaster on her shin. 'It's a long story,' she said.

Summer ducked beneath her mother's arm, danced out and grabbed Jude's hand, drawing her inside. The three of them stumbled together into the tiny living room. Claire perched on the arm of a chair while Jude flopped onto the sofa, and Summer cuddled into her lap. Jude stroked the little girl's hair, breathing in the flowery smell of her. A mixture of happiness and longing flared inside, but then the moment was gone – Summer never stayed still for long. 'Will you come upstairs, Auntie Jude?' commanded Summer. 'I want to show you my doll's house. I've just made some pictures to go on the walls.'

'Let your poor aunt rest a moment,' Claire said, glancing again curiously at Jude's cut. 'I'll put the kettle on, shall I? Have a shower and change, if you want.'

'I don't mind making the tea,' Jude said tentatively, but what she meant as a genuine offer of help was, as usual, interpreted wrongly.

'I can manage, thank you,' Claire said firmly. 'It's you who's in the wars today.'

Jude watched her push herself upright and limp into the kitchen. Although all the operations on her leg had made a difference, they had never entirely solved the original problem. After she was sixteen, Claire refused to endure any more treatment.

'Come on, Auntie Jude.' Summer ran ahead upstairs.

Claire called from the kitchen, 'I put some bedding out. Find yourself a towel in the bathroom cupboard.'

'Thanks.' Jude was looking round the living room, aware something was different. 'Ah! That's a gorgeous rug you've found.' Claire was so clever in the way she'd arranged everything.

Blacksmith's Cottage, on the edge of Felbarton village and dating from the seventeenth century, was tiny, higgledy-piggledy and thatch-roofed. As well as the kitchen and living room there was a small dining room downstairs that doubled as Claire's office, and upstairs were two bedrooms and a bathroom. With more than Claire and Summer in it, the cottage felt crowded, but Claire, who bought it two years ago, when the Star Bureau started to come into profit, had made the best of its quaintness, staining and varnishing all the beams herself and painting the lathe and plaster walls a soft China white. A woodstove had been fitted in the old fireplace, the surround decorated with brightly polished copper pans. The neutral-coloured sofa was brightened by a blue and white throw and cushions. The thick brown and blue patterned hearth rug was one of several pretty mats on the floor.

As Jude picked up her overnight bag and mounted the stairs she noticed something else new. 'These collages on the landing,' she called down, 'they're lovely. Are they from the shop?' There were two bright, almost mystical scenes of trees and stars made of bark and painted paper, the detail drawn in pen and ink.

'Do you like them?' Claire replied. 'Summer's got a friend called Darcey. Her uncle makes them. We took some for the Star Bureau and I couldn't resist doing a deal for a couple of extra for myself.'

Summer's room was decorated fit for a fairy-tale princess. Pale plastic stars dotted the ceiling. Jude knew they glowed green-white in the dark. Her niece's truckle bed was pink and white, with curtains of pink and silver muslin framing the bedhead. Claire had painted the walls with shy woodland creatures that seemed to peep round the vertical beams with large gentle eyes. Under the eyes of a pretty fawn, Summer sat cross-legged on the floor playing with a painted plywood doll's house. Jude dropped her bag on the mattress Claire had laid out and knelt down next to Summer to see properly. The house, she was astonished to realize, was an exact replica of Blacksmith's Cottage, down to the chimneys and the window boxes.

'Look, this is me,' Summer said, showing Jude a wooden doll dressed in an outfit rather similar to the one she now wore. 'And this is Mummy.' The Mummy doll wore a replica of one of Claire's long cotton skirts and tops and tiny dangling earrings.

'And this is Pandora.' The china cat had been painted with her real-life counterpart's exact black and white markings. Summer made them all dance through the doll's house. The two dolls had jointed limbs and Summer could sit them on chairs or, in the case of the little girl, make her kneel on the floor.

'They're amazing. Where did you get them from?' Jude asked, picking up a little kitchen chair to study it properly.

'Euan made them for me. He's Darcey's uncle.'

'Did he make the pictures on the staircase, too?' Jude asked. Whoever the talented Euan was he had clearly become something of a friend.

'Mmm,' Summer replied vaguely, lost in her game. 'Now you go to sleep,' she told the little girl doll, laying her on the bed in the replica princess bedroom. 'Or you won't enjoy school tomorrow because you'll be too tired. Sweet dreams, my darling!'

Remembering what Claire had told her, that Summer's dreams were anything but sweet, Jude reached out a hand and stroked the girl's hair. Should she say something? But now Summer had moved the Mummy doll downstairs and was making her feed the cat. The moment had passed.

'Have you ever been inside Starbrough Hall?' Jude, now changed into jeans and long-sleeved T-shirt, was watching her sister make supper.

Her sister, stirring a pan of risotto, shook her head. 'No, just glimpsed it from the road. What did you say you're doing there?'

'I'm valuing a collection of books and scientific instruments. They once belonged to an amateur astronomer. Look, I'll do that.' She took the saucepan for the broccoli side dish from Claire to fill from the tap.

'Thanks,' Claire muttered. 'So is it valuable, this stuff?'

'Some of it, yes,' said Jude, placing the pan on the stove. 'But it's really interesting, too. This man, Anthony Wickham, he lived at the end of the eighteenth century and I think he built the folly in the forest. He used it for stargazing. And when I went to see Gran last night, she mentioned the folly, too. So that's how I got myself in such a mess just now. I thought I'd go and look for it. Have you seen it?'

'I nearly went with Mum once, but we didn't quite make it. It's a ruin, people say. Did you find it?'

'Yes, eventually, and it doesn't look like a ruin. I found a foot-path and thought it would be straightforward, but then some idiot started shooting right near me and I panicked and ran.'

'You have to be careful about that,' Claire said, frowning. 'They must be killing foxes or rabbits or something; the pheas-ant season hasn't started yet. I hate it when it does – those poor birds, it's barbaric. But at least most people involved act responsibly.'

'Not whoever it was today. Anyway, I found the folly, but I didn't have a chance to get a proper look. There was a dead deer caught in barbed wire. Someone had shot it. And this man appeared and since he was holding a shovel I put two and two together. I got quite cross, actually, but then he was quite unpleasant.' Jude stopped, and tried to remember. 'Oh dear, it was a bit embarrassing. I assumed it was he who'd wounded the deer and perhaps I was wrong. He said he'd put it out of its misery. Anyway, he was very rude. Said it was private property and practically frogmarched me off his land.'

Claire laughed. 'It's like I said. You can't go nosing anywhere you like round here. You city types, you think everything's laid out for you.'

'I'm not a city type.'

'Yes, you are! Look at you. Going for a country ramble in a posh suit and stockings. Bossing some poor landowner who's merely going about his business. You're like that couple who've moved into the barn conversion down the road and complain about the smell of the farmer's fertilizer.'

'You've just said yourself the pheasant shooting is barbaric.'

'I know, and I wouldn't do it myself, but the land wouldn't be managed or the pheasants bred in the first place if people didn't want to go shooting. People from the cities don't see all that. And the government doesn't care about the countryside because there aren't votes for them there.' Claire banged a lid onto the simmering broccoli.

Why do we always argue about something? Jude thought, bemused. How did we get onto politics? She sighed and changed tack.

'Going back to the folly. Has Gran ever talked about it to you?'

'No, why, what did she say to you?'

'Something about someone she met in the forest there as a child.'

Claire tasted the risotto, frowned, and added a dollop of butter. 'I don't know anything about that.'

'Where's the gamekeeper's cottage? Any idea?'

'That? You must have passed it on the road from the Hall. On the left just before you go up the hill. I know who lives there. It's Euan, actually, the man who made those pictures.'

'The house at the bottom of the hill.' That was what the man by the folly said. Well, there could be other houses, but she hadn't noticed any. 'That might have been him I met,' she said. 'Euan. I think he was the man at the folly. Big? Curly dark hair. Quite sun-tanned.'

'It sounds like Euan,' went on Claire, regarding her sister with a watchful expression.

'But he's not the landowner, is he? The man who made the doll's house? Really?'

'I don't know what land he owns, but it's definitely Euan who lives in Gamekeeper's Cottage, and he definitely looks how you've described. He's become great friends with Summer. He came to the shop with the pictures at half-term, when Summer happened to be there. He had Darcey with him. She's in Summer's class. Summer's been over to play there. And once he took them out for the day. I invited him round here for supper to say thank you, and then last week he turned up out of the blue with the doll's house. He had made one for Darcey apparently, and Summer was cheeky enough to ask for one, too. You know how persuasive she can be. He's a really nice guy.'

'Is he?' Jude said doubtfully, thinking of her argument with him.

'Yes. He probably didn't like you accusing him of stuff.'

'I did have a reason . . . I was shocked, that's all. Oh hell, have I made a fool of myself?'

'I expect he'll forgive you.'

Claire seemed very supportive of Euan. Jude smiled and said, 'So, married, is he?'

'No, divorced, I think. But don't go thinking anything,' Claire said, prickly as a chestnut burr. Close as one too.

Jude put up her hands in mock defence. 'I wouldn't dream of it,' she said.

It was a long time since there had been a man in Claire's life. 'I'm too independent. I frighten them off,' she'd confessed a year or two ago after a couple of glasses of wine. Her relationships had often been short and fiery. Jude had seen her go in too deep too quickly with a man and then, before you knew it, she would be practically throwing saucepans at him, and he'd be on his way. No one in true honesty knew who Summer's father was. Claire had always refused to tell.

'That pop singer she met at the arts centre,' was their mother's belief, though Claire had never admitted it, but Jude thought she could be right. Jon, was his name. He'd had a mop of curly yellow hair and Summer's large dreamy blue eyes. Claire brought him to Christmas lunch at their mother's because he'd fallen out with his dad. It was the first Christmas since the girls' father had died, and they were finding it difficult enough to be jolly as it was. Jon had arrived late and Claire hardly spoke to him the whole time; he kept going outside to smoke odd-smelling roll-ups and then he'd left early. 'Without even saying a proper thank you,' Valerie whispered angrily to Jude and Mark that evening over the washing-up. Valerie and Claire had rowed about it and Claire had stomped up to bed and slammed the door, like she used to when she was fifteen. 'You can never say anything to her without her flying off the handle,' Valerie said bitterly.

'Perhaps you shouldn't have told her to "go out with someone decent for a change",' Jude observed with a sigh. She often thought how alike Claire and her mother were in temperament. Valerie could be petulant, too often overwhelmed by the responsibilities of motherhood, and she would frequently resort to screeching matches. Their father had been the calm one they all relied on. They all missed him terribly.

Jude had always hated having to make up for Claire. Ever peace-loving, she had been the well-behaved one, the child who worked well at school, went to university, landed a proper job and got married. Claire, in turn, intelligent but rebellious at school, hopeless at sport with her limp, had resented Jude for dutifully conforming. She'd walked out of the door when she was seventeen, but every time she got thrown out of the latest in a series of bedsits and rackety flatshares she'd be back home for a while.

After that Christmas, Jon made no further appearance, and a few weeks later, when Jude rang her sister and asked tentatively about him she said, 'Oh, him,' dismissively. It was a couple of months after this that she announced with a kind of grim delight that she was pregnant.

Having Summer made Claire suddenly grow up.

'How do you think Summer is?' Claire asked her now as she placed plates in the oven to warm. Jude couldn't see her face, but she heard a note of anxiety under her casual tone. She didn't think it an overstatement to say that Claire would die for Summer.

Once the baby came, it was plain to all that Claire had discovered a purpose in life. She'd given up her job at the vintage clothes stall on the market and started up her own business with her friend Linda; she had saved for a deposit and bought this dear little house, which she'd decorated so beautifully. She'd started to value her family, visiting their grandmother regularly, and relying on Valerie – as much as Valerie's flitting about allowed – for babysitting and grandmotherly treats. Valerie's move to Spain was turning out to be a much bigger blow to Claire than anyone would have predicted. And it wasn't just because of the babysitting. Claire genuinely seemed to miss her mother.

'Summer seems her usual happy self to me,' Jude replied.

'She is, most of the time,' Claire said, opening the fridge. 'That's what's so strange. If the bad dreams are because of stress, then she certainly doesn't show it in other ways.'

Jude studied her sister now, as Claire rummaged in a drawer for the kitchen scissors and cut open a box of pink grapefruit juice. At thirty-six, Claire was still elfin pretty, her streaked blonde hair as fine as Summer's, cut in a feathery mid-length style that framed her pointed face. Her clothes, acquired by skilful rummaging in charity shops and kooky bohemian boutiques, always perfectly showed off her slim figure, the colours in shades that complemented her English complexion. How could two sisters be so different? Jude wondered, catching sight of her own round face and thick gingery-blonde wavy hair in the shell-studded mirror above the sink.

'When did the dreams start?' she asked.

'About a month ago,' Claire explained. 'At half-term. Not every night. About one in three, though.'

'Do you know, they sound rather like the ones I used to have when I was little.'

'Really? I'd almost forgotten about those,' her sister said. 'That's why I asked to move into my own bedroom. You, moaning and groaning in your sleep. When did they stop?'

Jude shrugged. 'I don't remember. I suppose I grew out of them.' She didn't mention the one she'd had recently; it seemed to be a one-off.

'Perhaps it's a normal phase with Summer, then.'

The thought seemed to reassure Claire.

'Will you allow me to lay the table?' asked Jude.

'Yes, of course. There's a cloth in the top drawer. Here, Summer likes this.' She handed Jude the fruit juice. 'Shall we open the wine you brought?'

Jude cleared books and papers off the dining-room table, spread a gingham cloth and arranged two star-shaped candlesticks in the middle. Seeing Claire's laptop on a side table she was reminded of Beecham's and information she ought to send her boss. When she returned to the kitchen for glasses she asked Claire, 'Is the broadband connection up and running? I wondered if you could bear me doing a little work tonight? I've got to prepare for a meeting on Monday.'

'Of course,' Claire said. 'I think everything's working. Pass me that bowl for the broccoli, will you? I'll bring this through. Can you call Summer?'

'Mum rang last night,' Claire said, when they sat down to eat. 'Finally. It's incredibly hot out there, apparently. I mean really hot, nearly a hundred. The air-conditioning isn't working and the builders have bungled the plumbing, so they're staying with friends while Douglas sorts it out.'

'Poor Mum,' said Jude.

'Lucky Mum,' Claire replied sardonically. 'Remember, she has good old Douglas.'

Jude grinned. After years of helpless widowhood, their mother took up Latin American dancing and met a new life partner. Douglas Hopkirk, retired actuary, was in some ways like their father – calm, practical, reassuring. 'But he's so dull,' Jude remembered Claire complaining to her after they'd first been introduced to him. 'Nobody these days dresses like David Niven or says "Righto" and drinks Cinzano. No wonder his wife went off.'

'After thirty years of marriage,' Jude had replied. 'He must have had something going for him. He's very nice, actually. As long as you don't ask him about golf. He can bore for England about handicaps.'

'Or his tortoises. He went on to me half the evening about his wretched tortoises,' Claire had added with feeling.

'What have they done with the tortoises?' Jude wondered now. 'Can you take them on a plane?'

'They're with his daughter, but he's planning to get them to Spain somehow and breed from them. I already know more than anyone would ever want to know about their mating habits, thank you.'

'What do the tortoises do?' asked Summer, who'd been picking the mushrooms out of her risotto and piling them on a spare tablespoon.

'They, er, have to try quite hard to make baby tortoises,' Jude said quickly.

'Harder than people?'

'Sometimes it's hard with people,' she said, with feeling.

'You need a daddy to make babies, don't you?' Summer said. 'I told Emily's mum I didn't have a daddy and she says I must be a miracle.'

'You are my little miracle,' Claire said solemnly. 'We don't need a daddy.'

'Auntie Jude, if you want a baby you need a man to be a daddy.' Summer was too young to remember Mark.

'Eat up your risotto, Summer,' Claire murmured.

'Yes, I do, Summer. But it's not that easy finding one,' Jude replied. She had hardly talked to Claire about Caspar.

Summer regarded her with a serious expression, then said, 'I wish I could find one for you.'

'Thank you. That's very sweet.' Jude and Claire exchanged glances of suppressed amusement.

Claire, gathering up the plates, remarked to her daughter, 'If you develop a matchmaking talent, sweetheart, you'll always be able to earn your living.'

After supper Jude spent an hour on her laptop, studying the depressing monthly figures Inigo had emailed her and writing reassuring messages to the head of department. She promised to come into the office early on Monday and explained excitedly about the Starbrough collection.

She still hadn't heard from Caspar. She wasn't sure how much she minded. She remembered the comfort of his arms around her and how she enjoyed being seen with him, and then she did mind. It was good to be wanted again. Perhaps he hadn't been in touch because he was too busy getting ready for Paris. Or was it because it was Tate and Yasmin's party tonight? No, that was tomorrow. Whatever, she was glad she didn't have to go to it and meet more people she didn't really have much in common with.

On balance she'd rather be here. She was looking forward to sitting in that library again and talking to Chantal, going through the books and papers, finding out more about Anthony Wickham, securing the collection for Beecham's.

When she'd finished, which she reckoned would be early afternoon, since it would be Saturday and Claire would be at the shop, she'd collect Summer from her friend's house and take her somewhere. The beach was the most popular idea, if the weather held.

She was just about to close down her laptop when she remembered Cecelia, whose help she needed with the astronomical instruments. She found the address and opened a new email.

Hi, Cecelia,

I'm so sorry I haven't been in touch. I wonder where you are now – Cambridge, still? It would be great to meet and catch up, but I also need to ask your professional advice. When would be a good time? I'm going on holiday at the end of next week, but if there's the tiniest chance you're about before then that would be fantastic. Dinner one evening or a drink?

Much love,

Jude

Jude awoke disorientated in pitch darkness. The moaning that had woken her came again. Summer. Jude pushed herself up dizzily from the mattress and stumbled over in the direction of the noise. Now she could pick out her niece's face in the moonlight that leached under the curtains. Summer's eyes were closed but her expression was anguished. '*Maman, Maman,*' she whispered, 'where are you? *Maman!*' The last word was louder. She stirred and woke with a cry.

Jude sat on the edge of the bed, stroking Summer's hair and whispering, 'It's all right, it's all right, darling. It's only a dream. You're all right. Auntie Jude's here.'

'Mummy,' Summer cried out. 'Mummy.' Her face was pale and clammy.

'Mummy's asleep, darling.'

'No, I'm here,' whispered Claire, pushing open the door. Light from the landing fell across Summer's bed. Jude stood out of the way, feeling rather unnecessary as Claire comforted her daughter.

'I was frightened, Mummy. You weren't there. I couldn't find you,' the little girl sobbed.

'Don't worry, darling. You're awake now and I'm here. It was just a nasty old dream. It's gone now.'

After a while Summer grew peaceful and her eyelids fluttered and closed.

The women watched her for a while, then Claire pulled the duvet round her daughter and stood up.

'I'd take her into my own bed,' she whispered to Jude, 'but then neither of us sleeps. She's awfully wriggly.'

'I'll keep an eye on her,' promised Jude and they both went back to bed.

Jude lay awake for what seemed like hours. It was the same dream that she'd had, she was sure of it. Her heart quickened as she remembered. '*Maman!*' *Maman*, the French word. Running in the dark, tripping and falling into leaf mould, bruised, terrified, alone. Often as a child she'd woken to find her father there – not her mother – and was relieved to feel his comforting arms around her before he settled her down to sleep once more. Poor Summer. What could have set this off? Could a dream run in a family? It seemed unlikely, but what other explanation could there be?

She lay listening to Summer's gentle breathing, worrying and worrying, until the first birds began to sing and she finally drifted back into sleep.

Chapter 7

The next morning, when Jude turned into the drive to Starbrough Hall, she found herself following a Mercedes sports car that flashed silver in the sun. She parked next to it on the forecourt just as an elegant blonde woman got out of the driver's side. Could this be Alexia, Robert's wife? she wondered as she locked her car door, but a quick glance revealed the inside of the Mercedes to be pristine and there were no child seats. The woman said a cool 'Hi' and they agreed that it was another beautiful day. She didn't seem to know about the front door not being used, and Jude, though not confident of the way herself, suggested she follow her under the arch.

Jude knew most of the personnel at Christie's and Sotheby's, and she certainly didn't recognize this ice-maiden, but she couldn't stop herself checking. 'Excuse me asking, but you've not come to look at the library, have you?' She was profoundly relieved when the woman looked puzzled.

'The library? Why?' She didn't volunteer the nature of her business so Jude didn't elaborate.

'Never mind. Just an idea I had.'

Jude knocked on the back door. When Robert opened it the two setters bounced out, barking enthusiastically. Jude petted them, but the other woman backed away in alarm, so he called the animals in and shut them in a utility room.

Rachel Hore

'Come in, ladies.' He introduced Jude to the other woman, Marcia Vane, rather stiffly, then led them through to the hall. There he showed Marcia into what looked like an office and suggested Jude make her way along to the library.

'My mother's waiting for you there,' he said. 'I'm so sorry to be tied up again. Ms Vane rang half an hour ago and asked if she could call in.'

'That's fine,' said Jude, 'honestly,' and she walked into the library, pleased to find Chantal pouring coffee. She felt she needed a gallon after her broken night. This morning Claire had studied her daughter anxiously, but Summer had seemed her usual cheerful self, busy packing a pink rucksack with fashion doll paraphernalia to take to her friend's house.

'What excellent timing,' Chantal said warmly. 'I'm so sorry that it's just me again.'

'Oh that's really all right,' said Jude. 'I'm used to being left on my own altogether, so I'm very lucky that you're looking after me so well.'

'That wretched woman. Nine o'clock on a Saturday morning. Does she have no life of her own?'

'Pardon me?'

'That Marcia person.'

'Who is she?'

'John Farrell's lawyer – the man who's bought the woodland.'

'John. His name's John?' Definitely not Euan, then. So what was Euan doing up at the folly? Trespassing like herself, possibly.

'Yes, John Farrell. A businessman, we're told. Marcia Vane harasses Robert with endless questions about access and shooting rights. I wonder what she wants today? They ought to have sorted it all out when they bought the land, but she doesn't take the hint. That woman has the hide of a rhinoceros.'

'It must be what she's paid for,' Jude said, thinking that the rhinoceros skin in question would only be an appropriate comparison for such a polished, elegant woman as Marcia Vane if it came in the form of a beautifully tooled Hermès handbag.

'I suppose so.'

Jude couldn't have shut the door properly, because it suddenly clicked open. From outside in the corridor, they could hear voices – Robert's raised and agitated, Marcia's low and firm. Then came the sound of the dogs barking and a door slamming. Shortly afterwards, car wheels spun on the gravel and they watched the beautiful Mercedes reverse then tear off down the drive.

Chantal glanced at Jude, her eyebrows raised. 'Well, well, she didn't stay long,' she said.

'She didn't look very happy.' Jude stared down the drive at the speeding car, remembering the sight of Marcia's sullen face through the windscreen. Whatever was going on wasn't her business. She turned from the window and reached in her bag for the laptop lead.

Contemplating yesterday's computer list of entries, anno-tated with estimates, she guessed she'd been through most of the books now. She'd finish the others then devote the rest of the morning to the charts, the observation journals and the instruments. She quickly grew absorbed, and hardly noticed when Chantal excused herself to walk her dog.

She tapped in the last lot of particulars about the books and moved on to the journals. She had no idea whether they were worth very much – it depended on what they contained – but they might throw light on the rest of the collection. She would flick through them quickly and show them to her friend Cecelia.

As she put the last to one side, Chantal returned. Her expres-sion was grim and Jude said, 'Are you all right?'

'I spoke to Robert. It's just something that woman said.' Her face was stony, but she didn't volunteer any more.

Jude went over to the shelves of books to check whether there was anything she'd missed. There didn't seem to be.

'I've finished, I think. Just printing off the figures now. The books and manuscripts alone could be worth £50,000. The orrery, the globe and the telescopes – well, maybe another £50,000, but I need to ask advice. Look.' She passed Chantal the paper her mini-printer had spat out. 'If Robert's happy with these and would like to go forward, I can arrange for everything to be collected.'

Jude saw the look of unhappiness cross Chantal's face as she realized what this meant. That Anthony Wickham's collection would soon be gone.

'I'm sorry,' she whispered, going to sit beside her. 'It's sad. I do understand.'

'I know I must be brave,' Chantal said, hardly looking at the paper. 'These books and things have always been a part of my life here, of all that I've loved about Starbrough Hall, and with William gone it's like reopening a wound. It underlines that . . . I don't belong here any more.'

'Don't belong?' Jude hardly knew this woman but instinctively wanted to comfort her. 'Why do you say that? Your family live here and from what you say they love having you.'

'I know. And home is where the people you love are. But still, I am an outsider. You know, I thought about going back to France to live, but . . . ah, there is hardly anyone left of my generation of the family. My brother is dead, and I am not close to his widow or his children. Still, I have one or two old school friends in Paris it would be good to see more often. I went to a convent school near Notre Dame. The nuns were very strict but they weren't unkind. Oh, it all seems a very long time ago. A different world.'

'I can imagine,' Jude replied, pleased to see the sparkle return to Chantal's eyes as she recalled the past. Paris in the 1950s. It must have been thrilling. Jude imagined elegant *haute couture*, the Left Bank intellectuals, café society. Two neat lines of convent girls walking by the Seine, like in the Madeleine books . . . Jude wondered how on earth Chantal had ended up in rural Norfolk and whether it had been difficult to adapt.

'How was it you met your husband?' she asked.

'Oh, it was because of my aunt, *Tante* Eloise. She married an English army officer she met at the end of the war, and when I was twenty I was sent to stay with them at their beach house at Wells-next-the-Sea. My cousins were still young teenagers and I was supposed to help entertain them while improving my English.'

'We used to go to Wells for holidays,' Jude remembered. 'I love those pretty beach huts.'

'I do now. But I didn't like Norfolk at all at first. It was so bleak and featureless and it seemed it was always cold and raining. Me, I was used to the bright colours of the Riviera for my *vacances*. I was so homesick and my cousins squabbled all the time. One day, about two weeks after I arrived, I escaped and sat in a beach café and wept. It was there William found me.

'The poor man. Later, he confessed that he, too, had been very unhappy that day. He had motored to Wells with a girl he very much liked, and another friend, a man, and during the course of the morning it had become apparent that the girl much preferred his friend, and so he'd made his excuses and left them together. Which was marvellously generous of him. He was always like that, very modest.

'We spent such a lovely afternoon after I cheered up, just walking on the beach and visiting the town. And afterwards he walked me back to the house and I introduced him to *Tante* Eloise – dear Eloise, I do miss her. Well, that was the start of it all. Forty-six years he and I had together. I know we were lucky, Jude. Lucky to have met by chance like that. Lucky to have had so much happiness together.'

She was staring out of the window now, fondling the little dog at her side on the sofa. Then she glanced at Jude and gave her the kindest of smiles. 'I am sorry you had so little time together, you and your husband. Life can be so unfair.'

Jude said, trying to keep her voice steady, 'We were only married for three years, but we knew one another for much longer. We met at school in Norwich, you see.'

Chantal nodded. 'Were you ... attracted to one another straight away?'

'I think we were. I certainly was. And later, he told me that he liked me very much but that he didn't realize it immediately.'

It was then that the door opened and Robert Wickham entered. He took in the scene, the women sitting together, Chantal holding Jude's hand, and said, 'Sorry if I'm interrupting something. I'm informed that lunch is ready.'

'Please don't worry,' said Jude, rising to her feet. 'I've just been showing your mother these estimates.'

At lunch she explained: 'They are only estimates, of course. I told you I have to do further research. It's possible that we could achieve a higher figure, especially with a good publicity campaign to attract the right bidders.' They talked about this aspect for some time, Jude describing how they used mailing lists and websites and articles in the company magazine to seed a campaign in the media.

Robert seemed pleased with the figures and with Jude's proposals and said he'd like to think about the matter over during the rest of the weekend. They would communicate again on Monday once she was back in the office.

'Then, if you're happy, I can arrange for everything to be collected and catalogued,' she said. 'As I said, the instruments will need a specialist eye and I'll deal with that side for you.'

'That would be splendid,' agreed Robert.

'There is something I'd like to take now, if I may, though. The observation diaries. I have a friend, an expert, who might cast some light on what they contain.'

'And comment on their value, no doubt,' said Robert. 'Yes, of course, take them with you. I'll find something you can wrap them in.'

Jude drove away after lunch with a sense of satisfaction. If this job came off, as she thought it would – the very fact that the box containing the observation diaries was safely in the boot underlined that – Beecham's would be delighted. She would relish researching the background to the collection. It was one of the bits she loved most about her job: the history. It would be good, too, to see more of Chantal. Talking to her about Mark was painful, but she felt Chantal understood in a way that no one else did – even her widowed mother.

Now, finally, she could allow the memories in.

She remembered their first meeting. It was sixteen, no, nearly eighteen years ago now, the second day of Sixth Form. She'd seen him in the distance a couple of times, the new boy, tall, with a trendy lick of butter-coloured hair and an aura of pleasant self-confidence.

She and Sophie were dawdling their way downstairs after their first English Literature lesson, comparing timetables to see where they each had to go next. Mark, coming up the other way, had stopped to frown at a scrumpled paper in his hand, and the girls had to squeeze past.

'Sorry,' he said. 'Do you girls know where two-forty-three is?'

'Yeah, that's where I'm going,' Jude said. 'You must be doing geography, too. Oh,' she exclaimed catching sight of his map, 'you're looking at it upside down!'

He frowned, then saw what she meant. 'That's pretty stupid of me.' He turned it round and grinned up at her, sheepish.

Later, this was to become an oft-repeated joke. Mark, future geography teacher and explorer, couldn't read a simple plan of the school correctly. His best mate, Andy, repeated the story at their wedding with a pointed comment about who would be in charge in this marriage.

At the time, trying not to think that Mark's eyes were the bluest she'd ever seen, she blushed and mumbled, 'Anyway, it's up the other staircase. I'll show you.'

'Enjoy yourselves,' Sophie drawled. 'See you at lunch, Jude?' And she sashayed off in the direction of the language labs.

Jude and Mark sat together in geography for their entire sixth-form career. They borrowed one another's notes, felt pens and calculators. They moaned when Mr Bassett set them impossible homework and sat together on the coach for field trips on which they waded around in streams together to measure water quality. Once she fell asleep on his shoulder at the end of a long journey from the Peak District and woke to find his arm round her. She guessed he saw her mostly as a friend. Certainly geography was their only meeting point. Outside class they hardly saw one another. He was a scientist; she'd chosen history and English as her other subjects. She loved reading and creative writing and playing the flute in the school orchestra; he spent his weekends and holidays outdoors, skiing or hillwalking in the winter, sailing and kayaking in the summer.

In June of the Lower Sixth, she bumped into him at someone's birthday disco. He was with a bubbly girl with a gym-toned figure, whom he introduced as Tina. Jude felt unaccountably sad seeing them entwined under the swirling lights during 'Lady in Red'. It was because he caught her standing alone and off her guard that night that shy Rick Wansted at last plucked up courage to ask her to dance. How strange are the ways of fate. She and gentle Rick were to be together for the whole of the Upper Sixth, before fate intervened again.

At some point near Christmas, a classmate mentioned that Mark and Tina had split up. Jude didn't give the matter much thought – by that time she was half in love with Rick and his sinuous body, the sleepy, faraway look in his long-lashed eyes when he played guitar.

Jude and Mark swapped practice papers for geography revision and wished one another well for the exams themselves. When on the first day she caught his eye across the long rows of desks, he winked at her, before lowering his head to his work once more. His hair fell softly down his forehead and involuntarily something shifted inside her. For a moment she forgot which question she was on. From that time, Rick started to lose his hold on her.

In July the leavers' ball came round. It was a warm but drizzly night, so most people crowded into the marquee. She was with Rick, naturally, but they were part of a larger group, all dancing together, laughing, talking or lining up for photographs. She and Rick were drifting apart – both knew it, and it seemed sad, but not desperately so. Rick had a summer job picking fruit at his uncle's farm in Suffolk. Jude would work in a Norwich bookshop for a month before backpacking with Sophie round France and Italy. Then, exam results willing, they'd be going to university at different ends of the country.

Both recognized there would be new friends, new horizons, new loves. Neither wanted to tie the other one down.

Rick was bopping to Oasis with Sophie when Mark came up to claim Jude. After Oasis was finished there was Blur, and then the DJ put on 'Message in a Bottle'.

'Impossible to dance to,' Mark shouted in her ear, as the others roared the lyrics. 'Let's go and get a drink.'

They took their cans outside. The rainclouds were drifting away now. Jude, shivering a little in her skimpy black dress, peeled off her strappy sandals and did a little dance to keep warm. She glanced up at the sky. There was no moon, but between shreds of cloud stars were coming out.

'Ah, Jude. Freedom! I can't believe it. Leaving this place. I feel as though life's finally beginning.'

'You've only been here two years,' Jude reminded him, smiling.

'It seems like for ever. No more bells, no more uniform, no more calling Mr Sanderson "sir".'

'No one does anyway,' she said, laughing to think how their friendly headmaster would hate it, 'but I know what you mean. It's a fabulous feeling.'

'The world lies out there, waiting to be explored. There are seas to be crossed, mountains to be climbed.'

'In your case literally.'

'Absolutely. What else are all those long university holidays for?'

'Er. Revision? Earning money to pay the rent?'

'Well, yes, some of that. But I'll get sponsorship,' he said vaguely. 'And I've got it all worked out. I'm going to teach geography after uni. Then I'll still have those long holidays.'

'I think you're supposed to have a vocation to teach, aren't you?' she teased.

'But I do,' he said simply. And when she studied him curiously, she saw he was serious. 'I'm passionate about all that stuff. They need good teachers, people who will inspire children. I can do that.'

She believed him.

'I suppose, studying history, you'll end up teaching, too.'

'Not necessarily. There are lots of other careers that need a general arts degree. That's what Miss Eldridge said, anyway.'

'Don't lose yourself in the past,' he warned.

'But that's what I love,' Jude said, puzzled. 'Trying to understand what it was like, really like, I mean. To stand in other people's shoes, experience what they did, see their viewpoint.'

'What use is that? Surely it's the present that matters. Solving today's problems.'

'It helps us understand today.'

'We're so different, you and me,' Mark said softly. 'But we're still friends.' He ruffled her hair. 'You're special, you know that?'

'So are you,' she breathed, leaning in to him. Over his shoulder she saw that Rick had come out to look for her and she pulled away. Mark didn't seem to mind.

'I hope we go on being friends, you know,' he said. 'We could see each other when we're home.'

'I'd like that.'

'Promise?'

'Promise. Look, I promise on that star up there. The really bright one. You can't get more eternal than that.'

'That's probably a satellite. Not good enough.'

'All right, that one over there, then.'

He gave a mock sigh. 'It'll have to do, but there's a problem with promising on stars.'

'Which is?'

'Well, their light takes so many thousands of years to reach us, it may be that by the time we see them they don't exist any more. So promising on a star is ephemeral really.' He laughed, but Jude didn't. What he'd said about them being friends and special to one another had hit deep. Now he seemed to be making light of what he'd said. It was bewildering. After that evening, there was always a part of her that was waiting for Mark. It was just a matter of time. One day he'd be ready for her.

Ephemeral. That's what it turned out to be. The right moment had eventually come, but they'd had such a short time together. They saw each other several times through their university careers, when both happened to be back briefly in Norfolk. Mark was full of the places he'd been – fell-running in the Pennines, climbing in Peru. One Christmas he was talking about joining an expedition to the Himalayas. Maybe one day he'd try Everest or K2, he said, eyes shining. Neither guessed that this ambition was never to be realized.

Jude gained a first-class degree and an MA, moved to University College, London, to study for a PhD in eighteenth-century culture and society, then, the summer she responded to the advertisement for a paid internship at Beecham's, she heard that Mark had suffered a terrible accident.

He had been cycling in South America with a friend. Racing round a bend down a narrow mountain road, they'd collided with a lorry coming up. His friend was killed. Mark suffered a fractured pelvis. The surprisingly prompt arrival of an emergency helicopter, the skill of an Argentinian surgeon and Mark's subsequent removal to a London hospital combined to give him the best chance of a full recovery, but he spent weeks in the hospital bed, then months on crutches. Jude was not surprised to find that he had changed. He became more serious; guilt ate into him that it was he, not his friend, who had survived. This made him cynical, bitter even. During his time in hospital Jude visited most days and he came to expect her, relied on her to pull him out of his moods. They became closer and eventually fell in love.

'I always felt you were special,' he murmured to her the night she agreed to marry him. 'Right from the moment I met you, and you knew where to go, which classroom we should be in. You're my lodestar – that's the one that sailors followed, the Pole Star that took them safely home to harbour.'

'And I suppose you're like a shooting star,' she responded, managing to laugh despite the tenderness of the moment. 'Always travelling in unexpected directions.'

And, like a shooting star, he had disappeared over the edge of her world, taking all the light and leaving her in cold darkness.

Chapter 8

Summer's school friend Emily lived in a modern house half a mile out of Felbarton. Jude found it fairly easily, gathered up Summer and her rucksack of doll stuff and thanked Emily's mother, a pale, quiet woman with a baby on her hip.

'What shall we do now?' Jude asked Summer, as they walked to the car. 'The beach?'

Summer shook her head. 'Euan's,' she said. 'I want to ask him to make me a Jude doll.'

'Really?' How very touching.

'Yes, for the doll's house.'

'That's sweet of you. But surely we can't just drop in on him without asking.'

'He won't mind.'

'Are you sure?'

'Yes.'

'He might not be there.'

'If he isn't, we'll go to the beach.'

'All right,' Jude said, as she opened the back door of the car for Summer, where Claire had clipped in the booster seat. In truth she wasn't sure about this enterprise. The memory of Euan's annoyance at the folly yesterday and her own bluntness brought a blush to her cheek. On the other hand, perhaps she ought to take this opportunity to apologize. She turned the car round and they set off back the way she'd come, towards Starbrough.

'There! You've gone past!'

Jude slowed the car, and, checking carefully in her mirror, reversed into a small lay-by in front of a battered estate car. Now she understood why she hadn't noticed the property before. The drive on the other side of the road was half-hidden by a huge hedge that ran the length of the property. In the drive, in front of a wooden garage, stood a cement mixer and a hill of sand. To the right of the garage could be glimpsed the gable-end of the property. Jude stared up at it, taking in the flint walls, the slate roof and the square-hatched windows, their frames painted a fresh white. So this was the gamekeeper's cottage, where her grandmother had lived as a child. It gave her a strange feeling to realize this. She wondered how old it was – eighteenth century, probably.

She was just going to walk up the path and knock on the door when Summer surprised her by wrenching her hand away and running off along the side of the garage into the garden behind.

'Summer! I don't think you ought—'

'Auntie Jude, you've got to come round this way.'

Jude took a last anxious look at the closed door and followed the direction of Summer's voice.

Behind the cottage was a rough-cut lawn bordered by hedgerow. Summer was disappearing through a gap. Glancing briefly at the back windows of the cottage in case of accusing eyes, she hurried after her. At the gap in the hedge, she stopped dead in delighted surprise.

The small field beyond was sheltered by a row of poplar trees on the far side, their leaves flickering grey and silver in the breeze. It was what Jude had always thought of as a proper meadow – not with short juicy grass for grazing, but fragile, sweet-smelling grasses and delicate flowers for hay. And there was Summer running ahead through the flowers to . . . it was a real gypsy caravan.

She almost rubbed her eyes in disbelief, but there it was, parked in the middle of the field, its woodwork bright, painted maroon with white patterning, and with a pale-blue bowtop roof, straight out of a storybook. Its owner was sitting at the top of the steps, a newspaper open on his knee. At Summer's cry of greeting, he folded it quickly and stood up. He was definitely the man Jude had met yesterday.

'Euan, here's my Auntie Jude.'

'I think we've met already,' he said, coming down the steps. He and Jude stared at one another, then Euan put out his hand. After a second's hesitation she clasped it. His was a strong, warm handshake and although he didn't smile, Jude felt a tension inside her slacken. He released her hand and stepped back.

'Claire's sister, eh? If I'd known I might not have been so plain-spoken.'

'I'm so sorry about yesterday,' she said in a rush. 'I made a real fool of myself.'

He raised his hands in a calming gesture.

'You were upset and hurt,' he replied. 'I understand. And I was an idiot. Instead of explaining properly, I made things worse. I was already pretty churned up about the deer, you see, and it was the final straw to be bawled out for my good deed by some total stranger.'

'I'm sorry,' she said again. 'I was very frightened actually.'

'By the shooting, yes. That poor animal. I hated doing what I did, but sometimes it has to be done.'

Summer looked from one to the other in puzzlement. These grown-ups appeared to have met already. 'What happened?' she asked.

Euan sank down so that his face was level with hers. 'There was a deer yesterday near the folly. It had wounded itself very badly on some wire. Rather than let it die slowly and painfully, I had to kill it. And then your aunt came along and I'm afraid we had an argument about it. But we've said sorry now – haven't we?' He looked up enquiringly at Jude, who nodded.

Summer stared at him with huge eyes, trying to take everything in and for a moment Jude was worried, but then the girl said, 'Did it hurt the deer to be killed?'

'No, not a bit,' said Euan firmly. 'It was over quickly. Off to Happy Hunting Grounds.'

'I'm sorry for that deer.'

'So am I. It was being chased and very frightened. That's why it ran into the wire.'

'Who was chasing it?'

'I don't know.' Euan stood up and said to Jude, 'I've been worried about what's happening up there for a few weeks now. You didn't see anyone, did you?'

Jude shook her head. 'I just assumed it was you,' she said. 'That's why I was so angry.'

'I'm sorry. Like I said, I should have explained, but . . .' He looked so rueful, she rushed in immediately.

'You didn't think I'd listen. You're right probably. It was my fault really.' And finally they smiled at one another. He really was an attractive man, she thought, and now she realized that he wasn't like Caspar – apart from his build, that is, and the dark wavy hair. Euan's eyes were dark blue rather than Caspar's near black, and Caspar didn't have Euan's slow, patient movements and slightly diffident manner.

She became aware of Summer watching them thoughtfully.

'This little one's mentioned you, of course,' Euan said,

ruffling Summer's hair, 'but I'd no idea you were visiting. Are you just here for the weekend?'

'Yes. I'm going back tomorrow morning. I've been working at Starbrough Hall.'

'You're an auctioneer, I gather.'

'Yes. Books and manuscripts are my speciality. Claire told me you write, and I saw your pictures on her wall. They're lovely.'

'Thank you. They're a sideline really. I use them in my books.'

'Do you work in these woods? Yesterday, I assumed that you were the landowner but I gather he's called John someone . . .' She trailed off, embarrassed, remembering the haughty Marcia Vane and Chantal's outburst about the new landlord. She'd hate to think that Euan was employed by him.

'I must confess I was trespassing, too. Since I'm a naturalist, I'm afraid I allow myself to think, probably wrongly, that I can nose about up there if I don't disturb anything. I'm always walking about in the woods and it's seemed such a peaceful place. But recently . . .'

'The Wickhams, up at the Hall, don't speak well of the new owner.'

'If it's him that's indiscriminately shooting things, I'm not surprised.'

'That gibbet—' She stopped, remembering Summer was listening.

'I've seen it,' he said briefly, and Jude changed the subject.

'And you, you seem to be living out here? In the caravan, I mean.'

'Only for the moment. I bought the cottage last year, but it needs a lot of work, you see, and what with the rewiring and dust and the appalling smell of chemicals, it's much pleasanter out here – when it's warm enough. The cottage should be finished by September, though.'

'It must be lovely sleeping outside. I've never seen a gypsy caravan before. Especially one as pretty as this.'

'Would you like to come in?'

'I'd love to. What about you, Summer?'

'I've seen it loads of times,' she said in a superior tone. 'And I've cooked supper on the stove. It's called a queenie stove, you know.'

'Fit for a princess, then,' Jude said, trying not to laugh. She followed Euan up the ladder, and cried out with pleasure to see the roof's beautiful painted underside. 'Imagine drifting off to sleep looking at this ceiling.'

'It's not quite the Sistine chapel,' Euan said.

'Well, you're probably not allowed to sleep in the Sistine chapel.' Jude took in the wide bed and the painted chest and the little stove. Euan kept everything beautifully neat and clean. There was a heap of books by the bed and a hurricane lamp. Only the laptop computer on the bed placed the wagon in the twenty-first century.

'A cousin lent this caravan to me,' Euan said. 'It had sat in his barn for years. Chickens nested in it. We gave it a thorough scrub and a lick of paint on the outside and it was as good as new.'

'I love it!'

'I want to sleep in it. Why can't I?' Summer whinged. She had climbed up to look.

'She's always asking,' Euan told Jude. 'Maybe sometime when Darcey's here,' he said to Summer. 'Darcey's my niece. I sometimes babysit her when my sister's busy.'

Jude nodded, remembering.

'She goes to my school. Euan, can we show Auntie Jude the snake?'

'Certainly, Miss Grasshopper-brain,' he said. 'Jude, don't look so alarmed, it's just a harmless grass snake.'

'Snakes are not my favourite,' Jude replied with a grimace, 'but I'll be all right as long as I don't have to touch it.'

Summer led them back through the gap in the hedge and beneath the transparent-plastic roof of a large car port towards the other side of the cottage. This was full of cages and glass tanks. The grass snake was coiled lazily on a stone in one of the tanks, basking in a patch of sunshine. Summer gazed at it, mesmerized. Jude went round peeping into some of the cages. There was a young rabbit with a band-aged paw in one. 'I found it in a snare,' explained Euan. 'The idiot who had set it hadn't bothered to check whether they'd caught anything so the poor thing was catatonic and half-starved.'

In one of the larger cages, two downy owlets blinked sleep-ily. One, seeing Euan, clacked its beak expectantly.

'It's not feeding time yet, mate,' he told it. 'A neighbour brought me these. They'd fallen out of the nest. Usually it's best to leave baby owls for the parents to rescue, but their dog would have got them.'

He showed Jude a corner of the garden where he'd sunk a small pond liner into the earth. Dozens of young frogs swam in the water or nestled in the grass. 'Watch where you're treading. I raised these from spawn and am gradually transferring them to ponds in the area where there wasn't much this spring,' he told her, scooping one up.

'Oh, it's very pretty,' she said, surprised.

'See how delicate its skin is. And these beautiful markings are perfect camouflage.'

He passed the tiny frog to her and with some reluctance she let it sit in the palm of her hand, from where it stared at her impassively, before leaping off. 'Oh my goodness!' she cried, but fortunately it landed in the water. She watched Euan rescue another that had flipped onto its back and wondered how she could ever have thought this man was cruel.

Euan went into the cottage to make tea, and when he returned Jude was amused to see he obviously kept a stock of pink grapefruit juice for Summer. Summer took this act of homage as an appropriate moment to make her request.

'Would you make me an Auntie Jude doll for the doll's house?' Jude thought her tone a touch imperious, but Euan promptly agreed.

'An Auntie Jude doll? Of course, why not?' he said, looking Jude up and down as if memorizing her, which gave her an odd feeling. 'It'll take me a day or two.'

'That's very kind of you,' said Jude. 'Isn't it, Summer?'

'Thank you, Euan,' Summer sang out, with the air of a bored princess.

Little monkey, thought Jude, but Euan seemed amused at being bossed about by a nearly seven-year-old girl.

'It's my pleasure,' he said, and gave a mock bow.

'I'm very interested by your cottage,' Jude said. 'Especially because I think my grandmother lived here as a child. Is it still part of the Starbrough estate?'

'No,' he said. 'I bought it from Steve Gunn, the farmer next door. His father acquired it from the Wickhams along with the farm. I'd an idea it was connected to your family somehow. Claire mentioned your gran. Would you like to look round?'

'Love to,' Jude said, and, taking her tea, she followed Euan and Summer inside.

'The kitchen, you can see, is in a state of, er, transition.' This was a polite term for the fact that all the old fittings had been torn out and nothing had yet been installed to take their place. On a battered table, an old whistle kettle crouched on a double gas ring that was supplied by an ugly blue gas canister underneath. 'There's a scullery through there where I keep a cool box for some of the food. I'm learning to cope with pre-war conditions.'

'Like Gran's family must have done,' Jude remarked.

The big living room was furnished with one kitchen chair and a radio and smelt strongly of new plaster. He said, 'Don't touch anything, Summer, it's all still drying out and I don't want handprints, even yours.'

The situation was much the same upstairs, where there were three bedrooms and a smaller room that was being turned into a bathroom. 'At least the shower's usable now,' Euan said, and let Summer test the basin taps. The bedrooms had been rewired and replastered and there was a single bed in one of the bedrooms, and a desk with a laser printer and what looked like one of Euan's pictures in progress. 'At least I can use the electricity up here now,' he said. 'I sleep in this room when it's really cold outside.'

'It'll be lovely when it's finished,' said Jude, 'but it must feel permanently like camping.' As she was leaving the bedroom, a stack of books on a shelf by the door caught her eye. They were multiple copies of the same title. *The Path Through the Woods*. It sounded familiar and then she saw the author's name, Euan Robinson, and something clicked in her mind.

'This is you!' she exclaimed, picking one up and admiring the book's jacket, a woodcut picture of trees. 'Claire said you were a writer, but not that you were a famous one. I read a review of this only last week. A good one.'

'Glad to hear it,' he said, his eyes twinkling. 'And I'm not famous, I assure you.'

'Oh, but you wrote *The Lonely Road*, didn't you? I loved that book.' It was about living in the Norfolk salt marshes and beautifully, lyrically written. His books were non-fiction, part natural history, part literary memoir, and gave a wonderful impression of place.

'Did you?' he said, looking pleased. 'We were living up near Cley then. It was a wonderful, remote place out of season, and a marvellous book to write.'

Jude noticed the 'we' and remembered Claire said he was divorced. Euan turned away, muttering about checking where Summer had gone. She returned the book to the pile and, with a last glance around his spartan bedroom, followed him downstairs.

Summer, bored with DIY, had gone back out into the garden to see the animals. Jude and Euan watched her from the kitchen window and Euan said, 'I'd show you the folly, like I promised, but I don't like to take Summer.'

'I can understand that,' she said fervently.

'There's the shooting, yes,' he said. 'As I say, that started a few weeks ago; it must have been about the time that I took her up to look at the outside of the folly. Fiona, my sister, brought Darcey over for the afternoon and I thought it would be nice to ask Summer along. We went for a walk. I wouldn't have let them go up the folly, of course, but it's an impressive sight from the outside. The thing is, they didn't like it much. Said the place was spooky. Summer's face was quite ashen.'

'How strange. What was it she didn't like, do you think?'

'I don't know. The place does have an atmosphere, but I'd never found it threatening.'

'Did you mention it to Claire?'

'No, I forgot about it, to be honest. The children were completely fine by the time we came back here. So, no folly – unless you're around tomorrow?'

'I wish. But I have to drive back in the morning,' she said, with a regretful look. 'I've a christening to get to. I'm going to be a godmother for the third time.'

'Congratulations!' Euan said. 'Well, perhaps you'll be coming down again?'

'I hope to,' Jude said. 'Certainly if this business at Starbrough Hall comes off I'll be back quite soon.'

'Good,' he said. He sounded as though he meant it.

Just then, Summer stomped in looking furious. 'One of those owls tried to peck me. Can we go to the beach now?'

'I didn't think you wanted to, you funny thing,' said Jude, examining Summer's still-perfect finger. 'But yes, of course.'

'Will you come, Euan?' Summer asked, but Euan shook his head.

'No, I've got things to do. You spend some time with your aunt,' he replied.

Jude and Summer passed a most enjoyable couple of hours on the sands at Wells-next-the-Sea. Summer made friends with a young boy there with his grandparents, the children playing together in a shallow lagoon, trying to trap little fish and building a castle, which they decorated with stones.

It was as though the sea wind and the wide expanse of shore and the cries of sea birds had the power to blow all troubles from one's mind, or so it felt to Jude. Caspar, Mark, work, might all be a million miles away, matters of as little importance as she was on this vast beach. High above, wisps of cloud blew south, leaving a sky of luminous blue. The rising tide surged into the lagoon and the children abandoned the castle with shrieks of mock terror. On the way home, Summer fell asleep in the car.

Glimpsing the child's peaceful face in the driving mirror, Jude thought again about the strange dreams. It was interesting what Euan had said. That Summer hadn't liked going to the folly a few weeks ago. That might have been half-term. Claire had pinpointed half-term as the time that the dreams had started. Was the folly visit just a coincidence or had something about the place really frightened her?

That night Jude was woken by Summer murmuring in her sleep, and lay, listening and anxious, but the girl didn't wake and after a few minutes she quietened. Still, Jude couldn't sleep, and her worries bored deeper. Maybe the answer lay at the folly? Perhaps there'd be time to visit it in the early morning, on her way through to St Alban's. Deciding this, she felt more peaceful, and she slept.

Chapter 9

Stepping over the barbed wire and into the forest clearing was like breaching some magic circle. Early morning sunlight filtering through the branches striped the grass. The dew was nearly gone and the air smelt delicious, of earth and wood and vegetation. Once again, Jude was struck by the fancy that the tower was growing out of the ground like the trees, for the loose stones and bricks around its wide base suggested roots, and ivy clutched the walls.

The 'Keep Out' sign was propped up next to a ragged wooden door. If there had been a keyhole it had long since rotted, but she was dismayed to see an iron bolt with a rusty padlock. She should have thought that it might be locked. Maybe Euan had a key. She pulled at the padlock in frustration and, to her joy, the mechanism sprang open. The possibility of adventure flowered in her mind. She looked quickly about. There was no one to tell her she was trespassing. No one and nothing, only the conversation of birds and the sough of the wind in the leaves.

The bolt shifted easily enough, but when Jude pulled the door it resisted, and she saw its top hinge was broken. Lifting the door by the bolt allowed her to shuffle it open and she passed at last into the tower.

She hadn't a clear picture of what to expect, but something more attractive than what she now saw. The floor inside comprised chunks of brick embedded in bare ground to make a herringbone pattern. It was damp and uneven so that she stumbled in the half-darkness and almost fell. The smell was awful: damp, mildewy, earthy, old. Out of the shadows, a brick staircase wound upwards into cold darkness. A pale finger of sunlight fell across the bottom step, showing it to be crumbling and splodged with moss. From above came a scuttering sound. 'Hello?' she called up, not really expecting an answer. She waited. The tower waited. There was silence. Of course there was no one, she berated herself. Jude placed a hand on each wall of the staircase and one foot tentatively on the lowest step. It held, so she tried the next. She'd stop if it seemed dangerous, she told herself.

As she climbed the darkness thickened and her skin prickled. She transferred her hands to the steps above and walked on all fours, like an animal, her sense of balance gone, so that every few steps she felt as though she was falling backwards. She counted the stairs, nine, ten, eleven. They were comfortably deep, not too high. Fifteen, sixteen. She passed into a little patch of light from a window like an arrow-hole. She peered out, but all she could see was light glinting on foliage. On she went and her heart plunged in her chest as her hand missed its hold – a brick had gone. She edged round the gap carefully with her foot. Twenty-nine, thirty. What made her attempt this madness? Thirty-nine, forty. Now a pale drear light filled the air. She must be nearly there. Forty-five, forty-six, forty-seven. She was cold now, shivering with nerves. Another ten steps. She must be nearly at the top. And suddenly she emerged into a little round room. She sat on the floor, trembling, trying to calm herself and take in her surroundings.

The floor, like the rest of the folly, was brick. Wooden shelves and cupboards, some split and rotten, lined the walls. There were four small windows, spaced at equal distances round the room – one for each compass point, she thought – and a ladder in the middle that went up to what appeared to be a small trap-door. Once perhaps, the windows had been glazed, but now they were open to the elements. Rays of sunlight poured in through one and from the forest all around came an ecstasy of birdsong. Under the sunny window were a table and chair, both modern folding ones. Someone had been working there, for they'd left several sheets of paper and a reporter's note-book. She got to her feet and idled over to discover newspaper articles printed from the internet, and read about an expected meteor shower. The notebook was filled with scrawled notes and diagrams. And suddenly she felt that she wasn't just tres-passing on someone else's land, but intruding on something more personal: their work. Two hundred-odd years ago, this was where Anthony Wickham had worked. Now someone else came up here to think about stars. There was a strong sense of these people's presence. She felt uncomfortable, as though she should apologize and leave.

Crossing the floor back to the stairs, she passed objects on the shelves. There were a couple of paperback books, curled up with damp, a pen pot with a spray of dusty pencils. There were odder things, too. A great slice of knapped flint – the head of an axe or another tool, she supposed, picking it up and examin-ing it. A pair of men's spectacles glared at her, the tortoiseshell frames scuffed and dull. The elderly binoculars hanging on a nail nearby proved irresistible. She walked round the windows with them, one by one, looking for a view. Only through one could she see anything but trees. Amazingly, this window gave onto a vista of Starbrough Hall, like a doll's house in the distance. She scrubbed at the grimy lenses with spit and the hem of her shirt, and, looking again, could make out the library and the tiny figure of Robert walking away from his car and under the arch. It surprised her that she could see the house from the tower, but not the tower from the house. She wondered if this had always been the case or if the growth of the trees had lately made it so.

As she hung the binoculars back on the nail she glanced up curiously at the trapdoor. She knew her limits: it would be stupid to climb up alone and open it – what would happen if she fell? But she did long to know what was on the other side – open sky, perhaps, or another room like this? Regretfully, she lowered herself backwards onto the staircase, like a sailor descending a ship's ladder. She would have to come back another time with Euan. The thought was a pleasant one.

Emerging, trembling and dusty, from the bottom of the folly, she hauled the door closed, shot the bolt and hung the padlock exactly as she had found it, not locked but looking as though it were. It would be responsible to lock it, but then whoever had left it like that might be annoyed. A sudden picture of a child pulling it open and mounting the steps decided her, but when she squeezed the thing shut, it refused to stay locked. She left it. There was nothing else to be done.

She turned to walk back to the path, aware that time was moving on, but her eye was caught by something, a mound of fresh earth on the edge of the clearing. It was too big to be a molehill. She walked over, for a moment uncomprehending, then realized it must be where Euan had buried the muntjac. The earth was dark brown, rich in loam. Something yellow-ish stuck up from the soil. She pulled it out. It was a broken bone, the thickness of a hosepipe, evidence of something much longer dead than the deer. She dropped it, thinking nothing of it.

She stood up, looking around, troubled by a curious feeling she was being watched, but she saw no one.

Then, just as she reached the trees, she heard the sound of a vehicle's engine in the lane. It cut out quite suddenly, then doors slammed. All her terror at Friday's shots returned. She slipped off the path and made for a thick clump of hazel and brambles and hid. She was trespassing, and it might be the person with the gun. Thank heavens she'd been cautious enough to park her own car back on the road, and the newcomer wouldn't be looking for her.

Soon she heard a woman's voice, then the lower tones of a man. More than one person, then. From her leafy hiding place, she glimpsed them approaching, her eyes widening in surprise. It was Marcia Vane, today in tight white jeans and a low-necked top. She was accompanied by a tall, broad-shouldered man of forty, dressed more for the golf course than a country walk. What were they doing here at this hour on a Sunday morning?

They passed Jude's hiding place and she watched them stop at the breach in the barbed wire fence. The man gave an irritated cry and hunkered down to examine the broken wire. When he stood and spoke to Marcia, Jude could only hear shreds of their conversation.

'. . . definitely been cut whoever . . . they couldn't drive it in here.' The man threw open his arms, indicating the clearing. '. . . a few trees, I reckon.' Now they both stared up at the tower. The man walked across and gave the door an exploratory prod with his polished shoe.

'Heck of a job, John . . .' Marcia drawled. So he was Marcia's client, John Farrell. Or, Jude judged, by the intimate way she took the man's arm, something more than that.

Jude took the opportunity of their turned backs to melt away through the trees in the direction of the lane. They were clearly up to something, and she sensed it was better that they didn't know she was a witness.

Chapter 10

Jude arrived home in Greenwich at nine o'clock that evening, exhausted, but needing to ready herself for an early start the next day. The christening, at a church near St Alban's, had been followed by a big boozy party that had gone on all afternoon. By the time she left at six, the end-of-weekend traffic had brought the motorway to a standstill, then after her turn-off it had been a slow crawl across east London.

She unpacked, made her favourite comfort food – cheese on toast – and checked her emails while she ate. There was a reply from Cecelia, which she clicked on at once.

Hey, Jude (I adore writing that!),
    It's really good to hear from you. I'd love to meet up. Jude, it's the most amazing coincidence, but I'm working at the Royal Observatory down the road from you for a short time! Is there any chance you could meet me there after work one evening and maybe we can go for a drink or a meal in Greenwich? I'm pretty free – Danny's in Boston – so pick your day!
    Much love,
    Cecelia

She replied to this, explaining the situation and perhaps optimistically suggesting the next day, Monday, and was just logging off when her BlackBerry rang. It was, at long last, Caspar.

'We've been in meetings all day,' he said. 'And we've just had dinner in this amazing restaurant with the other guys. How was Norfolk?'

'It was fine, thank you,' Jude said in her chilliest tone. He hadn't been in touch at all since . . . Thursday, she supposed. But then she hadn't called him either. What did this say about them both?

'How were the star books?'

'Definitely worth the trip.' Her eye fell on the box containing the observation diaries that had somewhat riskily spent the day locked out of sight in her car boot.

'Good . . . Good . . . And your sister and everyone . . . ? Hey . . . you wouldn't believe who we saw in the restaurant. Johnny Depp.'

'No!' She forgot her coolness.

'Yes. With his wife and some other guys.'

'Really? What's he like in real life?'

'Pretty ordinary, I'd say. Nothing that a well-cut suit can't do.'

'Oh, Caspar! You're just jealous. Did you speak to him?'

'What do you take me for? Of course I didn't.' No, Caspar had too much of a sense of personal dignity to risk being snubbed. 'They must hate that, stars. People going up and treating them like public property.'

'Well it's the public that give them their success.'

'That's true, I suppose. Now, about next week. The holiday. Jude, I've got a very special ask. Would you mind if I didn't join you at the villa till Tuesday?'

'What, go down on my own? Oh, Caspar.' Jude was truly dismayed. 'Why?'

'Things here,' he said mysteriously. 'From what the guys were saying tonight they need us to get working on their British campaign straight away. I reckon I'd be free by Tuesday lunch-time. Look, you wouldn't have to drive down. I could cancel the ferry and you could fly to Bordeaux and Luke could fetch you. I'd pay.'

Jude felt suddenly very tired indeed. 'Caspar, no. That's not fair.' It was her main holiday this year. She wasn't sure about the whole thing anyway, and now he was ruining it. Suddenly she felt really angry. 'It won't be the same without you there. I don't know your friends and they don't know me. I was only going because you were.'

'But I will be there. Just a few days later. You'll be fine. The others will be really relaxed, you know. I'll ring Luke and Marney as soon as I get off the phone to you here. We'll sort it out.'

'No we won't sort it out, as you put it, Caspar. You're mess-ing me around.'

'You're angry, aren't you? Please don't be angry.'

'Are you surprised? You don't call me for days and then you tell me work is more important than our holiday. What am I supposed to think?'

There was a silence at the other end of the line. Then the tinkling of liquid falling on ice cubes. Caspar swallowed a mouthful of drink and said very humbly, 'I'm really sorry. I guess I've got so caught up in the work I'm on a kind of high about it. The trouble is, I've promised the guys we'll do it. Jack's all set up. I can't let him down. Look, can you think about it?'

'I'll think about it,' Jude said dully. She was really too tired and upset to think straight now. 'Can we speak tomorrow?'

'Of course, of course. I'm in and out of meetings, but we'll catch each other sometime.'

We'll catch each other sometime. Like passing comets or ships in the night. Was that what their relationship was like? Jude wondered, as she lay awake that night, too tired and jittery to sleep. She and Caspar didn't need one another, not really. Three or four months into their relationship and she couldn't say that she knew him very well. She'd told him about Mark, of course, and he'd been enormously sympathetic, shocked by the death of someone young and vibrant, but they'd not talked about it on any deep level. He hadn't encouraged her to, and she hadn't wanted to bore or freak him by talking about it much. That was a terrible indictment on their relationship, come to think of it.

And coming back home, that sense again of walking into what belonged to her and Mark – those memories were as comforting as the cheese on toast. She'd never allowed Caspar to stay here, had always arranged it that they ate in town and went back to his, or that it was sometime like a Sunday, when he'd want to go back home in the evening to sort out things for the week. But perhaps she ought to plod on with this relationship, put the work in and wait for it to come good. Maybe there could never be someone she could love with the same intense passion and sense of rightness that she'd felt with Mark. Just lying here in the half-darkness she missed Mark badly all over again, remembering all the nights when she'd turned over and snuggled into him and he, even in his sleep, had thrown a protective arm across her body.

What should she do?

Chapter 11

On Monday morning the office was electric with tension. It was only half-past eight when Jude walked in with her briefcase containing the precious journals, but Suri was already at her desk, head bent over a pile of dusty volumes, elbows tucked into her sides like a frightened animal trying to make itself as small and unnoticed as possible. She looked up at Jude's entrance, mouthed, 'Hello,' rolled her eyes and made a warning grimace. The sound of raised voices from Klaus's office told the rest of the story. Just at that moment, Inigo emerged, a look of tragedy on his face to make a Shakespearean actor proud. He hitched up the trousers of his ridiculous suit as he sat down at his desk, then started tapping away furiously at his keyboard, completely ignoring Jude's greeting. Klaus, meanwhile, hung in his office doorway, fingers hooked over the frame like a huge angular bird of prey, and regarded Jude with a fierce gaze.

'What's going on?' she asked, looking from one man to the other. Klaus summoned her with a brisk movement of his head and she followed him inside.

'Klaus? What's the matter?'

He ignored her question.

'Yes. Good morning, Jude. How was Norfolk? I read your emails, for which great thanks. We've definitely got the collection, haven't we? It would make a huge difference to our viability. I've taken the liberty of including some figures in the budget reforecast I sent upstairs this morning—'

'Did you?' Jude interrupted, a little alarmed. 'I'm pretty sure we've got it. I was going to check in with Robert Wickham today.'

'Excellent,' he said, rubbing the tips of his fingers together. 'You'd better look at this morning's figures for the year to date.' He scooped up a transparent document wallet and passed it across the desk.

It took her a few moments to absorb the lines of numbers. What glared up at her were the totals at the bottom. Actual against budgeted sales for the past six months. It was a shock. She knew Pictures and Furniture were having problems in the current climate, but Books were down nearly a million pounds on expectations, too. Klaus folded himself into his chair, gesturing to Jude to sit down opposite.

'We really needed Lord Madingsfield's collection,' he rasped, raking his fingers through his floppy greying hair. 'Those Audubon bird manuscripts particularly.' He glared through the glass wall of his office to the cowed figure of poor old Inigo. So that's what the row was about.

'It wasn't Inigo's fault,' Jude said, with a grudging sense of fairness. 'He's told you. Madingsfield has a cousin at Sotheby's—'

'I was just telling Inigo . . . I chose to call Madingsfield over the weekend,' Klaus interrupted in clipped tones, picking up an ivory paperknife from his desk and running his thumb down the blade. 'To say how disappointed we are. His story is a little different. He tells me in that dreadful oleaginous way he has that he didn't detect that Beecham's was "suitably enthusiastic" about his collection. I don't know what Inigo said to him, but it seems he didn't press the man hard enough.'

'But that's Madingsfield all over. He would blame us,' cried Jude. 'He would hardly come out straight and admit to nepotism, would he? Come on, Klaus, we know him of old.'

'Maybe, maybe not,' Klaus snapped, slapping the paper-knife down on the desk and making Jude jump. 'The point is that Inigo didn't go in hard enough.'

'But you've told us not to make unrealistic promises in these trading conditions,' Jude said, confused.

The phone trilled and Klaus snatched it up. 'Clive?' His voice was deferential now, nervous even. 'You're ready for us. Five minutes? Yes, yes. You've got all the documents I sent up? Yes, I understand completely. Very important. Good.'

Jude's whirling thoughts cleared. Klaus must be under tremendous pressure from senior management. He, like Lord Madingsfield, was desperate to parcel out blame. Today Inigo was in the firing line. Tomorrow, it might be her.

Klaus replaced the handset and reached for his jacket and his papers, his long face tense, miserable.

'Get yourself ready for a difficult meeting,' was all he said.

Jude went to collect her things.

'Inigo, are you ready? Suri, would you mind the phones?' Klaus asked, putting on his jacket.

Inigo refused to meet Jude's eye. All right, she thought, hurt, if that's the way you want to play it. It was apparent to both that the wheel of fortune had turned. Inigo was out of favour and today Jude was firmly in.

It was when they sat down at the boardroom table, with the chief executive and the finance director, that her eye fell on a handout in front of her entitled 'Suggestions to Deal with the Shortfall' and she felt her stomach flip. The first item, in bold type, was 'The Starbrough Collection' with '£150k' printed beside it. She shot Klaus a glare, but instead of shrivelling up in his seat, he frowned her into obedient silence.

Clive Worthington, Chief Executive of Beecham's UK, informed them tersely that he was interviewing the senior staff of all the different departments in turn to deal with the matter of a devastating downturn of income from recent auctions.

'You're not the worst department affected,' he said, looking at Klaus severely over the top of his reading glasses, 'but it's vital that you pull out every stop to meet these figures you've submitted. What's this latest entry? Starbrough? First I've heard of it.'

'Jude will explain,' said Klaus and Jude, her mouth dry with nervousness, described the collection of books and instruments that she'd inspected over the weekend.

'And this is a dead cert, is it?' Clive snapped. 'This collection coming to us?'

But before Jude could open her mouth to declare honestly that she was almost sure, Klaus butted in.

'Jude's promised me she'll settle the matter,' he said quietly. 'We think the figures are good to aim at.'

Drop me in it, you bastard, won't you? she thought.

'You could have warned me what you'd put,' she told him after the meeting. 'The sale's not even in the bag yet. And I told Wickham only a hundred thousand.'

'I don't see why it shouldn't make more, if the items are as you describe,' Klaus said in his smoothest voice. 'It's important to be bullish.'

'In this market? We haven't had anyone to look at the globes and stuff yet.'

'There's a lot of interest in this area. Anyway, it's going to help Clive bolster our position with New York. This is politics,

Jude. New York are asking us for job cuts.' His eyes glittered. 'Trust me.'

She sighed. He was, as usual, impossible. If he pulled it off he'd get all the glory; if it all went wrong, she'd get the blame. Trust him, indeed.

'If you can sew up the deal this morning, we'll discuss how to handle everything. To turn the Starbrough collection into a big sale the publicity must be bang on.' He marched back into his office.

Jude sat down and stared sightlessly at Wickham's observation journals where she'd laid them out on the desk. Please God there was a story in them big enough to make the difference. Aware that Klaus was probably listening from his desk – he'd left the door open – she picked up the phone and dialled the number for Starbrough Hall.

'Good morning, I hope I'm not ringing too early,' she said when Robert answered. 'I wondered whether you'd come to a decision. The team here are very excited at the prospect of handling the sale of the collection.' Company speak. She hated it.

'And we'd be delighted to let you,' came Robert's reply.

She almost leaped in her chair with relief. Instead she grinned hugely at Klaus, who was standing at his door, listening. He nodded back and mouthed, 'Well done,' at her.

But despite her exhilaration at her success, she had a sudden vision of Chantal standing in that beautiful, half-empty library looking desperately sad.

She spent much of the rest of the morning drawing up a letter of agreement, emailing the details to Robert for approval. Early in the afternoon he replied, accepting the terms. He ended his message with a PS: 'Do come and stay should you need to spend some time with the collection.' That was kind of him.

Klaus immediately summoned her and Bridget from Publicity to his office to schedule the sale and announce it. Bridget was seven months pregnant and in a hurry to get her deadlines sorted.

'If it's to be November we'll need a big feature for the autumn *Collector* by early August. Three thousand words, I'd say,' Bridget said. 'Would you do that, Jude?' *The Beecham's Collector*, a quarterly free magazine, was sent out to a mailing list of clients, media and other useful contacts. 'We'll use the piece as a starting point to create general media interest.' Jude understood that this should attract a wider range of potential buyers than the usual suspects.

'Jude, is there much of a story behind the collection?' Klaus asked, scribbling some notes.

'There could be; I just don't know yet.' She explained about the observation diaries and the charts. 'I'm showing the journals to a friend who's an expert in the field.' Cecelia had emailed saying that this evening would be fine.

'What would be fabulous,' Bridget said briskly, 'would be to showcase some discovery that this man made. Do we know anything about him as an astronomer?'

'He's not a known figure, I'm afraid,' said Jude. 'That's not what you want to hear, I know. I would love the opportunity to do some further research about him.'

'By all means,' said Klaus, impatient as ever. 'Then get everything up here and photographed.'

'It would be good to photograph the house and the library as well, if the owner is in agreement,' Bridget said.

'Excellent. Perhaps you'd sort all that out. And, Jude, that story. If there's one, find it.' There was a note of steel in his voice.

'Yes, sir,' said Jude under her breath. As she left Klaus's office she was all too aware of Inigo hunched at his desk, a gloomy expression on his face.

At five o'clock she left the office and threaded her way through the Mayfair side streets to Bond Street tube. But at Greenwich rail station, instead of turning right towards her house, she struck out in the direction of the park and climbed the hill to the Royal Observatory.

'How wonderful to see you! It's been far too long!' At reception, Cecelia Downham greeted Jude with a hug and showed her downstairs into a poky basement office, crammed with books and papers.

'What a fabulous place,' Jude said, looking around at everything. 'Straight out of a Dickens novel.'

'Isn't it wonderful? I'm contributing to an exhibition about the history of the Observatory, so I'm borrowing it for a couple weeks while a pal's on vacation. Here, have a seat. I'm sorry, it's like a yard sale in here.'

'So much for the paperless office,' said Jude, as Cecelia moved a pile of periodicals from an old chair, then set about making them both mint tea from a tiny electric kettle. A tall, stunning blonde with an East Coast accent, Cecelia always seemed an unusually glamorous figure for a researcher. In addition to being an excellent scholar she was enthusiastic about her subject and generous with her expertise. She was also a good friend, though she and Jude didn't see one another so often these days.

'Where are you staying? You don't go back to Cambridge every night, do you?' Jude asked.

'Danny has a friend with an apartment in the Barbican.' Cecelia's long-term boyfriend was also an academic, but they never managed to get jobs in the same place. Danny, though from Dublin, was currently a Professor of English in Boston, so one or other of them was always getting on a plane.

'You could have stayed with me,' Jude cried. 'Another time, you must promise.'

They chatted for a while, catching up from a year ago when she had visited Cecelia in the rooms of her Cambridge college.

'So what have you got for me?' Cecelia asked, indicating the briefcase Jude had brought.

'It's your period, Cece, late eighteenth,' Jude said, pulling the packages out, unwrapping the journals and handing them across the desk. 'Look,' she said, peeling the plastic off the last one and flicking through it to show her friend. 'Here's where the handwriting changes. There are definitely two people involved here. What I need to gauge is whether there's anything interesting about these from a collector's point of view. I mean, can we say Wickham made any contribution to the astronomy of the period? Oh goodness, I'm gabbling, I'm sorry. I'm under some pressure to make this into a big sale and I need a story. There'll be no problem paying you a research fee, by the way.' She sipped at the scalding tea while Cecelia flicked through the first volume.

After a moment, Cecelia frowned and said, 'I'll have a proper look, of course, Jude, but I can't pull a story out of the air.'

'No of course not,' Jude said hastily. 'I'm sorry. I didn't mean you should twist the facts or anything.'

'Since you emailed me last night I've been trying to weasel out something, anything, about your Anthony Wickham,' Cecelia went on. 'I hadn't heard of him before. I was trying to find if he was referenced by other astronomers. To be honest, I can't find anything yet. But I'll keep looking.'

'Thank you,' Jude said. 'That would be marvellous. I'll do some research of my own, of course.'

'Oh, and I've found someone to look at the globes.' She named an antiquarian based in Oxford. 'Mind you, I'd love to see them myself.'

'And you shall once they arrive,' Jude said, copying down the email address Cecelia showed her. 'But that won't be until I get back from holiday, I guess.'

'Where are you going on holiday?'

'France. Well, I think I am.'

'With your guy?' asked Cecelia, who, like most of Jude's friends, hadn't met Caspar but had heard talk of him on the grapevine.

'Yes,' Jude said uncertainly, dragging the teabag round in her mug by its tag. 'I'm not totally looking forward to it.' In truth, every time she had thought about the French holiday today, it was like imagining a great big block of concrete that shut out the light.

'Why ever not?'

She explained about Caspar's change of plan.

'It's quite a commitment, isn't it, going on holiday with someone?' She looked up at Cecelia, her expression anguished. I'm not sure I feel ready for it. Mark—'

'Jude,' Cecelia said gently, reaching out and touching her hand. 'It's a long time now since Mark. Four years.'

'I know, I know. Cecelia, do you think there's something wrong with me? Perhaps someone's heart can break so completely that it never mends.'

'Oh Jude, dear, don't sound so dramatic. Of course there's nothing wrong with you. Perhaps Caspar's just the wrong guy,' she said. There was a silence. She clapped her hand over her mouth. 'Oh God. Was that tactless or what?'

'Please don't worry,' said Jude miserably. 'I was only quiet because I was considering that you might be right.'

*   *   *

Jude was still wrestling with this revelation when Caspar rang that evening. She had sat down to watch the ten o'clock news, fed up with waiting for his call, and now she turned the TV sound off and watched the silent footage of estate agents' 'For Sale' signs, in a piece about gloom and doom in the housing market. She dreaded to think what implications this climate might have for antiquarian books.

'How did today's meeting go?' she asked politely.

'Yeah, it's gone well. What have you decided about France? Saturday or come with me on Tuesday?' He sounded as though he were brokering a business deal, not a love affair.

'Actually, Caspar.' She closed her eyes and plunged in. 'Will you think I'm awful if I don't come at all?'

'Jude! You must come. Don't be like that. Listen, if it's about my messing up the plans . . .'

She took a deep breath.

'Seriously, Caspar, I don't think it's right altogether.' And suddenly she was saying more than she'd originally intended. 'I don't think we're right.'

'Look, don't say that. I'll come back. I can get a plane tomorrow, at lunchtime probably. I can meet you at work. We'll sort this out.' She was surprised how distressed he sounded, but she'd already gone too far.

'No, Caspar. It's not as simple as that. I . . . don't think our whole relationship is right. I expect it's my fault. I'm finding it very difficult. Getting over Mark, I mean.'

'Mark? Your husband? Jeez, Jude, I know it must have been terrible, but it's been some years now . . .'

'Four,' she replied. 'Yes, everyone keeps telling me.'

'I suppose, I . . . don't understand. But, give me the chance. I'm . . . fond of you. Really. We could make something—'

'Caspar, no. I'm sorry.' She was surprised to hear his voice cracking, hadn't thought it would matter so much to him. 'I'm sorry,' she whispered.

She lay awake a long time that night. It was the right decision to have made about Caspar, she assured herself. Part of her grieved for him, but she also grieved for herself. Lying here alone it was Mark she missed most of all. In the darkest part of the night, the hour before dawn, she convinced herself that she would never be able to forget him, never find anyone who fitted her as well as he had. She would die alone. Finally, she slept. She dreamed she was walking up the spiral steps of a tower into darkness.

Chapter 12

When she woke the next morning, she felt exhausted, strung out. At some deep level she knew she'd done the right thing about Caspar, but it had taken all her energy. She got into work late and sat at her desk, trying to will herself into performing the day's tasks. There was so much to do. There were those two weeks' holiday booked, but, actually, it would be better not to take them considering Bridget's deadline. Yet she needed a break. As she looked over her notes on the Starbrough collection, checking facts and figures, she considered what would be best. What she wanted to do, needed to do, both from a work and a family point of view, was go back to Norfolk. In particular she might help with Summer, especially since her niece would be breaking up from school in another week or so. The whole thing sounded simple. However, Norfolk would hardly be a holiday if she was working at Starbrough Hall half the time, and sleeping on a lumpy mattress on Summer's floor wasn't something she could endure for more than a night or two.

She remembered Robert's invitation in his 'PS' to stay at the Hall and, slowly, a plan evolved. If the invitation had been sincere, and if Robert's wife, Alexia, didn't object, it would suit her all round to accept. Not least because it would make good sense to be on the spot if she was researching and cataloguing their collection, ready for the sale, and she could see lots of Gran and Claire and Summer while she was down there. Yet it was important that she had some holiday. She decided to speak to Klaus about it.

Klaus, with his eye for the main chance, saw the answer immediately. 'Why don't you go down there for three weeks instead of two? You can work for some of the time, then holiday the rest. You know I trust you. It'll be fairly quiet in the office. Yes, I like that idea. You can concentrate on the Starbrough collection, and that's vital at present. Then do what you like the rest of the time. And book the whole thing in as, I don't know, ten days' holiday. *Voilà!*'

Jude considered this. It was good of Klaus to be flexible, but it would be a strange sort of holiday. And yet thinking of the alternatives, being in the office, or taking the holiday and hanging around on her own in Greenwich, or patching together visits to friends at no notice, Norfolk seemed immensely attractive. She wouldn't impose herself on the Wickhams for the whole three weeks, but maybe they would have her for some of that period. She picked up her phone and dialled the number she was quickly consigning to memory.

It was Chantal who answered.

'Jude, my dear, how are you?' she said enthusiastically, but then she must have remembered the likely purpose of the call, for she sounded more subdued. 'I'm sorry, but Robert isn't here at present. Can I help at all?'

'I merely . . . wanted to discuss the next stage in the process . . . I'm sorry, Chantal, I know this is hard for you, losing the books . . .' she ended.

'Please don't worry,' Chantal replied with a sigh. 'Of course, it's your job. I will tell Robert you called.'

'Thank you. And, Chantal, I haven't spoken to my sister yet, but you can tell Robert I'm planning to visit Norfolk again very soon. To be frank, my holiday abroad has fallen through and I could call in on you to look more closely at the books.' She explained that she'd given Cecelia the journals and said, 'I could start the business of cataloguing. It would be nicer to do it there than bringing it back here. Unless that's inconvenient . . .'

'That's a wonderful idea. But if you go to your sister's you'll be sleeping on the floor again. No, no,' Chantal said, passionately. 'You must come to stay here. We have plenty of room, you know that, and it would be lovely to see you. I'll ask Alexia. She and the children came home last night, you know.'

'I couldn't possibly impose myself upon you all.' Jude crossed her fingers under the desk at the lie.

'Oh, you wouldn't be. Robert liked you very much and I know he'd be happy to have you stay for a week or two. And your time would be your own, there's no need to wait on us. You could work or spend time with your sister or your grandmother, whatever you wish.'

'That's enormously kind of you.' Jude thought longingly of the beautiful library, the conversations she'd had with this sympathetic woman. 'It would be wonderful. If you really think Robert and Alexia wouldn't mind.'

'I will talk to them as soon as they return, but I assure you there will be no difficulty.'

When Jude ended the call, she felt a great sense of relief, of rightness. Norfolk was where she needed to be.

Part II

Chapter 13

'I'm sorry, Caspar,' she whispered as the shreds of a dream fled, already forgotten. She opened her eyes.

She was lying in a big double bed between soft white sheets and sunshine was pouring into the room. A split second later she remembered where she was. Starbrough Hall was deliciously quiet. If she listened she could hear birds singing all around, maybe the distant purr of a passing car, but otherwise there was no sound. She rolled over to consult the watch on her bedside table. Eight o'clock. Not too embarrassingly late, then.

It was a perfect room to wake up in on a summer holiday, being on a corner away from the family bedrooms, with windows on two sides that admitted the morning sunshine. 'You really don't want dear old Max and Georgie bothering you at six o'clock,' Alexia had told her cheerfully the night before. 'And you'll have the bathroom next door all to yourself.'

Cheerful was exactly the right word for Alexia. She had a light, happy voice, and was attractive in a fair, healthy, bright-eyed way. Her calm, encouraging manner with the three-year-old twins was only slightly adjusted when she soothed her husband, who, Jude observed, liked his routines. A country-woman, the daughter of Yorkshire farmers, she also managed the housekeeping, the dogs and her grieving mother-in-law with equal facility. The accommodation of an unexpected guest into the household seemed not to trouble her in the slightest.

Jude was glad of the remoteness of her bathroom. As she ran water into the great claw-footed bath the pipes clunked and groaned so much she'd have been worried otherwise about disturbing the rest of the house.

She climbed out of the water, her mind as free and refreshed as her body. It was difficult in fact to believe that she'd arrived yesterday evening hot and dusty, the great rush of Friday-afternoon traffic adding an hour to her usual journey time. A good night's sleep, and the deep quietness of the place had quickly restored her. The trauma of Caspar and the stress of the office had quite melted away.

Downstairs, breakfast was in progress. Chubby golden-haired Georgie was pouring as much milk on the wooden table as on her cereal, chattering all the while; Max, neat and dark like his grandmother, shouted at his sister for splashing the book about dinosaurs he had open by his bowl. Alexia greeted her brightly; Chantal's small spaniel, Miffy, shuffled over to sniff her feet, waving his flag-like tail. Of the other inhabitants there was no sign.

'Come and sit down. Sleep well?' Alexia said, mopping up milk with one hand and stacking dirty bowls with the other. 'The tea's only recently made.'

'I slept wonderfully, thanks,' Jude replied, pouring herself some.

'Please help yourself to breakfast,' Alexia said. 'We're going swimming in a moment, aren't we, children? Like to get your shoes on now? Robert's out somewhere with the dogs,' she explained to Jude, 'and I don't think Chantal's been down yet. She's often awake in the small hours, poor thing.'

As she ate her cereal, Jude listened to the sound of the twins running up and down stairs, gathering jackets and plastic ruck-sacks, their chirpy voices squabbling over swimming goggles and towels. Then the back door banged, the car revved away and there was blissful silence.

She put her bowl in the dishwasher and made a piece of toast and some coffee, and reviewed her plans as she drank it. Three whole weeks in Norfolk, she could hardly believe it. When Robert had rung her at the office to repeat Chantal's eager invitation to stay, she'd confessed that she might be in the county for this length of time.

'You must come for as long as you like,' he said. 'After all, it's in our interests. And my mother seems to have taken to you. It will be nice for her to have somebody new about the place. She doesn't have much of a life, poor thing.'

This morning she would start work; however, Claire had rung yesterday inviting her over to supper. Jude had already told Alexia this, adding, 'I'd be glad to cook for you all occasionally while I'm here. Call it my contribution to the household.'

'Oh you needn't do that,' Alexia replied, but she seemed pleased that Jude had offered.

Jude took her coffee and her laptop along to the library. Everything there was as it had been, except for the journals that were now with Cecelia, but not for much longer, Jude thought sadly. Soon the shelves containing Anthony Wickham's books would be empty, the globe and the orrery would no longer grace the room. But the roof of the Hall would be sound. Robert, she'd learned at dinner last night, ran some mysterious import–export business, but it was suffering in the recession. This explained further both why he was around the house so much and why there was no money for the upkeep of the Hall.

She stood staring out over the park and, once more, her eyes were drawn to the line of trees on the hill. It was funny how you couldn't see the folly from the house, but you could see the house from the folly. Again, she wondered whether that had been the case when the folly was built. It seemed odd that, when follies were supposed to be decorative, you couldn't see it.

There were a dozen rolled-up charts in the cupboard and she knelt down to take them out one by one, then passed an absorbing hour while she tried to make sense of Wickham's plotting of double stars or objects he thought were comets. She jotted down in her notebook anything she thought might be interesting for cataloguing.

Then, underneath the last bundle of charts, she was surprised to find what looked like another volume of the observation journal, one she had obviously overlooked. She opened it and turned the pages. What a shame, it was mutilated. About a third of the leaves had been torn out of the back. The remaining two-thirds were entirely written in the newer handwriting, and when she turned to the first page she realized that the first entry was 10 March 1778. The volume followed the others in date order, in fact. How could she not have noticed the book before? She began to read and as she did her amazement grew.

Father wishes me to continue our charting of new nebulae and double stars, now that he can no longer. It is a heavy burden that I bear, but I will endeavour to carry out his wishes with all the skill and mastery that he has taught me. I will not fail him, though the nights are lonely and cold and he at least had me to help him. I have no one and must consult an atlas frequently, so that much time is lost.

4.30 in the morning, as the moon nears the horizon in Ursa Major, I saw Bodes Nebula, round with a dense brighter core.

Jude stopped to consider. 'My father . . .' So the second author was Wickham's son. Who was he? She'd have to ask Chantal.

Had Wickham died or was he away or incapacitated? She'd need to find all this out for cataloguing purposes. She continued to read.

24th March
Early evening, no moon tonight and the air is very still. In Taurus near Tau Tauri at 15´ distance a new star cloud or perhaps a comet.

In several subsequent entries, the diarist mentioned this new object, deciding that it was moving. By early April he concluded: 'Viewed at 278 magnifications bright and clear-defined. Possibly a comet. No previous reference in my father's notes.'

Eventually, it seemed, he recorded it as a comet, though he seemed to have some doubt.

After this, there were long gaps of time between diary entries and little of a personal nature. The observer mentioned a partial eclipse of the moon, the addition of a new nebula and, with notable excitement, a possible double star that Wickham senior had been tracking for some years.

Jude finished making notes and was about to put the book back in the cupboard when Chantal came in.

'Don't let me disturb you,' she said. 'I only wanted to see if you were all right.'

'I'm absolutely fine, and you're just the person I want,' Jude told her. 'I've found another volume of the diary – look – and need to check Anthony Wickham's dates with you. And those of his children.'

'Of course,' Chantal said, taking the book and examining it. 'It's a pity that it's damaged. I wonder who did that? Yes, I will look up the dates you need. But I can tell you right away that he did not have any children, not as far as we know, anyway. Or even marry. His estate passed to his nephew, you see. A man called Pilkington, who changed his name to Wickham.'

Jude stared at her in puzzlement. 'Then who is it in these pages who calls Anthony Wickham "Father"?'

'I have no idea. I will search for the family tree upstairs, if you don't mind waiting a bit. I have to hurry now. Last night, I had such toothache . . .'

'Oh, I'm sorry.'

'The dentist told me to come straight away. Will you be all right here for an hour or two?'

'Please don't worry about me,' Jude said. 'There's plenty I can get on with, I can assure you. Good luck with the dentist.'

When Chantal had gone, Jude settled down to work once more. She had reached the bottom of the cupboard now and was surrounded by scrolls and books. She bent down and looked right to the back of the bottom shelf, in case she had missed something. It wasn't a very well constructed cupboard, she saw. There was a piece of wood missing at the back and she could see the crumbling plaster beyond. Or was it plaster? There was certainly something. She reached in and put her hand through the gap, and felt paper. She grasped it and pulled gently, but it was stuck, so she shuffled herself round a bit and tried to fit her other hand into the gap as well, to find out what was holding it. She felt more paper. There seemed to be a whole wad of the stuff. She held it together and once more tugged. This time it moved, and she wiggled it out through the hole.

What she'd found was a thick curled-up wodge of pages covered in a faded handwriting, the same writing, she quickly realized, as in the journal she'd just been reading. She opened the journal towards the end, and, fitting the pages to the torn binding, saw that, amazingly, she'd found the missing leaves.

How extraordinary. But why had they been torn out? She tried to smooth out the pages she'd found, anxious not to damage the paper further, but they kept curling up again. At least they weren't damp, which was lucky really, considering where they'd been hidden. The writing was very faded, though, and difficult to read. With growing anticipation, she took her find over to the desk, turned on the lamp there, and tried to decipher the first line. It was a title. She thought it said 'An Account of Esther Wickham'. It wasn't a name she'd heard before. She began, with great difficulty, to spell out the first few lines. 'I was . . .' something – eight, perhaps. Goodness, was the whole document going to be as illegible as this? But when she peeled back the first page to check she saw that the writing on the next was darker and easier to interpret. Heartened, she turned once more to the first page and began to make out the faded letters. The voice was awkward at first, the sentence structure over-complex, but quite quickly it became more fluent.

An Account of Esther Wickham
I was eight years of age when I first came to know my father. How this could be, since I slept under his roof from infancy and ate his food and was cared for by his servants, it might be difficult to comprehend, but once you are acquainted with the facts of the case; and once you come to understand Anthony Wickham as I knew him, to appreciate the finely wrought workings of his mind, his – some say – unnatural devotion to a single passion, all will become clear.

In the very beginning, he was not my father at all. The filial bond was something we sought for ourselves late and forged together. This is contrary to the usual custom, which is that the names 'father' and 'daughter' come first, at the birth of the child, the closeness between them following after. In our case, it was some years after we became acquainted that he instructed his lawyer to give

*legal name to what we had already made real: in short, he adopted
me and made me his own.*

*Much of this he did not tell me until I reached my fourteenth
year, for he did not deem it suitable to burden a child with matters
that troubled its elders. Suffice it to say I was raised believing, once
I was sentient of these things, that I was his child, bone of his bone,
blood of his blood. That is what Susan, my nurse, urged me to
believe. The channels of her mind, I gleaned later, ran thus: since
I was brought to be raised under his roof, with no family name
to call my own, an armour of dignity must be joined together for
me. He had decreed I be called 'Esther', after the old mistress, his
mother, so Esther Wickham was what she bade the other servants
call me. As I grew I heard half-muttered rumours below stairs, and
remarks from my dear Aunt Pilkington, of whom I will tell more,
that I had no right to the name Wickham; that I was an orphan; or
that I was the master's bastard by some woman he'd met on one
of his infrequent journeys to London or Bristol, where he would
confer with other stargazers and from whence he returned laden
with learned books, and specula to grind lenses for new telescopes.
These rumours disquieted me and I would wonder about them, but
Susan bid me dismiss them as tittle-tattle.*

*The truth, as I say, I did not learn till I was grown. But perhaps
Susan was right to assert her version for while I was small it gave
me assurance. I was a nervous infant, prone to nightmares and
unaccountable ailments. I clung to Susan as though she were my
mother, and she to me, for she was blessed with no infant of her
own, nay, nor man, for who would have her, our Creator having
seen fit to make her homely, endowing her with a vast body and
a wandering eye, which caused the poor creature to be shy and
awkward with the stronger sex. But to me she was the loveliest
woman on God's earth, for as an infant she succoured my every
need and I wanted no other mother.*

Susan it was who comforted me in the night when I woke weeping from my dream. It was always the same dream, that I was wandering lost and alone in darkness, where the sharp claws of trees reached out to scratch my face or to pitch me to the ground. All around the cries of beasts grew closer, the smell of rotting loam filled my nostrils. The nights I had this dream, I would be afraid to sleep again, and Susan would ease her massive body in beside mine and fold me against her pillowy bosom until I quietened, half smothered. I cannot imagine she slept much, those times my demons visited, but she never complained.

Jude read this part over again with a curious feeling of unreality. The girl's dream was similar to her own and Summer's. How could that be? She considered the matter. Perhaps it was something to do with Starbrough. The folly itself was very atmospheric – an enchanted place, if one believed that sort of thing – but that didn't explain Jude's dreams. As far as she knew she had never visited the folly before this summer. Perhaps it was plain coincidence – dreams of running through dark woods and crying for your mother were, after all, the primal stuff of fairy tales – one had only to think of Snow White and Little Red Riding Hood. Maybe, way back, after humans became tillers of the ground, they began to fear the dark woods from which they'd emerged. She'd read that somewhere. She found her place on the faded paper and continued to read.

In those days my world was the nursery, the kitchen and the gardens around the house. I was forbidden to venture beyond the park on my own. Sometimes I played with the gardener's children, Sam and Matt, who liked to climb and run as boys will, and so I learned to climb and run, too, and if their sport did not please me, I would sit by myself to make nests with grass and kindling.

I fancied sticks and bits of bone were people and animals. Once Susan gave me some dolls made from pegs and dressed in scraps of cloth, which she'd bought from a Romany woman.

On the twenty-first day of July 1768, my sixth birthday, Susan shook me awake early in an unusual excitement and I rose to see by my window a magnificent doll's house, fitted with exquisite pieces of furniture. 'It's from your father,' Susan told me, in a tone of reverence. She explained that he'd glimpsed me from his window, playing outside with my sticks and grass, and sent for the doll's house all the way from London, complete with tiny dolls and finely wrought furniture – the windows even with little curtains, beautifully worked by slender cords, and the beds pretty counterpanes. My father did not visit the nursery to wish me happy birthday. Later in the day, Susan helped me form the letters of my name on a note of thanks. He did not reply. 'Your father is a very busy man,' Susan explained, 'with important tasks to perform. He has no time for little girls. But you see he keeps you in his mind.'

What came to occupy his time was the design and building of a tower which he might climb to study the stars. There was much talk in the kitchens about this tower and to me it sounded a thing of amazement. 'The folly', the servants called it. There was some precedent for such an edifice. The cousin of Mrs Godstone, our housekeeper, worked as a footman at a big house near Norwich and he told her the master had one fashioned like a heathen temple in his park. 'No good for anything,' Mrs Godstone's cousin the footman had said. 'Though it's handsome enough for the fine ladies and gentlemen to gawp at and fancy themselves in Rome or Arcady.'

Mr Trotwood, my father's land agent, was not at all pleased by this scheme. My father, having scant interest in his estates, left Trotwood to run Starbrough as he saw fit, and Trotwood had grown sleek and bullying in the doing. Yet now he was under orders to execute complex instructions about a silly tower that involved the acquisition of large quantities of fine brick, while his master made constant interference and the local men recruited to build it played surly. They hated Trotwood, who had made much trouble for himself in the village by his plans for improvement. One lad of sixteen he saw transported for poaching. Two families he turned out of their homes for not meeting the new rents. There was anxiety, too, among the villagers about the siting of the building, on the hill in a clearing that rumour had it was ancient burial ground. While digging the foundations, the labourers discovered human bones. After this they laid down their tools and refused to work. Trotwood was forced to bring in poor wretches from Norwich Prison for the task, since the master insisted that the project should continue. No one knew what happened to the bones, for the Rector would not have them in his churchyard. Some said that Trotwood himself reburied them in the foundations one moonless night.

It was during my seventh year that this drama was played out, and I remember often sitting under the table in the servants' hall, playing my favourite game with my peg dolls, that I was a princess stolen away from her parents, or teasing a cat with a piece of wool, and eavesdropping on the servants' gossip about the tower as they went about their work. Once there was much consternation, for one of the prisoners escaped. For days the women started at the arrival of any stranger and refused to leave the house alone at night, even to summon the coachman to his supper, or to fetch potatoes from the barn, but there was never any sign of the fugitive. Eventually it was said that he had made his way to Great Yarmouth and taken ship for Holland and so peace settled once more. Another time, one of the prisoners professed to have seen a ghost, believed to be the former owner of the ancient bones, so the men refused to work and Trotwood arrived at the house full of spleen, demanding to see the master, who was hunted down eventually in his workshop in the stable yard and who settled the matter immediately by raising their wages.

What did my father do in this workshop? Make his spyglasses, I was told, by grinding optickal lenses and mirrors.

Often, especially in the winter, when the nights were clear and sharp with frost, he never saw daylight, for he passed the long hours of darkness out in the freezing park with his telescopes, observing the starry firmament, and making notes in a large book. Then he'd sleep from sun up to sun down. Sometimes this gruelling routine caused him to sicken, and he'd lie abed for days, with the doctor visiting to bleed him, and great quantities of veal soup and gin taken up by Betsy the housemaid on a tray.

One autumn evening, the gamekeeper arrived at the kitchen with a brace of hares and the news that the folly was complete, and that very fine it was too, but only Jan, the coachman, was brave enough to climb the hill to see. It was ninety feet in height, he reported, 'most tall as the cathedral at Norwich', and with a room at the top, and, above that, a walled platform with a canopy, from which Mr Wickham might sit out of the weather, sweeping the heavens with his telescopes.

And this is what he proceeded to do. On several mornings, Mrs Godstone complained to Susan that the master had ordered victuals to be brought out to the tower at midnight and attempts had to be made to keep Jan or one of the stableboys awake to perform the task. Eventually, after Jan threatened to take his services elsewhere, Mrs Godstone made representations, and after that, my father took with him of a night a parcel of bread and cold beef or a capon that she packed after supper. And so a sort of equilibrium was restored.

As for me, I listened carefully each time the folly was mentioned, for it fascinated me more and more, the idea of this tower in the forest, and I longed to see it.

'Would you take me, Susan?' I asked her once or twice, but she always shook her head, and once she invoked the Lord's name.

'The forest is a godforsaken place,' she told me, 'full of savage beasts and spiteful spirits. You must never go there, and certainly

never alone, for if the spirits or the beasts don't get you then the gypsies will for sure.' At the time I was surprised at the passion of that speech. Later, much later, I understood.

But, in the way the Tempter works when something is forbidden, the idea grew within me, that I must see this folly, but I felt myself too young and insignificant to persuade any adult to take me. Then, in the summer that I turned eight, I talked of it to Matt, the gardener's younger son.

I have said before, that I was not allowed to leave the park. However, I had, the previous year, been sent to attend the small school in the village, which was run by the Rector's wife and their unmarried daughter. This new development had come about in the following manner: Mrs Godstone had been speaking to the master about acquiring new dresses for me, and he had chosen to ask how I fared. Mrs Godstone confessed that I received no schooling, though Susan had helped me to trace the alphabet on a slate.

The school, which gathered in a hall next to the church, numbered no more than thirty children, all told. There were few older than ten or eleven, for after that they were kept at home to help their families by tending livestock or scaring birds from new-sown fields. Matt was a pupil, but Sam, his brother, was already out helping his father. I often saw him, weeding the kitchen garden at Starbrough Hall. I was not the only child with well-made clothes. Hugh Brundall, Dr Jonathan Brundall's son, was there, and two fragile-looking daughters of an Admiral's widow sat together on the bench in front, ready with the answer to every question Miss Greengage contrived to ask.

She was a pale sap of a woman, Miss Greengage, with a hesitant way of speaking that the boys mimicked behind her back, but she possessed an enthusiasm for book learning, and every now and then she threw us some interesting morsel that made even stout George Benson sit up entranced instead of lolling in his seat and gazing out

*of the window. One of these occasions was a lesson about the move-
ment of the Earth within the heavens. Miss Greengage explained
the meanings of the names of the other celestial spheres which,
with the Earth, pursue their trajectories around the sun, and how
God the creator holds us all in a perfect mechanical pattern that
proclaims his glory. On certain nights, she explained, we should
watch for these fellow travellers, some of which might be seen in
the sky like bright stars. She drew a plan of this intricate pattern
on her slate board, but there were so many puzzled faces that she
stepped down from behind her high desk and reached for her shawl.
Since it was a fine bright day, she said, we would go outside and
make our own orrery.*

*Naturally, there was much excitement at this unusual event as we
poured out of the hall and across the graveyard to the green, where
Miss Greengage arranged us into a model of the planetary system.*

*George Benson was the sun, I remember; it was a sound choice,
for he was big and round and cheerful and could stand for long
moments without moving. Matt, the gardener's younger boy,
was a natural Mercury, small and restless. 'Esther, will you be
Venus, goddess of beauty and second planet from the sun?' Miss
Greengage asked me, and I proudly took my place in the orrery
between Matt and the Admiral's girls, who stood holding hands as
the Earth and its moon. Hugh was deemed a lordly Mars, god of
war, and other children I forget took the parts of Jupiter and ringed
Saturn. The little ones left over were set to be stars or comets, and
so, with Miss Greengage excitedly calling instructions, we began
to move in a stately dance, though the moon and the Earth would
collide, which set the little sisters into fits of merriment.*

*'Most charming,' said Miss Greengage, almost pretty in her ecstasy,
her hands pressed together under her pointed chin, and we paced our
orbits until we were dizzy and the Rector's wife rang the bell.*

'If you study the heavens tonight,' our teacher told us, 'you should

see Mars and Venus, the Lord and Lady of the Night, hanging like lamps, low on the horizon. Be sure to look, children. Work out their position, as I instructed, from where the sun sets in the west.'

Enthralled, I set myself the task that very same evening and, indeed, I saw the two bright stars over the hill top, just as she had said. It was at this moment that my love of stargazing had its genesis. My desire to see my father's folly grew.

Jude was interrupted in her reading by the sound of a car in the drive. Glancing at her watch, she saw to her astonishment that an hour had elapsed since Chantal left. And shortly she came into the library carrying a scroll of paper.

'I'm much better,' she replied to Jude's enquiry. 'He gave me a temporary filling. Now, I remembered where I'd put the family tree,' she said, laying it out on the desk for Jude to see. 'Look, Anthony died at the end of 1778 and there's no mention of a child.' She noticed the pages Jude had been reading. 'What have you got here?'

When Jude showed her the pages she'd found behind the cupboard, Chantal was amazed. 'I had no idea of the existence of these,' she said, inspecting them. 'Where did you say you found them?'

'Behind here.' Jude showed her the gap in the wood at the back of the cabinet, and, with some difficulty, Chantal knelt to feel along it.

'You could reach your hand down?' she asked. 'I never thought to try. I suppose at times everything has been such a jumble they just slipped through.'

'But why had they been torn out of the book?' Jude pondered.

'I've no idea. But it must all have happened a long time ago or I'd have noticed.'

'At least they've answered my earlier question,' Jude said

quietly. 'I asked you whether Anthony had a son, and you're right, he didn't, but he did have a daughter, an adopted one. Her name was Esther, and she's described the building of the folly.'

Chantal considered this. 'Esther. I've never heard of her before. Perhaps adopted children weren't included in family lists then. Where did she come from, does it say?'

Jude found the place in the diary. ' "was an orphan . . . or the master's bastard . . ." It's a bit of a mystery actually. Poor girl, not knowing. And she used to play at being a princess, it says later, so it clearly bothered her.'

Early in the afternoon, she emailed Cecelia about her new find, promising to send the torn journal to her on Monday and describing the battered pages she'd found that seemed to have been ripped from it.

> I must read these pages myself first – it'll be fantastic for my article – and I'll let you know what they say. What seems sensible is if I transcribe them as I go, then anyone interested can read them. In the meantime, as well as Anthony, we need to find out all we can about Esther Wickham.

She closed down her laptop, and feeling a little tired and head-achy, with a dull warning ache in her abdomen, she lay on her bed for a while. She thought about Esther's manuscript. Transcription would be a brilliant idea. Maybe she could do a little on her laptop every day. But not this afternoon. She was due over at Claire's later. For the moment, lying here was appealing, so she took a couple of painkillers and, after a while, drifted into sleep.

When she awoke half an hour later, she felt better and

decided to go for a walk. She'd not really seen the grounds around the Hall.

Chantal was nowhere to be seen, but Alexia, who was tidying up while the children napped, suggested she visit the gardens behind the house. 'There's not a great deal to see, I'm afraid,' she said. 'Though you can go round the stable block and the greenhouses and imagine how they used to be. And there's Robert's precious vegetable patch. You mustn't miss that – he's very proud of it.'

Jude explored the flower gardens and duly admired the neat rows of vegetables in the kitchen garden, then walked across the park, jumped the short drop into the ha-ha and picked her way across rough grassland towards the woods. As she came nearer, she saw an iron gate set in the flint wall that divided the park from the woodland. As she feared it turned out to be padlocked. She grasped the bars like a prisoner and peered beyond at a tantalizing path disappearing through the trees. Presumably it led to the folly. She turned away and began to walk down to the road, thinking she'd do a short circuit of the perimeter before returning to the house.

When she reached the road, she found it pleasant to sit on the low wall for a while under the restless trees, it being such a perfect, drowsy afternoon. In the fields on the other side mahogany-coloured cows were grazing. A light breeze cooled her skin.

A quarter of a mile up the road she could glimpse Euan's car, and at that very moment he came out of the drive and fetched something from the boot that looked like a strip of wood, before returning to the house.

She wondered whether he was just coming home or about to go out. Coming in, she decided, after a couple of minutes with no further sign. She slipped down off the wall and walked up the road.

Chapter 14

Euan was crouched by an open hutch in the old car port, and when he rose she saw he was cradling a rabbit in his arms. 'Jude, how good to see you. I didn't know you were down again.' His smile warmed her.

'I'm here for a week or two this time,' she explained, coming close to stroke the rabbit. It tried to struggle away from her. 'Oh, I've frightened it,' she said. 'I hope you don't mind me dropping in unannounced again like this.'

'Far from it,' he said, gentling the animal. 'Come on, boy, it's all right.' They were standing very close and the rabbit was quieter now; it waited, quivering, as Jude ran her fingers down its back.

'Is this the one you found in the trap?' She saw it no longer wore the bandage.

'Yes, look, its leg's almost healed. I'm wondering when to let it go.'

She ran her hand over the animal's ears that lay flat down its back, and her fingers brushed Euan's shirt, which gave her a surprising feeling of intimacy. The animal, as though indicating that it had the upper hand here, nuzzled deeper than she dared into that shirt. She said, 'I reckon it would simply follow you home again.'

He looked concerned. 'In that case, I'd have to find some-one who wanted a pet. It's impossible for me to keep them all. Especially if I go away. You're staying with Claire again, I suppose? I dropped by a day or two ago with the little doll

Summer wanted, but there was no one in, so I left it on the doorstep. I hope she found it.'

The mention of Claire was like a current of cool air between them. Jude stopped stroking the rabbit and stepped back.

'I haven't seen them yet, but I'm sure she was pleased. Actually, I'm staying at the Hall for the moment. Claire's house is so small it doesn't seem fair on them, and the Wickhams were quite insistent. I am going over to Blacksmith's Cottage later though, so I'll ask.'

'Thanks,' he said. He looked slyly at her. 'Hey, it's lucky you've turned up. I need a little help, if you have the time. You're not nervous of horses, are you?'

'Not particularly,' she said cautiously. 'Why?'

'Some men are coming to mow the meadow this afternoon, and I need to move the caravan. The farm horse, Robin, is used to pulling, and Steve said I could borrow him to shift it, but I rang to check and he's out, and the men are arriving in half an hour.'

'What do I have to do?' Jude said, a bit anxious. She'd not had anything to do with horses since she was a teenager, when she'd had riding lessons on Saturday mornings for a few months after they moved to Norwich.

'The most important thing is to hold Robin steady while I'm attaching the shafts,' he explained. 'Come on, I'll put this little fellow back and take you to meet him.'

Jude passed the next ten minutes cajoling the old carthorse with sugar lumps while Euan harnessed him, then they led him up the road, through the meadow, and somehow backed the horse between the shafts of the caravan.

'Where's it got to go?' Jude asked, as Euan checked the straps.

'Under the trees there, not far,' Euan said, with a nod.

When it came to it, Robin was more interested in nibbling the sweet grass than pulling, and the caravan wheels had settled into the soft ground over the rainy June, so several more sugar lumps and a mysterious-looking exercise involving Euan staring into the horse's eyes and blowing up his nostrils were required to coax him into action. Finally, the caravan shuddered up out of its resting place and, with Euan at Robin's head, proceeded to creak and sway in a slow wide circle until it came to rest under the poplar trees at the far side of the meadow. They were just disengaging the horse when a lorry was heard drawing up outside the cottage. There came an alarming clanking and grinding of metal on stone, then a small mowing machine, driven by a young man in a beanie hat, surged through the gap in the hedge. A portly older man followed on foot, breathing hard, his face flushed with exertion.

'Afternoon, Mr Robinson. You picked a good day for it,' he shouted. He gestured to the younger man, who killed the engine.

'Haven't I just, Jim. Jude, this is Jim Devlin, and that's his son, Adrian. Shall we let them get on with it? We'll have some coffee waiting when you've finished,' he told them.

'Tea for us, if you've got it, Mr Robinson,' Jim said. 'Strong enough to trot a mouse on, please, and two sugars.'

'Strong tea it shall be, then.'

'Coffee for me, please, Euan,' Jude said hastily.

As Jude followed Euan indoors, they heard the mower roar into action once more.

'What happens to the hay?' Jude asked Euan as they waited for the kettle to boil.

'When it's dry,' said Euan, spooning ground coffee into a cafetière, 'it's brilliant animal feed. Some I keep, some I sell to a local pet shop.' He fetched four mugs from the window sill and wiped them, dropping teabags in two and putting them to one side for when Jim and Adrian had finished. 'So what are you doing down here, "Auntie Jude". Exploring the dusty tomes again?'

'That's right. My boss has decided it'll be the saving of the company this year, so I'm here to do my homework.' She explained about the journals and about Esther and the article she was supposed to write.

'Fascinating stuff,' he said. He collected a milk carton from a cold box in his makeshift dairy and remarked, 'You'll be wanting to see the folly properly, I'm sure.'

'Euan,' she said, feeling a little guilty. 'I know you said it wasn't safe, but I'm afraid I went up the folly by myself in the end. Last Sunday, on my way home.'

'Did you?' he said mildly, pushing the plunger down through the coffee.

'Yes. I thought about stopping to see if you'd come, but it was awfully early.'

'That's fine. You're an adult.' He didn't look up as he poured the coffee. 'I don't want anyone hurting themselves, that's why I warned you off.' Still, he sounded a little off-hand.

'But you go up there, Euan. In fact I felt as though I was intruding. Is that your stuff up at the top? The books and the papers?'

'Yes. It's for my next book.' He brightened. 'I'm writing about the stars.'

'Really? That's quite a coincidence. I mean, given that I'm researching a stargazer. Anthony Wickham, the man who built the folly. Esther was his adopted daughter.'

'Ah, might be useful for my book then.'

'Is it non-fiction like your other books? What aspect of the stars are you writing about?'

'Oh, not the technical stuff, I'm no physicist, it's a general read, in the style of the other books really. It's about the cultural importance of astronomy. I'm passionate about the necessity of the stars to us as people. Living in cities and towns, and with so much artificial light, we're in danger of losing our connection to the night sky – that sense of wonder about the universe and our place in it. I want to convey all that to ordinary people, you know, get them to look up at the sky occasionally. I suppose that's an unspoken purpose of all my books, to make people fall in love with nature again.'

Jude thought how bright and animated he looked as he talked. 'Thanks,' she said, when he gave her her coffee. 'It sounds marvellous, like a book I'd love to read. So is the folly where you go to observe the stars? I noticed the trapdoor in the ceiling—'

'For heaven's sake, I hope you didn't go up there . . .'

He did look alarmed now and Jude said quickly, 'No, no, I'm not that stupid. Don't worry.'

'I know how it works, you see,' he explained. 'There's a particular trick to opening the trapdoor, and that ladder is not a good place to teeter while you try to work it out. Yes, I go up the tower like old Anthony Wickham to watch the stars, but also to think and write notes. I seem to get good ideas sitting in that little room,' he said, folding his arms and perusing her. 'There's something about the atmosphere. Not everyone likes it, though.'

'Summer, you're talking about? I know what you mean about atmosphere,' she said, her face sober. 'To me there's a strong sense of history, but then that's what I'm interested in. There's also certainly a – well, a presence. I thought about Anthony Wickham up there with his telescopes, whiling away the lonely nights. Though I couldn't say it was an echo of him I sensed. There wasn't much up there that looked as if it had been his. Not that I nosed around, of course,' she added.

'You have as much right to nose around as I do,' he said, leaning against the door frame, nursing his coffee. 'There are one or two things I've found on the site, though, and . . . that reminds me.'

He put down his coffee and went across to an old dresser against the far wall, which alone had survived of all the old kitchen furniture. He picked up something from a shelf and passed it to her. 'What do you think?' he asked.

'It's a coin, of course,' she said, turning the heavy piece of blackish metal. 'Maybe a penny.' She took it over to the daylight and examined it. 'A king's head. One of the Georges, perhaps, but I can't read which one.'

'It's George the First, I think,' he said. 'King of Great Britain from 1714 to 1727. I looked him up on the internet. I turned up the coin when I was burying the muntjac. I guess I should give it to John Farrell, since he is the landowner, but the website I looked at didn't say it's worth much and somehow I don't have him down as the sensitive collector type.'

A picture passed through Jude's mind of Esther's Mr Trotwood reburying ancient bones at midnight and the penny falling unnoticed into the hole. Where that idea came from she didn't know. There had been a small bone sticking out of the earth Euan had turned. She shuddered. 'I wonder whether there's ever been a proper archaeological dig round there,' she said. Just then she remembered another person who had seen the mound.

'Oh. Euan, there was something else odd. Have you come across a woman called Marcia Vane?' He shook his head, so she rushed on. 'She's the new landowner's lawyer, well, more than his lawyer, I think.' She remembered the easy way Marcia had laid her hand on John Farrell's arm. 'I met her when she came to speak to Robert Wickham. I just avoided bumping into her and a man who might have been Farrell last week, which would have been embarrassing. I ducked behind a tree and they didn't see me. I didn't quite get what they were talking about. Farrell was certainly annoyed that the wire had been cut.'

'Funnily enough, that wasn't me. I just bent it a bit to step over.'

'I wonder who did it, then?'

She examined the coin again and the profile of the first German King of England, who never learned to speak good English, trying to make sense of the worn lettering. The folly, Anthony Wickham, Esther's story, the coin. Everything led back to the past. She glanced round the kitchen, suddenly aware of the extraordinary fact, which she hadn't yet begun to assimilate, that her grandmother's family had lived in this house. There was so little that was original left now. The dresser might have been her great grandparents', she supposed. She must ask Gran. She must ask Gran lots of things. It was funny how she'd started talking about that gypsy girl she used to know. What was her name? Tamsin, that was it. That would have been the 1920s and 1930s, though. And Jude's great-grandparents had died in the 1950s.

'Who lived here immediately before you came?' she asked Euan.

'An elderly couple by the name of Herbert, I gather,' he said. 'They'd been here since the sixties when the husband was employed as gamekeeper. By the time Mr Herbert died the Wickhams had sold the land under us to the farmer – who realized there was so much work needed to be done to it he decided to sell outright and that's when I came along. Everything had been cleared out of the house before I moved in, in case you were thinking I might have found anything belonging to your family.'

'I was, vaguely. I was trying to imagine this place as it must have been when they lived here.'

She hefted the coin, which was warm and heavy in her hand. 'What's it like up there?' she asked. 'Right at the top of the tower, I mean? Is it open to the sky?' Esther's account had mentioned a canopy to protect Anthony Wickham from the weather.

'I'll take you one starlight night, if you like,' he said.

'I'd love that,' she said immediately. It never occured to her that this would cause trouble.

When she arrived back at Starbrough Hall, she went straight to her room to get ready for visiting Claire and Summer. She switched on her laptop briefly and saw that Cecelia had already replied.

I'd definitely like to look at the Esther Wickham stuff. How intriguing, a daughter who's been wiped from the family tree. I'd love to know her story. Well, I've been busy. I ran Anthony Wickham's name through the Royal Observatory archive catalogue. Click on this link to see what I've found! What sad people we are, both working on a weekend!

OK. Take care,

Cx

Jude immediately clicked on the website link Cecelia had given. The page that opened up described a batch of letters belonging to an eighteenth-century grinder of optical lenses and amateur astronomer, a Londoner named Josiah Bellingham. A dozen of these, the website said, were to Bellingham from Anthony Wickham, dated at various points in the 1770s. She clicked again to read the list of letters and couldn't believe her eyes.

Quickly she returned to Cecelia's email and pressed 'reply'.

Cecelia, if you could get me photocopies of these letters, that would be brilliant. I think we're on to something here. Did you see that the last six letters are from *Esther* Wickham? She really DID exist! The mystery thickens!

Chapter 15

'He's never asked *me* to go stargazing,' was Claire's petulant comment as she seized a piece of junk mail and tore it in two. She made stargazing sound like a euphemism for some louche assignation, Jude thought, but stopped herself from saying so out loud. It would only make matters worse.

She had arrived at Blacksmith's Cottage for supper to find her sister not long home and venting her tiredness and irritation from a mad Saturday in the shop on an innocent pile of post. *Rip* – there went a credit card circular.

'I'm sorry,' Jude said, almost regretting she'd mentioned visiting Euan. But if she hadn't said anything and Claire had found out, she'd have been in even worse hot water. 'I'm sure he would ask you if he knew you wanted to go. I suppose it's because of all the Anthony Wickham stuff. He can see it would be useful to me.'

'And don't *I* run a shop called the *Star* Bureau?' was Claire's whiplike comment as she yanked the plastic off a magazine, chucking the publication on the table.

Soul and Destiny, Jude read. 'Have you lived before?' ran one of the shoutlines. I hope not, she thought, one lifetime is trouble enough.

Claire glanced at her watch. She was due to fetch Summer from a birthday party down the road shortly.

'I won't go stargazing if you mind about it,' Jude said with a sigh.

'Why should I mind?' Claire replied.

'Something tells me you're keen on him.'

'Damn. House insurance renewal time already?' Claire cried, snatching up another envelope and tearing it open. 'Bills, bills, bills. What did you say?'

'We were talking about Euan,' Jude said. 'Claire, I'm trying not to put my great size sixes in this one.'

'There's nothing for you to put them in,' she replied. 'He's a lovely guy. I think Summer is trying to get us together.'

'Just Summer?' wheedled Jude, but Claire sidestepped the question.

'She misses having a dad, Jude.'

'But you said you were happy being just yourselves.'

'Well, yes, but she likes him so much. You should see them together.'

'I have. And I see what you mean. But what about you?'

'Oh, I don't think he's interested in me,' Claire said, tearing a flyer about a sofa sale into several pieces and letting them flutter into the recycling box. 'Anyway, anything he went into would be too serious, by all accounts. He doesn't play around. Darcey's mum, Fiona, said—'

At precisely that interesting moment the telephone rang and Claire snatched up the handset. Jude mused that she'd need to go carefully with Euan. She didn't want to upset her sister by leading him on in any way. She must keep everything on a strictly friendly basis.

'Hello? Hello?' Claire was saying down the phone. 'If you're the double-glazing people again I told you I don't . . . Oh, Gran, hi! How are you? Is everything all right?'

She met Jude's eye. Both women switched into alert at the possibility of a crisis.

'You're fine. Good. Yes, Jude's here,' Claire said, visibly relaxing. 'Do you want to speak to her?' She passed the handset over to her sister. 'I've got to fetch Summer,' she mouthed to Jude, who nodded.

Jude waited until the front door slammed – Claire never just closed doors – before saying, 'Gran, hello, it's Jude. How are you?'

'I'm surviving, thank you, Jude. Just because I telephone doesn't mean I'm dying.' Gran was unusually brisk. 'I want you to come and see me. I've got something for you.'

'Oh, what is it?'

'You'll find out when you come. I've been searching for it ever since you came last.'

'How intriguing!' Jude suddenly remembered that when she stayed there, over a week ago now, she'd heard Gran opening and closing drawers in her room after they'd gone to bed.

'It was such a stupid place to put it,' Gran muttered to herself.

'Gran? Can you still hear me?'

'Of course I can.'

'Are you free at all tomorrow?' She'd been invited to Sunday lunch at Starbrough Hall, but she could escape after that.

'Free? Where would I be going?'

'I can come late afternoon, if that's any good. Shall I bring Claire and Summer?'

'No, just yourself. Tell Claire it would be lovely to see them another time.'

What was up with Gran? Jude thought, and hoped fervently that Claire wouldn't feel excluded.

'It's . . . exquisite.' Jude held the necklace up so the evening light flashed on the row of gold stars studded with what looked like, but couldn't be, diamonds. There were six of them. 'Oh, what a shame, one's missing.' A link was damaged at one end of the row, as though a seventh had been torn off.

'Tamsin never knew when that happened,' Jessie said. 'She told me it had always been like that.'

'Seven for the seven stars in the sky,' Jude murmured, remembering the counting song her grandfather used to sing. The necklace was so dainty. 'These aren't real, are they, these stones? They must be zircons or something.'

Gran looked outraged. 'Of course they're real. *She* told me they were. I knew I'd put it somewhere safe, but I couldn't remember where. I hid it when that new plumber came, but it wasn't in any of the usual drawers, so I've had a fine old turnout. I went through the pockets of my old coats, and that fake tin I keep in the cupboard – oh, all the places I've ever put it when I've had men in – then this morning when I woke up the answer fell into my mind. Next door had a burglary a few weeks ago, and I had a bit of a panic. I'd put it where no burglar would ever look.'

Jude, trying to assimilate all of this, just smiled and shook her head.

'Under the carpet in the spare room,' Gran said triumphantly. 'In the corner, so there was no danger of anyone stepping on it.'

Jude laughed. Despite this tale of confusion, Gran's mind seemed sharper today. Perhaps it was remembering the challenge of outwitting all those poor, undoubtedly innocent tradesmen and the excitement of the find.

'Is it something you inherited?' she asked, studying the five-pointed stars. One, she saw now, had a goldsmith's mark on the back. It was gold, then, though the mark was very worn. It would take a specialist to make sense of it.

'Oh no, it's not mine at all. That's the whole problem.' Jude stared curiously at her grandmother, who went on, 'It belongs to the wild girl, you see. The girl I told you about. I've had it all these years.'

Jude felt bewildered. 'The wild girl? You mean Tamsin?'

'Yes, I told you, I took something from her.'

'But – a *diamond necklace*?'

Gran's expression hardened. She reached out her hand for the necklace and Jude gave it to her. 'She left it behind, Jude. It didn't seem like stealing at the time. We had a hiding place for it, you see, in the folly. And when she went away that last time and didn't come back, I found it. I told myself I was looking after it for her. I'd have given it back if she'd come and asked for it, but she never did. It was so pretty. I had wanted it from the moment she first showed it to me. So I put it in a little box under the floorboards in my bedroom and kept it there. Not even my sister, Sarah, knew about it.'

Jude thought of the refurbished floorboards in Gamekeeper's Cottage. Gran's hiding place would be gone now, nailed down and sanded. 'I went there yesterday, Gran,' she said, carefully watching for the old lady's reaction. 'To your old home.'

'There's a young man lives there now,' said Gran. 'I know about him. Claire's told me.'

'What did she say?' Jude asked, hoping to have some insight into what Claire thought of Euan, but Jessie was only thinking about her childhood home.

'That he's making something of the place.' Her expression was unhappy. It's upsetting her, Jude realized. Of course it would, imagining her old home being torn up and rearranged to suit modern purposes.

'But you've never been back there?'

Gran shook her head. 'Not since my parents died. I wouldn't want to. Better to remember it how it was. They were happy times mostly, oh yes, and I like to think of those. Until . . .' She stopped. For a moment she toyed with the necklace, held it up to see once more how pretty it was. Then she reached out and taking her granddaughter's hand in hers, tipped the necklace into her palm. 'Take it,' she said, closing Jude's fingers over it. 'I want you to find out what happened to Tamsin.'

'Gran,' Jude said softly. 'She would be so very old, and there's no guarantee—'

Jessie interrupted. 'Yes, of course, she's probably dead. Don't think I haven't thought of that. But there's a chance, isn't there? And, anyway, she might have children.'

'There's a chance,' Jude agreed, though privately she believed it to be a slim one. And any children would be getting old themselves by now. 'But I need to know more about her. What was her other name?'

Gran thought for a moment then said, 'Lovall. She must have been the same age as me, though she didn't know exactly when her birthday was. She was in my class at Starbrough, I told you that. She was such a gentle person, and quiet, but in natural history she knew the names of the animals and flowers, but sometimes they weren't the right names, they were the Romany ones.'

A name, a school, and a rough date of birth – Gran had been born in 1923. That was all the information Jessie could give about a girl she'd met in a forest nearly eighty years ago. A Romany girl with no permanent address, who had probably changed her name on marriage and was more than likely dead now. Oh well.

Jude wrapped the necklace in its tissue, and tucked the package safely in her bag. 'I can't promise anything, Gran, but I'll try.' It was all she could offer, but the expression of relief in her grandmother's eyes was reward enough.

Chapter 16

We're halfway through July already, Jude realized on Monday morning as she wrote a note to accompany the poor savaged final volume of the observation journal. She packed it up and drove to Holt, where she dispatched it at the post office to Cecelia, at her Barbican address. Then, since she'd arranged to meet Claire in her shop the following day, she browsed instead in some other antique shops and galleries for an hour. There was a lovely watercolour seascape with boats, which she bought to give as a thank-you present to the Wickham family when she eventually left. In the bookshop, she found a copy of Euan's new book. Then, walking back along the winding streets towards the car park, she noticed a small public library. 'Discover the history of where you live' a poster announced on the door. Deciding to do just that, she stepped inside.

'Where's your local section, please?' she asked a woman of about fifty who was pinning photographs onto a display.

'Right this way,' the woman replied and took her to over the shelves. 'Anything you were looking for in particular?'

'Do you have anything on Starbrough village or Starbrough Hall?' Jude asked.

'No specific book,' the librarian replied. 'But there might be something in these ones about Norfolk and Holt.'

'Thanks. I'll root around, then,' Jude replied, flashing a smile, and the librarian returned to her display.

Jude picked out the local volume of Pevsner's architectural history and turned to the index. The reference to Starbrough Hall was cursory and there was no picture so she put it back. A history of the area, published in 1998, proved more helpful. There was a page and a half that expanded on the information she'd read in the *Great Houses* book in her office – namely that the house dated back to 1720 when Edward Wickham, presumably Anthony's grandfather, built it on the site of Starbrough Manor, which had been destroyed by fire ten years earlier, only two years after the disastrous fire of 1708 that devastated most of Holt. Edward, it seems, was originally a local man who had retired to the area having made a fortune as a merchant of the East India Company. 'Edward's grandson Anthony built the tower in 1769,' she read with a leap of sudden interest, but a great deal of the rest of the information she knew already.

Its position, on a hill in the forest belonging to the house, was controversial, not least because it's always believed to have been the site of a burial ground dating back to the pre-Roman period. Unlike many other eighteenth-century follies, its purpose does not appear to have been merely decorative. References from Anthony Wickham's own writing indicate that he used it to view the night sky.

But then came something new.

In the 1920s an attempt was made to excavate the area around the tower and some items of interest from various periods were found, including Celtic jewellery, and these now reside at the Castle Museum in Norwich. At the time of writing, the Hall and the woods around are still in the possession of the

Wickham family, but the farmland was sold off in the early
sixties.

So there had been an archaeological dig, after all.

She went over and asked the librarian, 'You don't have
anything more about this excavation, do you?' She showed her
the passage in the book.

The woman spent a few minutes searching on a computer
terminal before saying, 'It looks as though we don't, I'm afraid.
Why don't you contact the museum in Norwich? A friend of
mine there would be a good person to try first. Her name is
Megan Macromber.'

'Thanks, I might do that,' Jude said, scribbling the name
down in her notebook. It wasn't an immediate priority, but it
might come in useful to know what was dug up in the 1920s.

Returning to Starbrough Hall, she spent a quiet few hours
in the library there, cataloguing, then started in earnest the
cumbersome job of transcribing Esther's memoir. The section
she'd already read was an easy job, but when she came to the
next part it took longer, not least because she kept stopping
to think about the story evolving beneath her hand. Esther's
voice, timid and formal at first, was growing in strength and
confidence as she proceeded.

For my eighth birthday my father sent me a hand-painted book of
pictures of birds and flowers and animals of our kingdom. I passed
many hours turning the pages, whispering the names to myself
and wondering at the delicate colours. I showed it to Sam, who had
taught me the country names of flowers, milksop and lords and
ladies, how to tell a male from a female jay, but he shook his head
over the Latin words in my book and declared them cold and dead.

'What does that word "veronica" say about the blue of a speed-ye-well?' he said with all the superiority of his ten years. 'And "Erinacea" in't as good as "hodgepig" – think how comical they look running on tiptoe.' But while I took his meaning, I still loved the strange sounds of these new words, and was glad I knew now why 'vulpine' meant fox-like, as Miss Greengage had told us, when the word sounded as if it should mean wolf-like, which instead was 'lupine'. Seeing 'vulpus' under a picture of a fox and 'lupus' by a savage-looking wolf made everything clear.

There came a series of long hot days interspersed by short cold nights without cloud. As we played outside, long into the evening, Matt and I marvelled as the sky turned from the deepest imaginable ultra marine to an exquisite indigo suffused with gold, out of which stars began to wink. It was always then, this breathtaking moment when the secrets of the upturned bowl of the night sky began tantalizingly to reveal themselves, that Susan would summon me to bed. So on one of these evenings we planned the final details of our adventure.

The chosen day was in the middle of August. I stole bread and cold ham from the larder while Mrs Godstone's back was turned, wrapping it in oilcloth and hiding it in a crock in the coolest recesses of the dairy, lest hunger should strike us. At bedtime I stowed warm clothes under my pillow. After Susan blew out my candle and I heard the squeak her left boot always made as she retreated down the corridor, I got out of my bed and pulled on my dress and jacket, and played silently with my dolls in the near-darkness until the house quietened. Then I counted to sixty slowly, thirty times, to be certain. When I slipped out of my room, the door clicked shut behind me, and I waited to see that no one had heard before flitting down the stairs, through the kitchen and the dairy, where I rescued my package, and out through a window that I'd left secretly unlatched. Some of the ham I threw to the dogs to silence them. I listened to them *snuffle about, their chains clinking in the dead air, then hastened across the cobbled yard and out into the park, where the sky spread out before me, the moon a glimmering slither amid the stars; I stood for a moment fancying it to be the curved spine of a dreaming fish in a wondrous dark pool speckled with light.*

Matt was waiting for me, hidden in the ha-ha as he'd promised. We walked together across the wide park and up the path through the woods feeling we were the only people left in the world. Gradually our eyes grew used to the darkness and we moved with confidence like other night creatures. Matt was certain of the route because he had consulted his father on the matter cleverly so as not to arouse his suspicion. 'I pretended an interest in the orchids,' was his explanation.

The path through the trees was at first narrow and brambly, then, as they became more widely spaced – beech and oak and chestnut – our progress became easier. Yet my foreboding grew. With every step my chest tightened. I clung to Matt's arm, unsure of the source of my fear.

'Esther,' he whispered. 'Stop it, you're hurting me.'

'I don't like it,' I managed to say.

'There's nothing to be frightened of.' But he clung to me, too, and I could tell I was making him nervous. 'Come on,' he said, his voice turning to a squeak. 'I think we're nearly there. Father said . . . Oh!'

Before us opened a clearing and in its centre moonlight fell on what appeared at first to be a gigantic tree thrusting upwards, taller than anything I'd ever seen. It was the folly: sinister, strange, fiercely alone. For a moment we could not move for awe, then Matt pulled at my arm and we stepped out of the shelter of the trees.

When we spoke of it later, we knew it to have been only a bat, but to see our terror when the thing broke out of the darkness upon us, you might have believed it the devil himself. I cried out and ran blindly. 'Essie, don't,' I heard Matt say, but I tripped and fell heavily, striking my head, and for a long moment knew only darkness and confusion, and Matt's voice crying, 'Wake up! Someone's coming.'

Then came a door banging and a man's voice – surprised, angry – and Matt shouting, 'Run, Essie,' though clearly I could not.

I felt a hand on my head, gently stroking my hair, and heard what I knew to be my father's voice: 'God dammit, it's the child.' I dared not move but felt his fingers search my wrist for a pulse, then he carefully rolled me over until my head rested in the crook of his arm. I opened my eyes and soon the shadowy contours of his countenance came into focus. 'Are you hurt?' he asked and he must have heard my whispered nay, for he carefully raised me to my feet. But my head throbbed and I staggered, so he steadied me and after a moment I felt better.

'Why in God's name do they let you roam the country in the dead of night?' he spoke, almost to himself. 'Have they sent you with some message, perhaps?' he asked. 'Is someone ill, or worse?'

'A message? No,' I stuttered, bewildered, then remembered our ham, grateful for an excuse. 'Though . . . I have supper for you.' I rescued the oilskin package, now somewhat crushed. He looked at it puzzled, but pushed it into his pocket. I glanced round but of Matt there was no sign. I prayed that he was safe and reassured myself that he must have run off home.

'Why would they send the child?' my father said to himself, but I could see his concentration was wandering. He felt inside his coat, pulled out a fob watch and angled it until it caught enough light to read it by. 'Come,' he said, putting the timepiece away. He took my cold hand in his warm one, and led me towards the folly. Now I was with him, I was no longer afraid.

'I'll take you home, but first I have some measurements to procure.'

*He led me through the door at the base of the tower and imme-
diately we were plunged into cold darkness. 'Wait,' he said, and
his voice was curiously deep-timbred in that place. There came the
scrape of flint and sparks flared into flame. I watched him light
a small lantern and wondered at the waves of light and shadow
lapping around the walls. A neat spiral of brick steps rose before us
and he gestured to me to go first. So up I went, feeling my way on
hands and knees, my fingers frozen with cold and fear. I climbed
for what felt like for ever, then suddenly we emerged into a circular
room with windows all about. There was a table by a wall, on which
another lantern burned, and it was by the light of this that I first
saw the world of this room in which I now sit.*

*It was, I imagined at the time and do still, like a cabin in a great
ship might be. It gave me also the sickening sensation I'd once felt
when I climbed a great beech tree as a dare of Matt's and felt it sway
in the wind. A wooden ladder led up to the ceiling and a square of
pale light. 'Up once more,' came my father's voice behind me, and
because I desired to impress him I overcame my reluctance and
placed my hands on the ladder rail. 'I won't let you fall,' he said
gently, sensing my fear, and so I climbed, glad of his shepherding
presence behind.*

*We came out onto a small brick platform, with a low parapet
around it and a canopy overhead and there – oh wonder! He had
rolled back the canvas to allow a telescope longer than a hay rake
and thicker than a man's thigh to point to the sky.*

*'Sit,' he commanded, indicating a small bench, and I sank down
thankfully on account of the swaying sensation and watched him
arrange himself on a high stool and compose his features, as he
grasped the spyglass and pressed it to his eye. Several minutes
passed thus with him staring through the glass, and I peeped
covertly about me all the while. Beyond the rim of the tower, the
tops of trees sighed and tossed in the darkness, nor did they ever*

cease. An owl called, another answered. From a long way distant, a vixen barked, an ugly sound. There was a small table by my father's side, on which were laid a large notebook, his pocket watch and some queer-shaped instruments and I watched him take one of these, hold it up to the sky and read aloud some figures from it. Then he scratched quickly in his book with a pen. This he repeated several times.

'I'm done,' he said finally, consulting his watch and dropping the pen back in its pot. He got off the stool, making to close the canopy. At this a great longing overwhelmed me.

'Oh may I see first?' I burst out, my shyness quite forgotten.

He contemplated me, again with that puzzlement, then shrugged and said, 'Why not?' I had to stand on his stool while he held me by the waist. When I applied my eye to the glass, at first everything was blurred, and then my mind must have grasped the trick, because I saw a bright smudge of bluish light. The intimate face of a star. My cry was involuntary.

'What do you see?' my father asked and holding the scope steady he looked where I had looked. 'Vega,' he muttered. 'One of the brightest stars in the sky. It's part of Lyra.'

'The magical lyre of Orpheus,' I breathed. Miss Greengage had read us the story of Orpheus in the Underworld, searching for his beloved Eurydice.

'You know the story?' He was amazed.

I nodded. 'It was given him by his father Apollo and his playing enchanted men and wild beasts alike.'

This amused my father for some reason. He adjusted the telescope. 'There,' he said, pointing to the sky. 'A line of four stars, and to the left a line of six. A box of four between. See it?'

'I think so.' He bade me peer through the telescope again to see the nebula of Hercules.

'Hercules. Do you know the tale of Hercules?'

I did not. Miss Greengage's mother had urged her to read to us from the Bible in recent months. I knew of Noah and his great Ark and Job covered in boils. I asked, 'Is there an Ark for Noah in the skies?'

He looked surprised, then divining the sincerity of my question, said, 'No, these star names are far older than Noah. Hercules the Strong was placed by his father Jupiter in the heavens in honour of his twelve labours.' He pulled the canvas canopy across its frame, then dismantled his spyglass and began to gather up his measures. 'Bring the journal, will you?' he asked, and I clutched it to my chest with my free arm as I descended the steps after him. I helped him lay out the tools of his study on the desk in the tower room, then he extinguished one lantern and raised the other to light our way downstairs and out.

'They call you Esther, as I asked?' he said, as he turned a great iron key in the door.

'Essie sometimes, sir,' I said.

'Esther, I prefer. After my mother,' he said. 'It was the name of a beautiful Jewish queen.'

I vowed never to be mere Essie again, but always Esther.

We set off through the forest together, he sure of his way despite the darkness. In his presence I felt no trace of my previous fears, but by the time we gained the park I was cold, hungry and exhausted. As he closed the gate I slipped into a faint. 'Here,' he said, offering me a strong drink from a flask, but I choked and spat it out, so he lifted me in his arms and carried me home. I remembered no more. When I awoke, I was lying in my own bed, the sun pouring in through the open curtains, and Susan was staring down at me in alarm. 'Why, you're dressed already,' she observed. 'Why did you go back to bed? Does something ail thee?' I did not disabuse her and slept most of the morning.

All the rest of that day I moved around in a haze. Part of me feared that last night had been a dream. 'Vega,' I whispered to

myself. 'Lyra. Hercules.' These names were real enough and I
clutched at them.

I looked for Matt that afternoon, but found only Sam, pruning
the low hedges in the herb garden. 'Mam couldn't wake him this
morning. He's taken a chill, she says.' I hoped fervently he would
be better soon. At least I knew that he had reached home safely.

Jude reached this natural break in the text, marked her place
and closed the journal, her mind filled with Esther's voice.
Anthony Wickham sounded such an intriguing man – lonely,
or at least alone, but tender and kind, and clearly obsessed with
the stars. She wondered if he really were Esther's father – somehow Esther's descriptions of him didn't give the impression of
a guilty Lothario hiding a secret love child – and if indeed he
wasn't, where and why had he acquired her?

Chapter 17

'The moon has a face like the clock in the hall.' The line from a childhood poem rose in Jude's mind the next day as she waited for Claire to finish serving a customer. They were going to have lunch together before visiting their grandmother in Blakeney. Jude was studying the clock on the back wall of the Star Bureau. Its face was designed like a large full moon, with small piggy features set in an expression of mock surprise. It stared down at the half-dozen visitors browsing the items on display as though saying, 'Well really, who do you all think you are?' It was vivid, witty, and though customers had often tried to buy it, not for sale. And looking at it allowed her to watch her sister out of the corner of her eye.

Jude rarely had occasion to visit the shop, though when she did she always loved delving in its trove of starry treasures. These ranged from delicate silver mobiles of the solar system to kitsch film-star T-shirts and plastic pocket-money toys. And it still amazed her, but also gave her immense pleasure to see Claire in her professional environment – efficient and effective instead of prickly and difficult. At this moment she was explaining calmly and earnestly to a young woman in a mini-dress and leggings why giving a name to a star in the firmament was such a wonderful thing to do. 'It's a fabulous sign of your love for someone special. I've done it for my daughter and my mum and my gran, and they were all so touched.' Claire clearly believed what she was saying, every word. She hasn't done it for me, it occurred to Jude, Claire's never named a star for me. And this dull thought bludgeoned home the distance between them.

She was fond of her sister, there was no doubt about that, and she supposed that her sister felt the same about her, but always there was this sense of Claire's resentment. It was more, much more than the simple biological fact that her birth had knocked little Princess Claire off her throne thirty-four years ago. It was about more than primal sibling rivalry to succeed and earn their parents' praise. After all, Claire had always refused to play that particular game. Some of it must be about Claire's disability, but since Claire's damaged leg had actually meant she received more in the way of parental concern and attention than her able younger sister, surely it should be Jude who was resentful. There was something else at work here, and Jude had never got to the bottom of it. She turned away, absently picking up and examining a delicate porcelain mug on which Van Gogh's famous picture of a street café under a starry sky was painted. It occurred to her she ought to buy something for Suri's birthday in a week's time. Not this, though. She looked about. A pretty string of fairy lights? No, too Christmassy. An engraved silver bangle caught her eye; it was just the sort of thing Suri would wear. It would look stunning against her tawny skin. She glanced at the price and then, as she pulled her purse out of her handbag, she tuned in to Claire once more.

'There's this lovely presentation box,' Claire was telling the girl, 'with a unique certificate.'

'Oh, the writing's so clever,' the girl exclaimed. 'Did you do that?'

'Yes, the personal touch is important,' said Claire, who had taught herself calligraphy as a teenager. 'This is where your star's name goes, here. And there's this chart of the night sky so you can see where it is. We only use stars you can see in the northern hemisphere, so your loved one can actually expect to see it, if only with a telescope. Here we write the coordinates, so they can find it. And there's this booklet about studying the night sky . . . oh, and my poem.'

'And it's twenty pounds for everything? I'll do that, then. It's my gran's sixtieth so the star will be called Trixie Tonkins.'

Jude, in the queue to pay for the bracelet, had to disguise a little snort of laughter with a cough. Clearly the idea of a noble celestial body named Trixie Tonkins also struck the girl as peculiar, because she asked anxiously, 'Do you think they'll accept that?'

Claire, commendably, kept a straight face. 'Of course. Astronomers use numbers rather than names, anyway, so they won't be bothered by what we do. The Star Bureau produces a register every now and then to publicize the names and, I've got to tell you, there are other companies that do this, but since there are more than fifteen million known stars, there're plenty for everyone who wants one.'

Jude had once had an argument with Claire about this. 'Don't you think you're conning people a bit? After all, stars won't ever officially be called by these names that people pay for. Is it legal?'

'I always explain,' Claire had replied fiercely. 'But people still seem to want to go ahead with it. It's more the symbol of naming a star, isn't it? It's a special thing to do for someone, a personal thing. Customers don't seem to care whether some nerd at NASA calls it by the name or not.'

'Money can't buy you love – or stars,' Jude muttered.

'Summer adores her star,' Claire said. 'She knows where to look for it and points excitedly when she thinks she's seen it. In actual fact, she can't see it with the naked eye, but you know Summer – she thinks she knows best.'

Perhaps that's why Claire's never given me a star, Jude saw suddenly. She thinks I'm a bit cynical. In fact, Claire was wrong, Jude did understand what Claire meant.

'Give her staff discount for the bangle, will you, Lol? Twenty per cent,' Claire's business partner Linda told Lola at the till. Linda's manicured finger moved quickly over the calculator. 'Twelve pounds, I make it.'

'Do you want a gift box today?' the shy teenager said, looking longingly at the bangle. 'It's really pretty, isn't it?'

'Yes, please. Oh, hold on a moment.' A book of fairy stories from a rack in front of the counter caught her eye. She pulled it out, thinking she'd never noticed any such collection on Summer's shelves. The illustration on the front of this one was lovely – a cuddly-looking wolf curled around a capable-looking Red Riding Hood. She turned the pages quickly. There was Cinderella in her coach, Snow White waking from her poisóned sleep, Jack swarming his beanstalk. Yes, she was sure Summer would love these illustrations; the characters seemed to leap from the page. The writer was a name she vaguely recognized. As to why it was in the Star Bureau, she saw the publisher was Little Star books. She smiled. Cheating, maybe, but why not.

'I couldn't resist stocking that one,' Linda remarked, as though reading her mind. 'It's not strictly speaking anything to do with stars, but we've sold two or three.'

The woman waiting to pay behind her gave an impatient sigh.

'It's irresistible,' Jude replied, making her decision. 'I'll have this as well, please. Sorry to mess up your calculations.'

By the time Jude had stowed away her credit card, Claire was ready. The plan was that they'd have lunch together in a little restaurant Claire knew, then drive their separate cars to Gran's, Claire picking up Summer from school on her way. Jude had felt guilty visiting Gran on Sunday without them, so she had suggested this arrangement.

'Lunch is on me,' Jude said firmly as they waited to cross the road.

'OK.' Claire shrugged as though she'd assumed this to be the case all along. This irritated Jude, but she was used to it.

In the restaurant they were served by the owner himself, who welcomed Claire warmly, kissing her on both cheeks. He was a jovial man, perhaps in his sixties, with a smile that crinkled the weathered skin around his sailor-blue eyes, and Claire flirted with him as he fetched the menus.

'What can I do for you lasses today?' he asked. 'Won't you introduce me to your friend, Claire?'

'She's not my friend, she's my sister,' Claire said, then saw the hurt in Jude's eyes. 'God, that came out wrong. Jude, this is Joe, lovely Joe, Linda's brother-in-law.'

Joe looked from one woman to the other, puzzled for a moment, then his face cleared and he nodded. 'I can see the likeness between you,' he said.

'Really?' Jude asked. 'Everyone says we're totally different.'

'Same expressions, same hands, same way of pushing back your hair, same smile,' he enumerated. The sisters looked at one another in disbelief. 'Takes a man of discernment to see it, mind you. Now, I recommend the cheese ploughman's. Or ploughperson's should we be calling it these days? The cheese is all locally produced. Then there's the seasonal vegetable tart . . .'

'I'll have that, thanks, Joe,' said Claire, twinkling at him, and Jude chose the ploughman's.

When Joe had left them, Claire said, 'So what did you buy in the shop?'

'Oh, this, for a colleague,' Jude said, bringing out the box with the bracelet.

'It's very pretty.'

'And then I thought Summer might like these stories since she got a magic star for reading.' She passed the book across the table and Claire looked at the title without opening it.

'That's very kind of you.' Claire looked a little anxious.

'Don't you like it? You were stocking it,' Jude pointed out.

'It's a beautiful-looking book. It's just that I've never really read Summer fairy stories. Her teachers say children can find them frightening.'

'Oh,' Jude said, a bit lost for words. 'I always loved them myself. These don't look very scary.'

'No, they don't,' Claire said, looking at the picture of Cinderella in her coach. 'Oh why not. It's very kind of you,' she repeated. 'I'm sure she'll love it.' Still, Jude was left with the feeling that her present wasn't entirely welcome.

Their drinks arrived. Her sister took a sip of cloudy organic apple juice. 'What's it like living the grand life at the Hall, then? A little bit more space than at Blacksmith's Cottage, I imagine.'

'But not as cosy. Seriously, Claire, it's alarmingly big. I'm not used to walking several miles of corridor to get to breakfast.'

'So how do they all manage there?'

'In what way?'

'Who does the housework and cleans the windows? It all seems very impractical.'

'There's just a daily cook and cleaner, I think. And Alexia's always very busy.'

'You'd think they'd rattle around.'

'They do a bit. And for years it must have been just Chantal and her husband, William, living there.'

'That must be strange. Having your son's family take over the house and you're still there.'

'I suppose so. A grand widow used to be moved out to a dower house, didn't she? In the bad old days, I mean.'

'A dower house – like for a dowager?'

'Yes, as in dowry.' The words were thankfully all that was left of that old custom where a wife was only as valuable as the money and lands she brought to the marriage. 'There isn't a dower house, though. Chantal told me she offered to find a place of her own here in town, but they wouldn't hear of it.' She considered the implications of this. Chantal, delightful though she was, must be used to the house being arranged and run in a particular way. If Alexia weren't such an easy-going kind of daughter-in-law, there could be difficulties.

Alexia hadn't changed anything round much, it occurred to her now. She thought of the drawing room with its formal furniture, the black and white photographs of long-dead family members set out on the piano and the bureau. Someone less tactful than Alexia might have brought in the interior design-ers. She didn't think it was merely a matter of there being no money. Even the dresser in the breakfast room was still lined with Chantal's mementos, though a modern corkboard on the nearby wall was covered with the messy paperwork of a busy young family: party invitations, lift schedules, digital snap-shots. She wondered what Alexia thought about the situation deep down. She'd not yet had much of a chance to observe.

Their food arrived and for a couple of minutes they concen-trated on eating. Then Claire said, 'You've never really said why you didn't go to France. I think you're mad, missing a chance like that. I haven't had a holiday for . . . ever so long.'

'We ought to go away together, the three of us, sometime,' Jude said on impulse. 'Visit Mum and Douglas in Spain maybe, once their place is ready.' But Claire didn't seem that keen.

'I can't leave the business really, can I?'

'Can't you? You and Linda seem to have help.'

'Lola? Yes, she's OK. And one of the mums from school, Jackie, helps out sometimes in the week with the online orders and the admin, but we can't afford to have someone else full-time and Linda gets a bit fed up, especially in school holidays when I keep having time off.'

'She doesn't have children, does she, Linda?'

'No, but her mum and dad are really old now and her mum has Alzheimer's.'

'Supposing you could get help in the shop, would you go?'

'Maybe. Summer would love it, I suppose.' Jude read it that Claire wouldn't. Thinking about it, a week or two cooped up with their mother would be tricky for Claire, even now that they got on better. The two sisters sat in silence for a moment, then Claire said, 'So why didn't you go to France with that Caspar guy? I thought you were keen on him.'

She was digging, Jude thought suddenly, reading her sister's thoughts. If Jude were still going out with Caspar, she would be safer to leave alone with Euan. Jude concentrated on piling chutney on her cheese, and remembered how upset she'd been that Caspar hadn't wanted to meet Claire. That, she saw now, was one of the things that sounded a warning bell about him. 'He's the first man I've been out with properly since Mark and —' She looked down at her food without appetite. Suddenly she decided to confide in her sister. 'Claire, I finished things with him. I'm frightened that I don't know how to be with someone any more. Every time I was with him I was comparing it to how it was with Mark. And there wasn't the same closeness. I wasn't at ease with Caspar. I was always wondering what he was thinking and whether he'd understood me.'

Claire studied her calmly, then remarked, 'He wasn't perfect, you know, Mark. You seem to think he was.'

What a strange thing to say. 'He was for me.'

'The trouble is you've put him on some pedestal, like he couldn't ever do a thing wrong. And then you compare every-one else to this ideal vision and they don't make the grade. How can they? You don't give them a chance.'

'Well you're the one to give me advice,' Jude retorted.

'That's different. I'm not looking for anyone else,' Claire said fiercely. 'Me and Summer, we're a big enough unit. It would take someone very special for me to change that.'

'Not Euan, then?' Jude flashed back. 'You seem to trust him with her.'

'I do,' Claire said, her voice softer now. 'Wouldn't you?'

Jude remembered his gentleness with all living things and nodded. She'd got the definite feeling that Claire was interested in Euan, despite all her protestations about going it alone. There was something troubling her though, about Summer.

'Claire, did you know Euan took Summer to see the folly once? Apparently she didn't like it.'

Claire looked mildly surprised, then said in an odd voice, 'Oh, why not?'

'I don't know. Euan said she was frightened by something. I'm sorry I forgot to tell you before.'

'She never said anything.'

'Well, perhaps it's a coincidence, then.'

'What's the coincidence?'

'Well, I just thought . . . I think it must have been around the time her dreams started.'

Claire stared at her, uncertainty in her face. Then she said, 'Mum wouldn't go there, you know.'

'To the folly? You told me you and she nearly went there once.'

'I fetched her over to babysit Summer – you remember that time she couldn't drive because of her knee?'

'A couple of years ago?'

'Mmm, it was just after Christmas. Well, I took a short cut past Starbrough Hall, and I remember the light was really strange; there was one of those winter sunsets when the sun is a scary red ball. I thought Mum was ill because she wasn't chattering away like she usually does, just staring out of the window at the countryside. I said, "Are you OK?" and she said, "Gran's old house must be somewhere about. I was looking for it." I hadn't met Euan then so I didn't know where it was. We must have driven straight past.'

'Easily done, given that huge hedge.'

'Anyway, we got to the top of the hill, and you know there's a tiny lane that goes off to the right? Foxhole Lane, Euan calls it.'

'It's the way to the folly. I didn't know it had a name.'

'Well, Mum made me turn up it and stop the car. It was getting dark and we couldn't see much anyway because of the trees. She said she was looking for the tower. She meant the folly, of course. "Why?" I asked her and she said something really strange. "I wanted to see if it was still the same." '

'The same as what?' Jude asked, leaning in closer.

'That's what I wanted to know but she didn't answer, just looked upset, so I said, "We'll have to get out and walk." I helped her out of the car and we got as far as the edge of the trees, then she changed her mind, decided we should go back.'

'I suppose her knee was hurting.'

'Yes, but, Jude, it wasn't only that. It was like she'd lost courage. I didn't push the point – I was getting a bit fed up actually. We were getting late to pick up Summer and it didn't seem a good idea, wandering around the woods at nightfall, Mum with her leg. Anyway, she seemed to cheer up once we drove off, so I forgot about the whole thing. Till what you said just now.'

'I didn't realize she even knew the folly. Perhaps she went there with Gran sometime. Why did she seem so apprehensive?'

'I don't know. Perhaps it's like with Summer. She found it . . . spooky. There are weird stories about it. Though Mum's not the type to be bothered by that stuff, is she?'

Jude considered the truth of this. No, Valerie could be quite matter-of-fact. She wasn't religious, she laughed at people who worried about breaking mirrors or seeing black cats. 'She likes horoscopes,' she said, remembering her mother always read the predictions for Virgo in the local rag. She took a certain pleasure in stretching them to fit her situation: 'good news at work' needn't mean a pay rise or a promotion at the surgery where she worked as a receptionist; it could be the grumpiest doctor in the practice actually smiling for a change or one of the nurses bringing in chocolate birthday cake. But believing in ghosts or funny atmospheres was not her usual behaviour.

'So what did Gran want you for on Sunday?' Claire asked.

Jude put down her knife and reached for her handbag. She brought out the small package and unwrapped it.

'She gave me this.'

Even scrumpled up in tissue the necklace looked beautiful. Claire didn't touch it; nor did she attempt to hide her expression of surprise, then envy.

'I don't mean she's really given it to me, Claire,' Jude rushed on. 'Just put it into my care. She wants me to find the person it belongs to.'

'The person . . . Who?'

'I'm as puzzled as you are. A girl, well, she'd be an elderly woman by now, called Tamsin Lovall. Don't look at me like that. I'm sure it's because I'm used to doing research that she's asked me.'

'I wasn't thinking that, Jude. I was just trying to work it out. Did we know she had this? She is a dark horse sometimes.'

'I know. She must have had it for over seventy years. And as far as we know has never breathed a word.'

'Do you think Mum knows about it?' Claire at last picked up the necklace and held it up. She noticed the damage immediately. 'Such a pity it's spoiled.'

Jude shrugged. 'Given how Mum and Gran are, I bet not. When do they ever communicate about anything tricky?'

'So where are you going to start? Looking for this Tamsin, I mean?'

'Do you know, Claire? I haven't a clue.'

'Look up Lovall in the phone directories?'

'Yes, but I bet there are loads of them. And her name might not be Lovall any more.'

Later, at Jessie's, Jude gave Summer the book she'd bought.

Summer squeezed herself onto the sofa between her mother and Jude and turned the pages. 'Do you like it?' Jude asked.

'Mmm,' said Summer, nodding. 'Can you read this one, *Cinderella*?'

Jude did, and they all listened. The story was beautifully told. Then Summer wanted *Snow White*.

'You were right, Jude,' Claire said when the story ended. 'You like your new book, don't you, darling?'

'One more?' Summer pleaded. 'Can we? Please?'

'Just one,' Jude said. 'Which do you want?'

Summer turned the pages until she came to a picture of two chubby toddlers, a boy and a girl, curled up asleep under a tree. '*Babes in the Wood*,' she said firmly.

'Oh not that one,' Claire cried suddenly. 'That's so sad.'

'It is a bit, isn't it?' Jude replied.

'I want it,' Summer commanded, so Jude, giving Claire an anxious glance, began.

' "There was once a man whose wife had died, leaving him to care for two beautiful little children, a boy and girl. Sadly, the man became ill, and knew he must die, and so he begged his brother to take the children after his death and to care for them as though they were his own. And so he died and the children became orphans. But the uncle was at heart a wicked man, and he plotted the children's death so that he might seize their father's wealth. He paid two villains to take them deep into the dark forest and kill them. Now one of the villains still had the trace of a conscience, and could not bring himself to murder these innocent babes. He quarrelled with the other man and murdered him instead, then ran away with the money they'd been paid and was never seen again. The poor babes were left lost and abandoned. They wandered about in the awful darkness until, weak with cold and starvation, they sank down senseless on the ground under a tree and there, in the darkest watches of the night, soft Death overtook them. Too late, the animals and birds of the forest took pity on them and covered them in leaves. And so when the villagers sent out search parties and they were found, it looked as though they were not dead at all, but only asleep." '

'That's horrible,' Summer said, taking the book and looking at the picture of the children, apparently asleep but in reality dead. 'I don't like that story at all.'

'Let's have tea, shall we?' Gran suggested brightly, and while Claire went to put the kettle on she remarked, 'Tamsin showed me that the forest wasn't a frightening place. Her family depended on it for their livelihood, you know.'

She sat back in her chair and her eyes took on that distant expression, as though she could see the past moving before her eyes.

'Did you meet them, Gran? Her family, I mean?'

'Oh yes, many a time. They camped up Foxhole Lane, not far from where we lived.'

'I know. It's near the folly.'

'That's right, dear. There were three, sometimes four, wagons. Tamsin didn't seem to have a mother, I think she'd died. Tamsin shared a wagon with her grandmother, Nadya, and her great-grandmother – I don't remember her name. She didn't speak much English and she looked like how you'd imagine a real gypsy to be, Jude, with big gold-hoop earrings and a very wrinkled dark-brown face and she smoked a clay pipe, same as the men.'

Summer was staring hard at Jessie. She asked, 'Did she wear a scarf thing on her head?'

'Yes, she did, dear,' her great-grandmother told her, amused. 'So did Tamsin's grandma Nadya. But in those days everybody wore scarves or shawls or hats when they went out. You didn't feel properly dressed if you didn't.'

Summer nodded and started turning the pages of her book again. Jude wanted to ask the little girl whether she'd learned about gypsies at school, but Jessie went on. 'They didn't ask me into the wagon – I felt it was their special place – but Nadya was very welcoming. If I went up there after school she'd give me a cup of tea with too much sugar in it and a heavy sort of cake. The great-grandmother would be making baskets and I used to like sitting and watching her; she was so quick and clever with her hands. Like when my ma made lace. Nadya came to our cottage door one spring, selling baskets planted with primroses, and my ma bought one with her lace money to be kind. When the blooms died, Ma planted the primroses in the garden and I was allowed to keep the basket.'

'I expect they got firewood from the forest, and hunted small animals,' Jude told Summer, remembering what had started Gran on this tack.

'That's right, dear, rabbits and even hedgehogs, and of course they knew all about the plants, which mushrooms you could eat and which leaves were good for medicine. Nadya tried to give me one of her brews once when I had a bad cough, but it smelt strange and I wouldn't drink it. I'm afraid Tamsin thought I was rude. Sometimes we got ourselves in a muddle like that because our lives were so different. Most of the time we played very nicely though. She was so dainty and pretty and she said such interesting things.'

'What did she say, Gran?' Summer asked. Claire was loitering in the kitchen doorway now, arms folded, waiting for the kettle to boil.

'Well, once she told me that she had three different names. Tamsin was only her public name. She wouldn't tell me the name her family called her, though I begged and begged, and even she didn't know the third name. It had been whispered to her when she was born, she said, and one day when she was grown up she'd find it out.'

'But I've got three names,' Summer said triumphantly. 'Summer Claire Keating. My friend Darcey's got four.'

'Tamsin must have been Tamsin Lovall at school, so I suppose she had four, too,' Jude said, smiling. 'Gran, did Tamsin mind going to school? Was it the authorities that made her?'

'Nadya wanted Tamsin to have her chance, was my impression. She couldn't read or write herself, but she was proud that Tamsin could. I'd have to help Tamsin with her school-work when she missed something, because her family couldn't. She'd never come into our house, even though I invited her, and I don't think Ma would have minded. She wasn't the sort to mind, our ma, but some of the local women were. There was this horrid skipping rhyme the other children called out to Tamsin. It went, "My mother said that I never should/Play with the gypsies in the wood." Of course, our teachers told them off if they ever heard it, but, well, you can't stop children, can you?'

Summer looked up from her book and said, 'That's a horrible rhyme, isn't it? I would never say that.'

'But I wouldn't be seen playing with Tamsin in school, oh no,' Gran went on. 'That wasn't very brave of me, was it?'

'No,' Summer said, a bit uncertain.

'They could be so cruel, the other children. There was one boy in particular . . .' Gran started fiddling with her hearing aid, which emitted a warning squeak.

Jude prompted, 'Who was he, Gran?'

'Drat this thing. Who? Oh never mind, it's not important.'

Jude sensed that it might have been, but tactfully asked instead, 'Tell me about the necklace. Where did Tamsin keep it?'

'Well, that's interesting. She wouldn't have worn it to school, of course, but once or twice she did at the camp. It was like her great-grandmother and the earrings. If they wore their valu-ables they wouldn't get stolen, would they?'

'No, I suppose not,' Jude said. But in the end, that's exactly what happened to Tamsin's necklace. Jessie had stolen it. Seeing Jessie's wistful expression she knew her grandmother was having exactly the same thought.

'I did love that necklace. Sometimes she let me try it on, you know, and we'd say that whoever had it was the princess and could choose what we were going to do that day. Once it was my turn, and I said I wanted to go up the folly. We often played near the folly, us children. Our da told us not to go up, though sometimes we did for a dare.'

There was a pause as Claire brought in a tray of tea and little shop cakes.

'Thank you, dear. None of us liked it much, the folly. It was damp and awfully gloomy.' She watched Summer peel the paper off a cupcake before continuing. 'Anyway, we climbed up to the room that day, Tamsin and me, and we played there, oh, some rubbish about fairies, and Tamsin found this little hiding place behind a loose brick. After that we used it sometimes to leave messages for each other and little presents. Just silly things like bits of cake or flowers. She once left me something one of her uncles made: two peg dolls tied together that looked like they were wrestling if you pulled the strings. Sometimes, you see, she didn't turn up at school, or her family had decided to move on, and then I'd go to look in case she'd left me something.'

Jude thought this enchanting, and Claire said, 'What a lovely idea.'

'I don't know when we first used it for the necklace. Not long after. Tamsin didn't want to, but I persuaded her. She let me take the necklace home, though I didn't show my ma – she'd have wanted me to give it right back. I told Tamsin that if I didn't see her the next day I'd put it back in the hiding place. And that's what I did. Of course, looking back now it was all a bit silly. Anyone else could have found it if they knew where to look. But at the time it seemed so romantic and I had foolish ideas in my head like young girls do.'

'How old were you when this happened, Gran?' Claire asked.

'Oh, we found the hiding place when I was eleven or twelve, I think.'

After tea, Gran fell asleep in her chair while Jude walked arm in arm with Claire out towards Blakeney Point, with Summer dancing ahead. The air felt lambent, magical. There is a special quality to the light out on the marshes in summertime, Jude thought; in the absence of wind, a stillness, and this, together with Gran's stories, put her in a strange, yearning mood.

They stood on a little spit of land looking across to the lonely last house right out on the peninsula and listened to a pair of skylarks in ecstasy somewhere up too high to see. Jude felt close to Claire in this place at this time; could forget that she'd said, 'Jude's not my friend, she's my sister'. But it was to prove a single, isolated moment.

When they returned to Gran's little house a text pinged into Jude's phone. Summer got to her aunt's handbag first.

'It's from Euan,' she cried, passing the phone to Jude, who scanned the screen quickly.

'It's about the stargazing,' she explained to Claire, watching her small bitter face. 'He says tonight would be good. I've got to meet him at midnight. I wish you could come.'

'Well I can't, can I?' Claire snapped, glancing at Summer. It was as though a fissure had yawned wide open between them.

Chapter 18

Angry with Claire, and telling herself she genuinely needed to experience stargazing at the folly for her research, Jude resolved to go, but it was hardly a difficult decision to make. She was already eager to see Euan again.

It was several minutes past midnight when she emerged from the trees by the folly and a three-quarter moon was rising, its missing segment a ghostly sketch. She was late because she'd become absorbed in reading Euan's new book, so she'd had to drive rather than walk, and when she'd got out of the car in Foxhole Lane her torch decided to die on her.

A tall figure stepped from the shadows by the tower. For a moment her heartbeat wavered, then the figure said in a voice she knew, 'Jude, I was worried you'd lost your way.'

'Sorry. I nearly did. My pesky torch.'

He stood back to let her pass into the tower first, shining his own torch to bathe the stairs in a red glow. 'Red light's better for stargazing,' he explained as they ascended. 'It doesn't destroy your night sight.'

She climbed more confidently this time, with the light and Euan a comforting presence behind her, and it didn't seem very long before they emerged into the little turret room. She glanced about, Gran and Tamsin's little hiding place a vague thought in her mind, but now wasn't the time. A square of moonlight on the floor announced that the trapdoor was open.

'Take your time with the ladder,' Euan said, 'and mind your head at the top.'

She was surprised to find that the summit of the tower was so confined – perhaps a dozen feet in diameter, and despite the waist-high parapet all round she felt vertigo kick in. She had to force herself to leave the ladder, and sat on the floor to adjust to her surroundings. The floor was of the ubiquitous crumbling brick and she was sure the tower was moving in the slight breeze, which made her feel nauseous. She tried closing her eyes but the sensation was worse so she opened them again to find Euan sitting beside her looking concerned, close, but not touching. She could feel the warmth of his body in the darkness and reached for his arm to steady her.

'Are you all right?'

She nodded.

'It was weird for me the first time. It gets better when you're used to it. Look up!'

She did and gasped in surprise.

'We're almost amongst the stars! I've never seen so many.'

'It's even better when there's no moon.'

Though this platform once had a canopy, now only a few of the brick supports remained and so it was open to the sky. And what a sky. Up above the trees, it was as though they were thrust up into a sparkling, shimmering dome.

'You really get the sense that we're on a planet, turning in space, don't you?' Euan murmured. 'Especially when the moon shows she's a sphere like that, not a flat disc.'

'It's as though the stars are alive and burning.'

'They are, most of them. I expect you know that being millions of light years away, we are seeing them as they were in the past. Some may not exist any more and what we're seeing are the ghosts of them.'

'It's too big a concept for us to grasp really, isn't it?' she replied, her voice husky in the cold air.

She saw, as though properly, for the first time, the misty ribbon of Earth's own galaxy, the Milky Way, made up, she knew, of hundreds of billions of stars, all eons of light years away. Giant words like eternity and infinity that people bandied around every day had suddenly taken physical shape before her. Now she remembered, as though it were yesterday, which in terms of their galaxy it was, a fraction of yesterday in fact, standing barefoot with Mark in the school field, making promises, which, in the end, humans being minute collections of molecules in a humungous universe, they were too insignificant and powerless ever to be able to keep, and she almost wept at the insight.

She glanced down for reassurance at the humble reality of her old jeans and trainers and became intensely aware of this other man, a near stranger in a scruffy anorak, who sat quietly, hands on knees, on the brick beside her. Studying those hands, considering their strength and their gentleness, brought her back into the world she knew, the tiny little world in which she could believe she was important.

'Are you all right?' he asked gently. 'You haven't said anything for ages.'

'Yes,' she replied. 'I think I'm all right.'

'Come on.' Euan pushed himself to his feet in one light movement, then helped her up, and moved to the telescope he'd set up on a tripod to one side of the platform.

'Is it safe?' Jude asked, eyeing the parapet.

'I think so, but I wouldn't lean on the side just in case,' he said, glancing absently, already absorbed by whatever he was looking at through the lens.

She shuffled towards him for safety, but merely catching a swooping view down towards the trees was alarming enough. She stopped and had to cast from her mind a sudden fearful image of Summer up here. But he hadn't brought her up, had he? She remembered what Chantal said about the accident that had happened once, forty years ago. It would be easy to fall, especially if you were drunk or high on drugs. The mere thought made her dizzy and she sat down on the floor again.

Euan said firmly, 'You need to come and look at this.' He helped her up again and held her by the shoulders as she found the eyepiece.

'I can't see anything. I'm too frightened. No, wait, hang on.'

What swam into focus looked like a topaz set in a heavenly wreath of mist and light.

'Oh my God. What is it?' she breathed.

'Arcturus,' he replied. 'The guardian of the bear. It's one of the nearest of the bright stars in the sky. Try looking at it with the naked eye. There.' Jude squinted to where he was pointing. 'You see a sort of kite shape? Well Arcturus is the bottom of that constellation, which is called Bootes, the Herdsman.'

'What's the sort of semi-circle to the left?' She was all right if she didn't look down, and he was holding her securely. She felt his breath in her hair.

'North-east, you mean? Corona Boreallis. The Greeks claimed it as the crown of Ariadne – the daughter of the King of Crete.'

'He of the Minotaur?'

'Yes. Now the biggest star in the Corona is a reverse nova. Every hundred years or so it'll fade suddenly, then recover. It's because of dark material erupting in it. I don't know very much about astrophysics so don't test me on exactly what dark material is.'

'Isn't it important for your book? I'm enjoying your new one, by the way.'

'Thank you. Only to some extent. I am interested, but as I told you my focus is our cultural response to the stars over the centuries: why we stargaze and why it's been so important to us to understand the cosmos. It's probably the oldest branch of scientific enquiry, you know, not that our distant ancestors would have understood our concept of science.'

'It puts us in our place, looking at the stars,' Jude whispered, but whereas just now she'd experienced dizziness and terror, this had settled to a kind of pleasant awe. With him holding her she didn't feel so nervous now; she was enjoying starting to make sense of the mass of dancing light above her.

They continued to look at the stars for a further half-hour or so and then, seeing she was shivering, Euan said he had a flask of coffee downstairs. 'Will you be all right on your own for a second?' he asked.

'Yes, I've found my stargazing legs,' she said, and it was true. She was quite happy here now, high above the troubled trees. And though it must be past one, she didn't feel the least bit tired.

She stood staring around the great bowl of stars overhead, observing the moon's progress across the sky and thinking how quiet it was. She tried to imagine Anthony Wickham sitting up here alone in the frozen night, calculating the movements of the celestial bodies. What was he hoping to discover? Cecelia hadn't found out much about him, or whether his findings had contributed to the great body of knowledge being built about the stars. What motivated him? She couldn't say. Though now she was beginning to understand the allure of the night skies.

Euan reappeared. 'This'll warm the cockles of your heart,' he said, pouring her a brimming cup. He'd put sugar in the coffee and she welcomed the sweetness. She took several sips, then passed it to him, and he drank, too.

'Do you come up most nights?' she asked.

'Only sometimes, if there's a clear sky. I found this place soon after I moved here, when I was casting around for an idea for a new book. I climbed up here on a night like this and was immediately struck by inspiration. I knew a fair amount about the stars already, and the whole idea for the book came into my mind practically ready made. It's quite rare for that to happen. And of course my publisher loved it. It's a magical book to research and write.'

'It's lovely when your interests are also your job. It's a bit like that for me, too. Or it would be if there weren't all the politics and the pressure to make money.'

She saw his teeth flash white. 'Well, we all have that, don't we? Food, mortgages . . .'

'Tell me how you got into nature study and writing. I've got this vision of you as a snotty-nosed boy trapping insects in matchboxes and hatching lizards on the dressing table.'

He laughed. 'It was a bit like that. I had what you might call a free-range childhood, out and about on my bike every day, and a very inspiring teacher who ran the natural history club. I read zoology at uni and became a lab rat for a bit – you know, research – but it didn't suit. So I moved back here and took a job in conservation.' He paused. 'It went on from there really.'

His words drifted off and she sensed he'd reached difficult territory. Telling her about writing his first book might mean talking about his marriage. He wasn't a man it was easy to know. He was friendly and open, and she felt so relaxed and natural with him, but there was still a part of himself he didn't easily give up. She respected that. Everyone had their own timing. She certainly did.

And so did nights of stargazing. Cloud was drifting over the moon. She drank the last of the coffee and suddenly felt very weary. 'I think I ought to get back.'

'Yes, of course,' he said. 'Well, I hope you've enjoyed yourself.'

'Oh yes,' Jude said fervently, watching as he dismantled the telescope and packed it into a bag.

'Good,' he said, and again that smile flashed in the darkness. He helped her onto the ladder, then came down himself, closing the trapdoor.

'You must come again,' he said, his voice echoing, as they went down the stairs. 'You're a good stargazing companion.'

'Thank you. I don't mind taking notes for you, if it helps.' Now why had she thought to offer that? It felt resonant of Anthony and Esther.

'How very kind. Are you staying long in Norfolk?'

'Apart from needing to pop up to London for a day or two sometime – oh, another couple of weeks.'

Such a short time really, she thought as she drove back towards the Hall. She must get on with more of that transcript tomorrow. She needed to start drafting her article for Bridget. And do something about that necklace in her handbag.

Chapter 19

The next morning after breakfast Cecelia telephoned. 'I've been reading those diaries,' she said. 'Jude, they are a really fascinating record of astronomical observation at that time. Wickham's most important contribution is these new telescopes he made. They meant he was able to look at the stars with significant magnification. I can also tell you that he was a very careful, objective observer. You can really get the impression of the development of scientific method.'

'That sounds encouraging,' Jude said doubtfully.

'But as to actual discoveries, this "story" you're looking for to help the sale, I don't know. He certainly identified a number of so-called double stars, but that's not going to sound very exciting, is it? I suppose what is interesting is what happens when the daughter, Esther, takes over from him. Her notes, though careful, are much more lyrical and passionate. She talks about the sky being "an ocean of stars" – that's a lovely image, isn't it? And she says here, wait a moment, that she feels "like a traveller among them". You really get a sense of her. But there is something else. Listen to this. She's talking about some object she's seen in the sky near the constellation of Gemini. "It is there again tonight. At magnification 460 I can see it has no tail so I question my Father's observance. It is no comet. I feel earnestly that it is something new." '

'I read about that. What was it?'

'I have my suspicions. If I'm right, well, it would be amazing. But I need to read to the end and check some other things before I say anything, and I might be a few more days doing that. Danny is over from Boston for a week and we promised ourselves a little trip to Paris.'

Jude was disappointed, but dredged up enough warmth to say, 'You lucky things,' and to mean it. Paris made her think of Caspar, but she felt no twinge of regret. It was curious that those few months with him already seemed an eon away.

She thanked Cecelia and said goodbye.

It was with renewed enthusiasm that she returned to Esther's memoir. She was quickly entranced by the young girl's voice.

It was nearing Christmastide Anno Domini 1772. One frosty afternoon I was amusing myself with the doll's house in my room when, glancing from the window at the sound of hooves, I beheld a carriage and pair swaying along the drive, the horses' breath billowing up in the icy air. The vehicle pulled up before the house and a youth sprang down to still the horses. The coachman handed from the carriage first a tall angular lady in a feathery hat then a skinny boy perhaps a year or two older than my ten summers. The lady stood glaring up at the house, as though inspecting it for deficiencies. I, it seemed, was one. For a moment her expression had softened, as though something in the mild lines of sandstone had appeased her, then her basilisk's eye caught my curious one through the glass and her whole body stiffened. I flinched as though struck and stepped aside. When I looked again she'd gathered her skirts and was marching towards the steps, the boy tagging after.

Suddenly, below, I heard the entire household roused into uproar. Mrs Godstone screeched for Susan; Mr Corbett, the butler, bade a footman: 'Fetch in the luggage sharp now, will you, man?' I crept out of the nursery, sly as a cockroach, and no doubt as welcome as one, to my hiding place near the top of the stairs. Downstairs, doors flew open and slammed shut, hobnails cracked on marble and a snarling female voice resounded through the marble atrium: 'Take me at once to my brother. And make up the fire in my usual room, will you?' My father's sister had arrived.

She had visited before, of course, but rarely for more than a day or two. On this occasion, Alicia Pilkington, second wife to Adolphus Pilkington esquire, gentleman farmer of Lincolnshire, brought their meek eleven-year-old son, Augustus, whom she referred to publickly as my father's heir. They stayed for the longest week I ever remember. And during that time they brought the household of Starbrough Hall to its rheumaticky knees.

Her bachelor brother, Alicia insisted with undisguised contempt, knew nothing of running a great house, and so it was her sisterly duty, she announced to Mrs Godstone, to investigate the systems, to audit the household accounts and to measure the thickness of the dust under the bed in her room, the room which she'd inhabited as a child and which must thus always be kept in readiness. With a precision the king's generals would admire in their quartermasters, she inspected the linen cupboards, the larder, the attics, the boot room, the cellars, the privies – but not Mr Corbett's pantry, the door of which he defended like a wild boar at bay. She passed judgement on every least aspect of the housekeeping from preserves to chamber pots – and it was not long before that basilisk's eye searched out me.

'Why does this child infest the family nursery?' she asked Susan while I loitered unhappily by. 'Can she not sleep with you and Betsy like any other serving brat?'

'The master does not think of her as a servant, my lady,' Susan burst out, bobbing hastily to lend deference to the remark. 'More as a . . . a connection.'

'A connection? In what sense a connection? They say she's some pauper's bastard. Why he doesn't give her up to the care of the parish I can never fathom.' This fresh view of my origins, and the accompanying look she gave me, which implied he should best have kicked me into a ditch to die, caused the blood to slow in my veins. 'Don't gawp at me so, you saucy imp,' she shrieked. 'I tell you, Susan, you'll do well to take her to your own bed. And teach her some manners, for the sake of God's angels.'

And so I slept a night on a thin pallet between Susan and Betsy in their room under the eaves, and I say slept, but shivered would be the better word, though Susan did her best to warm me with the thin blanket she could spare. 'Is it true?' I asked her. 'Was I really a pauper's bastard?' But she denied it heartily, telling me as before that Anthony Wickham must be my father. He had brought me home one summer's night and declared I be treated as his own. I saw through that right away; it might mean I was in truth his daughter, or it might not. 'I knew you to be well born,' she added, tucking the blanket round me, 'for though you were dirty and clothed in rags, your skin was as delicate as a petal and those rags were of silk.' I pondered this mystery as I tried to warm myself enough to fall asleep. Perhaps I was a princess after all, but I still longed for Anthony to be my father. In the morning, Susan pressed her lips together like two halves of a muffin and went to apprise my father of how his sister had treated me.

The next night I was returned to the nursery, but Father would have done well to have awaited his sister's departure, for it was then she first saw me as an obstacle to her ambitions, and though she would not dare touch me, she struck Susan across the face for flaunting her authority. And that proved her worst mistake with me for I could not forgive any who hurt my Susan. Thereafter Alicia Pilkington and I were bitterest enemies. That week I played tricks on her so subtle, so clever, she could not prove her misfortune was ever anything but accident, though she must have had her suspicions.

I laid green sticks in her fire so it smoked and made her clothes reek; I fed seeds of a herb Sam once told me caused dreadful itching through a hole in her mattress so she complained her skin was covered in bug bites. Most unkind of all, may God forgive me, was my treatment of poor Augustus.

Thin, pale Gussie added to the troubles of the household by falling into a fever on the third day of their visit. The weather was so bitter that Jack Frost nightly decorated the inside of my window and in the mornings I must break the ice in my ewer to wash, but in Augustus's room the fire was stoked up all night until the sweat ran down his face and soaked his bedding. Two nights crept by thus and the crisis passed, and since his mother returned to bullying the staff, it was I whom she deputed to amuse the invalid and this I did by telling him stories. Ghoulish tales about the burial ground on the hill, the horrific spectres that walked the woods and even, I assured him, ventured into the park. 'On any moonlit night I dare not look from my window,' I'd whisper, rolling my eyes, 'for fear of sights of such great terror I'd turn to stone.' Augustus would stare at me, his mouth a dark O in a face already white from illness. He refused to sleep alone and, to my chagrin, I was ordered to share his room. At every strange sound – the tremor of the glass in the window frame, or the creak of a floorboard, he'd sit up and clutch the sheets with his long girlish fingers. And in time I softened. My intentions towards him had been villainous – to get back at his mother – but gradually we became friends, and he confided to me his mother's expectations, that he inherit the Hall from his Uncle Anthony, since his father, Adolphus, had an elder son who was to inherit the Lincolnshire lands. I thought nothing of this at the time. He is a harmless sort of boy, my adoptive cousin, more like to his studious uncle than to his termagant mother or the portly country squire papa whom I met on a later occasion.

Apart from his intervention on my behalf, my father fastened his door to the turmoil of that week, keeping to his room or his workshop, his meals delivered by Betsy on a tray. It was too cold even for him to venture out to the folly, though the stars I saw from my window on those ice-bound nights must have tempted him; huge, they seemed, and glowing with their true colours, Arcturus creamy and Betelgeuse pinky red. For yes, I had been schooling myself about the night sky from a book I had found in the with-drawing room.

Two days after Aunt Pilkington's departure, Susan burst into my room, bright-eyed and breathless, gasping that I should make uncommon haste, for my father required my presence that very moment. She smoothed my hair and straightened my collar, then led me downstairs and out to his workshop near the stables, where she pushed me through the doorway and left me.

Father was there, sitting at a table busily polishing a large silver disk like to a salver. This, he told me without looking at me, was a mirror for a new spyglass and must be burnished this way with oxide of tin for many hours until it proved worthy to reflect the very images of the celestial gods. He had summoned me to assist in these endeavours, and I gladly set to, fetching materials as he ordered, placing by him a dish of tea Betsy had lately brought, all the while stuttering answers to his manifold questions about what I learned at the school and studied in books. Then he instructed that I read a passage to him from a volume lying open near his elbow.

I did so in a quavering voice. The book offered a queer postulation: that the whole universe might contain many stars like to our sun, and many planets, too, all inhabited by strange beings of God's creation such as we'd never yet encountered. I stumbled over the unfamiliar words and soon, not unkindly, he bid me cease, instead asking what I thought as to the ideas therein. Why, there are strange wild beasts on earth I've never seen, I told him, not sure what answer he required of me. 'There are some who believe a strange race inhabits the moon,' he said gravely, and I nodded, for I'd gazed at the moon many nights and believed I saw buildings and forests upon its surface. 'If so,' he added, 'what other planets might lie out there beyond our sight, and what manner of creatures might live there?'

Later, when he'd finished his polishing, he took me to his library and traced the paths of the planets of our solar system on an ingenious structure he'd had made after the great Lord Boyle's, named an orrery, which put me in mind of the game we'd played at school. Saturn was the strangest to me with its rings.

'Six planets circle our sun,' he told me, 'but some say there might be more.'

'I should like to find another planet,' I replied, my shyness quite gone. 'That shall be my ambition.' He was a quiet-spoken man, my father, often silent, alone in his thoughts. I liked it when he spoke with me for though he called me child he asked me questions as if I were his equal and never laughed at my answers or dismissed them as infantile. He needed to have someone to talk to of his interests, and, I like to think, found me useful in my limited way.

After that day, my life changed, and his, too, I believe. I still attended school and slept in the nursery and ate with Susan and the other servants, but sometimes the order would come down and Susan dispatched me to his workshop or his study. It was I who steadied his new spyglass as he coaxed the mirror and the eyepiece into alignment in its long wooden case, and I was present on the warm September evening that the men installed it in the folly, my task being to carry my father's notebooks then to wait quietly in the tower room listening to his impatient instructions as they laboured to fix it on the platform above. The task complete, he and I spent the precious hours until darkness fell poring over the star charts he'd drawn as he tutored me in his theories about the paths of planets, the nature of stars and comets, until moths came fluttering down through the skylight, drawn by the light of our lantern, and we *saw the stars were coming out. It was time to mount the ladder and watch the skies through his new glass.*

At first I could see little. 'Practice is the key,' my father said, laughing, seeing my moue of frustration, and after this night he brought me with him to the folly from time to time, though Susan complained at my irregular hours. 'The child is too tired to attend school, sir,' she scolded him, and because he trusted her with me he concurred and took me more rarely, for all my begging him.

The new spyglass was a marvel, revealing the skies to be filled with stars he'd not dreamed of before. My father became more absorbed in his work, often sleeping long into the day after a full night's viewing, so in a week of clear skies I might hardly be summoned at all to his presence. But then there would be periods of cloud, and the following year a winter so cold that birds fell frozen from the skies, and he'd invite me to his study where we huddled by the fire and he taught me mathematics, philosophy, and how to record my observations – all tools, he explained, to aid astronomy.

The mathematical symbols made little sense to me at first, nor did they for some long while, but I caught his passion to unlock the secrets of the heavens and persevered. By his teaching also I learned much about the fabulous monsters and tragic children of the gods commemorated by the ancients in the night sky. From there it was but a step to teaching me Greek and Latin, so I might read the old charts, and something of the wondrous new knowledge of opticks and the secret properties of light.

And so the pattern of our new life together became set. My eleventh birthday came, and I remember it well because the gardener's cat had had kittens, and he brought me a black and white one all to myself, which I named Thomas.

Sometimes, at little notice, my father would summon the carriage and dispatch himself with bags and boxes to Norwich or London, where I daresay he would meet with other stargazers or visit merchants of optickal instruments, for he would oft return nursing a crate packed with delicate lenses or mirrors and then he'd shut himself in his workshop for days at a time, experimenting and polishing.

It was on one of these occasions, in the late autumn of 1773, when he had been away nigh a week, that a pedlar woman came to the kitchen door one afternoon selling pegs and ribbons and the like. Betsy was much taken with a lace cap, which she bargained for, and Susan pleaded with Mrs Godstone to buy me some ribbons. I hung back, clutching my little cat Thomas, yet fascinated by the young woman's sun-baked skin and her fine foreign eyes and the lively movement of her strong lean body as she crouched to search her basket for the particular sky blue Susan demanded for my fair hair. And when Susan summoned me forward to try the colours, the woman seemed wary, studying me curiously as she waited for Susan to make her choice. When she bid us farewell, her eyes rested on me last of all as though she would commit me to memory, and this alarmed me.

Afterwards I sat in the servants' room as Susan hemmed my new ribbons, and listened to them gossip.

'Farmer said they were back,' Mr Corbett announced briefly as he built up the fire. 'He's setting up a watch at nights till they're gone.'

'Reckon it was they vagabonds took his birds last time, not the Romanies,' Mrs Godstone said. 'I chased them out of the tatty bed, remember?'

'Aye, well he's not taking chances.'

'Where do they live, the gypsies?' I asked, and I spoke so little they looked surprised.

'Why nowhere and everywhere,' Susan told me. 'They'll have pitched their camp up in a clearing off Foxhole Lane, I reckon.' Foxhole Lane led up past the folly.

How wonderful, I thought, to travel with a wagon and camp up in the forest. But less pleasant if I had no house to go back to in the morning. Still I was curious to see this camp and when I told Matt the next morning, he said straight away that we should go.

Instead of going home after school, he and I set off up the road past the gamekeeper's cottage, all the way up the hill to Foxhole Lane. There we hid ourselves among the trees and crept along like savages stalking a deer, skirting the path. The smell of smoke reached us first, then the crackling of their fire, and voices in a strange musical tongue and harsh laughter. We burrowed into undergrowth, peering out at a strange sight.

Three tents and two open wagons, once bright-painted mayhap, but now dingy and battered, were arranged in no particular order round a newly lit fire. Two women — neither of them the one who'd come to our door — were sitting on stools by the fire chopping up vegetables and casting them into a large cooking pot planted on the ground between them. A thin girl of ten or eleven fed sticks to the flames from a bundle she held. As we watched, a wiry man with a bow-legged gait emerged from the trees nearby and cast a brace of conies onto the grass by the pot. At this the older woman gave a harsh cry of satisfaction, immediately grabbing one up and starting to skin it, only stopping from time to time to toss bits of the steaming guts to a stubby little dog and to lick the blood off her fingers.

The girl brushed dirt from her hands and called to someone in the nearest tent. The doorflap twitched aside and two younger children, a black-haired boy of five or six and a pretty girl, two or three years younger than me, in a poppy-red headscarf, slipped out and followed her direction to search for firewood. All three were dark-eyed with sun-browned skin, but the girls at least were tidy and their dresses, though worn, neatly mended.

We'd been there only a few minutes when Matt caught his foot on a root and grabbed a branch to steady himself. At the sound the dog bustled over, barking. Matt shushed it in that natural way he has with all animals, and it skittered back to attend the rabbit-skinning, but the bow-legged man had already crossed the lane toward us. In a moment his eyes met mine through the leaves. 'Hi,' he shouted in surprise. Matt and I struggled out of the bushes and ran as if the black helldog Shuck was after us. For a while we heard the man crashing about, but then the sounds grew fainter and by the time we reached the road by the gamekeeper's cottage he'd given up the pursuit.

'Bloody gypsies,' Matt swore, when he'd recovered his breath, and spat most liberally into the mud. Swollen with pride at our adventure we swaggered home, where a furious Susan decreed I be given only bread and scrape for dinner for tearing my clothes.

I saw her again, the girl in the poppy-red headscarf, two days later. My father had returned from his latest excursion with a parcel containing two books that smelt new-printed, and news of a comet, and I begged him to take me with him to the folly that night to search for it. It was twilight when we arrived, and when we had gained the roof platform Father found he'd forgotten an astrolabe he very much wanted and I was dispatched to fetch it. It was when I flew out of the doorway at the bottom of the tower that I surprised her, just standing there, her eyes large with fear, her body poised for flight.

For a moment we stared at each other in the half-light, the girl and I. She was thinner than I, perhaps seven years old, maybe eight. 'Don't be frightened,' I whispered, but my speaking to her was too much, and she picked up her skirts and ran for the trees, though stopping once to look back at me. I waved forlornly, in what I hoped was a friendly fashion, but she continued in her flight.

I thought of her as I half walked, half ran back down to the Hall, not nervous now I knew the forest and its ways. There was some-thing a little familiar about her face, whether the heart-shape of it, *or the short upper lip, or the small straight nose, I couldn't say. The surprise, though, was that her eyes were not brown at all as I'd thought when I saw her at the camp, but blue. Unusual with the sun-burned skin and the black hair, but then what did I know about gypsies?*

When I returned in the gathering darkness half an hour later, breathless, but clutching the astrolabe, of her there was no sign, and caught up as I was in the subsequent excitement of locating the comet I completely forgot about her.

A few days later Thomas, my black and white cat, did not appear for his breakfast. Nor was he to be seen the rest of the day, despite my searching and calling. By the following morning, a Sunday, I was distraught, and before I could be caught and dressed in my hated best for divine service at Starbrough church, I slipped away across the park and into the trees to look for him. Young though he was, Thomas was proving a fine mouser, with a passion to roam. Perhaps he'd been caught in one of the gamekeeper's traps on his nightly hunting trip, from which he'd often return to build a line of fat corpses on the kitchen doorstep. It was, I admit, a small chance that he'd wandered so far, but Sam and Matt and I had searched the barns and the stables for him, and their father had promised to watch for him as he worked. Nobody, it seemed, had seen poor old Thomas dead or alive.

At first I took our usual path, which ran from the edge of the park, snaking through the scrubland and up where the trees began. I called and called for Thomas, stopping to inspect where I knew the gamekeeper set traps, but there was no trace of him. I had almost reached the folly, when my attention was caught by a tuft of white fur lying among fallen leaves by the side of the path. I stooped and picked it up. It was soft like thistledown – or cat fur – and as I stepped over some trailing brambles into a small clearing my worst fears were met. There lay the half-eaten corpse of a small animal amid matted clumps of black and white fur. I crouched beside what was left of poor Thomas, the tears already coursing down my cheeks. A fox then, it must have been. A quick death it was, I prayed. Kinder than lingering wounded in a trap, at least. The savage forest had taken my little cat. I wept.

As I wiped my teary face on my sleeve, I became aware of someone standing nearby and turned to see. It was the gypsy girl, her eyes wide this time with pity. She stepped over to crouch by the poor little corpse, and for a moment, despite the bright headscarf, she seemed herself like a small animal, the bones delicate under her tawny skin. When she raised her face to look at me, there were no tears, only that calm pity. She set about collecting twigs and leaves and handfuls of the damp forest earth, proceeding to lay them over poor Thomas, and after a moment I helped her, weeping all the while. When we'd finished, she took my hand and we stood together looking down at the burial mound and I thought about Thomas, how Father had picked him out of the litter for me before Matt's father drowned the rest, how Thomas clawed his way up curtains as a tiny kitten and liked a lick of butter as a special treat.

'Poor cat,' she whispered, and it was as though she'd heard my thoughts for she added, 'You will find another.' I glanced at her in astonishment and not a little dudgeon, but her small heart-shaped face was serious. 'You will.'

And she was proved right.

When I arrived home an hour later with my dreadful news, the household all comforted me. Thomas was a good cat, they said, but he'd a dangerous tendency to wander. Several days later, Mr Corbett came back from the village with a tiny tabby in a basket. On Father's suggestion I named her Luna, for in her grey and silver she was as pretty as the moon, and like the moon she remained fixed in her orbit. She never liked to leave the stable yard.

As for the gypsy girl, I saw her twice more that autumn. Once, the following week, she was collecting firewood near the folly, and she waved to me shyly, but when I made to speak to her she vanished like a fawn into the shadows. The second time I had climbed up to the tower room on some quest one afternoon at dusk. My skin prickling, I turned and was startled to find her standing behind me. 'How did you . . . ?' I began, but stopped as she glanced around the room, fear and curiosity doing battle in her face.

'Have you been here before?' I asked her, at once knowing it unlikely, for my father kept the tower locked, and she shook her head and mimed someone striking her. 'You are forbidden?' I guessed, and she nodded.

'We come here to see the stars,' I told her, and showed her one of my father's charts, and her eyes widened and she moved her finger over the map as though it meant something mysterious to her. I tried to coax her to climb the ladder, but she said, 'No,' and smiled, before retreating down the stairs once more. I was left staring at the chart and wondering what she'd seen in it.

A day or two after this, my father's agent, Mr Trotwood, came by to see his master and imparted with a ghastly satisfaction the news that the gypsies had moved on. The implication was that he'd had some hand in this. I was angry with him. The thought that I might not see the girl again saddened me and we had, as far as I could see, no quarrel with these people. Their only sin, it seemed to me, was to differ.

Jude finished typing, then read through the whole passage again, hearing Esther's voice, clear and strong, in her mind. Her origins were still clouded in mystery, but Alicia had offered another suggestion, that Esther had been abandoned by a mother too poor to look after her and was 'a pauper's bastard'. Actually that really didn't make sense. Not if she'd been wearing rags of silk. But *rags*? If she'd been well-born, why had she been wearing rags? Had her mother abandoned her or suffered some tragedy? Still, Susan had brought her up well; she seemed sure of herself as a person, loyal to those she loved, defending herself in lively fashion against those like Alicia who declared themselves her enemy. Her relationship with the man she called 'Father' was a touching one. He seemed to be coming to value his young charge, even to show a fatherly affection for her. Perhaps it was because of a meeting of minds – that she, too, was fascinated by the stars.

She glanced up at the portrait above the fireplace. If, as Chantal said, he'd been twenty-two when that was painted in 1745, he'd have been forty-two in 1765 when Esther came to the Hall, a middle-aged, childless bachelor; but the gentle wisdom in his expression, the book he held to denote he was a scholar, these gave a strong impression of his personality. He was a marvellous teacher, by Esther's account, and keen to make her his apprentice at a time when many would have dismissed her for her gender and for her misty origins. For despite being known as Esther Wickham, at this time it seemed that the girl had no legal existence, was a child with no name. And until this account had emerged from the dusty back of this cupboard, Esther Wickham had been lost to history. Jude's desire to remedy this was growing steadily.

She had tried to be true to Esther's spelling, writing in square brackets when she felt a word needed clarifying for a modern readership, and she double-checked everything now for typographical errors. Then she emailed the passage to Cecelia, realizing she was unlikely to reply for a few days because of Paris. She could hardly bear the wait. In the meantime she would print off what she'd done and show it to Robert and Chantal.

Chapter 20

The next morning, Thursday, brought a terrible shock. The post came while everyone was finishing breakfast. Robert opened the official-looking envelope and said. 'Good God,' then, 'I was right. Mother, I told you they were up to something.'

'Who? Not Farrell?' Chantal asked, her face suddenly tired and strained.

'What is it?' Alexia asked, coming in from the kitchen with fresh toast.

The letter was from the Council Planning Officer and it outlined the details of a planning application that John Farrell's company were making in respect of Starbrough Woods.

'That's why that Vane woman was asking about access. They want to turn it into a blasted holiday park.'

'What?' said Chantal and Alexia together.

'Surely they can't, not if it's always been forest,' Jude put in.

'All right, not quite a holiday park. But listen . . .' Robert tapped the letter with an impatient hand. 'Here we are . . . erect twelve single-storey dwellings on the west side of the route named Foxhole Lane for use as rented holiday accommodation and a single-storey lodge to be an office. The landscaping of the surrounding forest is considered desirable as is – my God, no – the demolition of the tower known as Starbrough Folly. I think they're relying on precedent that there has been building there before.'

'But it's a listed building,' cried Chantal, half rising in her chair. 'We checked that before. No, *tu ne peut pas* – you will not remember, you were only three.' She wasn't making any sense to Jude. 'Robert, it is listed. There are *les obligations*. You must write to them and tell how—'

'You're right, Mother, but their argument is that the structure is dangerous and beyond saving. They . . . where does it say . . . here! "Of no obvious historical or architectural interest".'

'But it is,' Jude cried. 'That's what I'm discovering. It's where Anthony Wickham and his daughter watched the stars.'

'I don't think they know that, Jude,' Robert said, passing the letter to Alexia to read.

'Then we must tell them,' Chantal said.

Shortly after this, Euan rang Robert to tell him he had received a copy of the letter. They discussed the matter for a while, then Euan asked to speak to Jude.

'It's vital to defend the forest,' he said, 'and Robert tells me the folly is listed. That's a relief to know, at least.'

'I don't think it's as straightforward as that,' she replied, and explained about the structure being dangerous. 'What do you think?'

'It's not dangerous enough for it to be knocked down,' he said. 'Surely. I know I'm always making a fuss, but, honestly, I wouldn't go up there if I believed it was going to collapse under me. It's just that aspects of it need to be repaired. The stairs need to be made good, and the roof area safe.'

'Well you'll have to get together with Robert and construct a counter-argument,' Jude said. 'And if I can find out as much as I can about the history of the tower, it might strengthen your case.'

'I don't want those holiday cottages, Jude, but I'd mourn the loss of the tower most of all.'

The phone rang and rang that morning. Other people in the village had also received letters, or had heard the news from someone else, and suddenly Robert found himself the leader of a group to save Starbrough from an unpopular development. It had until recently been Starbrough territory, after all, and Robert, it turned out, was leader of the parish council.

'It's not that we wouldn't all value the extra business,' said Steve Gunn, the farmer from Starbrough Farm, who tramped up to the Hall in his wellingtons rather than picking up his phone, 'but the traffic would be a blasted nuisance. They want an extra road built, don't they? And the forest is the forest. It's important in all sorts of ways. You know me, Robert, I might not agree with all these organic people, but we need the balance. They can't go tearing up the countryside and thinking it don't matter.'

'I'm with you on that one, Steve,' Robert said.

'So we need the parish council to do something about it. And that's you, Robert. Being the chairman and all.'

'And I intend to call an emergency meeting,' Robert said.

During the afternoon, Jude and Chantal walked in the gardens, which were bordered with beds of late peonies and flowering shrubs and seemed to be Chantal's domain. Chantal was still extremely upset about the morning's bombshell.

'I never thought something like this would happen. If poor William believed a man like Mr Farrell would get hold of the land, he'd never have sold it at all. I think we're to blame. Maybe we were naïve. And now we have put the forest and the folly in danger. Oh, Jude, it's all slipping away, all the things that have been important to me – this house, guarding the heritage. Robert doesn't see it in the same way I do . . .'

'But Chantal, you said you and your husband needed to sell the woodland to pay the bills. And Robert will fight the development plan. It is just a plan. I can't believe the authorities will accept it. Destroying ancient forest like that.'

'No, but I have seen how these things work. They'll come up with another plan and then another, until everybody's worn away and it's accepted. And who is going to defend the folly? I don't think the farmer really cares about that.'

'Maybe not, but Euan does, and I'm sure many of the villagers will. It's a landmark, something the village is known for.' Though it hadn't been recorded on her tourist map, she remembered. 'And Robert seems determined . . .'

'Robert is a good boy, but it's like I say. I can see his father in him. He doesn't have the same feeling for the past that I have – and you, Jude.'

They stopped for Chantal to grub out some weeds from a clump of soft white flowers.

'There, now the poor phlox can breathe,' Chantal said, allowing Jude to help her to her feet and brushing the dirt from her knotted fingers. She seemed calmer.

They stood for a while in silence, appreciating the birdsong and the sunshine. The warmth of the air and the scents of the garden imparted a sense of timelessness. All human activity came back to this: the endless cycle of growing and dying, becoming one with the earth once more.

Chantal said, 'This is where I came the summer William died. It was the only thing I could do for a while. Grow things. Here I could work and allow my mind to wander. It was very therapeutic. When the winter came, I would sit by the fire in the library and try to read Anthony's diaries.'

'I'm not a gardener,' Jude confessed. 'It was my work that saved me.' She remembered those first awful weeks after

Mark's death. The red tape involved in getting his body back from France, then the inquest in London and the funeral. The relentless flow of letters of condolence, the constant phone calls. She'd gone home to Norfolk for a while, but her mother, herself still in mourning for Jude's father, was of limited help, and Claire was struggling with a toddler and a new business. Jude's old school friend Sophie was a godsend, helping with practicalities and just holding Jude as she cried. But Jude knew the only thing that would save her was some structure to her life. After three weeks she returned to work and there it was easier.

Inigo hadn't started at Beecham's then; instead there was Gordon, a gentle character, nearing retirement. He and Klaus were both old school when it came to death – patting her hand and showing plenty of stiff upper lip. Some people would have found that cold, but to Jude being in the office was like shutting herself into a neat compartment: she knew where everything was and how to act. She could catalogue books and value collections, lose herself in the familiar routines. Her other colleagues by and large appreciated this. Jilly on reception gave her a huge, emotional hug when she returned, and some of the staff clubbed together to give her flowers, but after that they respected her obvious attempts to hold herself together and carry on. Occasionally something would trip her up: some well-intentioned acquaintance would offer some word of sympathy that pierced her heart, and she'd find herself rushing for the safety of the loos to compose herself. For outside the scraps of shelter she constructed for herself, the world was a howling wilderness.

Eventually, she found that she managed best if at some level she pretended that Mark was still in the world but not actu-ally at home; that he was just off on one of his expeditions somewhere, one of his longer ones when he was right out of contact by email or phone. And so she started to cultivate a little fantasy haven of their home, kept his pictures on the wall, his clothes in the drawers, as though one day he'd walk back in. A therapist would probably say that this was a terrible idea, that she was only delaying grieving, but Jude didn't care.

It was only a year ago that Sophie, on a visit home from the States, had persuaded her that she had to start letting go. One rainy Easter week, she and Mark's sister, Catherine, calm but firm, helped Jude sort through the drawers and cupboards. Catherine, white-faced, had driven away with a car full of stuff in suitcases and boxes to share between a local men's homeless hostel and a charity shop. Then Jude had flown back with Sophie to New York where she'd spent a lovely week in the family's apartment shopping till she dropped then eating out every night. It was hard coming home to London from that, and as she arranged her fashionable new clothes in the wardrobe and hung a Frick gallery poster in the hall, she felt she was merely moving into a different kind of grief rather than moving on as everyone told her she should be doing.

She recounted all this to Chantal now, knowing Chantal wouldn't laugh at her or pity her, but would understand. And indeed the older lady listened intently, respectful of Jude's need to talk.

'There was no one I knew who was in my exact situation,' Jude said. 'When someone young dies tragically people genuinely don't know what to say. We all knew it wasn't meant to happen. It was an accident. No one could be blamed, except perhaps Mark himself for doing these dangerous things. He knew the risks. There was always that comment hanging in the air. Yet who would have stopped him? Not me. Not anybody. His adventures meant so much to him.'

'You do have to let people be themselves,' Chantal said. 'Though it must have been hard for you being married to him. Every time he was away. The worry. William used to fly little planes. I refused to go up with him, and I hated it when he went, but I learned to put on the brave face.' She shook her head.

'Funnily enough, I didn't worry when he was away,' Jude said. 'It sounds arrogant, but I always knew he'd come back. He always did.' And he had. The whole story of their relationship had been about them being apart and coming back together. During school and university and after, they'd had other relationships, but part of her was always waiting for him. Because she'd known it was meant to be. And he'd never let her down. There was only once, after they became engaged . . . a shadow . . . but it turned out to be a silly misunderstanding really. Why did she remember it now?

'What a perfect summer day . . .' Chantal was murmuring.

Summer. A picture of her little niece rose in Jude's mind. It troubled her. Yes, she was worried about Summer.

'Chantal, there's something I meant to tell you. You know I described my niece's dream? And about the bit in Esther's memoir, when the workmen who built the folly found a grave or something and one of them thought they'd seen a ghost?'

'Yes, of course,' Chantal said. 'And that there was digging there in the 1920s and maybe they found some bones and you wondered whether this was the ghost? Why, do you think there's a connection to your niece? Surely not.'

'But it was her visit to the place that set off the dream.'

'Well, there have always been rumours about the place having an atmosphere. I don't believe it's a supernatural one. There is some kind of feeling about the tower, I agree, being deep in the forest like it is. And with its room at the top, it reminds one of Rapunzel's tower in the fairy tale, yes?'

'I hadn't thought of that,' Jude said. 'It's a very disturbing story. Imagine being locked in a tower with no door. And having someone climb up your hair would be unbearably painful. I always wanted to know why she didn't cut her plait off and use it as a rope to escape.'

'I expect the story was written by a man, my dear,' Chantal said, and Jude smiled, though she knew the answer wasn't so simple.

'But the stories about the folly,' she persisted. 'What do local people say? That it's haunted?'

'English people like their ghost stories, don't they? Some say they feel they are being watched. And Robert's grandfather was always sure he'd had a strange experience there when he was a boy. He said he had a strong sense of something there, watching him. Nothing more specific. And somebody at the inquest for that young man talked about there being an atmosphere. I'm sure I mentioned the accident?'

Jude did remember. 'What happened exactly?'

'It was the summer that Robert was three – 1970, that must have been. We were sailing up at Brancaster Staithe and we let him come with us in the boat for the first time. While we were away some young people broke into the folly one night and had a party there. Somebody fell from the top and was killed. They were all high on drugs at the time. The coroner was very clear. It was an accident and we weren't liable in any way because the place had been locked up and they were trespassing. The young man's family wanted the tower knocked down afterwards, but others didn't because it was so old and part of the history of the area.'

'What an awful accident. They don't say that he's one of the ghosts, do they, the young man who fell?'

'I haven't heard anybody say that, no. It was a terrible trag-edy, of course – he was only twenty – and dreadful for the family, but young people do such stupid things and it's diffi-cult always to protect them, especially when there is drink or drugs.'

Jude thought of the risks that Mark had taken. They'd always been calculated ones, though; as far as she knew he'd always followed the rules. On the occasion of his death the rock had unexpectedly crumbled under his foot and he'd slipped, drag-ging the following climber down with him. They'd not fallen more than twenty feet, but Mark landed awkwardly. It was bad luck, the mountain rescue people said. Many times she'd imag-ined it, tried to push the horror from her mind. The other man suffered no more than a broken ankle and bruising.

She thought of the young party-goer, and how it felt that first time, standing with Euan right at the top of the tower and looking down. She shuddered.

Chapter 21

That night she dreamed about the tower, about mounting the steps endlessly, up and up, never reaching the top, but knowing there was something important up there that forced her to keep going. She awoke the next morning filled with the certainty that the folly, somehow, held all the answers. To Summer's dreams, to the mystery of Esther. Everything came back to the folly. And now the folly was threatened by Mr Farrell and his horrible plans. She, Jude, must save the folly. It took a while for this after-dream sense of purpose to evaporate.

She still felt tired and heavy, as she took her now familiar seat in the library with her laptop, intending to transcribe the next bit of Esther's memoir. But trying to make out the hand-writing merely exacerbated the sharp pain growing behind her eyes, so she gave up.

Instead she curled up on the sofa and mused about the tower and all the things that might have happened there over the centuries. The building of the folly had disturbed an ancient burial ground, set in ancient forest. In some ways that was as terrible an act of vandalism as the one John Farrell now proposed in knocking it down. Then Anthony Wickham had spent night after night stargazing there. Maybe Esther, too, both of them imprinting their presence on the place. Down the years many others must have visited it, whether for the views of the house or just for the challenge of climbing it. Like ghosts, follies were an English

speciality, appealing to the traditional eccentric, amateur streak.
And a spooky atmosphere would undoubtedly add to the appeal.
She imagined children daring each other to go up it. Then there
were other things that had happened there. The archaeological
dig would have disturbed the ancient burial ground. The awful
death in 1970 . . . and those were just the things she knew about.
The place had certainly had an eventful history.

There was still so much to make sense of. It was difficult to
piece it all together logically. To begin with, perhaps she should
find out which pre-Roman tribe had buried their folk there. She
made a mental note to ask Chantal whether she knew. Then she
must contact the woman at the Norwich museum whose name
– Megan someone – the Holt librarian had given her, and deter-
mine the nature of the finds at the dig. She needed to discover
all she could about Esther and her mysterious origins. Was she
really a foundling, or could she be Anthony Wickham's love
child? And maybe other things had happened – oh, it was
impossible to know where to start with those.

Perhaps she could amass enough information to put a case
together for saving the folly. The possibility crossed her mind
that Euan could help. He would be able to argue the importance of the woodland, but he knew about the tower as well.
Although she had promised herself not to seek him out too
much, because of what Claire might think, she told herself this
thing was important. The thought of seeing him was a pleasur-
able one, and that made her feel guilty.

She brushed the feeling off and called his number. He
answered at once and her heart leaped when he sounded
pleased to hear from her. 'Come over this afternoon,' he said,
when she'd explained. 'The boiler men are here at the moment,
plus I'm trying to finish my word quota for the day.'

*   *   *

'Do you mind if we walk up to the folly again? I think I left one of my notebooks there the other night.'

'I was going to suggest we did anyway,' Jude replied. 'It might help focus my mind for my work. And we ought to help put a case together to defend the folly.'

They talked about strategy on the way. Euan said, 'It'll be important for someone to engage a structural engineer, but I'm sure the tower is basically sound. Otherwise, I'm afraid I'm not much use on the subject of its importance. That's your area of expertise. What I know about is the natural history. There are any number of important species of insects and plants around there.'

When they climbed up to the tower room, he couldn't immediately find the notebook, so Jude waited while he climbed up to the platform above. She wandered across to the shelves where he'd stacked several books and picked one off the top, a paperback guide to British wild flowers. She browsed through the section about orchids, interested by how different the wild ones looked from the exotic waxy beauty of shop-bought ones. As she replaced the book, she knocked the one below it and some pages become caught in a crevice at the back. She pulled them out carefully, then shifted the books to look at the wall. The brick behind, she saw at once, was loose. She guessed immediately what this was. Grabbing a battered tin spoon from a nearby shelf she teased away at the brick and edged it out, and then, seeing the one below it was loose, too, she pulled it out as well. Behind, was a small cavity. Gran and Tamsin's hiding place. It looked empty – no little messages or gifts. The space had been deliberately constructed when the tower was made, she decided, whether originally as a recess for a small lamp, or as a hiding place, she couldn't say. She ran her fingers around inside and discovered that it wasn't empty after all: a thin black packet lay there. She scraped it up with her finger-nails and inspected it, finding it to be an ancient piece of oiled canvas. Wondering if it was something to do with Tamsin, she tried to unfold it. 'Damn,' she breathed as it started to tear.

'Euan,' she said, as she heard him start down the ladder.

'I found it,' he said, fitting the trapdoor back over the hole. 'But some of the pages needed rescuing. They're a bit soggy.' He climbed down and came across. 'What have you got there?'

She showed him the hole and held out the little package. 'It might be nothing,' she said. 'I think Gran used this hiding place when she was a girl.'

'It might be something,' he replied, taking it from her and studying it. 'How curious.'

It was something, but something much older than the 1930s. Back at Gamekeeper's Cottage Euan left the package to warm on his new solar-heated water tank, and after that it was easier to open. Inside was a folded piece of vellum, which, when Euan had eased it apart with his penknife, turned out to be two small torn halves. Side by side they'd have fitted onto a post-card. Across them was sketched a complex diagram in faded sepia-coloured ink.

'What is it?' Euan asked.

Jude picked one up and stared at the marks round the circle and the lines intersecting it, the little scribbled symbols. 'It's a horoscope,' she said finally, squinting at it. 'Look, that symbol's meant to be fish – Pisces – and the squiggly lines must be Aquarius. I couldn't tell you what it means, though.' She stud-ied the paper for a minute or two longer then said, 'There's a date, look, along the tear. Seventeen sixty-something. July – what, the twenty-first? I wonder if Gran knew it was there in the hole?'

'Let's have a look.' It was Euan's turn to stare at the paper. He shook his head.

'The 1760s is definitely during Wickham's lifetime.'

'Could this be Esther's?' Euan said suddenly.

Jude considered. 'It would be neat if it were, but no one seemed to know her birth date.'

'Fascinating, isn't it?' Euan said. 'I wonder what it foretells.'

'Claire's the expert,' Jude said. 'She cast one for me once. It'll be a reading of the stars and planets on the date given, which quite often was a birth date. As to what they actually mean, that would be open to interpretation. I could never work out mine.'

'You mean I could look at one, maybe, but wouldn't be able to predict how many children the person would have.'

'It certainly wouldn't be as specific as that. More to do with predicting character. You know, like the Sun being in Aries, which rules the head, meaning you're a particularly rational being. I could take it and show Claire – if you don't mind.'

'Yes, of course, up to you, you found it. I can't imagine John Farrell would be interested.'

'I'm not giving it to him, whatever,' said Jude with feeling.

Later, she reread the early part of Esther's memoir, wondering if the astrological chart was anything to do with her. It must be! Her birthday was assumed by the household to be 21 July and it sounded as though that was the day that Anthony brought her to Starbrough rather than when she was born. But surely no one would think themselves certain enough of a date to cast a horoscope for it?

That evening she was due for supper at Claire and Summer's. It being Friday, Summer was allowed to have her friend Emily from up the road round to stay. Where Emily's mother had been pale and quiet, Emily was a solid child with strong colouring, tall for her age, and ungainly, with thick dark wavy hair worn in a ponytail on top of her head and a way of staring directly at people as though she were summing them up.

When the girls were safely out of earshot, playing some ball game in the garden, and Claire had brought in two mugs of tea, Jude laid the two pieces of the horoscope on the coffee table between them and said, 'What do you make of this?' She explained where she'd found it, and when she mentioned that Euan had been there, too, Claire glowered in silence. But the chart interested her.

She sat hunched over it for some time, then said, 'I'm not totally sure. It's different from any chart I've seen. How old did you think it is?'

'It's 1760 something. Look, it says there.'

'We can look at some of my books, if you like. There's one that has some historical stuff in it.'

Jude went over to the narrow bookcase. A great many of the books were on cookery and gardening and interior design, she saw, but the top shelf contained a guide to the night sky, the first of Euan's books, and several paperbacks, mostly popular ones, about astrology. She picked out the one serious hardback on the subject, a history of astrology, and ran a finger down the contents page. 'Astrology since 1700' was the title of one chapter.

'This one, I take it?' she said, holding it up for Claire.

'Yes. Dad gave it to me.'

'Did he? I'd forgotten.' Jude turned to the title page where was penned 'To darling Claire on her birthday, September 1996' in his dear sloping capitals. 'Good old Dad.'

'Pass it over. Thanks. He was good old Dad. I think he secretly thought it all rubbish. But he still gave me the book because he knew I'd like it.'

'I still miss him dreadfully,' Jude said, her voice dull.

'So do I.' Claire turned her head to look out at Summer and Emily, who were now bouncing on the trampoline. 'The other day I drove past that nightclub in Norwich where I used to work and remembered how I'd ring and he would always come down in the car to collect me, sometimes at one or two in the morning. Just to make sure I got home safely. It was horrible when he died. I felt like someone had . . . I don't know, pulled the ground away from under me.'

Jude tried to remember that first awful time, before the other awful time following Mark's death. When their father had his fatal heart attack, she and Mark were about to get married; there was so much still to be thankful for in life. But Claire, Claire had been as aimless as ever, drifting between jobs and men and now left in too-close proximity to a mother who wasn't coping, irritating the hell out of one another.

Jude waited for Claire to continue. They rarely talked like this – about deep feelings. Claire more often threw out barbed tendrils of the 'Mum talks to you more than me' variety rather than calmly discussing her anxieties. And so their conversations frequently got tangled up in guilt and accusation. Jude couldn't remember a time when Claire hadn't been a tight little ball of anger and frustration. The spiky child had turned into a pretty and wayward teenager, envious of Jude's solid successes yet disdainful of them, too. Now they both realized how much of an anchor their father had been in Claire's life; he was a kind patient man who'd steadied this wild pony, but never tried to break her. No one had ever wanted to do that. Claire had finally learned how to govern herself by having the responsibility of a child of her own.

Jude could never have predicted then that Mark would die, leaving her alone; that she and Claire would sit as they did now in the sunlit living room of a little cottage watching Claire's precious daughter, for whom they both felt such fierce love . . .

Just then, Summer rushed inside with her friend, announcing, 'We're going to play upstairs.'

'Fifteen minutes,' Claire called to them. 'Then it's bedtime.' She was flicking through the astrology book and found a page of illustrations. 'There are some charts here that might be useful. Would you like me to have a closer look later?'

'Yes, please,' Jude said. 'Anything you can work out would be useful.'

'I'll do my best.'

'I ought to go soon,' Jude said. 'Thanks very much for supper.'

'You're welcome,' Claire said.

'I'll go up and say goodbye,' Jude said, standing up.

She walked slowly up the stairs, admiring Euan's pictures on the way. They weren't great art, she had to admit, but they were attractive. He'd used the shimmering white bark so cleverly that it looked like a couple of trees, the moon and stars picked out in gold and silver ink between their winter branches on a gorgeous dark cobalt sky. She wondered which book he'd used them in.

'Oh no, how dreadful . . .' Summer's voice drifted down to her. Jude was immediately alert. She relaxed. Summer seemed to be telling some story, something about an accident. Jude walked up the last few steps and peeped round the door. Emily lay on the bed, turning the pages of a picture book, but Summer was sitting on the floor by her doll's house. She'd got the Jude doll and the Claire doll positioned by something on the carpet.

'Poor Thomas,' Summer was saying, her voice almost sobbing. 'He's dead. How can I live without him?'

Jude pushed open the door to see better.

Summer looked up, distress clear on her face. And then Jude saw what the dolls were standing over. It was the black and white cat, Pandora, stretched out on the floor.

She quickly collected her thoughts. Summer couldn't have said Thomas; that was the name of Esther's cat. Her mind was playing tricks.

'What's happened here?' she asked Summer gently, pointing to the little scene.

'A fox has caught the girl's cat and killed it,' Summer said. 'The other girl is going to help her bury it.'

'Oh Summer, what a sad story,' Jude stuttered. This had got to be some extraordinary coincidence. Summer couldn't know the story of Esther's cat. Had she mentioned it to Claire? Or to Euan? Maybe to Euan. That was it, and Euan had told Claire or Summer. She tried to remember if she'd told Euan about the latest instalment of Esther's memoir, but her brain seemed to have frozen.

'It's all right,' Summer said, misreading her aunt's distress. 'She's going to get another cat so she'll be happy again.'

'But where did you get this awful story?'

'I just woke up with it in my head,' Summer answered.

'She's always telling stories,' Emily said, without lifting her eyes from her book. 'She's such a liar.'

'No, I'm not,' cried Summer, indignant. 'I just wake up and know they've happened.'

'Know they've happened,' Jude echoed, her alarm growing.

'Yes, they've happened.' Summer stuck out her lower lip.

Jude moved some soft toys from the bedroom chair and sat down, suddenly weary.

'Is everything OK?' Claire stood in the doorway, arms folded, one eyebrow raised.

'Of course,' Jude said, glancing at Summer, who had now brought Pandora back to life to jump up and play. The little girl certainly didn't seem upset in any way.

'Claire, can I have a word?'

'Sure.'

Jude followed her downstairs and drew her sister into the garden. They sat together on a bench under a buddleia bush brimming with purple flowers. Earlier the butterflies had been poring over it. It was a peaceful golden evening, the air rich with flowery scents, an evening on which it was almost possible to think everything was all right. But it wasn't all right. Jude felt the knowledge like a weight in her chest.

'What's wrong?' Claire was looking worried now.

'Maybe nothing. It's just . . . Well, you know Summer's dream?'

'Yes. In fact I meant to tell you. I've made another doctor's appointment for her. Tomorrow. They have a surgery on Saturday mornings. I'll have to drop Emily off home, then go into work late.'

'Have you? I'm sure that's a good thing.' What would a doctor make of this new development though? Jude took a deep breath.

'Claire, I think she's dreaming about things that happened in the past. Not her past, I mean someone else's. Esther's. Things I've read about in this journal I found at Starbrough Hall.'

'Esther? You mean the stargazer's daughter? But that's nonsense. What's Summer got to do with Esther? That was a couple of hundred years ago.'

'I know. It does sound like nonsense. Listen, though. She was acting something out just now, something that I'd read in Esther's memoir. It was about a cat that died and a gypsy girl came to help her. And Summer said she woke up knowing the story. Where could she have learned it, Claire?'

'If that's all it is,' Claire said briskly, brushing a petal off her cotton trousers, 'you must have told it to her. Or she read something like it. Her head's full of stories, and that one doesn't sound very unusual.'

She's such a liar. That was what Emily said. Jude knew Summer to be a very truthful child. She must think these dream-things weren't just stories, but that they'd really happened.

'Claire,' she said urgently.

'What?' Claire's tone was impatient.

Jude saw that Claire just wanted everything to be all right. Well so did Jude. But it wasn't all right. She felt this strongly. It was partly that Jude had dreamed the lost dream, too. That was too much of a coincidence.

'Will you let me talk to her about it?'

Claire looked upset now. 'And put more silly ideas into her head? What are you trying to say, Jude? That she's possessed by something, or has lived before? That's too weird and I won't believe it.'

Considering all the other things you seem to believe, what's wrong with one more? Jude almost said, but didn't.

Instead, she sighed. 'I know. It's usually me telling you to be rational.'

'And now it's the other way round? But this is Summer we're talking about, Jude. Your niece, remember? It's no joking matter.'

Claire's face was pink, her eyes shiny. *How did we get to this stupid place?* Jude thought, alarmed.

'Of course it isn't,' she said, trying to make things right. 'That's why it's important. That's why I care so much.' But it was too late.

'You come here with your stuff about dreams and secrets from the past and stir everything up. You can't let me alone, can you? Summer's all I've got. I've made my own life, finally. I'm happy, and now you come and mess it up by coming out with all these ridiculous things.'

'I haven't messed it up,' Jude said helplessly, but Claire in this mood was unstoppable.

'You have,' she almost yelled. 'You always do. Everything's always gone right for you.' How many times in their childhood had Claire said that and in just that whiny tone of voice. She seemed to realize it, for she stopped and whispered, 'I'm sorry. Of course it hasn't.'

Mark.

'Yes, well. That's another thing I'm sick of, Jude. You've got to stop wringing your hands about Mark.'

'I can't,' Jude whispered. 'I don't know why but I can't. I've tried, you know.'

'Jude, I told you, Mark wasn't that perfect. He was a man. There are others.'

'He was pretty much perfect,' Jude mumbled. 'For me, anyway.'

Claire shook her head and said softly, 'No, he wasn't. He was just an ordinary bloke with all the ordinary faults.'

Jude looked at her sister and again there was that flutter of a curtain in her memory. Then it was gone.

'Come on,' Claire sighed, standing up. 'I must get those two into bed. You can talk to Summer sometime if you like, but there are no-go areas. I've read about that past life regression stuff in that magazine I get. It's not good, Jude. Too often the therapists put ideas in patients' heads by giving them biased questions. You can seriously mess someone up like that.'

'I know,' Jude said humbly. 'And I won't let that happen to Summer. Seeing the doctor's a good idea. Let me know what he says.' She followed Claire inside and picked up her handbag. 'I'm shattered, Claire. And I feel awful that we've quarrelled.'

'Don't worry,' Claire said, giving her a quick hug, but there was no warmth in it. 'Girls, Jude's going now,' she called upstairs.

Jude hardly noticed her surroundings on the drive home, so wrapped up was she in this new worry. Everything that was happening swirled round and round in her head. Esther. Gran. Summer. Tamsin. The folly. Euan. She drove past Euan's house, forcing herself not to give it a glance.

Chapter 22

On Saturday morning, Jude felt tired, listless and worried. She noticed Gran's necklace in her top drawer when she pulled out her make-up bag and felt guilty that she hadn't done anything about Tamsin. Following Claire's throw-away suggestion, she asked Alexia if she could borrow the Hall's phone directories and looked up Lovall. As predicted there were dozens of them. It was likely that Tamsin, even if she was still alive, had married and changed her name, but to show willing she rang the three 'T' Lovalls in the north Norfolk directory one by one. It wasn't an edifying experience. The first Lovall who answered was a woman married to a Mr Timothy Lovall. She thought Jude was trying to sell something and put the phone down on her. The second was rather deaf and clearly believed Jude to be a bit mad, and the third, a gentle-sounding Tom Lovall with a country accent, considered Jude's question but admitted himself at a loss to answer it. Dispirited, she gave up. Just to see what happened she tapped 'Tamsin Lovall' into an internet search engine and came up with an Australian volleyball star, an unlikely lead for an eighty-five-year-old woman, she thought, giggling to herself. She tried to broaden her line of enquiry by thinking who else who might have known Tamsin might still be alive. Gran was the only one of the Bennett children still living. Perhaps there was a school friend who'd be of some use. Gran had mentioned someone the other day – a boy. Who was it?

She dialled Gran's number. The phone rang and rang, and Jude was about to give up when a shaky faraway voice answered, 'Hello?'

'Gran, it's Jude. How are you? You sound a bit faint.'

'No, no, I'm fine.' Gran did sound a little dazed.

'Not still dizzy?'

'I seem to be all right today. What can I do for you?'

'I found your hidey-hole in the folly. It was behind two bricks, wasn't it?'

'Oh clever girl!' Gran sounded delighted. 'Was there anything in it?'

'A piece of oilskin.'

'Oh I remember that. We left it there.'

'It had an astrological chart in it, Gran, did you know?'

'Did it, dear?'

A piece of oilskin had obviously not seemed interesting to two young girls. Jude changed tack.

'I'm not getting very far with the question of Tamsin.' She explained about the calls she'd made. 'Do you know of anyone else still alive who might have known her? Anyone from school for instance?'

There was a short silence. 'I can't think of anybody. I lost touch with a lot of them, you see, when I married. Betty Morton is dead, and so's Joan . . . she was my bridesmaid.'

'There was a boy you started to talk about the other day.'

'Did I? Who might that have been?'

'Yes, someone who'd been unkind.'

There came another pause.

'Dicky Edwards,' Gran whispered. 'I don't think Dicky . . . I wouldn't want to meet him, Judith. I don't think he'd be any use.'

'Gran?' It was difficult to gauge down the phone, but Jude guessed that she'd touched some nerve. She looked at her watch.

It was only eleven o'clock and she wasn't doing anything much for the rest of the day. 'Gran, if you're not busy this afternoon, would you like me to come over and see you?'

Gran remained there gripping the receiver long after Jude had rung off. Dicky. He'd been a sort of dark shadow at the back of her mind for years, not one she'd wanted to give form to or a name. But talking to Jude about Tamsin the other day had brought him back in a flash of memory, and now she saw him clearly in her mind's eye. He had always been a big lad, tall for his age, and chubby, but when he turned thirteen or fourteen and helped his dad with the farm work the fat turned to muscle. Farmer Edwards was notorious as a shouter and a swaggerer. No surprises that his wife always looked cowed and fragile, and that his sons became bullies.

She fitted the receiver back into its cradle and sank into the nearest chair. It was all coming back to her now, in a rush of painful images. And the veil between past and present was too thin not to let them in.

Jessie was in her fourteenth year in 1937 when Tamsin returned to school after months of absence; she just appeared unannounced in the playground one misty February morning, standing shyly by herself. She'd changed. The girl was taller now, graceful as a doe, her liquid brown eyes large in a finely moulded face. Jessie, still small and flat-chested, envied her high pointed breasts, her delicate wrists and ankles. Tamsin was growing up. Jessie's schoolmates, turning for the most part into gawky adolescents with greasy skin, noticed it too, and treated her with the respect children often have for beauty. Dicky already broad-shouldered and with a man's voice, stared more than anyone, a troubling mixture of dislike and desire in his face.

This time, at the end of the day, Jessie felt confident enough to allow Tamsin to walk back with her, the pair of them loitering off down the lane together behind Jessie's brother and sister.

'Tell Ma I'm at a friend's,' she called to Sarah, swinging her satchel to her sister over the garden gate, then she walked with Tamsin up the hill to the gypsy camp. They didn't know that they were being followed.

Tamsin's family gave her a warm welcome: Nadya and the great-grandmother and the four men, one now with a pregnant wife, Kezia, in tow. Nadya pinched Jessie's cheek affectionately, and fed the girls tea and cake, and they petted the tethered horses and teased a fox cub that Tamsin's youngest uncle had caught and tied to a tree, from where it made hungry forays at the scraggy chickens that scratched the ground for insects just out of reach of the rope.

'What's he going to do with it?' she asked Tamsin, who shrugged and said, 'I don't know. He says he caught it scavenging. Jacko,' she cried out to the young man, who was whittling a piece of wood, 'you must let it go or it'll draw the vixen, and she'll kill the channi for sure,' but Jacko merely swiped at the nearest chicken with his foot and gave a careless laugh.

At twilight they all sat down round the fire and shared a rich dark stew that Nadya ladled from a big billycan, with a kind of flat bread to dunk in it. The men talked of who-knew-what in their guttural accents, and laughed and scowled, and Nadya sang quietly to herself. Nobody asked Jessie anything about her life, but she didn't mind. She sat close to Tamsin, and they shared her English textbook together by firelight, whispered to one another and listened to the men, Jessie mesmerized by the strangeness, feeling a part of it all and yet not a part, trying to ignore her conscience, which told her to go home.

Night was falling fast and the fox cub sat down and began to yowl for its mother, a heart-rending sound that went on and on, but the men only shouted at it or cajoled. The eldest of the men fetched a fiddle and attempted to imitate the noise. The fox cub still cried so the fiddler shrugged and started up a dance tune, first tentative, then faster and more rhythmic until toes started tapping and hands clapping and Nadya got up and began to dance. Jessie had never seen a dance so expressive, so wild and carefree. She clapped to the beat and watched the flash of gold jewellery in the firelight and the sparks flying upwards and thought this the most extraordinary experience of her life.

Then out of nowhere came a sharp crack.

The fox cub gave a last yelp, rolled over and lay still. The horses began to buck and screamed with fright.

For the smallest second everyone froze. Then came a frenzy of activity: the men rushing to soothe the horses, the women to hustle each other into wagons.

Between the whinnying and the shouting could be heard someone crashing about in the undergrowth, then came another gunshot and a man's laugh, receding into the distance. Jacko and the next uncle, Ted, each snatched up a brand from the fire and ran off in pursuit, but Jessie knew they were already too late.

There was something about that laugh that struck a chord in her, but at the time she didn't give the matter a thought.

'What did you do, Gran?' Jude cried, when Jessie told her all about it that afternoon.

'I was terribly frightened, dear. I simply picked myself up and ran off home without even saying goodbye. I knew the route perfectly, even in the dark. Back along Foxhole Lane, I ran, then all the way down the hill. I was in a fine old state, I can tell you, when I got back.'

She remembered her face, glimpsed in the bathroom mirror, all sooty and streaked with tears. Her clothes stank of smoke and strange food. Relieved she was safe, her parents were still furious. How dare she go to the woods at night? Especially to 'they gypsies'. But she thought they didn't mind the gypsies. Well there were limits, weren't there, and she'd crossed them by a mile. Anything could have happened to her, she might be dead or worse. A gunshot frightened her? Let it be a lesson.

She was banished to bed weeping.

As she lay awake listening to the vixen's cries of grief and thinking over the evening's events, Jessie remembered that laugh.

'It was Dicky,' she told Jude. 'He must have seen us go up the hill together. He'd have got the gun off his da.'

'What happened to him, Gran?' Jude asked, enthralled by this dramatic tale. 'Was he punished?'

'No, not then. I told no one anything at the time,' Gran said finally. 'I knew it was Dicky, and Dicky knew that I knew. I saw it in his eyes at school the next day, a challenging look. *What're you going to do about it, then?* that look said. I was scared of him. He had his gang, too. They'd lie, say he was with one of them. And I couldn't prove anything – no one had actually seen him – so what was the use of telling? I was sorry for my silence later, but it's easy to forget what it's like when you're very young, how weak and foolish you can feel. Things that look rational and easy to grown-ups don't look that way to children at all.'

'But didn't Tamsin help . . . ?'

'Tamsin didn't turn up to school the next day. Or ever again. I sent my brother Charlie up Foxhole Lane to look for her. He came back and said they'd gone.'

'So that was the last time you saw her?'

'Oh no, the gypsies still came to Foxhole Lane, but not for a while and when they did Tamsin told me she was finished with school.'

'And when did she leave for good and you take the necklace?'

Jessie's expression hardened suddenly and Jude wished she hadn't been so forthright.

'I'll come to that when I'm ready.' Jessie gave an impatient gesture and Jude knew that the conversation was over for the day.

Jude returned to Starbrough Hall with 'Dicky, presumably Richard, Edwards' scribbled on a piece of paper, but she knew Gran didn't think it would come to anything. To tell the truth, nor did Jude. If Dicky was still alive he was unlikely to want to help. She still had so many questions to ask her grandmother, though. Like, when did Tamsin eventually hide the necklace – presumably in the folly – and why? She arranged to visit again on Monday afternoon.

After supper at Starbrough Hall she rang Claire, still feeling bad that they'd quarrelled.

'I'm sorry about last night,' she told her sister. 'I wanted to ask how you got on at the doctor's.'

'I'm sorry, too,' Claire said. 'You frightened me, that's all. The doctor thinks Summer's fine, so I'm trying to believe him.'

'Well, I'm very glad about that,' Jude said, but uncertainty hung somewhere in the ether between them. She didn't think everything was all right, and she didn't believe that Claire did either, but she didn't want to disturb Claire's fragile equilibrium by saying so.

'Oh I took that astrological chart in and got Linda to look at it when we had a quiet moment,' she told Jude. 'She thinks it's very old, too. She found a book we sell in the shop and looked everything up. It's not a good horoscope, Jude. There's a lot about loss and tragedy and strength to overcome difficulty. I'd be worried if a child of mine had one cast like that. I'll show you in detail next time you come.'

'Thanks. Though I don't know what use it will be. We don't know who it belonged to, do we?'

'Your Esther, you thought?'

'It could be. If we're saying it's 1760 something. Your reading doesn't bode well for a happy ending to her story.'

'I suppose not.'

'Look, I'm not busy tomorrow. I could fetch you both and take you out to lunch somewhere, what do you say?'

'I'm sorry, we're busy tomorrow. People are coming to lunch.'

'Oh, that's nice. Anyone I know?'

'Yeah. Darcey and her parents. Oh, and I've asked Euan.'

'Oh.' Jude waited to see whether her sister would invite her, too, but she didn't and there was a silence between them again. She felt herself blushing and awkward, then managed to say, 'Well, some other time, then.'

'How about the evening?' Claire said in a rush. 'Come and fetch the chart then and I'll show you what Linda's written.'

'All right,' Jude said coolly. The lunch thing was silly. She felt furious with her sister, but also that she had no right to feel furious. It was as though she and Claire were engaged in some guerrilla warfare in which neither party would quite make their demands clear.

Chapter 23

On Sunday morning, Jude woke to the patter of rain on the window and a deep sense of loneliness. She tried reading a crime novel in bed for a while, then dressed and went downstairs to find she really was on her own apart from the dogs, the family having disappeared off to church. There was a note on the breakfast table from Chantal in her neat foreign handwriting explaining it would be just the two of them for lunch – the twins and their parents had been invited out. Jude breakfasted, catching up with yesterday's newspapers, then, not having anything else to detain her in the empty house, settled herself in the library and continued to transcribe Esther's writing. As ever, it was comforting to hide herself in her work.

Thereafter we grew close, my father and I. Often he was the same as he had always been – secret, lonely, alone. He would still disappear into his workshop for long periods, or I would find him in his study deep in a book, his food untouched on its tray. Sometimes he'd seem not to notice me and I'd sit there quietly with him conducting some research of my own, but then suddenly he'd say, 'Listen to this,' and read a passage out of some tome about the Via Lacta – our Milky Way – being milk spilt across the sky from the breast of the goddess Hera, or the latest method of calculating the temperature of the sun. The towers of books had grown all around us, and I sometimes felt he was like some alchemist of old, the instruments of his art lying washed up like jetsam on the piles of papers and charts all around.

No one was ever allowed to move anything. Betsy might bring in his food – that was all. She was not to clean. I alone was trusted to dust a little sometimes, but only if I replaced everything exactly as it was, he'd grumble, or else it might be lost irretrievably.

'Father, you require more shelves,' I sighed one day when he asked me to pick out a particular volume about opticks, and I was made to move twenty other books before I found it.

He looked around, blinking like an owl dazzled by daylight, as if he had never seen the room properly before. It was a dark narrow chamber at the back of the house, its aspect towards the stables. He'd chosen it when he was a boy, he had once told me, because no one else had any use for it. 'What say you, Father, we locate a bigger room to make a library?' I said excitedly, but he scowled.

'And where would we do that?' he replied, not possessing that kind of imagination, so I cast my mind about.

Later in the day, roaming the house, still thinking of the possibilities of this idea, I walked into a room I had hardly visited before. It was at the front of the Hall, looking out across the park. The room had no purpose, as far as I could see, beyond housing an elegant fireplace, a great wooden chest – empty – and a pedestal with a bust of Socrates upon it. In some ways it was no room at all, merely a sizeable anteroom where a certain class of visitor, an equerry with a message perhaps, might be ordered to await the master's pleasure, and there was, I saw, a reason for its dismissal – one side of the room bowed out a little, whether to some practical purpose or as the result of some structural weakness I could not say.

Still, the marble floor with its oval patterning pleased me, and when I stepped over to the window my heart lifted to view the forest in the distance and, since the sun had moved away and the sky was cloudless, I was sure I could just see the folly peeping above the trees.

*I turned and inspected the room once more, and suddenly saw in
my mind a revelation of how it could be. This would be our library,
and to solve the problem of the curved wall, it would be oval. Father
must be informed at once.*

The sound of a car on the gravel forecourt ripped Jude's absorp-
tion like a knife slashing a picture. She'd imagined she'd been
there in the eighteenth-century past, with Esther, seeing the
room as it had been before it was a library. And, in turn, sharing with the girl a vision of how it was now. What a curious
fancy, she thought, aware of Chantal's voice greeting the dogs.

Soon the door of the library opened. 'Jude,' she cried, 'I
thought you'd be in here again. You do work hard, dear. Are
you all right? Am I disturbing you?'

'Not at all,' Jude said warmly, her regret at the broken
moment wiped out by the desire to share her new knowledge.
'In fact you've come at just the right moment.' She showed her
Esther's papers. 'She's describing how the library was made. It
seems the whole thing was her idea.'

Chantal came and settled down beside Jude, who read
what she'd already transcribed and stumbled through the next
section of Esther's writing to find out about the making of this
extraordinary room.

*My father took little persuasion once I explained the scheme, and
my confidence quickly grew. By the following spring, in the year of
1774, the architect submitted his scheme for an oval room and the
work commenced. Soon Starbrough Hall lay under siege to carts
bearing sand and seasoned wood. Others drove away transporting heaps of rubble and dust. Half a dozen labourers arrived from
the village, then a number of fine craftsmen, fresh from fashion-
ing new buildings at Holkham Hall. These men all trampled grit*

down the corridors where Mr Corbett laid matting, and soon to breathe meant to choke on a chalky miasma. Betsy and I claimed we could taste dust in our food, but Mrs Godstone took umbrage at our complaints and Mr Corbett bid us hush.

It was the shouted orders and the hammering that drove out Father in the end. He took to living in the folly for days at a time, even sleeping in the tower room on a small mattress when he'd a mind. And so I was left alone to direct Mr Gibbons, the architect, a gentle man apparently with a daughter close to myself in years, who discussed matters with me in a grave and courteous manner. This pleased and surprised me. No one outside the house had ever treated me with such respect before, and I flowered under my new responsibilities. My father's agent, on the other hand, the odious Trotwood, deliberately flouted any instructions I gave regarding his labourers, his intention being to humiliate me. And so in time I learned discretion, using Mr Gibbons or the foreman instead to convey my will to him.

As the months passed in this way, I noticed how Mrs Godstone and Mr Corbett changed towards me. They remained polite and kindly, but there grew an uneasy distance between us, and there came a time when I no longer ate with them, but with my father, or, if he were away, by my lone self in the great dining room, with Betsy to serve. Even Susan treated me differently, calling me Miss Esther as often as not, which wounded me. She'd not shared my bed for some years, for I was no longer a little girl with nightmares who needed comforting, but now she took to knocking before she entered my room. 'You're becoming a woman,' she told me, when she helped me dress for dinner once. 'Nay, a lady. I always knew . . . And a lovely one.' All the old affection remained, I saw that in her eyes, but still, something important had changed. Father was treating me as the daughter of the house, and the household took their lead from him.

I felt the loneliness of it first when my old friend Matt began to touch his cap when he greeted me. We were shyer with one another, but then we were aware of becoming man and woman; at fourteen we could no longer play in the dirt as though we were children, nor did we wish to. He worked all the day with his father now, his daily clothes shabby where mine were fine and neat, his hands calloused, the nails ingrained with earth, while mine were clean and manicured. On high days and holidays I heard tell he met in the village square with other lads and they would drink too much ale and tease the wenches; our days of running off to the forest together were long gone and never mentioned. Sometimes this saddened me, for I longed for a friend of my own age.

By harvest time the main work on our new library was complete and the labourers slipped away to help on the farms. But there came a day late in September when the final details were complete. We stood, my father and I, admiring the rows of white-painted shelves and cupboards, the glass doors and the powder-blue painted ceiling. We remarked on the beautiful ornamentation picked out like white sugar piping, the sublime touch being a delicate oval centrepiece forged in plaster like a huge halo above our heads. We waited a week or two for the decoration to dry and the stink of lead paint to fade, then began the great task of transporting the contents of Father's study into its new home.

He would allow none to assist us packing the crates of books and papers, and once they were carried to the library I was allowed only to unpack and make suggestion, not to arrange. Finally Mr Corbett, with Sam and Matt and Jan the coachman, carried in the heavy desk and chairs, the globe and the orrery, and all was complete. That first evening I found him there already engrossed in his charts, a merry fire crackling in the grate, his supper as usual forgotten on a tray. 'Goodnight,' I called, but he gave no sign of having heard. I smiled to myself and closed the door quietly.

'There's no mention of this ceiling painting, is there?' Chantal pointed out. 'I wonder when they did that?'

'Maybe Esther will tell us in due course.' Jude closed down her laptop again, remembering how, for a moment earlier, it had seemed as though she had been inside Esther's mind, seeing the room as it had been, and imparting to Esther the vision of how it was now. It had been a curious experience; she couldn't explain it. Perhaps she'd fallen asleep for a short time and dreamed it.

There was still so much unanswered about Esther, but then she didn't know all the questions. Yet gradually, like pieces in a great complex jigsaw puzzle for which she had no picture to guide her, different snippets of information were coming together. Areas of detail were beginning to come into focus.

She glanced at her watch. It was half-past twelve. She had a sudden mental picture of Euan arriving at Claire's in a sports jacket and jeans, carrying a bottle of red wine. When she imagined him kissing her on both cheeks . . .

'Chantal,' she said quickly, 'had you anything special planned for lunch?' Since both of them had been left out of their families' arrangements today, why shouldn't they do something special and enjoy themselves?

'Not really,' Chantal replied. 'I thought we might finish some leftovers.'

'In that case,' Jude said, 'let me take you somewhere for lunch. I rather feel like it. Do you know anywhere that might take a last-minute booking?'

'The Green Man,' Chantal said promptly, her eyes sparkling. 'Yes, let's go out for lunch.'

The pub Chantal recommended was able to squeeze them in at the last moment. It was only a couple of miles away, so not far for Jude to drive, a lovely old building with wooden beams, that hadn't been too messed about by modern development. Their table was in the garden under a big canopy. They both ordered good old-fashioned Sunday roasts and a bottle of rich red Burgundy. 'My treat,' Jude insisted. 'It's so kind of you all to have let me stay at the Hall for so long.'

'No, we love having you,' Chantal cried. 'Alexia says what an easy guest you are and, anyway, it makes sense, with you working so hard on the sale. You are not having much of a holiday at all.'

'Oh, I'm seeing plenty of Claire and Summer,' Jude replied. 'Still, I must speak to Alexia and Robert. I feel I ought to find somewhere else to stay. It's very wearing to have guests.'

'Do speak to them, of course, but you'll find they agree with me. You must not go, Jude.'

Jude laughed. 'Well, it's very kind of you all.' Their lunches arrived and they began to eat hungrily.

After a minute or two, Chantal asked, 'How is the little girl? You said she was having some bad dreams.'

'They're still happening, I'm afraid,' Jude replied. She explained about the apparent coincidence of Summer knowing details of Esther's story.

'That is so strange. But you must have told her about it. There'll be an ordinary explanation. Especially, if, as you say, the doctor thinks she is behaving normally. Children of that age, they do have night terrors. I remember a time when Robert used to cry out for me in the night, and I would sit with him. William did not like him to come into our bed. In the morning it would be me who was tired. Robert was completely fine.'

'Perhaps that's all it is. Night terrors,' Jude said, but she knew she hadn't told Summer all about Esther, that was one thing.

And the nature of the dream was another. 'But why would they have started after Euan took her to the folly?'

Chantal shrugged. 'Coincidence,' she said briskly. 'Or perhaps there is something about the place that affected her imagination. So much has happened there. I believe these things can give an atmosphere.' Then she said, 'This young man you speak of, Euan, forgive me asking but you are becoming friendly with him?'

Jude put down her knife and fork, at a loss about what to say.

'No, I am intruding,' Chantal cried, waving her question away. 'He is very *charmant*. I just thought . . . I am sorry.'

'Don't be,' Jude said, taking a sip of wine. 'He is lovely. But I think he is already taken. My sister got there first. And I can't interfere.'

'He likes her?'

'I can't tell,' Jude confessed. 'It's hardly something one can ask. I think it might be at that delicate stage, you know, before anything starts, and I can't just march in and . . .'

'Ah, so you do like him.' Chantal's eyes sparkled wickedly.

'I find him . . . very attractive. As they say, I wouldn't kick him out of bed.'

Chantal gave a peal of delighted laughter, and several people turned to stare. She was very elegant and vivacious today, Jude thought.

'You see the problem,' Jude said. 'What do I do? What would you do? Woman to woman here, Chantal! Has anything like this happened to you?'

'I never had a sister, so this could never have happened, but relationships with your family, now those are important. No, you are right, you can't just march in and take . . . You will have to wait, my dear, wait and see what happens. Perhaps you should think of going away, forgetting about him. That would be the most honourable thing.'

'Would it?' Jude said feebly, feeling her energy drain away. Should she just go back to London and leave Claire and Euan to it? That was one code of behaviour. 'All's fair in love and war,' was another. But suppose she did get together with Euan, what would that do to her relationship with her sister, and with Summer?

While she and Chantal finished their lunch, Chantal talking about her very formal upbringing in Paris and how different it was from the way the twins were being brought up, Jude turned the matter over in her mind.

She didn't want to do the 'honourable thing' and vanish. Nor did she want to go into battle with Claire. It was difficult. She was always treading on eggshells over Claire, careful not to offend her, aware that Claire, though pretty, feisty and attractive, was also very vulnerable. But Claire wouldn't make sacrifices for Jude, she told herself now. Or would she? Again, the old resentments surged up. Then there was a key question. Euan was not some toy to be fought over. He had his own feelings and opinions. Surely the most important question in all this was what Euan himself felt.

Yes, the problem would sort itself out. She wouldn't go away, she'd sit it out. As Gran sometimes said, whatever was meant to happen would happen. With Mark, Jude had felt convinced that she didn't need to do anything to make destiny happen. Now, she was learning that it was important to make your own destiny. Not in brutal, selfish ways that swept other pieces off the chessboard, but making others aware of your needs and feelings, telling the truth as far as you could, working difficulties out between you rather than running away; these were grown-up, responsible ways of conducting your life.

'Thank you for a lovely meal,' Chantal said when they got up to go.

'And thank you for everything you've done to help me,' Jude said and kissed her.

Jude spent what remained of the afternoon making notes on some ideas for the article she was to write for the Beecham's magazine. She had characters for her story now, an idea of how to present the whole sale. It was incredibly exciting. The lonely stargazer and the tower he'd built, the little girl he found and trained to be his amanuensis, but who had her own mysterious tale to tell. What had happened to her and why hadn't she inherited the house? It would be marvellous to be able to say that the Wickhams had contributed in some important way to contemporary knowledge of the stars, but from what Cecelia had said so far that wasn't likely.

What she wouldn't write about was the connection this story had with her own family, about the dream. As well as being difficult to explain in a way that would be taken seriously, it would be wrong to bring Summer's experiences into the public eye. Anyway, Summer's story was still unfolding.

When Jude parked her car outside Blacksmith's Cottage at seven-thirty that evening, it was to find her sister's guests long gone and Summer weary after an afternoon running around in the sun. 'Is she OK?' Jude asked when she was told Summer was upstairs.

'Yeah, fine. I told you, the doctor said the same thing yesterday as last time. That there's no need to worry, young children often have periods of disturbed sleep or bad dreams. Since she's eating well and enjoying life there's really nothing to worry about. Full stop.' Claire, who seemed tired too, drank down the last of her tea and brought the cup down firmly on the table. 'I ought to feel relieved. I do feel relieved.'

But Jude didn't. 'Did you tell him about how the dreams started or that I had the same ones?'

'I tried to, but he wasn't really that interested.'

Jude sighed. 'I suppose it's not surprising. It sounds too outlandish.'

'It's got to be a coincidence the whole thing. Jude, your face, you look so serious. Do you still think there's something wrong?' Claire's eyes looked large in her face and for the first time Jude saw she looked done in.

'No, I was just wondering about you. Are you sleeping?' she said gently.

'Not very well,' Claire confessed, her hands wrapped tightly round the empty cup. 'I'm worried. I still don't quite believe what you say, but I'm worried.'

So am I, Jude thought grimly. Their differences about Euan faded into the background. They were both more concerned about little Summer.

'I'll go up and say goodnight,' Jude said, 'and then we can look at that astrological chart quickly. I won't stop long.'

'OK. Don't read her one of those dreadful stories,' Claire begged.

'Worry not. I'll find something light.'

Jude read her 'The Little Porridge Pot', about a woman with a magic food bowl who didn't know the fairy password and flooded the village with porridge. Not scary at all, just silly, and instead of sitting up in bed, Summer wanted to play with the doll's house while the story was being told.

She closed the book and watched her niece pack everything away.

'I haven't looked at the "me" doll properly yet,' she said. 'Can I see?'

'Here she is. Euan said he made her smart like when you go to work.'

The doll was wearing a semblance of a black skirt and jacket with a white blouse underneath. Jude laughed. 'Look,' she said, pointing to the gold ink dots, 'she's even wearing my earrings.' So that was how Euan saw her. The urbanite, the career woman. Part of her felt flattered, the other felt the distance between them. She sincerely hoped that when she smiled it didn't look as much of a smirk as that.

'What was the story you were making them do the other night?' she asked Summer. 'The one about the fox and the cat, I mean. When Emily was staying.'

'Oh that was a sad one, wasn't it? But the other girl was right, she did get another cat. It was a tabby called Moony and it never went running off like Thomas.'

A tabby. Moony: *Luna*. She even got the name almost right.

'Where did the story come from, Summer?' She almost asked 'From a book?' but realized that would be feeding her the answer.

'I told you,' Summer said, with that world-weary air that only a nearly seven-year-old girl could deliver so crushingly, 'I woke up with it in my head. Sometimes I do. Emily said I'm a liar, but she's the liar. She's just jealous, because Mrs Hatch put my creative writing on the wall and said everyone should read it.'

'Good for you,' Jude said, smiling. Then, 'What other stories have you woken up knowing?'

'Oh, lots. There's this gypsy girl, you see. She lives in the forest near the folly with her family sometimes, but then they put everything onto their wagons and ride away to faraway places, but she likes the folly place best because she's got a friend there. Her friend's called Esther. It's a pretty name, isn't it? If Mummy gets me another doll for my birthday I'm going to call her Esther.'

'What's the gypsy girl's name?'

Summer made a moue of her mouth as she thought. 'I can't remember,' she said. 'Wait . . . no, I can't remember.'

'Why do you wake up with these stories in your head, Summer?'

Summer shrugged. Jude wondered whether she'd say that she thought she, Summer, was the gypsy girl or Esther, or that one of them told her the stories or that she dreamed them. But she said none of these things. Instead, she said, 'I think the gypsy girl's called Rowan.'

'OK, that's a nice name,' Jude told her. 'It's a country name, too. A tree with red berries. Some people say it's magical.'

Summer brightened up and said, 'That's good, because her scarf thing is red.'

At this Jude practically lost her power of speech. Esther had written about the gypsy's scarf and it was poppy red. An obvious choice of colour perhaps, but it was Summer's certainty that was bothering Jude, and the fact that so many coincidences were stacking up.

She tried a different tack.

'Summer, have you ever been to the folly?' She knew the girl had, but again she was nervous of asking the child leading questions.

Summer nodded. 'Euan took me. I wouldn't go up in it 'cause I didn't like it. It was scary.'

'Scary?'

'Mmm, it made me think of something frightening. I don't know what, but I didn't like it.' Her voice squeaked suddenly.

'Poor dear.' Summer leaned against Jude, and Jude put her arm round her, ashamed. It would be wrong to pursue this conversation. What could it have been that was so frightening to a little girl, that Euan certainly hadn't detected about the place, and she hadn't either? The folly was atmospheric, in her view, but surely not frightening. She helped Summer clean her teeth and tucked her into bed.

'I'll get Mummy to say goodnight,' she told her.

'And tell her I want a drink of water,' Summer said. But when Jude got up off the bed Summer grabbed her hand. 'Don't shut the door, Auntie Jude. I don't want it dark.' At that she knew Summer was troubled, more troubled than she was letting on.

When Claire returned downstairs, she spread several pieces of paper and a large book out on the coffee table.

'This is what Linda found,' she said.

She showed Jude the different sections of the chart and the meanings Linda had jotted down. 'Look, she got them from here,' she said, showing Jude a page about eighteenth-century charts with some illustrations. 'The chart says the sun is in Aquarius here, and—'

'I'm not really sure I understand all that. What does it actually mean in terms of the person's future?'

'Nothing very definite. Linda's written here creativity, self-fulfilment, conflict, enemies and crisis. I told you it wasn't a terribly nice one, didn't I?'

'It's just, well, not very helpful, is it? In identifying someone, I mean, or finding what happened to them.'

Claire shrugged and said defensively, 'I can't help that, can I?'

Jude snatched up the book, another about the history of astrology, that Claire had left open. Two lines caught her attention. 'It says here that "astrology was not very popular in the eighteenth century." So it might be important that this chart was made at all. Who would have made it?' she wondered. 'And listen to this: "the discovery of a seventh planet, Uranus, in 1781, would have upset traditional astrological structures altogether". I suppose that's true,' she said, lowering the book. 'Which would make nonsense of this chart altogether.'

'Well maybe not,' said Claire. 'It would be incomplete. And as for who made it, why, traditionally, it was gypsies.'

Chapter 24

Jude felt absurdly pleased when Euan rang early on Monday morning, asking if she'd like to join him for a walk. 'I need to come up with a piece about orchids for a nature website,' he said, 'so I thought I'd go and see what's happening locally. Want to come?'

His voice sounded casual but Jude still couldn't help hoping he wanted to see *her*. For a second she weighed up the work she needed to get through versus a walk with Euan. It was no contest. She'd look at the notes for her article when she got back, though there wouldn't be much time. She remembered her arrangement to go over and see Gran later. Oh, she deserved a break.

'If you don't mind my complete ignorance of the subject,' she told him, 'yes, I'd love an orchid hunt.'

'Good. Come to the house in half an hour?'

When she arrived at the back door of the cottage he kissed her hello, but not so she knew it meant anything but friendship.

'How was lunch yesterday?' she asked as he shouldered his rucksack and they set off up the lane.

'Very nice,' was all he said. 'Your sister's a great cook. It's not often I get a full roast dinner.'

'Yes, she is,' Jude replied, wondering whether he was oblivious to Claire's charms or just keeping his cards close to his chest.

They climbed the hill, but this time Euan took a path to the left, on the other side of the road to the folly. This footpath was at first overgrown with nettles and brambles, but soon they passed into a thick, wooded area where the canopy blocked out the light and little could grow. It had rained sometime during the night. The trees dripped patiently, and everything was fresh and sweet-smelling.

'Where do we look?' Jude asked. 'I'm afraid I'm not very good at this kind of thing.'

'There won't be anything yet, but we might have luck further on where the trees thin out,' Euan said.

'Some of these trees are hundreds of years old, surely,' she said. 'Look at that oak.' It had a huge girth, having split into several sections so it was like three trees growing up together in one.

'It's still producing little acorns, isn't it?' Euan said, examining a leafy branch. 'I wonder how many new trees it's parented over the years.'

'Thousands, maybe.' There must be layers and layers of fallen leaves beneath their feet – centuries of oak leaves. 'It feels so ancient and mysterious,' she said. 'You can imagine Robin Hood and his men making merry here.'

'It is a good feeling here today,' Euan said, 'but it can be different. Think of all those fairy tales in which the forest is a dark and threatening labyrinth, where the trees reach out to grab the unsuspecting traveller, where fearsome animals lurk, where little girls and boys become lost for ever.'

She shivered. '*Like Snow White*, and *Babes in the Wood* and *Hansel and Gretel*.'

Stories she'd read to Summer.

And like the subject of the dream. Running through the forest, pursued by something dangerous . . .

'The forest has always been a metaphor for the wild, the primeval, hasn't it?' Euan was musing. 'For communities in villages and towns and cities I suppose that became particularly so. The forest would be the opposite of civilized – the home of the ancient, the pagan, the savage. The woodwose, the wild man of the woods.'

'He's different from the Green Man, isn't he?' she asked. 'I remember you wrote about the Green Man in *The Path Through the Woods*. He's a bit kinder, a sort of pagan fertility symbol, is that right?'

'Yes, think of Morris Men and real ale.' They both laughed at the genial folksy image this conjured up. 'The woodwose is darker, more elemental.'

Every now and then where the trees were sparser Euan would stop to inspect the grasses and wild flowers that flourished in the light.

Eventually, the trees began to peter out altogether.

'Eureka!' he said suddenly, and together they examined a group of plants like mauve spears, which were scattered amid the long grasses. He bent to part the greenery around the nearest one. 'This is known as the common spotted orchid. You can see why.' Jude sank down to study the plant he was twisting towards her. The spear, she saw, was in fact made up of dozens of tiny flowers, pinky mauve spotted with a darker purple.

'Even each individual flower is quite complex,' she said.

'Like tiny tiger lilies, I always think.' He took a camera out of the rucksack he was carrying and spent a couple of minutes photographing them.

'I would like to see some bee orchids,' he said, looking about, 'but we may not be lucky in this terrain. They're easy enough to identify – they really do look like pale purple bumblebees.'

'I wish I'd taken more notice of this sort of thing at school,' Jude said. 'I'm useless beyond obvious things like oaks and buttercups and daisies. I missed the nature rambles. I always had my nose in a book.'

'You did better than me in that respect, then,' Euan said. 'I was always desperate to get home from school and out into the countryside.'

'But you write books now,' Jude said, surprised.

'Yes, I'm sure my old teachers are astonished. But then I'm writing about things I care about. It's easy to communicate then.'

'You do write with passion,' she said. She'd liked that about the book of his she'd read, that the author's enthusiasm flooded out from the page.

'Thank you. Oh, look, there's a stag beetle. I'm glad I've seen him.' He took a notebook out of his rucksack and jotted something down with a stub of pencil from his pocket. 'It's for a local survey,' he told her. 'You know, it wasn't until I left formal education that I started seriously reading and writing and thinking properly for myself. I suppose it felt like exploring, rather than doing it because someone told me to. I've made some mistakes along the way, but I've carved out my own place in the world. It wouldn't suit everyone, but it seems to suit me.'

'You don't have a particular routine, do you?' Jude observed. 'After all, you said you're up half the night sometimes.'

'Yes, what with stars and moths and bats. I've been told I'm incredibly annoying to live with,' he said. 'Not least by Carla, my ex-wife. We married very young and then . . . Well, we found we wanted different things in life.' He smiled, but there was a ruefulness about the smile that made Jude wonder. 'It's not good for a sense of routine for me to live alone. I'm awake at odd hours, writing when I feel like it. Then someone might ring up and invite me to go and do something interesting that means I'm away for a couple of days and I have to find someone to come and feed the animals at no notice . . . Oh, by the way, I let that rabbit go yesterday. I took him to a warren near where I found him, and turned him loose.'

'How did he do?'

'He scuttled over to his brothers and sisters and started eating grass. No hesitation. Anyway, it's amazing really that those books get written at all. But they have to be or the bills wouldn't get paid.'

'Do you have to go and do talks and so on?' Jude asked.

'Oh yes, plenty of that,' he said. 'And the journalism. Especially when a new book is out. Shall we wander back now?'

They walked in silence for a while, and as if at the thought of returning to civilization, the whirl of anxiety started up in Jude's mind once more. Euan was stopping every now and then to inspect the insect life behind a piece of bark or to listen to the cry of some bird. When she became aware that he was looking at her, Jude turned with a smile and said, 'What? I'm not part of the wildlife!'

'Of course you're not,' he said, looking embarrassed. 'It's just that sometimes you look so sad.' He spoke lightly, but his expression, usually calm and confident, was suddenly vulnerable, as though she'd touched something in him.

'Do I?' she said. 'I'm sorry. There seems a great deal to be sad or worried about at the moment.'

'I wondered . . . forgive me. Claire told me about you losing your husband. That must be extremely difficult to recover from.'

She realized then that they hadn't spoken of the matter properly before.

'It was. It is,' she said. 'There are so many people, kind people who love me, telling me I've got to move on. But . . . I can't . . .' she trailed off. 'It's as though . . . I don't know, I haven't had the courage.' She laughed, not very convincingly. 'I expect I will, one day.'

He nodded, and she was relieved that he didn't mutter some cliché about time healing things.

'Actually, though, I wasn't thinking about Mark just now. I was thinking about Summer and what on earth to do.'

'Oh, Jude, I've been worrying about her, too. Claire was explaining the latest. I wish I'd never taken her to the folly now, but I've never had a hint of a suspicion of anything about it myself, so how was I to guess?'

'I don't think you can blame yourself, Euan. But it certainly makes me want to unravel this mystery as quickly as I can because perhaps then I can help her.'

'How are you getting on with the necklace story?'

'Not very far. Gran's told me a bit more about a boy who used to bully the gypsy girl, but that's all. I meant to tell you, she used to keep the necklace under the floorboards in your house. You didn't find any other hidden treasures, did you, when the bedrooms were being renovated?'

He shook his head. 'No, and the men didn't mention anything. Tell me more about this other gypsy girl.' Euan had stopped again, this time by a rotting log, where he absent-mindedly lifted a section of bark with his penknife to look underneath. They watched a millipede flow across his hand.

'Her name was Tamsin Lovall and Gran met her in the forest. She went to her school for a while.' She gazed around, suddenly able to imagine that first meeting. 'They used that hidey-hole in the folly for messages and presents. I've tried looking up Lovalls in the telephone directory, but that's as far as I've got. I'm so caught up with finding out about Esther at the moment, and Gran's telling me the Tamsin story in odd bits so it's difficult to concentrate on it.'

'I'd like to meet your gran,' said Euan, letting the millipede escape, and standing up. 'Seeing as she was brought up in my house. Claire's talked about her a lot and it sounds as though she must have a few good stories to tell.'

The second mention of Claire for some reason irritated Jude and she said impetuously, 'Why don't you come with me this afternoon, then? You might have better luck with Gran than I'm having.'

Jude rang Gran at lunchtime to ask if it was all right if she brought someone, but when they got to Blakeney she rather wished she hadn't mentioned that she was bringing Euan. Gran had clearly gone to a great deal of trouble to prepare for him, donning the pretty blue frock she'd worn at her birthday party and buying two kinds of cake from the village store.

'He seems very nice,' Gran whispered to her in the kitchen where Jude was helping her with the tea. Even the best teapot was ready, and a set of dainty tea plates.

'He is, Gran, and it's awfully kind of him to help us look for Tamsin.'

'Very kind,' said Gran, giving her granddaughter a worried smile. 'You are looking after that necklace, aren't you?' she asked. 'I wouldn't like to think of anyone else having it.'

'I've got it here, Gran,' Jude said patiently, indicating her handbag. Later she took it out and laid it on the table and Euan, who hadn't seen it before, couldn't take his eyes off it.

'How do you think your Tamsin got hold of it in the first place?' he asked Jessie over tea. 'It's a very valuable thing for a small girl to have.'

'She said her grandmother had given it to her, that it had been passed down through the family for years. It had never been sold, she told me, because it carried very good luck. They'd kept it safe, but no one knew where it had come from originally.'

'Why would she have hidden it in the folly? I'm a bit confused because you also said that she wore it a lot.'

'Gran,' Jude said suddenly, 'why did it get left in the folly? We found the hiding place in the upstairs room, did I say?'

'Yes, you did. We left presents for each other sometimes, and once when I borrowed the necklace I left it there for her to find.'

'And did she find it?'

'Yes, she did that time.'

Jude and Euan exchanged looks. They weren't getting very far with this line of enquiry, and Gran was crumbling a piece of cake on her plate, agitated. Jude changed the subject, asking her grandmother if she'd heard from her daughter in Spain. Yes, Valerie had rung a day or two ago. 'She's complaining about how hot it is,' Gran said. 'I told her before she went, but she never listens. Never did, you know.'

'Oh Gran, Mum is sixty now,' Jude exclaimed. 'Old enough to make her own decisions.'

'You never forget that your child is your child,' Gran said severely, 'and I do think it's very silly of her to have gone. Particularly at her time of life. But then I never could tell Valerie anything. Now I'm sure poor Mr Robinson would prefer that we change the subject.'

'I wish my grandmother were still alive,' replied Euan. 'She's been dead for over fifteen years, and I still miss her stories. You'd have liked her, I think.'

'Gran,' Jude said, having a sudden thought, 'might you have any photographs of Tamsin?'

'I don't remember one. There's a box of photographs in the loft. I can't get it down by myself, but you're welcome to try.'

'We'll get it down. Where d'you keep the hook for the trapdoor?'

The loft ladder was stiff from disuse, but they coaxed it down and Jude found the box behind a suitcase of Christmas decorations. They cleared away the tea things and placed the box on the table in front of Gran.

She lifted out some manila envelopes, which bulged with curled-up papers, and put them to one side. Then she picked up a small brown photograph album.

'My brother Charlie took these with his Box Brownie.'

The album contained page after page of black and white pictures and Euan and Jude perused them together. Some were a little out of focus, where the distance had been wrongly judged. Under each photo Charlie had written some jokey caption in white ink on the black sugar paper: 'Sparky's been at the cider again . . .' under a portrait of a dog rolling on its back, 'Snap!' below two girls, obviously sisters, in identical best dresses. 'That's Sarah and the bigger one's me,' declared Gran, after fumbling with her glasses.

'Look, it's the cottage!' cried Euan.

There were several pictures of Gamekeeper's Cottage, smoke coming from the chimney. Gran pointed out that in one the back garden was a vegetable patch, in another that the two children swinging on the gate were Sarah and her friend Ruth, that the man in a cap, smoking a pipe, in a photo entitled 'Da off duty' was definitely her father.

'No hedge back then,' Euan noted, looking at a shot taken of the road from the top of the house.

'And this is you?' Jude asked, showing Gran a solemn girl with dark hair and eyes, several years older than she was in the picture with Sarah and clutching a school satchel.

Gran peered at it. 'Nine or ten I must have been,' she pronounced. The caption was 'The dog ate my homework, Miss', and indeed little Jessie's expression was anxious.

There were no pictures of Tamsin.

'Gran, what else can you remember about her?' Jude asked. 'I mean, it's difficult to find out anything without a bit more information. You said her name was Tamsin Lovall. Can you remember her birthday or her parents' names, anything like that?'

'She thought her birthday was in September, and when she said at school that she didn't know the teacher chose a date for her, the twentieth. It's funny, isn't it, how I can remember that from all those years ago and I can't keep my own great-granddaughter's birthday in my head?'

'She's seven next month, Gran. August the twenty-sixth.'

Towards the end of the album were some shots taken up in the forest of Gran and some other children fooling about on a fallen log. 'Look, there's the folly,' cried Jude, pointing. 'And here it is again.'

'Oh yes. My, that's Sarah, of course, and Ruth, and my friend Beth, and there's Charlie's friend Donald.'

The folly was in the background. Against it was the very faint impression of another figure, but it was so blurred and faded it was impossible to say more than that it was probably female. 'Who's that?' asked Jude.

'Pass it here, dear,' Gran said, and she squinted at the picture for some time. 'I don't know,' she said finally. 'It's not Tamsin. Who would be wearing a long dress in that weather?'

Jude took the album back and stared. It was a long dress, it hadn't struck her at first, the figure was so faint.

'She's over-exposed,' Euan said, having a look himself. 'Or perhaps she moved at the wrong moment.'

And for some reason, as she stared at the figure, a shiver passed through Jude. 'Can we borrow this, Gran?' she asked. 'Just in case it jogs someone's memory?'

'Of course, dear. I know you'll look after it.'

The shadowy figure from the photograph remained to trouble Jude all that evening. It was of course, quite common, for a figure from one picture – whether accidentally or deliberately – to become superimposed on another, and she knew she shouldn't leap to silly conclusions. She was more worried about its relevance to Summer's experiences.

She sat in her room for an hour or so browsing internet sites about the meaning of dreams and about stories of people who thought they'd lived before, but found nothing very useful to this situation. Summer certainly wasn't presenting her stories as personal memories but as tales about someone else, someone separate from her. And none of the sites she'd looked at mentioned dreams being heritable.

'I still think you're making too much of it,' Claire said the next evening, Tuesday, when Jude visited and showed her Gran's photograph album, but Jude saw fear in her eyes. She could understand that. Who would want to believe that their little daughter might be being . . . well, haunted by something. It sounded medieval or like a scene out of a ridiculous horror film. Not that whatever was going on seemed in any way malevolent – thank heavens. She thought about the lost dream. The terror of it was about being lost, cut off from one's mother in a dark forest. A very small child might feel similar feelings after running off in a supermarket.

'There is something a little strange going on, you have to admit that,' Jude said.

'Don't, Jude,' Claire said, looking away.

'If I hadn't had that dream myself I would be saying the same as you – that children sometimes have periods of night terrors, and not to worry, they'll get over them.'

'I'm sure it's the fairy stories,' Claire muttered. 'I did tell you the school thinks they shouldn't read fairy stories, that they scare children by projecting adult fears on them.'

'What are they supposed to read, then? The history of any culture is all about myth and legend. And Summer loves them. She's always asking me to read her one.'

'The stories Summer's teacher gives the kids are chosen to reflect real experiences and empower them to work things through.' Claire sounded as though she were quoting official language.

'Admirable, I'm sure, and I don't know much about child-care, but surely a lot of the old stories haven't been imposed on children by adults. They go way back and address stock situations like stepmothers who prefer their own children and the penniless youngest son seeking his fortune. And you can't exclude fear of darkness and loss from life. Even the very youngest children have these fears, surely. Didn't you?'

'Oh yes,' Claire said. 'Do you know, my constant fear when I was little was that I didn't belong to the family at all? That I'd been a foundling, but no one dared tell me.'

'Really?' Jude asked, rather shocked. 'I'd no idea.'

'I suppose it's a common childish imagining, Jude, but I really, really believed it. It's certainly true I never felt . . . that I fitted in with you and Mum and Dad. I convinced myself at another point that I was adopted, but that no one dared tell me.'

'But that's nonsense,' Jude said. 'Of course you weren't adopted, and of course you were part of the family.'

'You may tell me it's nonsense, Jude, and it might indeed be nonsense. I probably knew the truth all along, but that didn't stop me making up the fantasy. I'm just telling you that that's how I felt. You don't listen, do you?'

'Sorry,' said Jude meekly. 'I was trying to reassure you.'

'You don't need to reassure me. Just accept my feelings about things. Mum and even Dad never did. I didn't fit into their boxes, you see. That's something I'm determined never to do to Summer – to expect her to feel or act a certain way. I want her to be herself.'

'She's certainly her own little person.'

'She is, isn't she? But it's funny, she's quite conventional in many ways. Liking dolls and animals and pretty clothes.'

'She's very imaginative,' said Jude, thinking of the stories she acted out with the doll's house.

Claire picked up the photograph album and studied the picture with the strange, shadowy figure. 'It does look very weird, doesn't it?'

'It does,' Jude said, 'but there's undoubtedly some rational, technical explanation involving camera optics and chemicals.'

'Yeah,' Claire said, dropping the album on the table. 'I've really had enough of all this. Jude, you'll tell me this sounds mean, but I'd rather you hadn't come and stirred everything up. I'm sick of it all.'

Jude felt as though she'd been struck. 'Me?' she said. 'I didn't—'

'Everything was all right before you came. Now there's all this nonsense about the folly, and Gran's stupid necklace. It's causing trouble. Summer was OK before you started digging up all this stuff about the folly.'

'No she wasn't. She'd been having strange dreams. You'll have to blame Euan for that. He's the one who took her to the folly.'

At that Claire turned her face away. Euan once again hung fire between them.

Outside, the skies opened and it began to pour down in torrents.

Chapter 25

It was a summer rainstorm that swept Alicia to our door the July I turned fifteen. She had visited twice since what Susan saw fit to name the Great Disturbance when I was ten, and on the first of these occasions my father had been forced to remonstrate with her, for Mrs Godstone had threatened to give notice at her interference. On this latest occasion, as well as Augustus, she brought her fat little countryman husband with her and the three of them stood dripping miserably in the hall while the driver's lad dragged in their baggage.

This time, I did not hide, but waited uncertainly on the stairs, wondering if, my new station in the household considered, they would acknowledge me. They would not. Augustus gave me one of his grave smiles, but his parents studiously ignored me and by now I had developed a sufficient sense of my own dignity to take umbrage.

Alicia walked with a stick now, since a fall from a horse that broke a bone in her foot some months before. This did nothing to improve her temper. Her husband limped, too, plagued by gout that etched lines of pain on his rabbity face. Only Gussie stood straight and tall, a quiet boy, too thin, with a book in his hand, altogether more like his uncle than ever.

'Where is my brother?' Alicia snapped at Mr Corbett.

'Why, he's gone to Norwich today, Mistress,' the butler replied.

He'd left at ten o'clock that morning, having received Alicia's letter informing him of her impending arrival. He'd not otherwise disclosed its contents, but whatever it was it sent him into a dark mood and instead of retiring to his study as usual after breakfast, he called for the carriage. Snapping rudely to Mrs Godstone's requests about dinner with a 'Whatever you think best,' and with no more than a glance at me, he issued forth.

From my window I glimpsed him striding back in, his clothes shiny wet, at past five that afternoon. He sought me out at once where I lay on my bed pretending to read, and brought me into the drawing room where Alicia, her husband and Sam were waiting, as though I was really his daughter, to be shown off to a doting aunt. At his order I sat down hesitantly on a couch.

'Well,' said Alicia, looking down her nose at me as though I were Monday's fish. 'If this is indeed how matters stand, we were right to come, were we not, Adolphus?'

'It seems so, it seems so,' Adolphus groaned, the poor man too preoccupied with finding a comfortable position for his painful foot even to look at me.

'It is indeed how matters are, Sister,' my father said, coming to stand behind me and placing a reassuring hand on my shoulder. 'I intend naming Esther my adopted daughter and my heir.'

My countenance must have showed a kaleidoscope of my feelings, for they stared at me, Alicia, her husband and son, with horrified fascination as my father's words found their mark. I watched her face grow dark as the sky outside and then the storm broke loose.

'That one is not fit to be your daughter,' she screeched. 'She's some pauper's brat and the world will know her as such. Give her money, if you like. Pay her off. Find her some rich Johnny who will discount bad blood for the sake of a pretty face. How can you betray your family and your good name? Think of Augustus, think of your noble father . . .'

'You may provide for Augustus, you've wealth enough. Esther has nothing. And damn my drunken father's memory. My lands

are mine to dispose of as I will, I tell you, and I plan to give them to someone I care for. All my life I've suffered your bullying, hectoring ways and your letter today was the last of many last straws. I have no quarrel with Augustus. He's turned out remarkably well considering his parentage, but I . . . have . . . had . . . enough.'

Never had I known him show such emotion. Nor, it seemed, had Alicia, for she sat there, the breath punched out of her, able only to say, 'Well . . . well . . .'

They left again the next morning, Augustus's half-turned face a ghostly half-moon through the rain-spotted window of the carriage. And I felt sorry for him then.

My father did not turn out to see them go, nor did he leave his study for that entire day, and I dawdled miserably, stepping out in the garden between showers, to quarrel with Sam who forgot himself and called me 'come-uppity', and wondering what everything meant.

But as evening came and warm gusts wicked away the storm clouds my father stepped forth to view the stars, and I with him, hurrying to match his eager pace.

What did you mean last night, Father? I wanted to ask. How can I ever become your daughter? But something in his demeanour dissuaded such questioning. Only when we reached the tower room, made splendid and otherworldly by tongues of liquid gold from the setting sun, did he speak with a gravity and eloquence I'd never known before.

'It is true,' he said, 'that I drove to Norwich yesterday and hailed my attorney as he left the court to dine. I have ordered him to draw up documents to name you my daughter and my heir. The deed is not yet done, however. He insists he must study his papers and books for impediments and such fiddle-faddle — but it will be done and done soon. I am tired of Alicia's greed and her constant haranguing. And I desire you to have Starbrough Hall and to continue my work when I am gone.'

'When you are gone? Don't speak of it, Father,' I said with sudden alarm. 'You're not ill, are you?' Is that what hurried him?

'Nay, I am not ill, child, just weary. And those who study the stars come to know of how small and insignificant we are, like ants or beetles on the face of lonely rocks spinning eternally in infinite space. How the hand of fate might strike us in our futile insect purposes without warning or pity.

'When I found you, Esther, it was one of those moments of destiny. I have no wife, nay, nor ever wanted one.' He chuckled then. 'Suppose she turned out to be like my sister, what peace would I have in life?

'I was returning from a meeting in London one evening in July in 1765, and as we passed through the forest the driver – not our man Jan but another – stayed the horses and informed me there was a child in the road. Curious, despite myself, I stepped down to see. The man brought to me the most pitiful bundle and I saw it was a tiny trembling girl. Your clothes were shredded, my dear, into filthy rags; your tender skin was scratched and bloodied, your hair a matted tangle, your eyes huge with terror. Stricken with pity, I took you in my arms and wrapped you in my blanket but your trembling did not cease. I ordered the driver to continue our journey and in the rocking of the carriage you slipped finally into exhausted sleep. It was then I noticed you clutched something tightly to your chest. Gently I unpeeled your tiny fingers and brought it out to see. It was this.'

He went over to the wall and I was surprised to see him remove a brick from it, to reveal a secret recess. From this he took a velvet-covered box and held it out to me. 'Here,' he told me quietly. 'The time is right. Take it, it's yours.'

At first I thought I'd opened a box of living, sparkling starlight, then I saw it was a necklace, a necklace of stars. Seven of them. Seven diamonds set in gold, hung on a golden chain. For a long moment I could not speak.

Jude, who was sitting on her bed, reread the sentence with the sensation that she was falling. A necklace of seven stars. Like Gran's, but complete. It couldn't possibly be the same one. It was a coincidence, that's all. But the mystery of Esther's origins – at least, the mystery of how she came to Starbrough Hall – was finally solved. Esther had been a foundling. A foundling in silk rags. She sat back against the pillows for a moment as she gathered her racing thoughts, then eagerly read on.

'I know not where you came from, Esther, nor, to tell you all truth, did I seek to learn. Of that I am ashamed. I believed the hand of destiny delivered you to me, I, who had no one and thought I needed no one. But I was no use as a father. I kept you as a possession, had no sense of how to treat a child. It was enough for me that you were fed and clothed and cared for by a good woman like Susan, who loved you. You were there, mine, but I was free to continue my life as I had made it. I kept you as you had kept that necklace, a treasure I could take out and look at as I wished. God forgive me.'

His account bewildered me. I was too naïve then to know how parents and children should be. He had never hurt me and I always believed he had cared for me, even if from afar. Just as he accepted me, I accepted him for what he was. And we had come to know each other in our own time and our own way and now, for the first time, the love between us was acknowledged, made real.

He drew me to him, awkwardly, pressed my head uncomfortably against his collar bone so my cap fell off, but I minded not. 'Little Esther,' he murmured. 'I named you after my mother, whom I lost when I was small, and because while some say Esther translates as "myrtle", others say it means "star". You might know that the myrtle plant bears a star-shaped flower, so the two meanings are in nature wrapped into one.' He was the dry scholar always, but I felt the warmth of his lips through my hair.

We returned the necklace to its hiding place and set to work. That night we swept the skies together with a new sense of closeness and endeavour. Lyra, I remember, the great lyre of Orpheus, was particularly bright, as though it sang not to lure the dead from hell but the living into new life and happiness. And for the first time he trusted me to write notes in his journal to his dictation.

There seemed to be nothing more written about the necklace for the moment. Jude, still clutching Esther's book, pushed herself out of bed and took the box containing the necklace from the top drawer of the chest. She spread it out on the white duvet and found the place again in the text. 'A necklace of stars . . . Seven diamonds set in gold, hung on a golden chain.' Of course, one was now missing and the description was frustratingly vague, but still, every instinct screamed to her that the two necklaces were one and the same. But she couldn't know that, could she? The testing, scientific part of her mind insisted that she could not. Gran's might be a later copy, or one of several made at the time. She noticed again the goldsmith's mark on one of the stars, very faint, but there nonetheless. She'd have to ask Gran's permission, of course . . .

The following day, Wednesday, after one call to a colleague at Beecham's and another to an auction house in Norwich, she drove into the city, parked the car in a multistorey car park and made her way through the backstreets to a brightly lit jeweller's shop near the cathedral.

'Would you be able to give me some information about this?' she asked the woman behind the counter, who, by her tailored suit and assertive air, Jude took to be someone of seniority. She unwrapped the necklace to show her.

'You're not looking to sell, are you? We only do valuations for insurance purposes,' the woman said briskly, studying the necklace briefly through a magnifying glass, then scrutinizing Jude as though judging whether she was a jewel thief disposing of loot.

'I completely understand,' Jude said, holding the woman's gaze, and wondering if it would make the situation worse or better if she said she worked for an auctioneer's and so knew something of these things. 'I don't want to sell, though it would be useful to know its value. This is something that's been in the family and I'd like to know more about it. When it was made and, if possible, by whom. You'll have noticed the goldsmith's mark here.' She turned over the central star.

'Mmm,' the woman said, after taking another look. 'It's a nice piece – or would have been but for the damage. Have you ever thought about getting it cleaned and having a replacement star made?'

'I've only just been given it,' said Jude, 'so, no.' She couldn't tell the woman the truth, that it didn't, if Gran were to be believed, belong to her family at all.

'We're very busy at the moment. I can get back to you in a week.' The woman wrapped up the necklace and pulled a pad of forms towards her. 'Your name?' she asked.

Jude gave the details required.

'Any quicker than a week and I'd be most grateful,' said Jude. A week seemed an age to wait. 'My grandmother is most anxious to know,' she added quickly. 'She's very unwell at the moment, and worry makes her worse.' This wasn't completely untrue. Remembering Gran's concern that she didn't let the necklace out of her sight she'd rung her that morning to tell her what she was planning. Gran had been slightly doubtful about handing it over to strangers – even a reputable jeweller's – but had reluctantly agreed on the basis that it might help trace Tamsin.

Jude emerged from the shop with a receipt for the necklace and a guilty conscience, but also relief that the woman had promised to be as quick as she could. What should she do now? She checked her watch and saw it was only mid-morning. A coffee would be nice, and maybe a bit of shopping. But as she walked up through the cobbled streets she glimpsed the castle and remembered something else she should do. She flicked through her notebook and found the name. Megan Macromber.

Chapter 26

'This is all I can find.' Megan Macromber, an assistant curator at the Castle Museum, had glowing plum lip gloss, serially pierced ears and a formidable knowledge of Norfolk history. She placed a cardboard box that had once held twenty-four baked bean cans on the table between them and offered Jude a chair. Jude sat down and read the grimy label pasted on the top of the box: 'Starbrough Folly, Holt, June 1923'. While Megan began to unwrap packages from the box, Jude pulled out a newspaper cutting she spied tucked down one side. The picture on it showed a middle-aged man, the hair from whose head seemed all to have flown to his upper lip, posed on one knee at the foot of the folly, displaying some old bits of pottery and bone with all the pride of an angler with a prize-winning fish. 'Cambridge archaeologist braves local legends to uncover the past,' the heading said.

'What have you got there?' Megan glanced at the cutting as she laid some shards of pot on the table and started to unwrap another package.

'It says, "Tradition has it that the area is haunted",' Jude read out, ' "and locals advised Mallory not to dig there." '

'Mallory?' Megan said to herself. 'Charles Mallory. Where've I heard of him?'

She resumed unpacking the contents of the box. A ring made of bone, some ancient coins, a couple of gun cartridges of more recent origin, all these she laid on the table. Then came a small, tightly wrapped parcel, which took ages to unroll.

'Wonder what this was off!'

Jude, seeing what Megan held out in the palm of her hand, drew a sharp breath. It was tiny – the size of a 5p coin. The gold setting was twisted, and it needed a good clean, but there was no doubt in her mind. It was a star. A star studded with diamonds.

'Megan,' she gasped, 'you're not going to believe this, but I know what this comes from. It's part of a necklace I've just handed over for valuation. My gran's had it in her possession for years and years.' She quickly explained.

Megan held up the little twisted star and said, 'It would seem sensible for you to have it, though of course I can't just give it to you. Look, you say the necklace is with a jeweller. When you've got it back, why don't you bring it in for me to see? By then I'll have found out the procedure. There must be forms and things in these cases.'

Jude said ruefully, 'There always are.'

'But this necklace,' Megan persisted. 'You said it's connected to the Wickham family? If you want to find more about this Esther, have you looked round the church in Starbrough? It would be a start. And the parish records will undoubtedly be in the archive at County Hall.'

On the way back to Starbrough Hall, Jude, still marvelling that she'd found two clues about the necklace in quick succession – in Esther's account and in the box at the museum – returned to Starbrough Hall through the village, and decided to follow Megan's advice. There wasn't much to the village centre: a huge church loomed over a half-square of eighteenth-century cottages, and the green with the ancient oak and its encircling bench that she remembered seeing as a teenager. She parked the car by the church and opened the lychgate to the churchyard.

The church itself, fortunately unlocked, was light and airy. Its central point of interest was a huge medieval stone font at the beginning of the aisle, with a figure carved on one side. Jude stood back to view this properly. It was of a man with unkempt hair and a beard, brandishing a club-like weapon. A cardboard label resting on the lid of the font explained that it was a woodwose – a wild man of the woods, its pagan-sounding purpose to chase away evil spirits. It seemed to be the oldest part of the church, she discovered as she wandered around. The choir stalls with their beautiful carved decoration were fifteenth century, according to another label, but most of the memorials around the walls dated from the eighteenth century onwards. She was interested to see several for members of the Wickham family – a Victorian magistrate named William, a Richard Wickham who'd died of his wounds in the Boer War. She could see nothing for Anthony or for anyone called Esther. Having looked at everything, she left the building, pulling the door closed behind her.

The oldest part of the graveyard was dominated by a large tomb ringed by iron palings on which faint details about various Victorian Wickhams were recorded, but nothing further back than that, indeed there were not many eighteenth-century gravestones at all. There were no Esthers, not even Anthony's mother, only a Stella, the wife of Hugh or Hugo someone, the dates too faint to read confidently, and an Essie George, who'd died in 1850. Around the other side of the church were the twentieth-century graves; she supposed her Bennett great-grandparents, the gamekeeper and his wife, were among them. At the far side of the burial ground an old man in shirtsleeves was clipping a hedge and she made her way between the graves towards him. At her greeting he lowered his shears and took a moment or two to consider the question she asked.

'They'll be somewhere over there,' he replied, pointing his shears at an area she'd not searched very thoroughly. 'My da passed away in 1957 and that's where he got put. My ma, too, when she couldn't stand being without him any more.' He shuffled along the rows of graves, his shears swinging dangerously from one sinewy hand, and she followed at a safe distance. They found the grave quickly enough: the stone cross reading 'James and Rose Bennett', and giving their dates. At the base was a memorial flower vase that had obviously housed nothing but spiders for years. Jude vowed to come back sometime with some cut flowers or a plant. It gave her an odd feeling standing here looking at the names, that she had a special connection to the people buried in this place she'd never visited before, people she had never met but who still belonged to her.

The old man was walking slowly back to his work, when she thought to ask something. ' 'Scuse me.' He turned, with an enquiring look. 'Do you know of any travellers, any gypsies buried here? There's one in particular I want to find, Tamsin Lovall. I don't suppose that name means anything to you?'

He thought for a long moment, then said, 'Not Tamsin Lovall, no, but there's maybe another Lovall. Come with me.'

He led her through a gate in the hedge and out onto the green.

The wooden seat around the ancient oak tree was made up of different sections bolted together, some newish, others with broken arms or missing slats, silver with age so they appeared almost part of the tree itself. Some of the seat-backs bore small metal memorial plates in varying states of legibility.

'See if you can make out that one,' said the old man, pointing to a mottled plaque on one of the older sections.

'Ted Lova . . .'

'Could be Lovall, d'you think? There was a Ted Lovall.'

'Could be,' Jude said uncertainly. She walked around the tree, looking for other names. There was only one that really interested her.

'Marty Walters,' Jude read aloud, '1950 to 1970. Only twenty.'

'Summer of 1970, it happened,' the old man said. 'Nearly the whole village put in something for the seat. They were sorry for his family, you see. Terrible accident, terrible.'

'He was the boy who died at that party,' Jude said, with a sudden sense of shock. 'Where did his family live?'

'Now you've got me. Up Sheringham way, I believe. Somewhere on the coast, anyhow. But he died at the folly.'

The church hadn't, after all, told her anything about Esther. There were still the parish records, she supposed, but she didn't have any definite dates to help her there.

Back at the Hall, there was nobody about, so she went to the library where she'd left her laptop. She paced the room restlessly for a while, looking out of the window to the point where the folly must be, trying to link up all the connections in her head. It was no good. Sitting down at the desk she took a piece of paper and wrote down what she knew:

Esther, daughter of Anthony Wickham. Had necklace when
      found in 1765.
Befriends gypsy girl in forest c. 1775?
Gran meets Tamsin Lovall c. 1933.
Takes necklace from her (how did Tamsin's family get neck-
      lace and how did necklace get broken?)
2008 – Gran gives me necklace.

She stared at the notes with a feeling of frustration. How on earth had the necklace (assuming it *was* the same one) gone from Esther's possession to Tamsin's a century and a half later? Were the two gypsy girls from the same family line? It was difficult to imagine how a valuable necklace could have been transferred safely down the generations when the temptation must have been to sell it. Where would you keep a necklace in a wagon, anyway, where it wouldn't get damaged or lost? Though it had got damaged. She started to doodle a picture of a caravan, drawing patterns on the roof like on the one Euan slept in, but she wasn't much of an artist and the perspective was all wrong.

She sighed and pushed the paper away. She needed to think what to do next, but she had other things to be getting on with. And she was collecting Summer from school that afternoon.

She logged on to her laptop and resumed work on the synopsis for her article. Half an hour later she emailed it to Bridget McLoughlin, the editor of Beecham's magazine, saying she knew she had further research to do, but that she thought the story should be the personal one – about the pair of star-gazers, father and daughter. What did Bridget think? At the last moment, before she pressed 'send', she added her boss, Klaus, as a recipient. Best to be on the safe side.

The doodle of Euan's caravan again caught her eye. Where would he have got a gypsy caravan? He'd told her he'd borrowed it from someone – his cousin, she thought he'd said.

'How did your cousin get to have your caravan in his barn?' she asked Euan that afternoon when she dropped by with Summer. They had found him asleep in the caravan but he insisted he didn't mind Summer calling him awake.

'It was there when he bought the farm,' he replied, as they walked across the field to the cottage. 'The people who sold it to him had Romany connections, I gather.'

'I don't suppose you could find out what their name was, could you? I don't know where we can track down these Lovall people.'

'I'll try, but there are other ways, you know.'

'Tell me,' she said, immediately interested.

'All right, why don't we go and meet the travellers here, on the edge of forest? They might know something. They've probably been coming here for generations. They used to camp up Foxhole Lane, as you know, but that blasted John Farrell moved them on to a site on the other side of the forest, right by the main road.'

'Do you know them?'

'Of course. I've often met them on my wanderings.'

'Well that would be great. When could we go?'

'This afternoon, if you like,' said Euan, yawning. 'Can you let me have a quick shower and a cup of coffee first?'

'What about Summer?' They watched the little girl outside talking to the owls.

'She could come. Why not?'

'I don't know.' She felt very protective of the little girl at the moment, that was all. 'Oh, why not?' If they were friends of Euan's they'd be all right.

The encampment on the edge of the forest numbered only three caravans, modern ones, not the painted wagons like Euan's, and a couple of the cars that pulled them were parked untidily on the nearby verge. An elderly woman hanging up washing on a line stretched between two of the vans watched the *gorgios* approach, then, recognizing Euan, nodded to him and rapped on the nearest vehicle calling, 'Barney!' then something incomprehensible. After a moment a dark lean man, of thirty-five or forty emerged, pulling on a jacket over a T-shirt and jeans. Euan had got to know Barney, he'd explained, the last time the Romanies had passed through. Steve Gunn usually made a point of giving him work, and Euan, seeing him constructing bird coops, had got him to do some cages.

'Euan,' he cried, with a white flash of a smile, and he came forward to grasp the other man's hand. 'Good to see you. And you have brought your family?' His expression was an amused puzzlement.

'No,' said Euan, with a delighted laugh. 'But I wish they were.'

'We're friends of Euan's. I'm Jude,' Jude said, stepping forward and offering her hand, 'and this is my niece, Summer.' But Summer stayed close to Jude, holding her hand, and would only take shy peeks at Barney. She tugged at Jude's blouse and Jude bent down to listen to the girl whisper.

'Summer would like to know about the caravans,' Jude said gravely. 'I think she was expecting them to be more . . . well, colourful and horse-drawn.'

'Like Euan's,' Summer was brave enough to say.

'Ah,' said Barney, his face regretful. 'Euan's is beautiful. Liza here –' the woman pegged a bright cotton shirt to the line and came over to listen '– she lived in a *vardo* as a child, but these are much easier to look after, eh, Liza? And it was a hard life for the horses. The busy roads and often nowhere to graze. The children liked the horses. I'm sorry my two are not home yet for you to play with, Summer.'

'Are they at school?' Summer asked, forgetting her shyness.

'They go to school in Starbrough, yes,' Barney said. 'Is that your school, too?'

Summer shook her head.

Rachel Hore

'Summer and her mother live a few miles away in Felbarton,' Jude explained, 'but it's interesting that your children are at Starbrough.' She looked at Euan, who nodded encouragement. 'Euan says your family have been coming here for many years, and I wondered if you had heard of a girl – well, she'd be a very old lady now if she were still alive – who knew my grandmother when she went to school in Starbrough back in the 1930s. Her name was Tamsin Lovall.'

Barney looked doubtful and turned to Liza, speaking to her in a mixture of English and that strange, harsh language. Jude wondered if the old lady was his grandmother and how old she might be; her skin was wrinkled like a raisin, but she was still quite agile.

The old lady nodded slowly and said to Jude, 'I know a Lovall but not your Tamsin. My father's sister. Her man was a Lovall, Ted Lovall.' She said something else Jude didn't catch.

'There's a bench in Starbrough with his name on,' she told Euan.

'Is there?' Euan said.

'Yes, I've seen that,' Barney said. 'Perhaps he was well-known hereabouts – was he, Liza?'

'I believe so,' Liza replied, with a chuckle. 'Especially at the Red Lion. He gave up travelling right at the end of his life,' she told Jude, 'and he liked to earn a pint or two telling his stories.'

'There was some bad feeling, further back, I think,' Barney said. 'Some of the family – maybe your Tamsin was one – chose to settle during the war. There was work locally and those were difficult times for Romanies; there was such suspicion of anyone foreign-looking moving around.' He spread his hands. 'Inevitably there were harsh words said about betrayal of family and the traditional way of life. Me? I like the life, but I have sympathy for those who give up. It's very hard and there is so much hostility to us.'

'Is Farrell still trying to move you along?' Euan broke in, his voice low and urgent.

'Yes. And the police were here last week,' Barney said. 'Something about stolen birds. "Routine", they said, "very regretful". Yeah, routine that we're the first people they check. I almost laughed. "The only bird you'll find here," I told them, "is the chicken Margrit bought at the supermarket. But you can search us if you like." And, do you know, they didn't even look? That constable was all right, wasn't he, Liza? Said he was sorry and looked really embarrassed. Then he wants to ask us questions – turns out his family were Romany way back. So we have a good long chat about how he could find out about them. You see, people are not always what you expect. But there are some who go round life like they wear blinkers. They only see what they want to see, and that is usually bad.' His eyes blazed briefly, then returned to their gentle friendliness.

'Now, your Tamsin Lovall. It is possible that she or her family still live nearby. Have you tried advertising in the newspaper or on a website?'

'No,' Jude said, wondering why she hadn't thought of that before. 'I suppose we could.'

'Otherwise, I will ask about, but I can't promise,' Barney said. 'It was a long time ago.'

'Thank you, Barney,' Euan said. 'I knew you'd try. Liza, thank you.'

'That is fine, Euan,' Liza said. Then she added something in Romany and gestured to Jude, repeatedly holding out her hand.

'She wants to read your palm,' Barney said, chuckling.

'Go on,' said Euan.

'Should I?' Jude said.

'Yes. You must give her a coin. Here's one.'

Liza clasped each of Jude's hands in turn, studying the shapes of the fingers and the joints before examining first the right palm and then the left, tracing the patterns of the lines and the fleshy mounts. 'You have a strong will, very strong,' she pronounced finally. 'But something is holding you. Escape it and you make your own destiny. Very good.'

'You must ask her about love,' Barney said, looking from her to Euan, which made Jude feel hot in the face.

'The love line is broken,' Liza said. 'Something sad, huh? Then a fork, see here? You must decide.'

'No tall dark handsome strangers?' Jude said lightly, laughing, but Liza didn't smile.

'I cannot tell you the future, only what you can make from it,' she said. 'And you, little one.' She made a coaxing noise as though to a small animal and Summer, with a mixture of fear and fascination, held out her hands.

Liza examined them both, stroking the fear away, then held them together palm to palm for a moment as though blessing her. 'Look after this special little one,' was all she said to Jude.

'I will. What about you?' Jude said to Euan.

'Oh, Liza's already pronounced over me,' he said. 'Some of it seems to involve giving up beer and chocolate, I'm afraid.'

'You're having me on,' Jude said, as Liza smiled. 'I don't think she means that kind of heart trouble.'

He smiled, but Barney said quite seriously, 'It is possible to diagnose some conditions from the hands. The length of fingers is—' He broke off.

A car was approaching, and they watched it slow right down as it passed. The driver, a hulk of a man in a shirt with rolled-up sleeves and hair as trim as a mole's leaned out of the window and swore fruitily at the 'gypos'. Liza and Barney ignored him, their faces blank like statues, but Jude, infuriated, took a step towards the car, her fists clenched. Euan grabbed her arm and held her back.

'That's not the way to deal with it,' he growled as the car sped off with an anguished roar.

'I wasn't going to hit him!' she said, shaking him off, still angry. 'I can't believe you didn't say anything.'

'It only makes things worse. Believe me, I know.'

Summer looked stunned, so Euan put his arm round her and said, 'He was very rude to our friends, wasn't he? Not a nice person. But everybody's all right. Come on, time to go. I bought some mint chocolate ice cream, Summer, to celebrate the new fridge freezer, so let's go home and make cones.'

While Summer wandered outside in the garden, looking at the animals and dreamily licking a huge ice cream, Euan and Jude lolled in deckchairs with mugs of tea.

'Thanks for stopping me back then. I really wasn't going to hit him, just give him a piece of my mind, but perhaps you were right. Poor old Liza and Barney, putting up with that abuse.'

'I know, but Summer was watching, and anyway, you can't deal reasonably with people like that. You don't know what they'll do. He might not have hurt you, but he might have got out and swung a punch at me.'

'At you? Why?'

'A strange logic some blokes have. Despite years of every-one talking about equality, they still think the men should be in charge. He'd blame me for not controlling you properly. Or it might be against his code to clobber someone else's woman, so he'd hit me by proxy because I was with you. You have to remember, too, Barney would feel humiliated if someone else, especially a *gorgio* woman, tried to fight his battles. Male pride. It's ancient. Don't underestimate it, Jude.'

'It's all very silly,' she said, with a moue. 'But what's going to happen to Barney and Liza and the others? I can't imagine living like that. It's so . . . precarious. Aren't they allowed to stay on that patch of land?'

'No. Farrell wants them off. They only have an odd right of tradition. Which isn't a property right, I'm afraid. The Wickhams, when they owned the land, were, by all accounts, most generous to the gypsies. But up on Foxhole Lane they were in the way of Farrell's plans. He's letting them stay by the main road at the moment and the council's now involved and trying to negotiate a permanent site for them, but . . . Well, you saw that driver's reaction. I won't get on my soapbox, but since the 1960s and 1970s, government legislation has made it more and more difficult for Romany communities to live a trad-itional travelling lifestyle. And people are still so prejudiced.'

'I suppose the bad habits of other kinds of traveller haven't helped. Rubbish and crime, I mean.'

'New age raves on Yarmouth beach? No, that's not the Romany way. Nor is fighting back like you tried to do just now, Jude. You're very passionate when roused, aren't you?'

Jude thought he was mocking her, but his face was serious.

'I hate seeing injustice, that's all,' she said quietly.

'I've noticed that. And you're very protective of your family. I like that, too. Though perhaps you don't need to be.'

He was leaning forward in his chair now, his hands locked together, intent on what he was saying.

'You're very defensive about your sister.'

'I suppose I am. I've always felt so . . . sorry for her, you see. You know, because of her poor leg, but also . . . life has seemed a huge battle for her. She's never found her way. Until she had Summer. Summer's given her a purpose. But we've never been at ease with one another, Claire and I. I suppose she's fond of me, but . . . there always seems to be that edge. I don't know why I'm telling you this. It's not something I've said to anyone else, even Mum. Well, least of all, Mum. She's one of the people I've had to defend Claire against.' It felt natural and hugely liberating to confess all this to Euan, and yet she didn't know where it was all leading. He seemed to care about Claire, that much was obvious. She felt wan, her energy leaching away.

'Perhaps – I hope you don't take this the wrong way – but perhaps that's part of the problem. That you pity your sister. People sometimes resent being pitied. And, let's face it, it sounds as though you've needed as much sympathy as she has. She's very strong, Claire. I admire her enormously.'

Jude stared at Euan. Admiration. That implied respect, yes. In the old days it also meant romantic love. She felt a miserable sting of jealousy.

Now she felt she was losing him, she noticed anew the spring of his wavy hair, the clear blue eyes in the tanned face, the deft sculpting of his nose and lips, the pulse at his throat as he studied his big hands, powerful hands that could dig and build, but were also gentle enough to cradle a wounded animal. He glanced up, across the garden, and she followed his gaze.

Despite her dismal mood she had to smile. Summer was trying to stem a lava flow of melted ice cream, catching it in her mouth as it dripped from the cone, while squeaking that it was cold. At the sound of his deep, relaxed laugh Jude was dashed by a wave of desire.

Summer finished eating and started to wipe her hands on her trousers.

'Summer, don't. Come and wash,' Jude called. She fetched her inside to the sink.

When they came out again, it was to find Euan had started to tend to the animals in their cages and she took this as a sign that they should go. It was half-past five, she realized.

'I ought to get Summer home,' she told him. 'Thanks so much for taking us to see Barney and Liza.'

'I'm sorry it was so little use,' he said, collecting up the mugs and rescuing Summer's cardigan from the ground. 'What did you think of his idea of advertising for the Lovall family?'

'I thought I'd do that. Would the local paper be best?'

'I think so. If you emailed, they'd probably print it very soon,' he said. 'Newspapers seem to like that kind of letter. It interacts with the readership, I suppose. Well, Summer, shall I see you again soon?'

'Yes,' Summer said. 'Thank you. And do you remember you said I could sleep in your caravan one night?'

'I do,' he said.

'Well, can we do it soon?' she ordered. 'It's the holidays at the end of the week.'

'So it is. We ought to celebrate. I'll speak to your mum,' he promised. 'I take it you'd like Darcey, too?'

'Yes,' Summer said.

'Yes, please, little monkey,' Jude muttered.

After she'd dropped Summer off at Claire's, she drove back to Starbrough Hall, mentally framing the phrases for the letter to the paper. It was too late to send it tonight. The next day's letters page would have been put together by now. She'd do it tomorrow morning. Instead, after supper, she transcribed some more of Esther's journal.

It was not long after our library was finished that I met the gypsy girl again. It was winter and almost a twelve-month since her people had last been seen in Starbrough Woods. The pedlar woman came to the kitchen door again, and this time she brought with her the girl I thought of as my friend, and her elder sister. Susan called me to come and see their wares, for she knew I should wish to choose the lace for a new gown she was sewing for me. I smiled at the girls, but they were shy, and only the little one would meet my gaze. The elder, who must have been closer to me in age, was swarthy of skin and stocky of build, quite different from her birdlike sister, though handsome in a lusty way, I own. I looked at every piece of lace they carried and chose a matching collar and cuffs. Then, on impulse I bought half a dozen lengths of ribbon, to make presents of to Betsy and Susan. I had never seen Mrs Godstone wear anything so frivolous as a ribbon, so for her I chose some clothes pegs and for the men-servants pots of evil-smelling salve for cuts and grazes. For these I paid out of a purse of money my father had presented to me, and in this way I discovered the pleasures of giving.

Several days passed and Jan the coachman brought sobering news. One of the gypsy men, he thought named Luca or Lucas, lay dead after an argument about a horse. The murderer, some ruffian at the inn where they had both been drinking, had been taken into custody. My father was summoned to attend the inquest since Luca's people were residing on our land. I heard later that he paid for the poor man's burial himself.

Late the next evening I was upstairs preparing for bed. Going to draw the curtain I noticed a strange glow over the forest, also billows of black smoke. I ran to the door, crying to the household that the forest was afire. All were awake in a moment, doors banged, people shouted and all was panic. Mr Corbett and Jan hurried out with my father, armed with brooms to beat the flames, while I pulled on my cloak and went with Betsy to alert the neighbours and to bid Mr Trotwood raise assistance from the village. This done, we joined a party of people heading in the direction of the forest, intending to see what help we might offer. Before long we could follow the smoke and the flames till we could hear folks' cries, then when we gained the camp at Foxhole Lane we saw an awful sight. One of the wagons was alight and half a dozen figures *staggered around, struggling over possessions or with one another. Two drunken gypsy men lurched about with barrels and stools and clothing, which they'd cast into the heart of the fire. Meanwhile several women pulled them off again, assisted in this by Mr Corbett, Jan and my father. The women scolded and cried, the men were swearing and laughing. It was a verily a scene from hell.*

Then, standing well apart from the flames and the choking smoke, I saw the children huddled together, their faces golden in the firelight, their mouths great Os of horror. I called to Betsy to help me, and together we went to comfort them.

'Can we take them back to the house?' I asked Betsy, but they would not leave their people and instead Betsy set off to fetch Mrs Godstone with blankets and sustenance. The older girl cradled her brother while I looked after my friend. The poor dear thing trembled in my arms, terror in her eyes, and I tried my best to reassure her, until the pedlar woman, their mother, saw us and came instantly to claim her from me.

It was an hour before men from the village arrived, to beat out the flames and an hour after that before the blaze was overcome and Jan and Mr Corbett caught the terrified horses. Then, since there was nothing more the gypsies would have from us, we left them alone to their damaged chattels and their grief.

'It's their custom 'tis the trouble,' my father told me as we set off for home. 'When a Romany dies they burn his wagon and his possessions. His brothers went too far tonight.'

And I could not banish from my memory the terror and hope-lessness in the little gypsy girl's eyes as I tried to comfort her.

That night Jude took ages to get to sleep, instead worrying over the events of the day. What bothered her most was her conversation with Euan. She allowed herself to remember his deep blue eyes, his quirky mouth and tender expression, and this gave her a delicious warm feeling, but then his words about Claire interfered with that fantasy. She tried to stop thinking about Euan and concentrate on Claire. Did she really patronize Claire or see her as an equal when she wanted to help her? She did find Claire unbelievably irritating sometimes, and had always thought she was being a good sister when she tried to ignore this. What really caused this imbalance between them? What did Claire feel about her? Had Claire never named a star for her because she didn't love Jude enough? She brooded on. Claire rarely showed any interest in what Jude was doing – her studies or her work – and never had. Perhaps this was jealousy or perhaps Jude mattered little to her.

Euan admired Claire, he'd told Jude that, and now Jude wondered if he had deeper feelings for Claire. She hadn't really seen them together enough to judge, certainly not for any length of time. She hadn't had the opportunity to pick up those little glances and gestures that gave these things away. She did believe, though, that Claire hoped for more than friendship. And the two of them certainly shared a love for little Summer. Euan was a natural with children and Summer adored him.

The thought of the three of them together – Euan, Claire and Summer – sent a surge of jealous anguish through her, then a kind of dullness set in. No, at that moment what she felt wasn't pity for Claire, but instead that old resentment she'd felt sometimes as a child, when Claire had monopolized attention in some way, or as a teenager, when boys had been attracted to her sister's feisty prettiness rather than Jude's quieter, kinder charms. It was a long time since she'd felt that teenage jealousy, but every now and then she was surprised to find the old patterns of anger and envy still lay beneath the surface. She wondered if you still felt them when you were Gran's age. She sighed and turned over, trying to get comfortable.

They'd both tried to be closer, more caring of one another, since Mark died, she could see that. Summer had been nearly three and Claire was struggling with the Star Bureau and saving up to buy a home. Claire had tried her best to comfort Jude; had rung her up frequently and made a point of visiting her sister at their mother's whenever Jude came home. They'd definitely become closer because of it. But their relationship had somehow slid out of kilter again, and part of this, she knew, was to do with Euan. Round and round went her thoughts.

Euan was Claire's friend originally, the voice of Jude's conscience whispered again. No, she'd been over all this with Chantal. She should just aim at being normal, friendly, with Euan and see how things turned out. But perhaps whatever turned out would drive a sword between the sisters? Oh damn it all.

She'd read a magazine article about sisters recently, and it emphasized this contrary feeling they have for one another, a mixture between jealous rivalry and great caring. It said sisters were immensely important to one another and yet evoked the worst sort of hatred and jealousy in each other, generated originally by infant competition for parental attention. Also, the article said, position in the family was very important. It seemed to imply that the elder sister was likely to be the steadier, bossier one. Funny, but in their family, it was the other way round. Claire was less confident, often complaining that their mother was more interested in Jude, even that she loved Jude more. It would be interesting to talk to Mum about this sometime. Which led to another frustration – it was hardly a conversation to have down a mobile phone to Spain.

The following morning, though tired, she felt steadier again, and composed her letter to the local paper. It began:

I am trying to contact the family of Tamsin Lovall, a childhood friend of my grandmother who was born Jessie Bennett and who is anxious to hear news of her.

She stopped typing, thinking long and hard about which address to include. In the end, after quickly checking with Robert, she gave her name care of Starbrough Hall. Gran was vulnerable and might be confused by post arriving from strangers, and the name Starbrough Hall might be recognized by Lovalls.

She emailed the letter, and was just opening her catalogue file in order to write descriptions of a few more books when Megan from the museum rang her on her mobile. Jude was surprised to hear from her. They'd left it that Jude would contact her again once she'd recovered the necklace from the jeweller's.

'I couldn't wait to tell you,' Megan breathed down the phone.

'What is it?'

'Charles Mallory. The archaeologist. I looked him up when you'd gone. I knew there was something odd.'

'Odd?'

'Yes. He died. Soon after, I mean. I thought I'd read about it somewhere; it was treated as a big mystery at the time. I asked a friend at the newspaper archive to check for me and he's just rung back. A couple of weeks after that piece you found about his archaeological finds, it seems Mallory simply vanished. It was assumed he'd gone home to Cambridge, but eventually he was reported missing by his college. No one seemed very sure where he was last seen and then they found his car down a lane near the harbour at Brancaster Staithe. His body had been washed up further along the coast some weeks before, but not identified until then. No one ever knew whether it was an accident or something else, whether he'd killed himself perhaps.'

'How very peculiar. You don't suppose there was a curse,' she wondered, 'like with Tutankhamun's tomb?'

'It makes you think, doesn't it?' Megan replied. 'That's why I rang you straight away. It sounds too silly, though. It's more likely, isn't it, that there was some ordinary explanation? He was a bit eccentric by all accounts – that silly moustache – and perhaps he was depressed or something.'

'The curse thing isn't easy to assess. He'd have to have believed that he'd been cursed and show psychological effects.'

'I don't think my friend found anything like that. Anyway, it doesn't help you about the necklace, does it?'

'No, but thanks for letting me know. I'll ring you as soon as the necklace is ready.'

Afterwards, Jude considered that, strange though it might be, the story of Mallory fitted in with all the other strange things reported to have happened at the folly. After all, he had disturbed the ancient burial ground and taken away some bones. Perhaps something had affected his mind – he'd looked perfectly happy and proud in the newspaper picture. If it had been an isolated incident in the story of the folly, then in all probability Megan would be right and his death was likely to have been an accident. But add it to all the other stories, and it looked more sinister.

She forgot about the matter when she opened her email inbox to see separate messages from both Bridget and Klaus. Both were appreciative of the idea for the article that she'd sent them, but she had to laugh at their very different concerns. Klaus was interested in angles to hook certain types of bidder and wanted to be certain she would emphasize the uniqueness and importance of the items themselves. Bridget, on the other hand, produced a useful list of editorial suggestions with regard to shaping an interesting story. Still, both were happy with the general approach, though Bridget said somewhat wistfully that she wished there was more hard information about the astronomical discoveries.

'I'll do my best, Bridget,' she wrote back. She, too, wished she had something. It was time Cecelia got back to her with her possibly exciting piece of information. She sighed then settled down to type the next piece of transcription.

Chapter 27

After breakfast on the twenty-eighth day of January, in the year of our Lord 1778, my father set forth for Norwich to attend a great meeting at the Maid's Head inn. Noblemen, clergy and gentry, he informed me, from the length and breadth of Norfolk, had been summoned to discuss opening a subscription to advance a regiment in these critical times for the King. Since I professed no knowledge of the matter in question he acquainted me with the revolt in our American territories and how their defence against the rebels drained money and men from our realm in no small measure. A demonstration of support for King George was forthwith required, he declared, and every Englishman worth the name should open his heart and his purse to the cause.

He returned after nightfall, tired and agitated. The meeting had been a long one, with much dissent and fierce argument, but he had put himself down for 25 guineas and duty was done.

After dining well on boiled mutton and caper sauce, he retired to his library and from thence, I fondly believed, to bed. But when I sought him out after breakfast next morning he was not to be found, in either his library, or his workshop, or his rooms. Betsy was questioned, who declared his bed not slept in, nor clean shirt assumed. Mr Corbett organized a search of the house and outbuildings, but I knew by instinct exactly where he must be. I called to Sam in the stables, and we half ran, half walked across the park and up the hill through the trees to the folly. There, as I suspected, we found the door unfastened.

I cannot imagine where I found the strength to mount those stairs with my whooping breath and giddy sense of terror at what I might find, but mount them I did, to find all my fears justified.

My father lay sprawled at the foot of the ladder, his lantern smashed across the floor. With a bleating cry I ran to his side. His body was warm, praise God, despite the winter chill, but his pulse was weak and while his eyelids fluttered at my touch he did not wake. His face was bleached as pale as last night's new moon.

Sam ran back down at once to fetch help. I set about folding my cloak, but when I raised his head to slip it underneath for a pillow, my fingers found dried blood and a hot swelling above his left ear. 'Father,' I whispered, 'Father, wake up.' I wept a little and as my tears fell on his forehead, his eyes opened for a moment and his lips moved.

It seemed an age before we heard shouts, then footsteps slapping on the stairs. Sam brought his father and Mr Corbett, and soon stout Dr Brundall arrived, panting dangerously so I feared he might pass out like my father and then we'd need to get two bodies down those stairs.

They gave my father water and the doctor, now recovered, dressed his wound, pronouncing it 'hardly serious', then they wrapped him in blankets and gently lifted him down the stairs where Dr Brundall's son and two of their servants had ready a stretcher to bear him home.

All that day and the following one, too, my father lay senseless on his bed, but at dusk the day after that, his eyes opened and focused immediately on the moon rising beyond his window. 'Father,' I whispered, and his eyes met mine. His fingers stirred on the coverlet and I placed mine over them and breathed a prayer of thanks. In the days after that he grew steadily stronger, taking gruel and the soup Mrs Godstone made and which I fed him, letting no one else.

They moved a wooden cot into the room so I might sleep nearby and attend him if he woke in the night. Matters continued in this way a fortnight before Dr Brundall declared the immediate danger to be past. We waited anxiously for further improvement, but there was little. My father was a broken man.

February ebbed away, and my father could not leave his bed nor did he speak. Then one day early in March, he found his voice, stilted and rusty as though long buried underground. He could only pronounce single words, 'yes' or 'no', 'meat' or 'water' and an early instruction to me was 'read'. I leaped up at once and flew downstairs, where I ransacked the library shelves for exactly the right book. I chose the Arabian Nights, which Father had purchased shortly before his accident, and I came to feel like Scheherazade herself as I held his attention night after night with my stories. When he'd had enough he'd bade me 'out', meaning not that I was dismissed, but that I should extinguish the candles. I'd retire to my room leaving the curtains open so he might see the skies in the lone watches of the night.

One day in the middle of March he managed 'star' and 'book' and mimicked writing, so I brought his observation diaries and we passed an hour or two revisiting all he had seen. Far from soothing him, as I had hoped, it made him agitated, and it was out of this event that my idea arose: that we would carry him out to the park one night to view the stars. Needless to say, this plan was met by the household with horror. Suppose he fell or caught his death? But my father was enlivened by the idea, and seeing as good spirits are vital to good health, I insisted that it was his will. It was agreed by one and all, however, that Dr Brundall should not be told. This was not easy, as the good doctor very often visited the house, and once he brought Father's attorney with him, Mr Wellbourne, on what business I do not know, though Mr Corbett was called to witness my father's signature on a document. 'His writing was so feeble it was piteous to see,' he told me.

The first night outside he was laid on the same wooden cot on which I'd slept during the first critical days. Soon after that, Mr Trotwood was sent to Norwich to purchase a Bath chair. Father, having no strength in his limbs, was unable to grasp a telescope, but Sam, who was good with his hands, devised a frame to be attached to the chair to hold one. This done Father had only to move his head to view through the eyepiece. I would sit by him and set down his stuttered observations in the book as usual. Many nights he was too tired even for this, and instead on occasion I would set forth by myself. I loved to sweep the skies for comets; however, none of the telescopes from his library showed the treasures of the skies as clearly as the great reflector in the folly, and I dared not venture up there alone. It was therefore arranged for it to be transported, with great trouble, back to the house and Sam constructed a stand for it in the park. It was the best we could achieve, but the park was not as good as the tower, which stands away from the lights of buildings and closer to the stars. It was lonely too, and cold outside; my clothes were often heavy with dew or stiff with hoar frost.

One freezing night towards the end of March I saw for the first time what seemed like a tiny disk passing close to Taurus. The following evening it was there again and I looked for it every clear night after that, measuring its progress towards Gemini. I believed it to be a comet but, if so, an unusual one with its regular shape and no tail. I did not realize what I had found until many months had passed.

Jude reached the bottom of the page and turned it over, only to realize with dismay that there was no more. Esther's story had finished! But how could it have? It didn't feel finished. Although the sentence was complete, the story wasn't. It was dreadful. She needed, she *had*, to know more. Anthony had died later in the year; that was common knowledge. But what had happened to Esther and the comet-thing she remembered reading about in the observation journal, she still had no idea.

She sighed. This would have to do for the time being. There might be sufficient for Bridget's article. But still, she felt desolate. She closed the computer file containing this latest piece of transcription and emailed it to Cecelia.

How was Paris? You'll be amazed by this final bit. What do you think it could be that they found?
  Longing to hear from you.

With luck Cecelia would get the hint.

When she logged on during the evening a response pinged into her inbox.

Jude, Thank you for this, which is fascinating. I've read all the observation journals and I have sent you those letters you needed. It'll be your turn to be amazed. They should be with you tomorrow. Ring me when you've read them. There's lots to talk about.
  Oh, and Paris was wonderful.

On Friday morning a thick envelope addressed to Jude in Cecelia's stylish handwriting arrived by special delivery. It contained photocopies of half a dozen letters in Esther's italic hand, so familiar to her now.

'They're the ones from the Cambridge library,' Jude explained to Chantal.

They repaired with them to the library where Jude spread them out on the table. They were all signed 'Esther Wickham' and addressed to one Josiah Bellingham.

'Remind me of who he was?' said Chantal.

'A London watchmaker and a grinder of optical lenses,' Jude told her. 'An amateur astronomer of some reputation. He lived and worked in Whitechapel in the second half of the eighteenth century. I think Anthony Wickham bought equipment from him to make telescopes. Yes, look, that's what the first letter says.'

14 May 1778

Dear Mr Bellingham,

I write to you at the instigation of my father, Anthony Wickham of Starbrough Hall, who you will perhaps remember having many times bought from you lenses and specula for spyglasses. You will be surprised at my writing instead of my father, and to learn that my purpose is not to order goods from you but to crave your advice.

You may not know the sad news from Starbrough Hall, but on 28th January inst. my father met with a terrible accident which has left him gravely cast down. Although he has recovered somewhat, thank God, he is yet an invalid, unable to rise from his bed without assistance or to walk, unable to write or to speak more than a few words. We pray that his progress will continue.

These last weeks he has proved hale enough to continue his stargazing, and this he has been determined to do. Many nights have we repaired to the park and now I must tell you of a curiosity we have seen. A strange object like a comet but with no tail or a nebula, but it moves, visible in the quartile near Tau Tauri. This we viewed with 460 magnifications, very well defined, and with 278 magnifications, sharp and a small star nearby.

My father's suggestion was to write to you as the best of his acquaintances to investigate this further. He also believes you are an honourable man.

'So wouldn't claim the credit, I suppose,' Jude muttered.

Bellingham must have replied in friendly fashion, because the next letter to him was dated a few days later and merely answered a few questions Bellingham had about measurements. Jude concluded from it that he hadn't been able to find this object through his own telescopes but was planning to visit an acquaintance who possessed a better telescope. The third letter indicated that this contact couldn't see it either, or had concluded it was a nebula. 'It's important to watch it over a long period of time,' Esther had written. 'A month, maybe, though it is now faded from the sky.'

In July she wrote to him again, asking if there had been any developments, then again, to remind him in August.

In the final letter, dated October, the tone had changed. Bellingham must finally believe her for she said that she'd be eager to hear back from him 'as soon as you have consulted with the Astronomical Society. I have never written such a thing as a paper and fear I would need significant assistance.'

After lunch, when she was alone in the library, Jude rang Cecelia as requested.

'The transcription you sent me yesterday, and Esther's letters to Bellingham exactly confirm my interpretations of that torn diary you sent me. Jude, it's amazing. Has the penny dropped yet?'

'Not really, I'm afraid,' Jude replied. 'You'll have to tell me.'

'What she saw,' Cecelia said, and Jude had never known her so animated, 'was the planet we call Uranus. Just think, Jude. She saw it in 1778! Three years before Herschel discovered it and gave it a name. Though I don't think it was called Uranus for a while. He and his sister Caroline thought it a comet at first as well, you know.'

'So Esther really was becoming a skilled astronomer.'

'Building on her father's expertise, yes. If she hadn't so good a telescope she wouldn't have been able to see it. I should also add that she wasn't the only one before Herschel to have reported seeing this strange object. Herschel was the first to study it properly, though, and to draw official attention to it and that, I suppose, is the really important thing about a scientific discovery – to recognize its possible significance and to follow it up. Think of Isaac Newton staring at that falling apple. People have always seen apples falling but no one before saw it as anything but commonplace. But he had the background knowledge and the intellectual curiosity to go away and experiment endlessly and construct from it the theory of gravity.'

'So why is it important that Esther saw this comet or planet or whatever you are saying it is? After all, someone else discovered it a couple of years later, named it and took all the glory.'

But Cecelia wasn't to be swayed. 'In the history of astronomical discovery I suppose it's not important. But in the context of the story around this collection you're selling it's fascinating. And being an historian of astronomy, I am really interested. It's part of the whole endeavour of scientific discovery at the time and Esther, let's face it, is unusual being a woman. You know about Herschel's sister, Caroline, I suppose?'

'Not really,' Jude confessed.

'She's a prime example of both the possibilities and the limitations for women operating in the man's world of intellectual discovery. William Herschel was able to escape a very restrictive upbringing in Germany and set up by himself as a musician and amateur astronomer in Bath. But he had tremendous trouble being allowed to bring his little sister to join him – she was expected to be the family skivvy. When she eventually came, her job was to be his assistant in what was often gruelling physical work. He ground his own mirrors and built his own huge telescopes – like Wickham – and she had to help, and she was only this tiny little woman. She took part in the stargazing and noting what they saw. She did get public recognition for her contributions and even became something of a celebrity for discovering a comet – the first "lady's comet", as the writer Fanny Burney put it. But part of the celebration of her was the fact that she was a bit of a freak – a female astronomer – and it was more common to hear her referred to as "the great William Herschel's sister". It might even have helped her cause that she was so modest and tiny and self-effacing.'

'I wonder whether Esther was,' said Jude with a little smile. 'The way she must have bossed that household about to do things for her father!'

'Yes, considering she was, as your latest transcriptions told me, a foundling and might have been regarded as the lowest of the low, she seemed to earn everyone's respect and obedience. If she was spirited she must also have been very clever and tactful. It is interesting to speculate what might have happened if her father hadn't had that accident. They might have made discoveries that rivalled Herschel's. It's useless to speculate, of course. It's much more interesting to read the correspondence with this man Bellingham. I wonder whether he did anything more about the matter of the strange object she talked about.'

'I don't know.' Jude felt despairing. 'There is no more of Esther's account to read.'

But when she ended the call and thought about all that Cecelia said, she felt brighter. At last there was something significant to write in her article. Esther and her father had made an important discovery, and their work deserved to be presented to the world. She could hardly wait to sit down and revise the synopsis of her article and let Bridget know. But there wasn't time for that right now. She had offered to cook the evening meal.

Their meal was early to accommodate the twins and because Robert had to rush off to chair an open meeting of the parish council. Chantal was to go with him. While doling out strawberries and cream, which followed roast chicken – the twins' favourite – Jude volunteered to put Max and Georgie to bed so that Alexia could go too, but she gently refused.

'It's not really my sort of thing,' Alexia confessed. 'Robert will do very well without me. Why don't you go, Jude? You won't be able to vote or anything, but you do know about the folly. And you've done enough, cooking us this lovely meal.'

Robert added, 'Yes, you'd be useful actually, Jude. Would you mind saying a little piece about the folly?'

Jude, who sometimes had to address auction rooms, agreed.

About fifty villagers gathered in the village hall opposite the church. Euan was an early arrival. He sat with Jude and Chantal but was immediately engaged in conversation by the woman sitting on his other side. Jude, in between nodding and smiling at Chantal's many acquaintances, was glad of a quiet moment to scribble a few notes on what she needed to say. As Robert called the meeting to order, she looked around for John Farrell or Marcia Vane, but there was no sign. Whether or not they knew about the occasion, she saw that they wouldn't have been welcome. For once the meeting started it was clear that most villagers were against the development, and certainly all of them hated the idea of the folly being knocked down. 'It's our best-known landmark,' one of the parish councillors put it.

Here, Robert invited Jude to speak, referring to her somewhat vaguely as a 'historical expert' from London. Jude, at first hesitantly, duly described how the tower had been built for stargazing and that significant discoveries had been made from it that added to the bank of knowledge at the time.

'Don't forget, too,' she went on, warming to her subject, 'it's an important piece of architecture. Follies, as you might know, were a feature of the eighteenth-century great house, a way by which landowners demonstrated their wealth and sophistication. Starbrough folly is a particularly fine, listed, example.'

After this, Euan spoke out against the development, beginning, 'This application is another example of the creeping destruction of something vitally important: our rural heritage. Bite by bite, we are eating away at our precious wild places. If we start interfering with the habitat of the red admiral and the bee orchid we will lose them. And lose them, remember, for ever.'

When he'd finished and the applause died down, Robert chaired a general discussion then summarized by saying, 'It's fairly unlikely that the planning authorities would allow the area to be built on extensively, but we can't rely on that supposition. I propose that we resist the demolition of the folly and the development plan in its entirety. However, Farrell might fight back, asserting that, given the folly, there is a precedent for building there.' It wasn't long before this proposal was enthusiastically accepted, then Robert agreed to draft the necessary letter and the meeting was closed.

'Like a lift up the road, Euan?' Robert asked him as they walked to the car.

'Thank you,' he replied. In the back of the car, his arm stretched across the back of the seat, Jude felt terribly aware of him.

Robert was praising his contribution to the debate. 'It's a vital aspect of the defence,' he said. 'Perhaps I can consult you when I write that particular paragraph.'

'Sure,' Euan said.

'In fact, would you like to come to dinner tomorrow night? We can sketch it out then. I'm not as good on bee orchids and whatnot as you are.'

'I can call in tomorrow during the day, if you like,' Euan said, 'but I'm afraid I'm busy during the evening.'

He said to Jude. 'Actually, Darcey, Summer and Claire are coming round. Summer finally got me to agree to her sleeping in the caravan, and Claire's gamely volunteered to borrow my tent.'

'Oh, that sounds fun,' she said. Her sister hadn't said anything about this when she'd spoken to her on the phone earlier, and, once again, she felt oddly left out.

Euan, perhaps sensing this, said, 'The tent's got two sleeping compartments. Why don't you come, too?'

'Thank you,' she replied, then regretted it, not feeling sure whether they really wanted her there. 'Perhaps I ought to say no. I'm not great in tents,' is what she should have said. But Euan was so enthusiastic when he said, 'Great! We'll have a barbecue. My sister and her husband might be free, too.'

It was just a kids' sleepover, Jude remonstrated with herself as she lay awake later that night. But Claire was being so odd at the moment, and she guessed she'd be intruding.

She'd warned herself to stand back, though it was ridiculous to think she needed to. Just a couple of weeks ago she had broken off from Caspar because of her allegiance to Mark; it didn't make sense to be resentful of Claire's interest in Euan. And . . . now it came back to her, what she'd tried so hard to forget, the very thing Claire must have been hinting at when she said Mark hadn't been perfect. Jude had trampled it down in her mind for years, believing it best, the only way forward if she wanted to keep Mark. And of course once Mark died, forgetting was part of the process of his sanctification in her memory. And now she'd taken the lid off the memory, there was no replacing it.

Their father had died nearly eight years before in October 2001, just after she and Mark had become engaged. He was sixty-one, their mother still only fifty-four. Mark and Jude, who were due to marry the following June, spent practically every weekend between the funeral and Christmas visiting Valerie, and Claire often deserted her rented bedsit to keep their mother company. What Mark must have thought of this household of weeping women, he was too sympathetic and tactful ever to have voiced, but he noticeably took every opportunity to get out of the house by volunteering to make supermarket trips, fill Valerie's car with petrol, fetch dry-cleaning or go on myriad other errands. These were all tasks that Valerie's long-suffering husband had performed and which Valerie had neither the energy nor the desire to attempt herself yet.

Claire tried to help by washing and ironing and helping their mother with her hair and make-up, but all too often she found herself snapped at and rebuffed.

'You have a go with her, then,' she'd moan to Jude and retreat to her old bedroom with her tarot cards and a box of tissues. Valerie didn't try all that harder with Jude, but Jude didn't mind so much and kept calm.

She was very much aware that Mark seemed able to manage Claire. He'd tease her in what Jude had assumed was a brotherly manner; he would put his arm round Claire easily. He had a sister, Catherine, a year or two younger than himself, and showed a friendly way with women that Jude had always appreciated. So she didn't take much notice of how he and Claire were with one another.

But it was now that a certain cameo rose out of the confused images of that awful period, a period that she usually tried to blot from her mind.

She and Valerie had left to drive over to Gran's for the afternoon, but a mile or two out of the city, Valerie realized she hadn't got her handbag and insisted Jude turn round to fetch it. Jude was annoyed; why couldn't her mother exist without her handbag for the afternoon? She slewed the car to a halt out in the road, then, remembering that the key was in the handbag and Mark was out seeing an old school friend, stomped down the side path to find the spare key in its hiding place in the greenhouse. She glanced in through the living-room window and a flicker of movement caught her eye. She stared, and Mark stared back. He was lying on the sofa, and Claire was stretched out across him. Numb with shock, Jude got the key, grabbed the handbag from the hall and tore off without speaking.

Later that evening he insisted to Jude that Claire was exhausted from crying. He had been preparing to go out when she had come to the front door, and finding everyone out had sat down to talk to him about their father and how difficult Valerie was being, and ended up weeping uncontrollably. What else could he do but comfort her? That was all. Jude was overreacting.

Jude was so angry and uncertain, she spent that night on the sofa bed in the box room. She just wanted to be on her own, she told Mark, while she thought things out. But as Mark stuck to his version, and her memory of what she'd seen faded into all the other confused events of that time, she came to accommodate it and let the matter go. Anyway, Claire started referring to someone called Jon she'd met through her evening job behind the bar in the arts centre and soon the crisis was over.

It's funny. It was only now, thinking about Claire and Euan, that she remembered it at all. If Claire had been trying to bring the matter up, what on earth were her motives – kind or unkind? Was it really some strange attempt to knock Mark off his pedestal and make Jude come to terms with the fact that he'd gone? Was she trying some trick of one-upmanship in the game of love? Or was there something else she was trying to convey?

The revelation that struck her then was too awful to be borne, and she thrust it away.

Chapter 28

On Saturday morning, Jude felt tired and grouchy. Tonight she'd agreed to go camping and she didn't think Claire would be that pleased. She was weary. In some ways she thought she'd be better off going away. She'd been at Starbrough Hall two weeks, two of her precious three weeks of working holiday, and she ought to decide what she was going to do with the rest. It was difficult to see how she could take a proper holiday as such. She could pass the time in Greenwich, she supposed. There was research she could do from there, then make arrangements for the books and the scientific instruments to be packed up and brought to the office. Yet part of her felt bad at the idea of leaving Summer when she was so troubled. And there were so many ends left untied – the business of Tamsin Lovall, for one.

Perhaps she ought to stay. Despite assurance from Chantal, she felt squeamish about letting the Wickhams have her for a third week. They must be pretty fed up with their guest by now, though they were kind enough not to show it. And staying with Claire was not, at the moment, a comfortable proposition, and not just because of the lumpy mattress.

She turned on her laptop to see if she had any messages. It seemed not, until she noticed that an email from Cecelia dated the day before was sitting in her spam box. It must have gone there because the title was in capital letters with half a dozen exclamation marks. YOU MUST READ THIS!!!!!! She clicked on it quickly, and the message she read made her forget all her thoughts about leaving.

Hey, Jude,

I went to the British Library after we spoke, and just for fun I fed 'Josiah Bellingham' into the catalogue search engine. And what came up – ta da! – but his unpublished diary. I ordered it up straight away and – well, you won't believe what I found. I've copied out the relevant bits out for you and here they are!

Jude quickly downloaded the attachment and began to read.

From the unpublished diary of Josiah Bellingham, maker of optickal instruments and supplier to the Astronomer Royal.

31 December 1778

I left my sister Fawcett's this morning after breakfast and rode for two hours, reaching Starbrough Hall at eleven. There I found my journey to be wasted, Wickham being several days dead, God rest his soul, the girl vanished, and Wickham's harpy of a sister, one Mrs Adolphus Pilkington, in situ with her husband and their son, a thin bookish spawn by the name of Augustus. None recalled seeing the letter dispatched two days before announcing my impending arrival. I stated my business: to learn more about a strange comet or nebula the woman Esther had seen in the sky. I had written to the gentlemen of the Astronomical Society on the matter, I told the Pilkingtons, and they had bid me explore it further. Mr Pilkington, a genial enough gentleman, though he limped badly from gout, bade me dine with them, which we did well on mince pie and rabbits smothered in onion. On questioning them both I learned a sorry tale. Wickham, being a childless bachelor and a person of solitary habits, had come, in the manner of a foolish old man, to dote on a poor foundling girl he'd rescued from the roadside and she had used her wiles to tame him like a lamb on a string. He had lately named her his adopted daughter. Since his terrible accident in the tower, of which I was already acquainted and which left him helpless, she had made him her puppet and refused to entertain his beloved sister and the bookish nephew, being the rightful heir. Here Madam Pilkington muttered in aside that the girl had been in some way involved in the accident, but her good husband assured me later in private that there was no evidence for this. I enquired after the whereabouts of the girl. 'Gone,' was all they'd say. It appears that soon after the Pilkingtons arrived, she'd fled the scene they knew not where or what goods or money she might have taken with her. 'She was a wicked girl,' Madam Pilkington asserted, 'and Starbrough Hall is well rid of her.' I do not think I like Madam Pilkington.

At this outburst the maid waiting on us at table dropped her burden of plates with a crash and fled the room weeping. 'You'll see how distressing even the mention of Esther is to them,' intoned the wretched dame as she rose from the table. Only I saw the look of pure hatred the butler darted her as he hurried to repair the mess.

My instincts screamed at me to leave, but my intellectual curiosity was not yet satisfied. Were there notebooks, I asked, which I might consult regarding my mission? Madam Pilkington didn't know and by her tone didn't care, but she gave me leave to enter Anthony Wickham's library. I was struck at once by the beauty of the room, its unusual oval shape and the range of scholarship displayed on its shelves. Luxuriant as a cow in clover I grazed the shelves, lifting out one delight after another, then examined the collection of spyglasses, marvelling how he had constructed such wonderful instruments from the lenses I'd ground for him. That I'd

*not met with him again before his death seemed suddenly tragic,
and the girl's mysterious disappearance a damned nuisance and a
puzzle, for I discerned that this pair, the Pilkingtons, were hiding
information from me. Still, what could I, a mere acquaintance of
the dead man, do about any of this? I discovered several journals
stacked on one shelf. Two more lay on the desk. I perused all these
and noted their contents, but the most recent entry was from over
a year ago and there was no mention of the strange celestial object
of which the girl had written to me. Any more recent volume, I
discerned, must be missing, and a further search proved fruitless.*

My work here was done.

*'Should the girl Esther reappear, I should be glad to correspond
with her,' I told the Pilkington harpy. 'Or if you discover the final
journal book, send for me. It may be that your brother's work yields
discoveries germane to our knowledge of the skies, and if so I should
be glad to represent it to the authorities on his behalf. Your servant,
sir, madam,' and so I departed with mixed feelings – of relief at
leaving these people, but also of deep unease.*

*I passed the night at the market town of Attleborough. At one
o'clock I was woken by a huge storm of hail and snow and a wind
so great I felt with a great terror my bedstead rock under me. It was
another day and a night before the weather turned clement enough
for me to set forth for London once more and home.*

So Bellingham did come, Jude told herself, closing the file. But
what on earth happened to Esther? She missed showing him the
planet that she and her father had found; that was awful. She
emailed Cecelia, asking, 'What you've found is both wonderful
and terrible. Is that all? Were there no further relevant diary
entries?'

There was no immediate reply. She rang Cecelia's mobile,
but only got a message to say she should try again later. She

prowled up and down the library, thinking and thinking what she should do next. In particular, had Esther written any more, and if so had it survived?

She stared at the cupboard. She'd found the wodge of pages fallen down a gap at the back. What if she hadn't got them all out? She opened the doors, took out all the charts and pushed her hand through the gap at the back, trying to feel about. The arc her fingers traced met with nothing but brick and mortar dust. She retreated, nursing scraped knuckles, and considered the possibilities. Of course, if need be, she could ask Robert about removing the back of the cupboard, but that seemed an act of vandalism and she ought to try to see if it was justified. Surely, she thought, anything that had dropped through the gap couldn't have fallen very far. If only she could see . . .

She went to find Alexia and asked to borrow a torch and a hand mirror. Alexia, whom she found on her hands and knees clearing up the play room, came immediately to help. At first Jude, angling the mirror and shining the torch about, could see nothing much at all, but then . . . there was some paper lying just out of reach. Eventually, using a wire coat hanger and some double-edged sticky tape Alexia brought her, she netted a dozen more pages in the familiar handwriting.

'But that really seems to be it,' she told Alexia.

'Thank goodness,' Alexia said. 'I don't like loose ends.' And she went back to sorting toys.

Jude eagerly began to read.

I can hardly bear to write of those last days. As the season of Advent prepares us for news of a joyful birth at Christmas, in Starbrough we prepared ourselves for my father's passing. He was too weak to be taken outside that autumn, nay he had lost the will to sweep the skies and he ordered the great telescope to be returned to the

tower, though I kept the precious specula in their box in the library
for polishing. I tended him carefully those days, as though he were
an infant, helping him eat what little he would, and washing him,
with Betsy's help to turn him, though he was light now and so piti-
fully wasted you could see the blood move in his veins.

He slept much of the day and near Christmas Dr Brundall
visited and told me it was only a matter of time. I should send for
his sister, and though it riled me, so I did. None could say I shirked
my duty there.

They did not come immediately, the Pilkingtons. They dallied.
Only later did I find out why. And so it came to pass that their
carriage drew up outside just after the post-horse left Starbrough
Hall bearing letters announcing its master's death. With them
was Mr Atticus, an attorney from Norwich. Not Father's ancient
Mr Wellbourne, but a young man with a plausible manner and a
mercurial brain. They all crowded into my father's bedroom and
contemplated his poor meagre body with a horrifying disinterest.
Only Augustus showed distress, turning as pale and inert as the
corpse. I drew him from the room and tried to comfort him with
what few broken words I could find.

Alicia's voice flew about the house with orders that beds be made
up and furniture rearranged, that the parson be summoned to
discuss the funeral. It was her obvious lack of grief that incensed
me most. She offered no consolation for Susan's tears nor Mrs
Godstone's faded weariness, but instead complained about over-
cooked herring and undercooked puddings and ordered Father's
favourite old greyhound be shot, for the sight of its mange offended
her. I told her, as calmly as I could, though I was fair stirred up,
that I'd like to speak to Parson Orbison myself about the burial, for
Father had once told me he wished to be buried by the folly and this
I would like to arrange if he would allow it. At this she stormed
about the room, shouting about respectable Wickhams being buried

in the churchyard and I said, 'It's no good losing your temper, ma'am, I'm merely repeating his wishes,' but that did not make her see reason.

Finally she calmed down a bit and said we'd see what the parson said when he came, then she called Mr Trotwood and entrusted him with a letter to be taken directly to Mr Wellbourne in his chambers. 'He must visit us tomorrow to read the will, should it suit him,' she told us, but if the tone of her letter were as sinister as her words, he would know that it must suit him very well.

Mr Orbison visited as darkness fell and stayed to dinner. Since the ground in the churchyard was hard as stone, he said, he could only imagine it would be worse on the hill where frost had lain thick these past weeks. And he would not, he added, holding aloft his wine glass like the Holy Chalice, have anything more to do with a place that was so obviously a pagan graveyard. Alicia's eyes gleamed with triumph and her smile was like the flicker of a snake's tongue. I dared say nothing more on the subject.

The following morning when Betsy opened the door to Father's lawyer, Mr Wellbourne, an icy draught blew through the house. We all sat in the dining room, he and Mr Atticus at opposite ends of the table, Alicia and Adolphus to one side, myself and Mr Trotwood on the other. The rest of the household stood around the room and Mr Corbett fed the fire. Early in the proceedings Augustus was found listening at the door and his mother snapped at him to come in and hold his tongue.

Mr Wellbourne read the will in his cracked, whistling voice. It seemed to continue for pages and pages, but eventually he came to the meat. Alicia was granted the sum of £3000, some items of furniture and the portrait of their mother hanging in my father's chamber. Several hundred pounds were to be shared amongst the staff. A donation was made to the Royal Astronomical Society. The rest: house, lands, chattels, money, were bequeathed to Esther

Wickham, 'my adopted daughter'. There was a collective sigh from the servants as Mr Wellbourne laid down the papers and removed his spectacles. Susan caught my eye and smiled. Mr Corbett winked, I swear it. I looked at Alicia. Her face was as tranquil as a summer's day before a storm, but seeing the threatening wisp of cloud in her eye, I knew a deep fear.

At the other end of the table, Mr Atticus harrumphed and began. 'Mistress Pilkington, Mr Pilkington, Mr Wellbourne, if I may. I must declare this will null and void forthwith.' The room fell still as the frozen park outside. 'You say, sir, that it was drawn up and signed last April, but this was after Mr Wickham fell and sustained the blow that eventually killed him and I am of the opinion that he was not of sound mind. I have written evidence from the doctor who tended him.'

'Dr Brundall?' cried Mr Wellbourne. 'But he is one of the witnesses to the document.'

'You will see here this letter dated the thirtieth of April last.' Mr Atticus held up a single sheet. 'It is in response to one Mrs Pilkington wrote Dr Brundall concerning her brother's condition. I quoth: 'I advise you to put off visiting your brother, for he is still weak, easily tired and occasionally muddled of mind.'

'I tell you,' repeated Mr Wellbourne. 'He witnessed the will. Why would he have done that if he judged his patient to be of unsound mind? We must interview him to clarify the matter.'

And so the argument went round and round. Mr Atticus demanded to see the original will which Mr Wellbourne said was drawn up before my arrival, but Mr Wellbourne had left it in Norwich. Alicia put in that she would honour all bequests made to servants in the new will, which lightened the atmosphere in some quarters of the room but not mine. The matter was adjourned until the old will be found and Dr Brundall made an affadavit. The carpenter arrived with the coffin and so the meeting dispersed.

That night I sat for an hour with Father in his room. He was dressed in his best suit and arranged in the open coffin in such a manner that he appeared merely asleep. I wept for him and kissed him farewell, for tomorrow the hearse would come and the coffin be closed and we'd follow him to the churchyard where he, the star-keeper, who had swept the heavens and explored the highest reaches of the human mind, would be buried in a dark hole to be gouged in the frozen ground. At eleven o'clock I retired to my room and, worn out by the sorrow and anxiety of the day, slept deeply without dreaming.

The writing here was less firm, and blurred in places as though by tears, and Jude stopped reading and sat staring into the distance, trying to imagine what it had been like for Esther, to lose her beloved father and feel she was losing everything. Awful. Should she read on or stop and transcribe the bit she'd just read? Read on, she decided, but at this point there came a knock on the door and Euan came in.

'I won't disturb you,' he said. 'I've come to see Robert. Just wanted to confirm with you that tonight's on. Fiona and her husband are coming for supper and I've told Claire she'll have a tent mate.'

'Was Claire all right about it?' Jude asked.

'I think so. Why shouldn't she be?' Euan asked, sounding surprised.

'Oh, no reason.' She changed the subject. 'Euan, I've found some more pages of Esther's journal. It's awfully sad. I must tell you—'

'And I'd love to hear about it. But Robert seemed a bit impatient. I'd better go. See you this evening. I said seven o'clock to Claire.'

Do you really not know why Claire would mind, you marvellous man? Jude mouthed, as he went off to Robert's study. She slumped in her seat, all energy suddenly gone. Perhaps he was completely unaware of her sister's interest in him. Or of hers. She sighed. Well, she'd have to go to the sleepover now. Heck, when had she last slept in a tent?

She was turning back to Esther's memoir when the door opened once more. It was Alexia again.

'How are you getting on?' she asked Jude.

'With Esther? Oh, fascinating. I—'

'Good, I am pleased. I've just bumped into your friend Euan rushing down the corridor, and he tells me you're camping this evening. So I thought I'd come and ask you if you needed anything. I've got a couple of sleeping bags if you want to borrow one. Would you like to come and choose?'

'Oh, thank you,' Jude said, standing up. She'd have to finish reading Esther later.

'I kept mine from Guides,' Alexia told her as they went upstairs, 'though you might prefer Robert's. It's warmer.'

'I imagine you would have been a jolly good Girl Guide,' Jude said, laughing. 'Always prepared.'

Alexia smiled and performed a mock salute. 'I think we've got a lilo somewhere, too. Anyway, let's get you kitted out.'

'Alexia, you're amazing,' Jude told her as they reached a spare bedroom full of fitted cupboards, from which the mistress of the house started dragging items out. 'You put up with an extra guest for two weeks, and pull sleeping bags out of hats, all without seeming to mind a bit. But I must be a real nuisance.'

'Honestly, you're not,' Alexia said, giving her a hug. 'I've always loved looking after people. It's the one thing that really makes me happy. And I meant to tell you, if you want to stay next week as well, please do. We'd love to have you!'

'Are you sure? You must have read my mind.'

'I've already talked to Robert about it. Of course we're sure. Now, there's that one and this one, and I might even have a blow-up pillow somewhere.'

Jude packed herself an overnight bag and was ready by six. At last, she told herself. She simply must read the rest of Esther's memoir; she had to know what happened. She slipped along to the library, settled herself at the desk and began to read. She read and she read it again, and only when her phone rang and it was Euan to ask where she was, did she push the pages away reluctantly and leave the house. So deep in the eighteenth-century past was she, it was as though Esther walked beside her all the way.

Chapter 29

It was difficult to drag herself out of her thoughts, but if anyone could do it, it was Claire, flirting with Euan.

'Will you put the tent up for us, Euan?' Claire wheedled, as bossy as her daughter.

'I think I can manage that.'

'And can we *possibly* borrow your shower in the morning?'

'Yes, I can allow that, too.'

'And – how about breakfast in bed?'

Euan threw back his head and laughed.

'It's all right for you, you're sleeping in a nice comfortable room.'

'I'm almost tempted to come and join you. The smell of paint in the cottage is awful.'

'Well, if you don't mind sharing my sleeping bag . . .' Claire said, fluttering her eyelashes.

Jude listened to this exchange with some amazement and not a little envy, that her sister possessed this easy teasing way with men. Euan just seemed to be friendly, as normal.

The evening, despite Jude's fears, was a great success. Darcey's parents, Paul and Fiona, joined them. First Euan cooked burgers and sausages on a barbecue in the field. They all ate them with rolls and salad. Ice cream and fruit followed. Paul had brought his guitar and they sat around the glowing barbecue singing silly songs from Paul's extraordinary repertoire. Then, it being nearly nine-thirty and the little girls eager to start the next part of the adventure, Paul and Fiona said goodbye and Euan made hot chocolate, which they drank looking up at the stars, which were just starting to burn overhead. 'My star's over there, I think,' Summer said.

'Darling, you can't possibly see it,' Claire said, 'though you're quite right, it is near Arcturus in Boötes.'

'I don't mind not seeing it. I think it can see me,' Summer retorted, which Jude thought a nice sentiment.

'I expect it's watching over you,' she told Summer.

'And me,' Darcey echoed, not really understanding.

Claire helped Darcey and Summer into their pyjamas and anointed them with insect repellent, then Jude elected to read to them from the book of fairy stories that Summer had brought with her, though Claire wasn't very pleased about it and stomped off into the house, her limp pronounced accusingly. The girls chose *Rapunzel*, so Jude adjusted the hurricane lamp and settled herself in the bed with a girl either side of her.

' "Once upon a time," ' she read, ' "there were a man and a woman who longed for a child of their own. They lived next door to a nasty old witch, and usually they kept out of her way, but one day when the woman looked out of her window she saw some most delicious-looking salad growing in the witch's garden and she wanted some very badly indeed. Eventually, one moonlit night, she persuaded her husband to gather her some, but the witch caught him at it." '

Jude went on to tell how he bargained for their lives, and that the price was to give her their first child. 'When a little girl was born to them, the witch came and took her. She named her Rapunzel and when she was twelve and very beautiful the witch took her far away and locked her up in the top of a tall tower without a door and with only one window.'

'Why did she do that?' asked Darcey.

'Because the witch thought she was precious, a thing to be kept safe and all to herself.'

'That's not a good thing to do to someone,' said Summer. 'If she'd been free she might have liked the witch.'

'I think she was such a nasty old witch no one liked her,' said Jude firmly. 'Fancy taking away someone's child like that. Now, shall we get on with the story?

' "Rapunzel grew up to be very lovely. She had very long, strong golden hair, which she kept tied in a single plait, like a piece of silken rope. And every evening when she came to visit her in the tower, the witch would cry out from below, 'Rapunzel, Rapunzel, let down your golden hair,' and Rapunzel would unfurl her lovely plait and allow the witch to climb up it." '

There were no further interruptions from the girls, and Jude read how one day a prince came riding by and saw the tower and was enchanted to hear the beautiful voice of a girl, singing. When the witch came he hid behind a tree and saw how she climbed up the tower with the help of the owner of the voice, who was the prettiest girl he'd ever seen. After the witch had gone, he stood below her window and cried, 'Rapunzel, Rapunzel, let down your golden hair,' and you can imagine Rapunzel's astonishment when a handsome youth climbed up her plait and stepped through her window. Of course, the two of them fell in love, and for many days afterwards the prince visited Rapunzel in secret and she agreed to be his wife. They discussed over and over how on earth he could free her.

'And now comes the horrible part,' Summer told Darcey.

' "One day, when the witch climbed up to see Rapunzel, the girl complained and said, 'The other one doesn't pull my hair so,' then clapped her hand over her mouth as she realized that she'd betrayed her lover. The witch pretended not to have noticed her slip, but after she left the tower she hid herself in the forest to watch. When she saw the prince cry up to Rapunzel, and her darling captive respond eagerly to his request to let down her hair, she threw herself into a fair old rage. But when she'd calmed down again, she thought up a plan. The very next day she went earlier than usual to the tower and climbed up Rapunzel's hair. This time she overcame Rapunzel, tied her to a chair and cut off her plait with a single swish of her knife and kept it for herself. Then she banished the girl to a desert." '

'How did Rapunzel get to the desert?' Darcey asked, confused.

'Same way she got up into the tower in the first place,' Jude answered. 'Magic.

' "The prince came and waited as usual, but when the witch did not visit Rapunzel at the set time he shrugged and went to stand under the window and called up. The silken rope of hair snaked down and he grabbed it and started to climb. But when he came to the window it wasn't the beautiful face of his beloved he saw, but the wizened, warty old features of the wicked witch. 'I curse you to see beauty no more,' shrieked the witch and she let go of the plait so that the young man fell. He landed in a bramble thicket where the nasty thorns, obeying the witch's curse, scratched out his eyes." '

Aware of the girls' own horrified eyes upon her, Jude glanced ahead to the next paragraph. No, it was going to be all right.

' "The prince wandered blind in the wilderness for many years, relying on the kindness of people he met to feed and clothe him, and searching for his lost wife. Eventually, he stumbled through a desert and found her, living in a humble hut with their twin children. She recognized him instantly and embraced him, and her tears of pity at his blindness and his rags fell upon his face. His eyes were healed and he saw her, worn by sorrow and hardship, but still, to him, his beautiful Rapunzel." '

She put the book down and they all sat quietly in thought for a moment.

'Come on, it's time to snuggle down now,' Jude said. The bed, with its soft mattress, was made up with sheets and a duvet with a cover in a patchwork pattern that complemented the paintwork. 'This is so lovely, isn't it?'

'Mmm,' said Darcey, who snuggled down straight away.

Summer lay on the nearer side of the bed, quietly looking up at the ceiling, her eyes shining in the dusky light. 'I'm so glad Rapunzel and the prince found each other,' she murmured.

'And that he was made better,' Jude agreed. 'It's really a story of how love wins through over everything, isn't it? Things weren't just happy ever after, though, they probably some difficulties to overcome first, but at least they were all together . . . Now, how are we going to manage things here? Will you two be all right if I shut the door? You'll still get some moonlight in, but it'll be warmer.' There were insect nets nailed over the window openings, and a curtain above the doorway, so everything could be adjusted for comfort. 'I'm going into the cottage for a very little bit to chat to Euan and your mum, Summer, but then we'll be sleeping in the tent, so you'll know where to find us.

Summer nodded sleepily. Jude so hoped she wouldn't have bad dreams tonight.

When she went into the cottage, she knew at once that something had happened. The atmosphere was charged with tension. Claire and Euan both glanced up at her unhappily. 'Is something wrong?' she asked.

'No, we're fine,' Claire said quickly, and looked away. It was bewildering. Jude didn't know whether her presence was welcome or not.

'Have some more wine,' Euan almost ordered her, so she perched on the edge of his new sofa and made small talk.

When the mood failed to lighten she left half the glass undrunk on the coffee table and said, 'Anyone mind if I use the bathroom? I'm off to bed.'

'Me, too,' said Claire.

She and Claire crept out to the field together ten minutes later. Claire peeped into the caravan, then went straight into the tent without a word. Jude looked, too. Both girls seemed to be sleeping peacefully.

Jude changed quickly into pyjamas and bedsocks and got into her sleeping bag, then lay listening to her sister settling herself. 'Goodnight,' she called and Claire mumbled a reply. Feeling surprisingly warm and comfortable Jude lay thinking over the day's events, and less comfortably about Euan and Claire, though she couldn't make sense of that. She tried various hypotheses, then pushed the matter away. Her thoughts moved on to the final part of Esther's memoir. She hadn't had a chance to tell anyone about it yet; she hadn't really assimilated it herself, it was so awful and astonishing.

Chapter 30

I rose early the next morning, dressed myself in my black, and was breaking my fast alone when a letter came. Seeing from the familiar hand that it was from Mr Bellingham. I returned to the dining room and opened it eagerly. The message it contained put me in such confusion I had to sit down. The news was just as my father had hoped. Bellingham was interested enough to make representations to the Astronomical Society about the strange comet we had seen and intended to visit us a few days hence. We should be recognized for our discovery! But how terrible that it was too late for my father! I read the letter once more and paced the room, considering. Eventually, I decided. I would not give up our quest. I would stand in my father's place and present our findings with confidence, no matter that I was just a girl. Nor would I apprise the Pilkingtons of his visit, not yet. With luck my inheritance might be proved and they departed for home disappointed by the time he came.

I heard footsteps in the hall and hurriedly concealed the letter in the drawer of a console table. Not a moment too soon for the door opened and Augustus came in. He stopped, hand resting on the door knob, embarrassed to find me there alone.

'Isn't my mother downstairs yet?' he asked awkwardly.

'I have not seen her,' I replied. I felt suddenly sorry for him, this tall, skinny ghost of a boy, caught up in the whirl of his mother's ambition. He had admired my father. Had anyone ever asked what he wanted in this matter? I thought not.

The day passed in a haze of grief. We all shivered through the funeral itself and the lowering of the coffin into the cold earth, then pretended to be civilized and sociable together over a cold collation in the dining room. It was surprising how many relatives my father still had – mostly elderly cousins or their bedraggled relicts who came out of either curiosity or some vestige of family feeling, or because they were glad of a free dinner. It was a dismal affair, coloured only by the livid glances that Alicia shot me every time I crossed her line of vision.

After the last carriage departed with its last drably dressed occupant, I slipped away to the library to be quiet and alone. There I found the latest of the observation journals and passed an hour or two marking up the relevant passages ready for Bellingham's visit. It struck me as I did so that it would be useful to sweep the skies tonight for the object in question. It might have moved into Gemini from Taurus, where we'd seen it last March. Suddenly it seemed important to find out. Last night, I'd noticed from the sanctuary of my room, the skies had been cloudless and the wintry stars burned bright, their colours clear. Tired as I was, I was fired with a desire to try tonight.

Supper consisted of the remains of the funeral breakfast. Only Uncle Adolphus ate with appetite, breaking open a bottle of the best port from my father's meagre cellar. The rest of us picked at our food in stiff silence. I wondered whether Alicia had received communication from her Mr Atticus today, but if so she wasn't saying. Father's Mr Wellbourne had attended the funeral, of course, but for some reason he had not come on to the Hall afterwards and there had been no opportunity to speak with him. My future depended on a struggle over a legal document. No one had suggested what might happen to me should Alicia's side win. I did not think I could stay on at Starbrough Hall, even if she would allow it. But where else could I go? I took another gulp of my port for warmth and courage and excused myself, saying I was going to the library to read and from thence to bed.

Once safe in the library I made my final preparations. Quite how I was to carry the specula, instruments I needed, the journal and a lantern, I did not know, but then I remembered a small handcart, generally kept in the stables to carry firewood and straw and the like. I waited for time to pass, and when ten o'clock struck and the house gradually settled into silence, I crept out into the dark. I threw the yard dogs some bread so they should not bark. My little cat rubbed up against me in the moonlight. The warmth of her fur and the stamping and snorting of Castor and Pollux in their stalls and the sweet smell of their manure were all so familiar and comforting I almost wept at the thought that I might ever have to leave.

The cart had side rails to which I could secure my packages with string, and was so light I could half carry it round to the side of the house and thus avoid trundling it noisily over the stable yard, though my hands near froze on its metal handles. Thick gloves and cord were two more items I must fetch.

One by one, I brought out the astrolabe and the box containing the specula and tied them firmly into the cart. A bag containing a lantern, some smaller instruments and the journal fitted neatly on top. I felt for the key to the tower, deep in the pocket of my dress. It was time to depart.

By this time skeins of cloud had started to drift across the nascent moon, telling me to hurry, for thicker might follow and the night be wasted. I set off, dragging my little cart, squeak, squeak, squeak, across the park, down a slope across the ha-ha, bumping it over the rougher ground towards the woods. The task proved awkward, the cart's cargo rattling alarmingly over every hummock, and once I gained the narrow path up through the wood, the wheels caught on brambles and bracken. What seemed like hours later, but was

probably half of one, I reached the tower, unlocked the door and lit
my lantern. Then came the task of transporting everything up to
the top. Twice, I had to mount those steps, then to climb the peril-
ous ladder and push open the trapdoor to attain the platform. All
this I managed without slipping or dropping any part. This done,
I set off down the steps for the last time to fetch the last package.

It was when I was walking upstairs again that I heard a
rumbling noise below and stopped, alive to a sudden terror. Before
I'd decided whether to race down or retreat up, there came the
slam of the door and the clink of the key turning. I was locked in.
Was the danger within or without? The shriek of metal on metal
told me someone had slid the outside bolt. Without. I ran down
the stairs and dashed straight into the cart. Bruised and shak-
ing, I picked myself up and banged on the locked door with my
fists and shouted. Then waited. And shouted again. And waited.
There was nothing and nobody.

And that had been the end of Esther's memoir. It was so frustrat-
ing. There had been only one more piece of paper, tear-stained
and crumpled. On it Esther had written in an uncharacteristi-
cally untidy scrawl just three short sentences. Jude had read
them several times in the library and now, as she lay in the
dark, she tried to remember them. Yes, that was right:

I have been here three days and three nights without food or water
or fire. No one comes. I fear to die here alone.

It was as though she heard Esther's voice in her head.

And drifting into sleep now in the warmth of the tent the
same thing happened as had that time when she'd read about
the creation of the library; it was as though she were there with
Esther, experiencing what happened next . . . as in a dream . . .

On the first night, Esther told herself that it would be all right in the morning. Whoever it was who'd imprisoned her here would be back to explain and let her out. It was a jape, perhaps, or an accident, or done to scare her. She wondered who could have followed her here. The gamekeeper, perhaps, thinking with the master dead that it could only be an intruder. Most likely it was something to do with Alicia. She considered the matter over and over. They'd be looking for her. Susan would search. So would Sam and Matt. Someone had to.

Finally, for courage, she forced herself to continue in her purpose. With some difficulty she wound back the canopy, fitted the specula to the telescope and searched the skies for the curious object she'd found. But tonight there was no sign. It was too late in the year, she decided; a gibbous moon was rising, dimming the stars, and as the night progressed a curtain of thick cloud blotted them out altogether. It began, very gently, to snow. Esther pulled off her gloves to catch the flakes in her upturned hands and lick them up thirstily. Then she climbed down the ladder, shutting the trapdoor, and went to curl up on the small mattress her father kept there. It was damp, but she laid a piece of oil cloth over it and wrapped her cloak around her. She slept fitfully.

The morning was drear and cold, the air smelt of metal. She climbed to the top of the tower, but all she could see was a thick mist. She cried out for help again and again, but her voice sounded small and dull, and when she listened there came no answering call. She half-crawled all the way downstairs and tried the door once more. It was still locked, and all her kicking and shaking barely disturbed its great oak solidity, nor was there any gap to insert a lever, even if she could find something to lever with. She retired upstairs once more.

Next she pulled the journal out of its bag and tore out several pages. On each she wrote a message, then she found two small

lumps of flint her father had collected and kept, and a bit of brick,
wrapped a paper round each one and dropped them from the roof,
praying she'd not be unlucky enough to hit any person or animal.
If she was still there this evening – she hardly dare think of that –
she could light a candle, but there were only a couple left, together
with a collection of stubs, so she wouldn't waste them now. She
paced the room, hardly knowing what to do with herself, panic
rising and ebbing, only to rise again, as she struggled to master
her fears. Twice she gave way to bouts of sobbing, but when she was
calm again she told herself, 'This will not do.' She would survive
this. Whoever had left her in this plight would not prevail. Her
mutilated journal lay on the table. There was a bottle of ink and
several pens in a cupboard. As it had many times before, as they'd
sat out on the roof together, she and her father, the ink had frozen.
Now she warmed the bottle in her hands, then seized a pen, dipped
it in and drew the book towards her. Like Sir Walter Raleigh and
John Bunyan when they were prisoners, she would keep her sanity
by writing. And if she were found too late, then all could read her
story. It would be the story of her life.

She began to write.

'An Account of Esther Wickham . . .'

For three days she wrote out the details of her short brave existence,
lived as it had been within the confines of Starbrough Hall and the
village. In her fifteen and a half years she had hardly been beyond
it, never seen Norwich and its fine Norman cathedral, never visited
Yarmouth to see the herring boats come in, never seen the vast
North Sea crash on the shingle. But she had surveyed some of
the greatest secrets of the universe, had studied the infinite skies
above all, seen other planets, seen stars winking at her from who
knew how many millions of miles and millions of years away. She
was young in years but old in knowledge and wisdom. She was a

girl who'd lost her beginnings and might soon know her end. She finished her account with a terrible sense of grief; she'd lost the man she'd come to love as her father, and who had rescued her and learned to love her. She'd probably lost the home he'd intended be hers for ever. She remembered with a terrible pang of anticipated loss that today was the day Josiah Bellingham said he'd come – he'd go without seeing her or learning more about the great discovery she and her father had made. She'd lost that, too.

Finally, as dusk gathered and the third night fell, she put down her pen. She had one candle left and a little oil. She would stand the lantern on the roof tonight and hope someone would see it.

Outside, in the caravan, Summer was dreaming, too. She cried out once, but Esther and Claire merely stirred in their sleep. And Summer's dreams and Esther's began to merge . . .

And in the morning, when the women awoke, Summer Claire Keating had gone.

Chapter 31

Daylight. Jude heard Claire stir, then unzip her compartment and crawl out. She eased herself uncomfortably over onto her back – the lilo had definitely leaked air in the night – and willed herself to get up. It was hot in the tent and her sleep had been troubled; unrecognizable remnants of dreams still floated through her mind, dreams full of violence and howling loss. She remembered suddenly the uncomfortable scene last night, when she'd gone in to find Claire curled up, tired and emotional, on Euan's new sofa, empty glasses everywhere, and Euan standing awkwardly by the window, a bottle of lager in one hand. Neither said what had happened, but Jude was still sure something had. Both parties had seemed relieved when she decided to go to bed and they'd followed her example.

'Darcey, where's Summer?' she heard Claire ask outside. 'Has she gone in to the loo?'

'I dunno,' she heard Darcey reply.

'I'll go and look.'

A worm of worry started to gnaw away in Jude's mind, something to do with her dream. She disentangled herself from her sleeping bag and, shuffling into her trainers, crawled out of the tent in her pyjamas. She went to the door of the caravan, where Darcey was sitting up in bed, her thumb in her mouth.

'Hi, did you sleep well, darling?' she asked the girl.

'Mmm,' Darcey replied. 'Where's Summer?'

'I think—' Jude started to say, but Claire's voice cut across hers.

'Jude, I can't find Summer.' Claire was loping towards them across the meadow.

'Is she not. . . ?'

'She's not in the cottage. Euan hasn't seen her.' As if at the mention of his name, Euan appeared, in jeans, pulling a T-shirt over his tanned chest, his face tired and unshaven.

'Have you found her?'

Claire shook her head quickly. She looked anxious.

'Summer?' called out Jude, and she started searching the perimeters of the meadow. Suddenly they were all calling and searching.

'The animals,' Jude cried, and ran over to the cages to see if Summer was studying the grass snake or talking to the owls. She wasn't.

'Summer? Come out now, please, you're frightening us.' Claire's face was pale, her voice trembly, full of unshed tears. Jude felt a cold touch of dread.

They searched the cottage again, then Euan combed the grounds, Darcey trailing after him, whingeing tearfully. Claire was manic, limping up and down the lane, calling, her breath in whooping pants. Euan phoned his sister, who said she'd be along at once. Then he took Darcey back over to the caravan, and Jude brought her something to eat and they gently questioned her. Had she seen Summer at all that morning? 'No.' Had she, Darcey, woken up at all in the night? 'Yes, no, maybe.' When Euan persisted, she turned her face into his chest and shook her head fiercely. 'I don't know,' she wailed.

Euan looked up at Jude. He seemed to have aged years in a few minutes, but managed to stay calm. He tried again.

'Darcey,' he asked gently, 'did you see Summer at all after Jude left you last night? Did she say anything to you?'

'I don't remember, I don't remember,' said Darcey, and she began to weep noisily and messily. Euan cuddled her and dug a paper serviette out of his jeans pocket to clean her up.

'Don't worry, darling, we'll find her,' Jude said. 'Euan, I must go and help Claire,' she said, getting up. 'Do you think it's time to ring the police?'

Euan nodded once and said in a low voice, 'In these cases there's no time to be lost.'

In these cases. Jude felt the blood rush from her face. That meant he thought Summer had been. . . . No, surely she'd just wandered off.

'Here's my phone,' she said, her voice croaky with emotion. 'Do you mind doing it? I must tell Claire.' She ran out of the meadow just as Fiona's car pulled up outside the house.

Claire was standing by the gate, her face drawn, her slender body trembling. 'Claire, dear,' Fiona said, starting towards her.

'Claire, Euan's calling the police,' Jude said quietly, putting her arm around her sister, thinking how light and thin she was. Claire didn't resist as they drew her back into the meadow to the caravan.

'They're on their way,' Euan said crisply. Fiona took Darcey from him and cuddled her. 'Look,' he said, 'can we go over what you think happened? Who was last to see Summer?'

'We looked into the caravan when we went to bed, didn't we, Claire?'

Claire nodded, glassy-eyed, her gaze roaming the trees around the meadow as though hoping Summer might emerge any moment, her pretty face stained with the juice of early blackberries, her honey hair in a glorious tangle, a dewy bunch of wild flowers in her hand. But no one came.

'And were they both there?'

'Yes, I think so,' Jude said. She tried hard to picture what they saw – yes, two little heads on the pillows, an arm flung across the edge of the bed, the fingers limp in sleep.

'Had she been nervous about anything before she went to sleep?'

'No, I don't think so.' Jude shook her head. 'I read to them both. Here.' She leaned into the caravan and rescued the book from the top of a little cabinet. '*Rapunzel*.' She turned to the story. There was the wicked witch with her pointed chin and hooked nose. There was the beautiful innocent girl and then, yes it was a bit gory, the prince with his face being torn by thorns.

Claire let out a cry. 'You read her this!' she said. 'No wonder she gets nightmares.'

Euan looked from Claire to Jude, surprised at Claire's outburst. 'Claire, ssshhh. It doesn't help to blame anyone.'

Jude felt stunned. Could the story really have upset Summer so much that she ran away? If she *had* run away. If she had run away she would be found and brought back. Jude wouldn't mind taking the blame, as long as Summer was brought back. But the thought that her sister was blaming her in any way was still horrible. She couldn't look at her. Her eye fell instead on the book. The pictures were a bit scarier than others in the book, she thought now. Suppose Summer had had bad dreams after seeing them last night and it disturbed her? But surely in that case she'd have cried out for help, not run off somewhere. She'd be too frightened to do that, surely.

The police came: a woman sergeant, oddly called Bride, and a constable who looked little more than a boy. They went over the story several times with Claire, Jude and Euan, asking many questions and conducting their own painstaking search of the premises. 'Look, for goodness sake,' Euan said, his cool cracking. 'She's not here, damn it, and we need to be out looking.'

'Of course, sir, we're merely trying to establish what we're dealing with here,' said Sergeant Bride.

She and the constable went off to look in the trees beyond the meadow. Soon Euan came back into the room to say he'd heard the woman speaking urgently on the telephone.

'We need to be out looking,' said Claire, standing up, a wild look in her eyes.

'Sit down,' ordered Euan. 'You're in no state to go rushing off.' She struggled briefly with him then gave up.

'I've got an idea,' Jude said quietly. All through the questioning, her mind had been working away. It was something to do with her dream, but she couldn't remember properly. 'Could she have gone up to the folly?'

'Why would she have done that? She was frightened of the place,' said Euan.

'I know, but I thought . . . reading about Rapunzel and the tower last night. Perhaps there's some connection. I mean, if she had one of her nightmares.'

'She's never done that before, though, has she? Gone off, I mean.'

'No, but then we're much closer to the folly here.'

'You mean it's calling her or something,' said Fiona, with a humourless laugh.

'It doesn't sound very likely to me,' said Euan heavily.

'Oh, who cares?' Claire cried out. 'It's a bloody awful idea, but it's an idea. Let's go and look.'

At that point the police officers re-entered the room. Sergeant Bride said, 'I've been speaking to HQ. They've recommended bringing a unit in.'

'Oh God,' said Claire, slumping in her chair.

'We ought to visit your neighbours, sir, and ask them to search.'

'I don't really have many,' said Euan, then he said, 'Well, there's Starbrough Hall, then Starbrough Hall Farm on the road towards the village. And another cottage between the farm and the village. I don't know the names of the people there.'

'I'll take Claire up to the folly,' said Jude. 'We'll walk in case we see . . . anything on the way.' She then felt she had to explain to the police officers about the bad dreams. 'We're afraid she might have sleepwalked,' she told them. They looked a bit sceptical, but the sergeant told the constable to accompany them. 'It's the only lead we have,' she told him.

Claire said suddenly, 'We haven't checked if any of her clothes are missing. She couldn't have walked off in her bare feet, could she?'

Jude wondered briefly whether sleepwalkers ever stopped to put shoes on, but when Claire, with a sudden spurt of energy, hurried outside, she followed. When she got to the caravan she saw Claire was sitting on the bed with Summer's capri pants and T-shirt laid across her lap. She was holding the little girl's cardigan to her face and her eyes were closed. Hearing Jude, she opened them again. 'Her sandals are gone,' she said happily. 'That's good, isn't it?' Then looked desperate again.

'I'm sure it's good,' Jude said, soothing. 'Come on, let's go and look.'

The constable seemed to have vanished somewhere, so they set off alone.

They half walked, half ran up the lane, Jude holding Claire's hand, until they came to the footpath sign. Jude hesitated. Would the child really have taken this wild and difficult path, or would she have hung on until she got to the easier lane to the folly? 'Think,' she told herself. Perhaps the thing to do would be to go up this footpath and come back by the lane.

'Up here,' she ordered Claire, plunging down the over-grown path.

It was even more overgrown than when she'd been down it last, and, stung by nettles and prickled by brambles, she came to doubt that Summer would ever have ventured this way.

Claire obviously felt the same. 'This isn't right. Can we go back?' Jude stopped, considering the path ahead. It didn't look as though anyone had passed through here for ages.

From behind there came a shout, and Euan came crashing through the vegetation. 'You might as well keep going,' he said. 'It'll be quicker now than going the other way round.'

As Jude had found last time, the going got easier as they passed into shady broadleaf woodland, and the loamy path widened. When they reached the gamekeeper's grim gibbet, Claire recoiled with a squeak of horror. 'Oh my God, I hope she didn't see that,' she whispered. 'It would have really freaked her.'

But they saw no clue that the little girl had passed this way at all. It was with some despondency that they came out into the sunlight of the clearing, but then Jude's heart leaped with hope.

'Look,' cried Euan.

The door of the folly was hanging open.

Claire started towards it, in her funny, hopping kind of run, and ducked inside. Euan caught up with her and started to climb the stairs first, while Jude helped her sister, not knowing whether to hope or to dread what lay ahead. When they stag-gered up round the final bend to meet Euan at the top, his face told his news. Summer wasn't there.

'Oh no,' cried Claire, collapsing on the floor, her breath coming in great rasping sobs.

As Jude tried to comfort her, Euan checked the roof. 'I shouldn't think anyone's been up here, but I'm just making sure.'

He pushed open the trapdoor and a shaft of sunlight fell down across the two women, like the hand of God in a medieval painting, Jude thought, dazzled, feeling transported into some other reality. A terrible other reality if Summer wasn't ever found. She had a sudden vision of the new course their lives would take if. . . .

'No, no one,' grunted Euan. She heard, rather than saw him close the portal, and when the gold swirls faded from her retinas, she found herself staring at a point in the wall behind the bookshelves where a brick had been pulled aside. The hiding place.

'She *has* been here,' Jude cried, getting up and hurrying over to the hole. 'We left it closed. But how did she know about this?'

'I don't know,' Euan said, stepping off the ladder and coming to join her. 'I never told her.'

He peeped inside. 'There's nothing there,' he said. 'What would she be looking for?'

'And how do we know it was Summer anyway?' Claire cried out harshly. 'It might have been someone else altogether. Summer was frightened of this place. Surely she wouldn't come alone and willingly . . .'

Her words hung in the air. Everyone thought at the same moment: what if she hadn't been alone? What if someone had brought her here . . . by force?

'Ludicrous . . .' he muttered to himself under his breath. 'Who else knew about this place and the hidey-hole. It's totally ridiculous to think anyone . . .'

Jude thought. Who else knew, indeed, apart from Gran? She cast her mind with difficulty over all the people she'd met at Starbrough. Who would know about the hidey-hole and to whom would it matter anyway? None of this made any sense.

Claire was clearly thinking the same thing, though, since she'd never been up here before, she was even more at sea than Jude.

'We still can't definitely say that Summer came here last night can we?'

'Or this morning,' Euan said absently. He started hunting around the place, looking for clues no doubt, Jude thought. But he found nothing. No trace of a little girl in Barbie-pink pyjamas.

Jude stepped over to help Claire to her feet. Her sister was silent, disconsolate, staring at the floor. As Jude put out her hand her eyes followed the direction of Claire's gaze. There was a small patch of crumbled mortar dust by the wall near the top of the stairs. In the middle was planted the perfectly formed print of a very small shoe.

'Don't touch it,' Jude whispered urgently as Claire put her hand out towards it. 'Look, we'd better get out of here in case the police . . .'

The others both looked at her, as through fog. The fog cleared.

'I think Jude's right,' Euan said slowly. 'Claire, we ought to go back without disturbing anything further.'

They both helped Claire down the stairs, then, each holding a hand, led her out of the clearing by the route that Euan had taken Jude that first time they met, to Foxhole Lane and down to the road. Jude's gaze flittered as they walked, looking for . . . well, anything that might say what had happened to Summer. As they reached the junction of the lane with the road a police car drew up and two officers, one the very young constable, got out. Euan took them back in the direction of the tower to show them what they'd seen. The women continued down the road to the cottage.

When they arrived it was to find the house transformed into an incident scene. There was a police van, another police car and several other vehicles, a German shepherd on a leash, and the sergeant was organizing a team of local people, including Robert and Steve, the farmer, to start searching the area. Fiona had been allowed to take Darcey home. Claire was sent to find an item of Summer's clothing to give the dog a scent, then she and Jude were told to sit on the sofa in the living room while a detective asked them more questions, and tried not to listen to the people all around them studying maps, talking about ditches and storm drains, the crackle of police radios, the endless recitation of the meagre scraps of information about Summer's movements of the night before.

The hours passed with agonizing slowness, and yet Jude didn't want them to go quicker. The longer Summer was missing, the worse the prognosis would be. 'Why can't they find her?' Claire wailed again and again, and Jude concurred heartily.

Euan returned after several hours, the young constable with him. He told them in a low voice how the folly had already been turned into a crime scene, with blue and white police tape and a forensic specialist in attendance. At the news, the blood drained from Claire's delicate features and she sat as still as a porcelain doll.

Jude, though quite as anxious, thought what to do. The idea of ringing their mother passed briefly through her mind. She rejected it for the moment, but when the first journalist arrived – from the local television news – she knew she'd have to tell Valerie before she got wind of the crisis from some other source. But when she made the call to Spain there was only an answerphone; she left a bland message about ringing Jude back. That was all she could do for the moment.

The detective returned to question Jude and Claire and Euan once more, going over and over the same facts, and Jude, despite Claire's frowning looks, stumbled briefly through her account of Summer's bad dreams and weird knowledge of events long past. The man clearly didn't know what to make of this, but did his best.

'So you're saying that she was maybe frightened after you read her the fairy tale and might have sleepwalked or something?' he asked.

'Possibly. But . . .' If only she could remember her own confused dreams from last night. 'Look – I know it sounds daft – she might have gone off, I don't know, on some quest to do with this story I told you about. She got quite caught up in it, you see. It seemed very real to her.'

'This girl from the eighteenth century,' he said unhappily. 'It sounds a little strange.' Jude knew he wasn't convinced. She couldn't blame him.

When he finally left them, Claire turned to her fiercely.

'I wish you'd stop all that nonsense. Couldn't you see he didn't believe a word of it? It's just crazy.'

'Claire, we've talked about this before. You agreed—'

'I didn't agree anything. If you hadn't stirred everything up Summer wouldn't have got upset.'

'I didn't stir things up. It all started before I came here. Her dreams, I mean.'

Claire's eyes slid to Euan, who stood up and said shortly, 'I'm going out to help look. I can't sit here.'

'It's you as well,' Claire cried. 'It was when you took her to the folly that the dreams started. And she wouldn't have gone to the folly last night, I know she wouldn't, not of her own accord. She hated the place. Someone must have taken her there.' She looked hard and cold at Euan, who flinched. 'Maybe you took her. For all we know it was you.'

There was a complete silence, then Euan said, 'Thank you for that vote of confidence. Now I'm going out to look for your daughter.' And he was gone.

'Claire. How can you have said that?' Jude whispered harshly. 'You know it's nonsense. You know.'

'It's you that's talked the nonsense,' said Claire bitterly. And she covered her face with her hands and began to sob uncontrollably.

The day passed. Then the night, which they spent in the tent again because Claire wanted to be close to where she'd last seen Summer, though neither of them slept much. In the small hours Jude woke and heard Claire whimpering. She shuffled her sleeping bag into the compartment where her sister lay and snuggled into her. Surprisingly, Claire allowed her to comfort her. Jude wondered when this had ever happened before. Claire had never played the protective elder sister, had never cuddled Jude when she cried. There was just that time after Mark died, when she came and hugged Jude as though it were the most natural thing in the world, and Jude had wept into her shoulder, letting her feelings go for the first time since the accident. And now the person Claire loved best in the world was lost to her and it was all they could do to cling to each other, Claire with the kind of desperation Jude had never, thankfully, seen in her before, and hoped never to again.

Was it really only yesterday she'd burned with jealousy of Claire? It seemed so long ago. And now she wasn't jealous at all. Nor did she feel pity, because what Claire was feeling was what Jude was feeling, too. Summer was precious to all of them. And now they might have lost her. For this brief moment there was nothing between them. And in this moment of pure truth, Jude dared to ask the thing that she had never asked, indeed had never even acknowledged as a conscious thought before.

'Claire,' she said, 'I know this is stupid, but a couple of nights ago I had the weirdest idea. That – you'll say I'm crazy – Summer's father . . . was Mark.'

There was a silence that went on and on and on. Finally Claire cleared her throat and said, 'You're crazy. How on earth could you think that?' and turned over, edging away. And a wave of despair swept over Jude.

At first light, police reinforcements arrived and the search resumed. The mood was darkening and there were shreds of talk about abduction now. The footprint in the folly might indicate Summer had gone there of her own volition, or that she'd been taken there. Jude overheard the detective say 'no signs of a struggle', which somehow wasn't as comforting as it might be. The nature of the police questioning was changing, too. Who did Summer know? Who did Claire and Jude know? Did Summer use the internet? Did she ever wander off by herself? Jude couldn't tell from the set expressions of the questioners whether Claire's answers were helpful to them or not.

At some point in the dreary confused hours, Jude thought to ring Chantal. She was slightly comforted to hear the woman's warm sympathy. 'I have been praying for the little girl. I am sure she will be found safe. Do not give up hope.' Jude had to cut the call short because her voice kept breaking as she thanked the woman.

Euan returned after a day of searching the forest. He was exhausted and somehow a husk of his usual self. He sat, hands clenched together, arms on his knees. Claire wouldn't look at him. At one point he told her, 'I will search and search and search until we find her. I will bring her back to you,' but Claire merely shrugged.

In the early evening, the detective came with the young constable and formally asked Euan to accompany him to the police station for questioning. He was assured that he wasn't being charged with anything. Euan went, a shambling figure with the dust of the day still on him. Cameras flashed as he got into the police car and was driven away.

'Claire, sometimes I really hate you,' Jude whispered into the door jamb, but not loud enough for her sister to hear. The tears were falling down her face.

She knew with absolute certainty that Euan had nothing to do with Summer's disappearance. But though in her mind she'd been over and over the events of that fateful evening she couldn't remember something that she knew was there but was dancing just out of her reach. It was something, she knew, to do with the folly.

Chapter 32

Summer thought it was lovely going to sleep in the caravan, smelling the comforting, familiar scent of the painted wood, trying to make out the patterns on the ceiling, still faintly visible in the dying evening light. She was warm and comfortable and safe, with her best friend, Darcey, gently snoring next to her. She thought over the story Auntie Jude had read her and briefly imagined that she was Rapunzel in the tower, but she didn't think she'd ever let something like that happen to her, so she imagined instead what it might be like to be the prince and to save someone you love from something bad. With this not unpleasant thought she sank into sleep.

She dreamed, not this time the lost dream. She was running through a forest all right, but she wasn't crying for her mummy, she was running to help someone. She had a strong sense that something wasn't right, someone was in danger and she had to find them. It was something to do with the folly, she knew that. She had to get there and help.

Still deep in her dream, she sat up in the darkness, pushed the bedclothes back and swung her feet to the floor. A toe prodded something. A shoe. She bent down and grasped it, fitted it onto her foot, then felt about until she found the other and put that on, too. She pushed open the caravan door and felt her way down the steps. She knew the way up to the folly from here, and now she tiptoed past the tent and ran across the meadow

– a little frightened, but not much for it was important to be brave tonight, like a prince. The owls, shuffling in their cage, saw her, but she didn't notice them. She turned left out of the drive and walked all the way up to the junction with Foxhole Lane, for she knew the footpath would be nasty and brambly.

And now she could sense more strongly the urgent summons to the folly. Part of her didn't want to go. It had been spooky there. But another part of her mind knew she had to find Esther and help her. Before it was too late. It was very dark under the trees, and misty, and she shivered, but then the mist cleared and she could make out enough to see her route. Quickly, she went, past several wagons huddled in darkness at the side of Foxhole Lane and the word *Rowan* formed in her head, then on she went, along the narrow path towards the folly. There were times in life, she knew from storybooks, when you had to do the thing you were most frightened of.

When she reached the folly, the door was unlocked. It swung open easily on new, well-oiled hinges. She started to climb the sturdy brick steps.

In the safety of the tent, Jude's eyes had briefly opened then fluttered closed. She had sunk once more into sleep.

It must have been past midnight when Esther heard the key turn in the lock downstairs and the door handle turn. Her flash of hope was immediately followed by a prickle of fear of who or what it might be. She flew across the room and flattened herself against the wall next to the doorway and listened to the sound of slow footsteps trudging up the staircase, louder and louder. A man bearing a flickering lantern loomed in the doorway, spiky shadows leaping up round the walls. When he lowered the light she gasped with relief, 'Oh, Mr Trotwood, it's you.'

He looked her up and down, somewhat warily, but with no surprise.

She said in a rush, and not without a catch in her voice, 'I got locked in. I don't know how. I expect you've all been looking for me. You saw the light, I suppose.'

Mr Trotwood ignored her, but held up his lantern to inspect the room, noticing the mattress and the book open on the table. His expression hardened. He turned to her and said, 'You'll be hungry, I expect.'

'Why, yes,' she said. 'I've had nothing for three days.'

'And cold, I should think.'

'Yes, I have been.' She pulled her cloak around her, with growing alarm at his strangeness.

He made a little noise in his throat, the meaning of which she couldn't gauge. He dropped the bag he'd been carrying on the floor near the wall.

'Mr Trotwood, thank you so much for rescuing me, but can we go now?'

She moved towards the doorway.

'Not so fast,' he said, very quietly, and seized her by the arm. She stiffened, terrified.

'The mistress is finding you, shall we say, inconvenient.'

'What?' she said, then, absorbing his words, 'Was it you who shut me in here?'

'No,' he said in his slow deliberate voice, 'but somebody did a useful job, didn't they? Come on,' he ordered, twisting her arm painfully behind her back. 'Up here, there's a good girl.' He pushed her to the ladder.

'No!' she cried. 'Leave me alone.'

His response was to clamp a leathery hand over her mouth with a hissed, 'Don't give me any more trouble now, yer little upstart.'

He hauled her up the ladder one step at a time as she fought and flailed and tried to cry out. Finally he got her out onto the roof. 'It's over you go,' he cried, dragging her towards the parapet. 'Then they'll say, "Poor little thing, grief-stricken after the old man's death," and you'll be out of everyone's—' He gave a sudden cry and kicked out, nearly letting her go. Someone had bitten his leg, damn them to hell. He swung round to see a girl, thin, ragged. Where had she sprung from? He kicked at her again and she fell sprawling across the platform. The moonlight shone on her face and Esther saw with surprise that it was the gypsy girl.

With Trotwood's attention elsewhere, Esther took her opportunity. She bit his hand hard. He tore it away with a cry. She twisted out of his grasp and stepped back, tripping over the telescope stand and nearly falling. He advanced. She grabbed the telescope and yanked part of it loose, then wielded it like a cudgel. He put out both arms to snatch it from her. Rowan launched herself at his legs, making him stagger, and Esther hit him on the shoulder with her weapon. He reeled, then recovered himself and kicked Rowan away. She scrambled to her feet. Both the girls were facing him now, Esther with her nasty weapon. He backed away, then edged sideways, perhaps intending to deal with Rowan first. What happened next was a surprise to them all. His foot caught in the top rung of the ladder and he pitched sideways, his head hitting the parapet with a great crack. For a moment he lay like Goliath hit by the stone, blood pouring from a cut on his head.

After a while he sat up, dazed, but the girls were past him. They scampered for the ladder like two frightened mice, Rowan getting down first, then Esther, who lowered the trapdoor and bolted it behind them. Then they waited in fright below, clutching each other, listening to Trotwood bang on the trapdoor and roar curses. After a minute or two of this he desisted suddenly. They heard a thud, shufflings and then a groan. After that, silence.

The two girls looked at one another. The gypsy girl's eyes were huge in her thin face. She put out her hands and took one of Esther's and stroked it gently.

'How did you find me?' Esther asked. 'I'm so glad that you did.'

The girl uttered two harsh syllables, and when Esther frowned uncomprehendingly, she mimed a little scene.

'You were asleep,' said Esther, watching closely, 'and somebody woke you. No, you had a dream?'

The girl nodded, and mimed running and panting.

'You came as quickly as you could? Well, I'm glad you did.' The girl pulled out of her skirt pocket a small piece of brick with one of Esther's messages still wrapped round it. It was soaked, the writing indecipherable. 'Yes, that's mine. Thank you, oh thank you.'

They both listened in case of any sign of life from the roof, but there was none. Then Esther noticed Mr Trotwood's bag. There was a dead rabbit tied to the strap. She eagerly undid the buckles, hoping for food. Inside was a pistol and a lump of fruitcake wrapped in a cloth. She placed the pistol on the desk next to her journal, untied the rabbit and gave it to the girl, who received it with a show of pleasure, then she divided the cake between them. Both of them ate hungrily.

Esther picked up the pistol. She'd never handled one before, but she fiddled with the catch then fitted her forefinger over the trigger and pointed the gun shakily at the window. Yes, she thought she could do it if she had to. She marched over to the ladder, climbed up and pushed at the trapdoor. It would not move. There was something weighting it shut. She gave up and came back down, returned the pistol to the desk with some relief. She wasn't sure what her intentions had been. To rescue him, bring him down the tower at gunpoint, perhaps.

Outside, the wind was beginning to get up. Esther went to a window and watched the snowflakes beginning to fall. Then she said to herself, What shall I do?

Trotwood had confirmed her worst suspicions, that not only did Alicia wish to deny her the inheritance of the Hall, but she had hoped to deprive her of her very life. And Trotwood had supported her in this. Who else would, among the servants? Obviously not Susan, who loved her like a daughter, and she couldn't imagine Mrs

Godstone or Corbett taking against her, or Betsy. But the more she thought about it, the more frightened she was at the idea of going back. She had no one of any power or influence to support her and now there was the problem of Trotwood, lying dead or dying upstairs. It was an accident, of course, in the end. He'd slipped and cracked his skull, but it could still look bad for the two of them, very bad.

The other girl finished the last crumbs of cake, then snatched up Trotwood's bag and rummaged in the side pockets. All she could find was a couple of wizened apples. She handed one to Esther and began to eat the other noisily. Esther watched her small white nibbling teeth with fascination. The girl's headscarf had slid back on her head and in the lantern-light Esther saw that the hair was paler where it sprang from her scalp but streaked with dirt or tar. Seeing her curiosity, the girl quickly pulled the scarf forwards.

Esther began to pace the room, rubbing her arms for warmth, her thoughts whirling like the snowflakes outside. What should she do? There was surely nowhere for her to go. The servants couldn't help her. She thought of Matt. No, she couldn't endanger him. It suddenly struck her how truly alone in the world she was.

Now the girl uttered, 'Esther,' and said something in her strange tongue, gesturing towards the stairs.

'You want me to come with you?' Esther said. The girl nodded, then her gaze alighted on the pistol and the apple cores.

Esther took her meaning. She returned the pistol to the bag, which she laid against the wall as it had been. Then she set about collecting up every piece of evidence that she'd recently been there, tidying the ink in a cupboard, placing everything she'd brought with her back in her bag. She hesitated over the journal, then wrapped it in an oilcloth and took it to the hiding place in the wall. She opened it and saw the box containing her necklace. She forgotten all about it, but she might need it now. She opened the box and lifted out the string of stars, her heart leaping to see the beautiful sparkling charms. Quickly, she

undid her cloak and slipped the necklace round her neck, looking
up to see Rowan's expression of amazement and, yes, desire. The
box went into her bag, then came the problem of fitting the journal
inside the hidey-hole. It simply would not go. She stood in an agony
of indecision. The journal was precious, with its record of discovery,
but it belonged with the others, back at the Hall. She'd leave it in a
cupboard. No one would know how long it had been there. But the
account she'd written of herself might be useful one day.

Eventually she placed the book on the desk and tore out the pages
she'd written over the last few days, wrapped them in the oilcloth
and packed them in her bag. Then with one last glance around the
room, she followed the gypsy girl downstairs.

It was snowing quite heavily still, although the wind had finally
dropped. They loaded up the little cart and set out across the clear-
ing, knowing the snow would cover their tracks. Once, Esther
skidded and fell and when Rowan helped her up, she felt the neck-
lace slip from her neck. Holding her glove in her teeth, she felt for
where it had caught in the lace of her dress and pulled it free. She
was clutching it in her hand, just as she'd done nearly fourteen
years before, as they vanished together into the forest.

The only trace of Esther was a little gold star that lay winking
in the snowlight.

When Summer awoke, she was curled up under a tree, the early
dawn light starting to filter down through the leaves. She had
awoken because she was cold. The remnants of her dream fled
in the face of her surprise and fear and she sat up, crying out for
her mother and looking all around. When no one answered she
called again, and again, then threw herself to the ground and
curled up like a caterpillar waiting for danger to pass. Tears
zigzagged across her face and for a while she drifted between
sleeping and waking. Then she felt the lightest of touches on

her shoulder, like the caress of a falling leaf. 'Mummy?' She raised her head and at first could see no one. Then she heard a giggle and caught a movement behind the next tree. Not Mummy – but, curiosity overcoming fear, she rose to her feet. The other child, if child it was, ran ahead to another tree, but Summer could only detect the movement, not see the girl – she sensed it was a girl – herself.

'Who are you?' Summer called out, then whimpered, 'I want my mummy.'

She thought the girl beckoned, then saw the leaves move and the giggle came again, from further along the path. Summer started to follow. 'Where are we going?' she asked, but the girl did not reply. The light was stronger now, and the birds were in full voice. Summer felt much calmer. She didn't know where the girl was taking her, but she understood it would be all right. She pictured her mummy's face in her mind and knew, just knew, she'd find her soon. Her mother had said to her once after they'd become separated in a supermarket, 'Darling, if you ever feel you're lost, don't worry, I'm looking for you. I'm always looking for you.' Her mother would be looking for her and she'd find her. And in the meantime, this girl, for she could see her properly now, was helping her. They wandered together all day, the girl showing Summer where blackberries grew, and where clear water flowed. They played together, hiding games and catch, and once they made a dam in a shallow bubbling stream. Then came times of realization that she was still lost, and she'd panic and cry, and the girl would make soothing noises and caper around, trying to make her smile. When evening came once more she sank exhausted on a mossy bed and the girl covered her with dry leaves.

She was awakened on Monday morning – not that she knew it was Monday – by the sound of a passing car. She sat up and looked around and saw she was lying near a road. Of the other girl there was no sign. When she got to her feet she recognized where she was. A little further along the road, on the other side, stood the gypsy caravans. She could even see Liza, sitting on the steps of her van, reading a newspaper and eating toast. She wondered what to do, suddenly lacking courage. Relief and fear rushed over her in equal measure. She sat down in the grass again and wept.

There came the roar of another car, the jangle of music. The car slowed, the music stopped and a man's voice cried, 'Hi there. Are you OK?' She looked up, dazzled. It was a lovely sports car, her favourite kind of blue, with the roof down and a small dog of indeterminate lineage standing in the back seat waving its tail. She'd always wanted a little dog. The driver was a man with curly blond hair like hers, and sunglasses. He took these off now, and she saw his face, all smiley and snub-nosed. She liked him at once, but remembered what her mother had told her about not getting in people's cars even if she knew them. But this man didn't ask her to get into the car. Instead he said, 'I'm sorry you're sad. Do you live over there?' He pointed to the gypsy caravans. She shook her head and whispered, 'I want my mummy.'

The man thought for a moment, then he said, 'Look, will you stay exactly where you are, next to my car, and look after it for me? I'd like to ask that lady over there for help.'

Summer nodded, so the man checked for traffic, then got out of the car, his little dog leaping out after him. He crossed the road and jogged over to the caravan site and Summer saw him speak to Liza. And then they were both hurrying back towards her.

And Liza put her arms around her and called her darling and Summer knew she was safe.

Chapter 33

Jude would never ever forget that first rush of relief when the policewoman said, her voice cracking, 'She's found. She's OK.' After the release of tension it was like her body was filling up with fizzy champagne. There was nothing more to worry about in life, ever ever again. She and Claire clasped one another, Claire laughing and crying alternately. The worst had been contemplated and the worst had gone away. Then the euphoria ebbed and questions rose in her mind. When could they see her? Where had she been for the last two nights? Was she really all right?

'She's being taken to hospital just to check her over. We're to meet her there. Come on.'

When they arrived at the big hospital near Great Yarmouth, they were taken to a small white-washed office, where Summer was sitting with a nurse, who was trying to entertain her with various brightly coloured toys. She went at once to her mother and they hugged each other and Claire started crying all over again.

'I'm OK, Mummy, don't fuss,' Summer said, and it was Claire who needed comforting.

Out in the corridor, a youngish man with wavy blond hair, and an elderly woman with gold-hoop earrings, sat waiting patiently. Jude had been too anxious to give them a second glance on the way in, but now she recognized Liza, and the man, too, looked vaguely familiar. Claire, who was gripping Summer's hand, seemed to know him too, because she said, 'You!' and her other hand flew to her cheek. Jude couldn't quite place him. Was he another of the gypsies?

'Hello, Claire,' the man said softly. 'It was me that found her. Well, and Liza here, of course. Are you all right now, little one?'

Summer nodded and leaned into her mother's side.

'It was you who saw her first, young man,' Liza said. 'My eyes aren't as sharp as they were.'

'Claire, this is Liza,' Jude said. 'Do you remember I told you about taking Summer to meet her?'

'Liza, thank you. Thank you, both of you,' Claire whispered. Then she turned and said, 'Jude. You'll remember Jon?' She looked anxiously at Jude, and Jude did remember. She turned to the man in wonder. 'Yes, I met you one Christmas, I believe. We were, er, worried because you left without saying goodbye.' He'd looked different then, when he'd been going out with Claire, that time after their father's death. Trying so hard to be cool he'd come across as plain rude.

'Yes, well I'm sorry about that,' he mumbled. 'I guess those days you didn't see me at my best.'

'Snap,' Claire remarked drily.

He'd certainly changed for the better. He was wearing neatly pressed stone-white chinos and a crisp pale blue shirt. The hair, though still longish, was neatly styled and his blue eyes were lively, intelligent, but with a touch of seriousness. And as Jude saw him properly she knew the truth immediately, and a great burden slipped away.

Claire seemed quite anxious in his presence, kept looking nervously at Summer.

'How was it you found . . . ? Did you know . . . ? I didn't . . .' she kept starting to say, and Jon broke in.

'Look, this is going to sound ridiculous, but I'll try anyway. Your sister, Jude – well I didn't know her name was Gower. It didn't mean anything to me when I saw the letter.'

'What letter?' Claire asked, confused.

'The letter in the paper. About Tamsin Lovall.'

'Oh goodness,' said Jude, 'that letter. I didn't have a chance to see it had been printed.'

'What on earth are you both talking about?' asked Claire as though they were mad. Summer, tired, had started a little rocking game at her side, threatening Claire's balance.

'I maybe forgot to tell you. Liza here and her son recommended that I place a letter in the local paper asking if anyone knew any Lovalls and, in particular, Tamsin.'

'So what's that got to do with Jon?' Claire asked. 'Summer do stop jiggling. I know you must be shattered. We'll be going in a moment.'

'I was on my way to find Judith Gower,' said Jon simply. 'You see, Tamsin Lovall was my grandmother.'

'You've got to tell him, Claire,' Jude said, arms crossed, as she contemplated her sister. They were back in Blacksmith's Cottage and had just seen Sergeant Bride and her boss off the premises after two wearying hours of discussion and filling in forms. The police, after hearing Summer's own rambling account about gypsy girls and towers, had settled for the easier explanation that she had suffered a nightmare, sleepwalked and got herself thoroughly lost. Euan, they were told, had been immediately released and the case more or less closed. Summer, meanwhile, bathed and fed by Jude while Claire was still talking, was soundly asleep upstairs.

'Tell him what?' Claire snapped.

'Well, the truth.'

'The truth being . . .'

'It's obvious, isn't it? You were right to tell me I was crazy thinking it was Mark. It's as Mum and I guessed at the time. Come on, Claire. Jon's her father, isn't he?'

Claire grunted and turned away.

After a moment, she said, 'Yes. Yes, he is. And yes, I suppose I will have to tell him.'

'I wouldn't be surprised if he's guessed already. After all, they look similar, and he can do his maths, I'm sure.'

'Great,' said Claire gloomily. 'Now he won't leave us alone at all.'

'Did you see the adoring way he looked at her, though?' Jude asked, unable to resist teasing. 'Another conquest for Princess Summer.'

'Oh really, Jude.'

'She is very charming, your daughter.'

'She'll be worse trouble than I was. So, I tell him. And I'll have to tell her. Then what?'

'I expect he'll want to see her from time to time.'

'And interfere. Just what I was frightened of.'

'Oh, come on, Claire, what's so bad about him becoming involved? Summer will have a father. And what a lovely one at that. I hope you don't mind me saying, but he seems to have grown up a bit since he last graced us with his presence.'

'Yeah.' Claire seemed lost in thought for a moment, then sighed and said, 'I suppose so. OK, I'll tell him. But Jude, please don't say anything to anyone else about it yet, to Gran or Mum. I have to tell Summer first and I want to do that in my own time. Maybe let her get to know Jon a bit first. It's not going to be easy for any of us.'

'OK, it makes sense.'

*   *   *

Euan phoned Jude's mobile half an hour later when Claire was upstairs. Jude took the phone out into the garden. 'Is Summer all right?' were his first words.

'Yes, yes, amazingly she is, thank God.' As he didn't seem to have heard the details, she explained about an old friend of Claire's finding the girl near the gypsy encampment.

'Are you back home? How are you?'

'I'm fine. They let me go pretty soon after she was found. Police car home, many apologies, sir, that sort of thing.'

'I can't believe that they took you in the first place.'

'It's routine, Jude, you mustn't worry about it.'

'Or that you're being that nice about it.'

'Yes, well . . .' he said. 'Your sister was very stressed.' Both of them were thinking of Claire's accusing words.

'I don't believe she meant it. Not when she stopped to think.'

'I know,' he said, 'but it hurt. Very deeply.'

'Euan, this might not be the time, but what happened between you? The night Summer disappeared, I mean. I came into your living room and, well, you could have cut the atmosphere with a knife.'

'I think you'll have to ask Claire about that. It wouldn't be gallant of me . . .'

Jude sighed and closed her eyes. 'I thought as much,' she said, but a guilty feeling of delicious relief welled up in her. Euan changed the subject.

'Where did Summer say she'd gone?'

'It's still a bit of a mystery, Euan. She doesn't seem to remember. Someone was shut in the tower, is what she says, and she had to let them out. Then a girl looked after her in the forest and they played, and then she woke up near the gypsy caravans, and we know the rest. It sounds extraordinary, but – well, everything she said tied in with a dream I had the night she disappeared. Only I forgot about it in the morning, the dream I mean. It must have been the shock or something. I'm so sorry, I'm rambling. Everything's happening at once and it's so . . . oh, confusing.'

Euan brought her down to earth by saying patiently, 'So she thinks she was in the forest all that time? And she didn't even hear us calling for her?'

'Apparently not. And you'd have thought she'd have hypothermia, but you should see her, she's absolutely fine. She says this girl put leaves over her – leaves, Euan. Like the folk tale.'

'They sound like a couple of very lucky Babes in the Wood. Who was the girl, do you think?'

'I've no idea. Summer thinks she was a gypsy, but it certainly wasn't Liza's great-granddaughter. *She* was out with her mother all day yesterday and fast asleep in her parents' caravan at night. Hang on a moment.'

Claire had stepped outside, clearly wishing to speak to her.

'Is that Euan?' Claire whispered. 'Could I talk to him when you've finished? If he can face it, I mean.'

'I'll ask him,' Jude said, her face impassive, then she spoke into the handset: 'Euan, will you have a word with Claire?'

There was a silence, then Euan said, 'Yes, sure.' He added, 'I'll see you soon, then?'

'Of course,' replied Jude. 'I'll ring you.'

She passed her phone to Claire, and went inside, not wanting to hear their conversation. She couldn't help, though, watching her sister pace the garden, her expression agitated. Once she pressed her forearm to her face as though trying to stem tears. Another time she heard her cry, 'No, you've got me all wrong.'

'Hi.' Jude spun round at the sound of a man's voice. 'Heck, who put that there?' Jon was rubbing his head and frowning at the low doorway to the living room. 'Sorry to make you jump, Jude. The front door was open but no one heard me knock.'

'Oh dear,' she said. 'Are you all right? I'm glad you've come.'

'I wanted to find out how the little girl is,' he said.

'She's absolutely fine,' Jude repeated, 'not least thanks to you.'

'Asleep, I imagine,' he said, seeing her glance upstairs.

'Dead to the world,' she replied, then immediately thought what an unfortunate expression that was in the circumstances. 'Are you really a Lovall?'

'That was the other thing I wanted to see you both about. Yes, I am. Descended from one, anyway.'

At that moment, Claire finished her call and walked in slowly from the garden. She looked exhausted, Jude thought tenderly. Exhausted and sad.

'Oh,' Claire said, seeing Jon rise to meet her. 'You again. I'm sorry . . . I didn't know you'd come.'

'Are you all right?' asked Jude, putting out her hand for her BlackBerry.

'Yes,' Claire replied, giving it to her, her voice steady. 'I'll tell you about it later.' She half fell onto the sofa and sat hunched up like a small, bruised waif, her legs tucked under her.

'More tea, I think,' said Jude firmly, and she went off to make it, pushing the kitchen door to and deliberately clunking about, glad when the noise of the boiling kettle drowned the rise and fall of voices from the living room. Even so, when the kettle switched itself off she couldn't help hearing his anguished cry: 'You should have told me I had a child. I had a right to know.'

'Don't you see?' Claire replied, her voice passionate. 'I had to protect her.'

'From me?' he cut in. 'From *me*? Did you think I'd drop her or – or try to take her from you or something?'

'I didn't *know*. I couldn't predict how you would turn out. But I didn't trust you then, Jon. I could hardly trust myself.'

Stuck in the kitchen, Jude didn't know whether to pretend she wasn't listening, or to blithely interrupt. The problem was solved for her by Claire, who came in. 'So I've told him,' she remarked, picking up two of the mugs.

Jon had gone out into the garden where he stood legs apart, arms folded, looking at the full-blown roses, their petals starting to fall.

Jude watched as Claire took out the tea, nudging his arm to get his attention with such a tender, natural gesture Jude wondered where it came from. Jon turned slightly and Jude was entranced to observe the ease of the look that passed between them, though Jon still looked cross and Claire prickly. They're like a long-married couple, she thought, which really was extraordinary considering that as far as she knew they hadn't seen each other for seven or eight years. Jude and Mark had shared that feeling. They might not have met up for months or, like that time leading up to their engagement when he was away on his travels, a whole year, but they had just picked up where they'd left off every time. Still, she hadn't kept the secret of an unexpected baby from Mark. This might, she suppose, either draw Claire and Jon together, or drive them further apart. She wondered if it were too tidy to hope for the former. Jon did seem quite transformed from the casual young man she'd met that Christmas Day nearly eight years ago.

She drank up her tea and decided she should go. Though desperate to hear about Tamsin Lovall and to tell Claire about her Esther dream, never mind to learn what had gone on between Claire and Euan, she was reluctant to play gooseberry to Claire and Jon.

This time it was Jon's turn to rescue her, for when she went outside to say, 'I probably ought to get back,' he exclaimed, 'But you haven't told me yet. Why you were looking for my nan. That's why I came, you see. That's why I was driving down that road at that time and saw Summer. Heck, Claire's told me I rescued my own daughter! And I was coming to find *you.*'

'Coming to . . . I still don't entirely follow this. How can Tamsin be your grandmother?'

'Look,' Jon said, 'I'll start at the beginning.' He leaned against the trampoline and told them the story.

'An old friend of our family showed my dad the letter you put in the paper on Friday about Tamsin Lovall. I didn't know her name had been Lovall then, but this friend remembered her and said that it must be her, and I was amazed because I didn't know she'd been a Romany. Dad had never told me. He said it was because she'd been secretive about it and he respected that.'

'I take it she is dead then, Tamsin?' Jude said quietly.

'Yes, years ago, when I was five or six,' Jon said. 'I don't really remember her at all.'

'Oh, that's so sad,' Jude cried. So all these years Gran had been worrying pointlessly. Tamsin, from whom she'd taken the necklace, had been dead; she must have died comparatively young. 'When was that?' she asked. 'Sorry, I can't work it out because I don't know how old you are.'

'Same as you,' chipped in Claire. 'He's thirty-four, aren't you, Jon? April the fifteenth, I remember. Aries. Fire sign, same as me.'

Jon looked at her with an expression of amazement.

'It's all right,' Claire added hastily. 'I never expect men to remember birthdays and things. I'm a Leo – twentieth of August.'

Jude hardly noticed this conversation. She was thinking: so Tamsin died nearly thirty years ago. And Gran hadn't known. Nearly thirty years, probably, she'd had that necklace on her conscience. But she'd have wanted to return it to the family, all the same.

'Anyway,' Jon said, 'Dad tried to ring you on the number given in the paper. And it came out as number unobtainable.'

'Oh?' said Jude, surprised.

'Yeah, look.' He pulled a wallet out from his jacket pocket, extracted from it a small rectangle of newspaper and passed it to her.

'Damn, they misprinted the number,' she said, annoyed.

'Yeah, and it only says Starbrough Hall, Norfolk, so Dad didn't want to send a letter in case it didn't get there, and since he only lives up at Sheringham and I had a day off work, I said I'd drop it in at the Hall. So here's the letter.'

He handed Jude a white envelope with her name on it. She opened it, read it through quickly, then stood deep in thought.

'Here, let me look,' said Claire and Jude gave it to her.

Dear Miss or Mrs Gower,

I read your letter asking about Tamsin Lovall. That was my mother's name before she married. She always said she was Romany, but when she was eighteen or nineteen she met my father in Great Yarmouth where she'd gone to be a nurse, it being wartime. He was a Navy rating and they met at a dance, and got married soon after, when I believe I must have been on the way. She never went back to her family. I think she quarrelled with them about the nursing. She had three children, me and my sister and brother, but sadly passed away in 1980 shortly before her 57th birthday, of cancer. My father, George, died in 1999. I'm afraid I don't remember her speak about your nan, but then she never talked much about her childhood. I think she didn't want people to know about her being a gypsy and to think she was different. She was a shy woman and never liked to stand out in any way. I would however be interested to meet someone who knew her when she was a child, if you would care to contact me.

I remain yours truly,

Frank Thetford

Claire passed the letter back to Jude. 'I'm so confused,' she said. 'Who's George and who's Frank?'

'George was my grandfather. He's the one Tamsin married. Frank's my dad.'

'And you're her grandson.'

'Which means,' said Jude, finally bringing it out into the open, 'that Summer is Tamsin's great-granddaughter. Jessie's and Tamsin's. My God.'

'And you came to find us just in time to rescue Summer.'

The chain of coincidences was so astonishing they all just stared at each other.

Later that day, Jude drove back to Starbrough Hall, longing for her bed. When she reached Gamekeeper's Cottage, she stopped the car, thinking she ought to go and help Euan deal with all the mess. There were no other cars there, not even Euan's. She knocked at the door, but there was no answer. She walked past the animals and into the meadow. The tent was gone and the caravan shut up. There was no sign of Euan at all. Feeling suddenly very sad and alone, she walked back to the car and continued on her way.

The next morning, she was just finishing telling Chantal everything that had happened when her phone rang. It was the jeweller's shop in Norwich to tell her the necklace was ready.

'It's definitely from around 1760,' the jeweller told her later, when she arrived to pick it up. 'And our researcher can pinpoint the goldsmith's mark to a shop in Hatton Garden. If it was complete and in good condition something like this would be worth, oh, about nine or ten thousand pounds, but as it is, not more than five thousand. I've written you a letter here to explain it all, and we'd be able to arrange for a replacement star to be made if that's what you decide.'

'Amazingly, we found the missing charm,' she told the jeweller. And in the remnant of a dream a little star twinkled on new-fallen snow.

'Oh well done. That would give the necklace further value, of course. If you want to bring it in it would be a privilege to do the repair. This is a very pretty piece.'

'Isn't it?' Jude said, bringing out her purse to pay the woman. 'Can you tell me one more thing, would this design have been common at the time?'

'It says all that in the letter. Here we are, "Although stars became popular later in the century as interest in astronomy became fashionable, at this earlier period they were more rare. This item is believed to be unique, not least because the jeweller specialized in commissions for individual pieces." '

So the likelihood that the necklace had been Esther's was strong. But where had the baby Esther got it from? And now it would be Frank's. Then Jon's. And just maybe, eventually . . . Summer's.

The dream was starting to come back to her more strongly now.

Instead of walking back to where she'd parked the car, she set off for the Castle Museum. She had some forms to fill in.

*   *   *

It was Wednesday before Euan called her, after an exhausting day of dealing with the photographer that Bridget from the office had sent down to photograph Starbrough Hall generally and the library in particular.

'I'm staying at Fiona and Paul's,' he told her. 'A rest seemed called for. Are you busy tomorrow?'

'Yes,' said Jude, 'but it would be wonderful if you came and joined in.'

'In what?' he asked.

'A rather amazing gathering,' she replied. 'At Starbrough Hall. The Wickhams have been so kind. We didn't have anywhere else big enough, you see. And the Hall is so important to the story.'

And she explained.

Part III

Chapter 34

'The whole thing is like a huge 3D jigsaw puzzle,' Jude told Euan on Thursday morning. They were sitting in the library at Starbrough Hall, where she was showing him the transcripts of Esther's memoir. 'It does my head in just to think about it.'

'Perhaps writing it down would help,' Euan suggested. 'Can I use this paper? A flow chart would be best. Look, here is Esther at the top on the left.'

'And the gypsy girl, I'll call her by the name Summer came up with, Rowan, on the right.'

'Here's the necklace under Esther's name, then we'll do an arrow to Rowan because she must have given it to Rowan.'

'Then we have to suppose that Rowan passes it down her family, who are all Romany, until it's Tamsin's turn to have it in the 1930s.'

'And that's when your gran, the gamekeeper's daughter, takes it off her and keeps it. We'll write her name, Jessie, down here on the left near the bottom, then your mum's name, Valerie, then Claire's and yours, then Summer's.'

It was on the tip of her tongue to tell Euan about Summer and Jon, but she'd promised Claire not to.

'Then under Tamsin's name, Frank, Jon.'

They both stared at the chart they'd drawn. 'What this suggests is that the necklace should be given to Frank, as Tamsin's eldest child.'

'There's still so much we don't know, isn't there?' Jude said. 'I mean, Esther writes about being locked in the tower but we don't actually know, unless we trust my weird dream, how she got out of it and what became of her afterwards. There's certainly no evidence that she was ever connected with Starbrough Hall again. Augustus inherited it, and Chantal's shown me the family tree. There's no Esther. And of course, we can only guess that Tamsin is descended from Rowan.'

'It seems likely, though,' Euan said. 'How else would Tamsin have got the necklace?'

'So the only clues we have,' Jude said, 'are hardly going to stand up to historical scrutiny. It's my own imaginings, and what Summer said happened when she went missing. She still insists that someone needed to get out of the folly and that she was then looked after by some other little girl. Euan, if I hadn't had strange dreams like Summer's when I was a child I could more easily dismiss it. But there's something very weird at work here and I'm not prepared to just dismiss it.'

'And yet you can't possibly put it in your magazine article about Esther. You can't.'

'Of course I can't. Apart from the question of historical evidence it wouldn't be fair on Summer. But maybe, just maybe, we could use it as a hypothesis to lead us to further hard evidence. Let's assume that Esther did escape. It's quite plausible that she went off with Rowan and her family. Certainly if Alicia cut her out of her father's will and Esther felt her life threatened.'

' "Off with the raggle-taggle gypsies, oh". No, I'm not laughing at you, Jude. It sounds very, I don't know, romantic, that's all. Can you imagine her having to live a life on the road after being the daughter of the Big House?'

'It would have been incredibly hard for her.'

'So perhaps she did something else, but I don't see how we find out.'

'No, nor do I at the moment.'

They were both silent, thinking their own thoughts.

Then Euan looked at his watch. 'What time do we have to fetch Mrs Catchpole?'

'Gran? Just after lunch. It's incredibly kind of the Wickhams to invite us all here.'

'It would have been a crush at your gran's. And you're right, it's very appropriate since Starbrough is where it all happened. But are you sure you want me cluttering up the place, too?'

'Of course I do,' Jude said, placing a hand on his arm. 'You're part of all this somehow.'

'Do you know, I feel I am,' he replied, smiling at her.

Sitting in the huge armchair in the drawing room, propped up with cushions, Gran looked, thought Jude, like a small nervous child. Chantal was at her most charming, pouring tea into beautiful porcelain cups, and even Miffy did her best, coming to press her doggy warmth against Gran's legs.

'When are they coming?' Gran asked Jude anxiously, for the third time, twisting her worn wedding ring.

'Any moment,' Jude replied, and Euan, standing at the window, said, 'They're here now,' as Jon's blue sports car rolled up the drive. There followed a few minutes' mayhem because the twins let the setters out and Summer was frightened to get out of the car, but Robert grabbed one dog and a neat, slightly portly man who could only be Jon's father got out of the car and caught the other, and Claire and Summer climbed out of the back. Jon took a carrier bag out of the boot and passed it to his father. Then, the front doors being open as was appropriate for such a special occasion, Alexia came down the steps like the gracious chatelaine she was and swept them all up into the house.

Frank and Jon were introduced to Gran, who, now they were actually here, had quite forgotten her nerves and received them like a queen. Chantal seated Frank in the chair next to Gran's, and while Alexia took Summer to show her the twins' playroom, the adults tried to encourage the conversation that Gran had needed to have for so many years. They learned that Frank had a job as a driver for a big garage and car showroom in Yarmouth. He was a quietly spoken man with very bright eyes – like Tamsin's, Gran said suddenly at one point. 'I can see her in you.' They seemed to know a lot of the same places and remember local events and notable people. Jude saw his pride in Jon.

Jude managed to gather the threads of the family's story. Frank's wife had left when Jon was thirteen. Frank had no job at that time and let everything slide. By his late twenties, when he met Claire, Jon had left school with paltry qualifications, played in several bands, none of them successful, and was drifting. Then, a few years later, an opportunity presented itself. He saw a band of local lads playing in a pub and thought they had something. He offered to give them a few tips about who to talk to, how to present themselves, and before long found himself their manager. Now, two successful albums later, they were touring and he was building up his own small record label of other groups.

'He's really making something of it, aren't you, boy?' Frank said.

Jon looked embarrassed.

'Hence the manager's flash car,' Claire commented, but she was clearly impressed.

Frank glanced at Claire, and looked as though he wanted to say something else, but then decided not to. Instead he picked up the carrier bag he'd brought with him and extracted a photo album. 'There're pictures of my ma in here,' he said, opening it and holding it so Gran could see. 'This is her in her nurse's uniform, and that's her wedding, of course. Here she is holding me as a nipper and this is us on the beach at Sheringham, I believe.'

Gran turned the pages in silence, a strange sort of expression on her face, as though she wanted to see the photos but was frightened of the feelings they awoke in her.

'Your da looks a good man,' she told Frank, who nodded. 'Were they happy?'

'I believe so, yes,' he said.

'She deserved to be happy,' Gran muttered. The album was passed around and Jude at last saw Tamsin – dark hair tied back severely under her nurse's cap, deep-set dark eyes, a shy, serious expression.

'How was it exactly you knew her?' Frank asked. 'She never said much about her life before she met my da, except that she lived in a *vardo*. That was her word for a caravan. She liked to talk about the *vardo* and the various horses that had pulled it. There's a picture of it somewhere. I found it again after she died. It might be at the back here.'

The photograph was stuck inside the back cover. Gran stared at it for some time. She hardly noticed when Frank gently took the album from her and passed it to Jude. The photograph was creased and a little blurred, but it showed a wagon very like Euan's, in black and white, with a slender girl, presumably Tamsin, sitting upfront next to a muscly, weatherbeaten man who was pulling on a cigarette, his other hand holding the reins.

'That was Ted, one of her uncles,' Jessie said.

'The caravan is like yours, isn't it?' Jude murmured to Euan, who studied it closely before passing the album to Claire.

'It is, isn't it, but that really would be too much of a coincidence,' he said firmly.

Claire passed the album to Jon and then Chantal, then stood up.

'Mrs Wickham, would you mind showing me where Summer's gone?' she asked, and the two women left the room. She didn't like to be parted from Summer at the moment. Jon muttered something about checking on them and followed. Euan rose and quietly went over to the far window where he stood, hands in pockets, looking out over the park. Gran still sat silently turning her wedding ring.

'What is it, Gran?' Jude asked softly.

Frank, probably thinking she was tired, started to make his excuses, but Gran motioned to him to stay. But still she said nothing, so Frank gave a sort of harrumphing noise and said, 'Mrs Catchpole, I know something bad happened to my ma. She was always a very private person, haunted by something, I'd say. My da told me as much, too. Somebody hurt her badly, didn't they?'

Gran looked at her and Jude was moved to see her eyes glistening with unshed tears.

'Seeing those photographs . . . Of course, it brings it all back. But, yes, that's what happened. It was when she and I were fifteen.'

Gran was quiet again for a moment, then looked straight at Frank. 'I've not talked about this for a very long time. I hope you'll understand. It's been a burden to me all these years. If I'd told on him earlier it might have been stopped.

'Well we went up to the woods one time by ourselves. We met some soldiers, three of them. I knew one of them from school, Frank. His name was Dicky Edwards. He'd always been a bit of a bully and we could tell right away they'd been drinking.

Yeugh, the way they looked at us. Well we were frightened, and it turned out we were right to be.'

Jude could hardly bear to listen as Gran continued the story. The girls made to run, but the men caught them. They'd struggled and Gran had been lucky enough to land a kick that made her captor let go and clutch himself in pain. 'Leave her, we've got the gypo,' shouted Dicky, and young Jessie had staggered off in the direction of home, horrified at the thuds and screams behind her. She'd reached home whooping for breath, hardly able to get out her story to her startled mother. Her father was called and the farmer, who both ran up to the woods, then somebody got the message up to the Hall and the police were summoned, but it was all too late for Tamsin. Jessie's mother told her she'd stumbled back to the encampment, bloody and bruised. Mrs Wickham had fetched the doctor to her and a search was set up for the lads, who were caught as they got off a train. But when the sun rose next morning, Tamsin and her family had gone and for many years no gypsies came to Starbrough Woods.

'And when she didn't come back I took her necklace,' Gran muttered. 'I knew where she kept it and I took it. Jude, do you have it, dear?'

Jude took the box from her handbag and gave it to Gran, who opened it.

'Frank,' she said, 'this was your ma's. I don't know where she got it from, but when she vanished I left it in the hidey-hole in the tower for her, thinking she'd come back. Then when she didn't I took it. I've kept it all these years. I'm sorry.'

What Frank made of this confusing account, Jude couldn't guess, but he took the box from Jessie and looked down at the lovely necklace, complete with the seventh star, which the museum had returned to Jude and the jeweller had, as a temporary measure, quickly cleaned and fitted back into its place. There was an expression of uncertainty and wonder in his face. 'Is it real?' he asked.

'It most certainly is,' said Jude, smiling at Gran's indignant expression. 'They think it's from 1760, or about then. That's what the jeweller said.'

'What would I do with it?'

'It's a kind of family heirloom. I suppose you keep it and pass it down the family.'

'There's just Jon.' Frank looked down at the necklace, then put it down on the table and passed a hand across his face. 'All this,' he said. 'I can't take it in. It's horrifying . . . what happened to my ma, I mean. Dreadful. No wonder Da never said much about it.'

'I suppose it might have been seen as shameful back then.'

'I don't know,' Frank said, 'I don't know. I expect he was wanting to protect her. He did that well.'

He sat sunk in thought for some time, then Gran said, 'I could never forgive myself, you see. I should have told on Dicky before. And then I ran away and left her.'

'What could you have done, Gran? Maybe the same thing would have happened to you.'

'That's what I told myself, but I still feel dreadful about it, dreadful.'

While they were speaking, Euan came over from his watch by the window and sat with them, turning the pages of the photograph album. When a silence fell, he said, 'Do you know, Frank, I think this caravan of your mother's might be the one in my garden. I said it was a coincidence, but, well, Jude, look at this pattern. Then there's the carving here and a chip out of the fretwork just here, can you see?'

'Where did you get your caravan from?' asked Frank.

'It's not mine, only borrowed,' Euan told him. 'My cousin has a farmhouse up near the coast at Sheringham, and he found it in one of the barns. Do you suppose your mother's whole family settled in the end?'

'I don't know,' said Frank, 'though perhaps I could find out. There are websites, I expect.'

'A whole other story,' Jude said, and Euan smiled, clearly pleased at the thought.

Robert and Alexia had laid out a big buffet tea in the musty old dining room for the occasion.

'I can't thank you enough for doing all this,' Jude told them. 'It's so important to Gran.' They watched her holding court at one end of the table, Frank and Chantal asking her about her childhood on the estate here. At one point Jude heard her ask Euan how he'd changed the cottage where she'd been brought up.

'It's been very jolly having you all,' Alexia said, reaching to remove her son's leftover pizza from the greedy gaze of one of the dogs. 'I think it's the first proper party we've had, isn't it, Robert? Apart from the twins' birthdays, of course.'

'Yes, I believe it is. And it's most appropriate that it's a celebration of what one might call the Wickham inheritance. Jude, you've done a most marvellous job of uncovering such an interesting episode from our past.'

'There are still a few gaps in the story, but I'm doing my best to try to fill them. Then I'll be able to finish my piece.'

'This is the one for the Beecham's magazine?' Alexia asked vaguely.

'Yes, it should help a great deal to build interest in the sale.'

Jude was going home the following day; she was due in the office on Monday. Over the last couple of days she'd started drafting Bridget's article. She'd finish it over the weekend, she hoped. The challenge was to keep to the word count. It was practically writing itself.

Now she looked round the room. It would be awful to leave this place. There were those loose ends to tie up; she was looking forward to finishing her piece and preparing for the sale, but she'd miss being here, part of life at Starbrough, and Claire and Summer and Gran.

She'd uncovered a wonderful story, about a girl who'd found a father and helped him in his endeavours, who'd discovered something of shattering importance – another planet – only to have everything snatched away from her. Jude believed most earnestly now, after Summer's experiences, that Esther had escaped from the tower, but what had happened to her afterwards was a mystery she had to try to solve. No one knew where Esther had come from – or where she went. Like a comet, there was just the brief bright glimpse of her life in her memoir, only for her to disappear once more into shadow.

She went to speak to Frank, who was now standing on his own, sipping a glass of beer. 'Frank, I hope it's not cheeky of me to ask, but could I borrow that necklace for a short while to take back to London? I need to have it photographed properly, you see, for a piece I'm writing about this house.'

'That should be all right, yes, you take it. It's not my sort of thing really. I only accepted it because it was something of Ma's. What I'd do with the thing I don't know. Jon won't want it, will he? I wish he'd find himself a young lady. About time he started a family, I reckon. Liz and I were married with him running round our feet when I was his age.'

Jude longed to tell him that he did have a grandchild, Summer, and they were watching her now, not running around but looking after the twins, ordering them to finish their drinks and play hide and seek with her.

'Nice little girl, that one,' Frank remarked. 'I remember meeting your sister once with Jon. She's changed a lot, hasn't she?'

'So's your son,' Jude said feelingly.

'It's good when they find what they're meant to do in life,' he said. 'But that little girl . . .' He let his words trail off and Jude wondered if he'd guessed.

As if she'd heard him, Claire appeared at their sides. She said to Frank, 'Gran's so happy that she's met you. I can't believe the difference it's made.'

'She's a very interesting lady, she is,' Frank said. 'We've been having a good old gossip, putting the world to rights. And she's very proud of her granddaughters. You, Claire, she's particularly proud of you, she says, with your shop and such a lovely little girl.'

'Yes, well,' Claire said, colouring slightly, but Frank had said just the right thing for she looked happier and more confident as she said, 'I haven't always been lucky really. But they say it's what you make of what happens to you in life, don't they?'

Jude smiled to herself at hearing Gran's old saying, and moved on, leaving them talking. There was plenty to talk about.

Just at that moment, Alexia walked in holding Jude's handbag, which she had left in the hall. 'I could hear your phone ringing,' she said. 'But I just missed it.'

'Oh,' Jude said, searching for the handset.

She stepped out of the room, read the display with some surprise, pressed a button to return the call and when it answered said, 'Hello, Mum, how are you?'

'Well, fine, dear, but we wondered where everybody is. Your gran isn't home, Claire's phone goes straight onto answer and you left me such an odd message. Is everything all right? Where are you?'

'Norfolk,' she said. 'Don't worry about the message. Panic over. Claire and Gran are with me. How is everything out there?'

'Dear, we're not in Spain any more, we came home. I couldn't cope at all. The heat, water shortages . . . it was simply dreadful. No, we got a flight back this morning. I did email you about meeting us at the airport but you clearly didn't get it.'

'No, I'm afraid not.' Jude couldn't help laughing at her mother's assumption that the world orbited round herself. 'So you're at home now?'

'Just having a cup of tea then we must pop out and buy something for supper.'

'Hold on a moment,' Jude told her. She searched quickly for Alexia and found her in the kitchen and explained. 'I wonder if you'd mind if they came for a short while. Everyone's together, you see, and it's a real opportunity. Douglas's home is only five or six miles north of here.'

'Why not?' Alexia said. 'The more the merrier.' But Jude thought for once she looked just a tiny bit weary, and was sorry. But this was too good a chance to miss.

'Mum,' she said down the phone, 'finish your cup of tea and bring yourself and Doug over. You know where Starbrough Hall is, don't you? You're going to get a bit of a surprise.'

'Starbrough Hall?' her mother said, sounding doubtful, and Jude remembered suddenly what Claire had said once about her mother knowing about the folly. 'I suppose so.' Jude heard her confer briefly with Douglas then say, 'We'll pop in quickly, if you think nobody would mind.'

After tea came the tour of the house. Chantal led a party that included Frank, Jon and Claire, Euan and Summer. Gran said she'd rather stay sitting, and Jude wanted to show her the library. 'If I was young I'd have a good go round,' she told Jude.

'I never saw much but the kitchens before, but once there was a party in the garden and I peeped inside that big living room when no one was looking.'

Later, they all crowded into the library, too. Gran was in the big chair by the fireplace, surveying everyone.

Frank hovered by the orrery, fascinated as Chantal explained how it worked. Claire said she loved the ceiling best, with the personifications of different constellations. Euan pointed out to Summer who they all were and she repeated, 'Gemini, Aquarius, Aries,' to herself like a mantra. Max and his sister ran about or crawled over the furniture, Robert crossly nervous that they'd break something.

'Why are there only six planets, then?' Frank was asking, and Chantal explained that these were all that had been discovered at the time it was constructed. 'This is why Esther is important. It was she and her father who first discovered a seventh, but they themselves never recognized what they had found, and, anyway, it was never made public.'

'Ah,' said Frank.

'Chantal, when it gets darker, perhaps we could try using a light source in it?' Euan put in.

'What a good idea,' she replied.

Jude in the meantime was showing the journal to Claire, then took the memoir out of the cupboard. 'Esther wrote this when she was imprisoned in the tower,' she explained, showing her. 'It's bits out of this that Summer seemed to know.' But Claire regarded it nervously, as though it might convey some horrid curse if she touched it.

'I'm still not sure that can be true,' Claire said, glancing at Summer, who was with Frank, looking at the orrery. 'All I know is that, for the last couple of nights, since she . . . she went missing, she hasn't had any nightmares. I'm crossing my fingers . . .'

So whatever it was might have gone, Jude said to herself. She daren't voice this out loud in case it alarmed Claire. The idea that there might have been . . . well, something. Maybe a psychologist could explain it neatly away. Jude certainly couldn't.

'When's Grandma coming?' asked Summer, not in the slightest bit interested in any of the books and papers Jude had spread around her. It was now an hour and a half since Valerie had phoned.

'I'm sure she'll be here soon,' said Claire. 'They'll have lots to do if they've just got home.'

'Perhaps they've gone shopping first,' Jude said, looking at her watch. 'After all, it's getting a bit late.'

She heard Frank say to Chantal, 'Yes, we ought to be getting along home, let you good people have a quiet evening.'

'Oh, we're enjoying ourselves, aren't we, Robert?' Alexia broke in. 'Do stay a little longer if you can.'

'I think they're here,' cried Summer, running to the window and lifting the blind. 'Yes, Grandma! Grandma!' She banged on the window with her soft little fist, then skipped to the door, where she waited for Alexia to open it. Chantal followed, with Jude and Claire, hurrying out into the hall and down the steps. There a very smart couple were getting out of a polished navy saloon car. Summer hurtled forward.

'Darling,' cried Valerie in her gorgeous husky voice, and opened her arms wide to catch her. 'How pretty you are. Let me look at you. Isn't your hair lovely with those slides like that. Ooh, and I wish I could find shoes like yours. They don't make them for grown-up ladies, darling.'

She turned to the row of smiling women. 'Claire, Judith, darlings, I'm so sorry we're late. And . . .' She embraced them in turn. Douglas, affable and correct, shook hands and kissed cheeks, and Jude introduced them to Chantal and Alexia. Chantal immediately admired Valerie's pretty suit and drew her into the house, Summer hop-skipping ahead. Jude watched them go, noticing, to her surprise, that her mother's high-heeled sandals were dirty with mud. Definitely odd. She went to help Douglas with some bags of gift-wrapped parcels stowed in the boot.

'I'm sorry we're on the late side,' he said gravely. 'I expect Valerie will tell you. We had a little stop on the way.'

'Oh,' said Jude, thinking of the mud, 'nothing wrong, I hope.'

'No, we had enough of that earlier. The airline lost my golf clubs. A damn nuisance and I've filled in endless forms. No, Valerie had a bit of sight-seeing to do. Curious, really. Now if you could take these presents . . . you know Valerie, can't pass a shop.' He lowered the boot lid and said no more about the mysterious diversion, so Jude asked him about Spain as they went inside and he told her briefly about the stressful time they'd had. 'We really should have waited until the villa was finished. I regret taking her there too soon. She really found it quite impossible – hot and confusing – and I don't blame her. I can hardly forgive myself.'

In the library, Valerie, like a scented bird of paradise alighting amidst the dowdy colours of the English country house, moved from kissing her mother to shaking hands with Robert. 'Little darlings,' she murmured, on meeting the twins.

'Mum, this is Frank Thetford,' Jude said, and Frank greeted Valerie with a vigorous handshake. 'My ma was an old friend of your ma's, which is why we're here,' he explained briefly, 'and this is my son.'

To say that Valerie was surprised to set eyes on Jon would be an understatement. The blood drained from her face. Claire had the grace to push forward and bale Jon out. 'Mum, I know you remember him, don't you? We met up again recently. Actually, he's really helped with Summer, and . . .' She clutched, involuntarily, at Jon's arm. Jon gently took her hand and enfolded it in his. Valerie, however, was looking from Jon to Summer and back again, her lipsticked mouth an O of disbelief. Jude saw Frank start to do the same thing. Claire rolled her eyes.

'Does she know?' Valerie said to Claire finally.

'Summer?' Claire said, trying to be nonchalant and merely sounding sulky. 'No.'

'What?' asked Summer, sensing the grown-ups were up to something.

'Nothing, darling. I'll tell you later,' she said sternly.

'Well, I think he's a very nice young man,' contributed Gran, whose hearing aid was working perfectly today.

'Has everyone guessed?' Claire said, glowering.

'I'm afraid we just assumed,' Robert blurted out, blushing. 'The likeness is . . . undoubted.'

'Well,' Frank said, 'I'm delighted, young lady, most delighted.' And he and Claire hugged each other awkwardly.

'What's everyone talking about?' asked Summer crossly, and was furious when people just laughed.

'I promise, darling, that I will tell you later,' Claire said, bending to hug her daughter.

Jude heard Frank say to Gran, 'And now I've a little girl to give that necklace to!'

At that moment Alexia and Chantal entered the room with trays of drinks and plates of food from tea for Valerie and Douglas, and everyone regrouped, chatting. The children decided they'd had enough of boring adult conversation and Alexia left the drinks to take them off to watch DVDs.

'There's someone you haven't met yet, Mum, Douglas,' Jude said, and stepped over to bring Euan into the circle. He'd been waiting quietly in a corner of the room, watching proceedings, but apparently perfectly comfortable.

'I expect you'll have heard of Euan. He's the naturalist and author.'

'Ah, yes, a neighbour of ours went to hear you do that bookshop talk,' Douglas said as Euan shook hands with Valerie and her husband most charmingly, and they chatted for a while about books and Spain, which Euan seemed to know a little about. Now it was Jude's turn to roll her eyes, because Valerie beheld him with great interest, and asked him at one point how long he'd known Jude.

'Mum,' she said, trying to broaden out the conversation, 'you'll be amazed but Euan lives in the house where Gran was brought up.'

'Gamekeeper's Cottage? Why, we passed that just now, didn't we, Doug? And I wanted to stop and look because Claire had said it was being done up, but Doug said we ought to get on.'

'We'd already stopped once, Val.'

'Where did you stop, Mum?' Jude leaped in to ask.

Valerie glanced at Claire as she said, 'I wanted to see the folly.'

'I didn't realize you knew the folly,' Chantal said, coming over with a tray of kir and snacks.

'Oh I know it all right,' Valerie said. She met Chantal's eye with raised eyebrows and Chantal looked puzzled.

'I did tell her we were probably trespassing, didn't I, old girl?' Doug put in gently, as he passed drinks round.

'It is not our land you were trespassing on,' Chantal said. 'I'm sad to say it belongs to someone else now.'

Claire chipped in, 'Why the change of heart, Mum? You didn't want to go there last time.'

'I didn't have the courage. But ever since, I've been thinking about it, and when we came past just now, I got this funny feeling that we had to stop and see where it happened.'

'Where what happened, Mum?' asked Jude.

'It was you, wasn't it?' Chantal said in a low voice, clutching the empty tray. 'You were at the inquest. I didn't recognize you till now.'

Valerie looked about the room. Gran was petting Miffy. Euan, Frank, Jon and Robert had gone to stroll round the grounds. She twisted her glass nervously. 'I never told Claire and Jude about it,' she said. 'It was too awful.' She took a large sip of her kir and gazed distractedly round the room.

'Mum?' Jude said, seeing tears in her eyes.

'Sorry, dear, I'm a little tired. It's been a long day.'

'Perhaps we should be going,' Douglas said, looking with concern from Valerie's anxious face to Chantal's pale one.

Claire broke in crossly, 'No, Douglas. Mum, you can't say that something awful happened, then go off without telling us what. Do you think we're going to get a wink of sleep all night wondering what it is? Well, we're not. You're so selfish.'

Douglas opened his mouth, then closed it again when Valerie said petulantly, 'Oh I suppose you're right. I need to sit down though.'

It occurred to Jude, as they all settled themselves, faithful Doug next to Valerie, that her mother was on some level enjoying all this attention. But she forgot this uncharitable thought as soon as Valerie began her story because she realized instantly that it was part of the bigger story, the one their family had all become caught up in.

'When I was very young,' Valerie said, 'I was a bit wild, wasn't I, Mother?'

'You were certainly that.' Gran had been listening quietly. She knew this story already, Jude guessed, startled.

'But we had so much fun. It happened when I was twenty. One July it was the birthday of someone in our crowd, a boy called Ian. Hayes, I think his other name was. I haven't seen him since. He found the most marvellous place for a party. An old deserted folly, he said, and the really good thing was, the owners were away. And he organized it – music and booze and so on – and I came with this lovely boy I was seeing at the time. I'd got very fond of him in fact. His name was Marty.' She paused, a sad, faraway expression in her eyes.

Marty, Jude remembered. The name on the bench in the village. The boy who died.

'Mum,' Claire said impatiently, 'do go on.'

'After the pubs closed we all drove up in the darkness and it felt like the middle of nowhere, really quite spooky, and we left the cars down this lane and followed a line of lights Ian had laid through the woods. It was a bit mad, us girls in our silly shoes and short skirts and Marty carrying this crate of beer. Ian had got a big bonfire going, and there was this tower thing – really romantic, but, as I said, very spooky, too. So we did all the usual things you do at parties and, of course, a few naughty things went on—'

'The doctor at the inquest said most of you had been smoking cannabis,' Chantal interrupted, her tone clipped and icy.

'Yes, well,' Valerie flicked her wrist dismissively. 'What else did you expect?'

'It was a factor when his family tried to sue us,' Chantal told everyone.

'That whole business wasn't anything to do with me.' Valerie tried to pull the hem of her skirt down over her chubby knees but it wouldn't quite reach.

'Mum,' pleaded Claire, 'do go *on*.'

'I forget how much time passed before Marty suggested we go up the tower. Ian said it was locked, but Marty could never be told anything and someone had a toolkit with them in the car and they got the door open. About half a dozen of us went up – I didn't want to but Marty did, so I went too, and Ian and some others. It was a long way up and we were all a bit squiffy and giggly and the girls kept squealing, then we reached that little room and everyone crowded in. Marty thought it was amazing, but we girls didn't like it and wanted to go down. All I can say is the place didn't feel good, as if we'd disturbed it with all our racket. The other girls and one of the boys went down, but Marty shone his torch about and saw there was a ladder up to a kind of hatch door in the ceiling. Ian held the ladder and up Marty went. He opened the door and hauled himself through and . . . that was the last time I saw him alive.' She stopped, her manicured hand covering her mouth.

Chantal said in a low voice, 'He fell, didn't he? That's what they said. He shouldn't have gone up there, especially the state he was in. He went too close to the edge and lost his balance.'

'He fell,' Valerie said, facing Chantal with a stubborn glare. 'But we don't know why. They wouldn't listen to what Ian said at the inquest. Ian climbed the ladder, too, he said, just in time to see Marty with a surprised expression on his face. He wasn't looking at Ian, but at something Ian himself couldn't see because the trap door was up in the way. Marty stepped backwards and lost his balance and tipped over the parapet. I heard him scream all the way down. Oh I'll never forget that scream. I tried to get up the ladder after them, but Ian was scrambling back down and we could hear a terrible din of people down below so we rushed off down the stairs. Near the bottom I missed my footing and flew through the air. After that I knew nothing till I woke up in hospital the next day, my head covered in bandages and a terrible ache in my insides.'

'It was dreadful, simply dreadful,' Gran said. 'And we hadn't even met this boy. We didn't know about him. Her father was beside himself, but I told him, at least she's all right. Maybe it'll be a lesson to her.'

'But some people said it was our fault,' Chantal said, visibly upset. 'That's what's difficult. Of course, I can understand the family . . . so grief-stricken. But demanding we knock down the folly and pay them reparation. That was unreasonable. Fortunately the judge agreed. My husband was very generous to pay costs.'

'Are you all right, darling?' Douglas was stroking his wife's hand.

Valerie nodded. 'All that was nothing to do with me,' she said, then pressed her lips together. 'And it wouldn't bring Marty back.'

'No, of course not.'

Everyone was quiet for a moment. How sharp emotions were still, nearly forty years after this tragedy. Jude wondered why her mother had never mentioned it before, such a significant event in her life.

'What do you think happened on the top of the tower, Mum?' Claire asked.

'Marty and Ian had certainly been drinking, I can't argue with that – and smoking stuff, too. I didn't like those joint things – they made me feel sick – so I remember everything quite clearly. The room in the tower had an odd atmosphere, I can tell you that. I don't know what to make of Ian's version. Marty could have just lost his balance and fallen. Ian couldn't have pushed him or anything; he hadn't left the ladder. But as to Marty seeing something that surprised or frightened him, I still don't know that I believe that. I felt sorry for Ian, though – the coroner didn't seem interested at all.

'I left home a few months afterwards, moved to London and found a job as a secretary. Soon after that I met your father. I kept all that a secret from him, I'm afraid. I suppose I thought he might be put off me. He was so . . . decent and straight, wasn't he, your dad? After we were married it became harder to bring it up. Especially since . . . Well, it's something I never told anyone except Marty. Your Gran knew, of course, the hospital made sure of that. I was pregnant at the time of the accident. Three months, they said it was. I lost Marty's baby.'

There was a shocked silence after this. Finally Jude muttered, 'Mum, that's awful.'

'Awful,' echoed Claire. Then asked their mother in her direct way, 'Was Marty pleased that you were pregnant?'

'He wasn't,' their mother admitted. 'But he was getting used to the idea. I like to think we might have come through it together.'

Jude glanced at Douglas, but he didn't seem in the least bit piqued by his wife's dreams of a long-ago lover. Of course, he'd have his own stories of romance – even Douglas and his tortoises and his golf clubs. Other men wouldn't be so rational; they would react with automatic jealousy. Lucky Mum. Jude was becoming more and more impressed by her new stepfather.

'That makes me feel funny,' Claire whispered. Perhaps she and Jude wouldn't ever have been born if Marty hadn't died.

She noticed that Gran was beginning to doze off. Chantal tactfully withdrew, murmuring something about feeding the dogs. Only Douglas still listened quietly to Valerie, Claire and Jude untangle the snare of past misunderstandings.

'I was very frightened when I found you were on the way,' Valerie told Claire. 'It brought back all the memories, you see, and I couldn't tell your father, it was too late for that. I was scared of wanting you too much – in case it all went wrong again – and then when you were born, and with your poor leg, well, I got this idea it was my punishment for having gone wrong the previous time and I was so upset. There was so much anxiety for me . . .'

'. . . you forgot there was a little baby that needed cuddling and loving,' Claire said, heavily.

'I suppose that's it,' Valerie said. 'But you were a very irritable little baby. You wouldn't suck, then you got colic. And the teething was simply dreadful. I never knew a child could have so many teeth.' She picked up her handbag and took out a tissue to wipe her eyes. The prim way she sat with the bag on her lap was like one of those brave women in the 1940s films, who, after tragedy and disappointment, permed their hair, put on another layer of lipstick and got on with their lives. Keep up appearances. That was Valerie and she wasn't going to change now. Jude felt a little rush of love for her. Valerie was brave in her own way. 'You have to make the best of things,' she'd always said.

To everyone's surprise, Claire started to laugh. It started off as a bitter laugh, but then it gained pace and volume and became a laugh of relief, and then simply uncontrollable giggles. Jude caught it next, then Valerie. Only Douglas sat, a little bemused, but smiling to show willing.

'Oh dear, I'm sorry,' Claire said, wiping away tears. 'It's not really funny, is it? I'm sure if I hadn't had Summer and didn't know what it all felt like, I'd probably have stormed out of the room in a rage by now.'

'You were always good at storming out,' Valerie said. 'I never knew such a cross child. I had simply no idea what to do with you. Your father was so much better at it all so I left it to him. But look at you now – so beautiful and with a wonderful daughter of your own. I'm so proud of you, I really am. But I can't take any of the credit for it.' And she started laughing again. 'I'm sorry, Douglas, you must think we've gone mad. Jude, darling, I'm so sorry, I don't mean you to feel left out.'

But Jude, who had never doubted her mother's love, merely said, 'I don't. Honestly. But we'd better smarten ourselves up quickly. I can hear the men coming back!'

Summer opened the door and ran into the room. Then came Robert and Frank with the twins, Max carrying a football, then Jon and Euan, in a deep discussion about something that broke off when they saw the women all pink-faced and flustered. Gran woke up with a start.

'Is everything all right?' Euan asked.

'Oh yes,' said Claire, and she started giggling again.

'We'll blame the kir,' Jude said, trying not to follow suit.

Douglas rose to his feet and said, 'You've had a good turn about the grounds, I hope?'

'Oh yes, we've been discussing estate management,' said Robert. 'And playing penalties, of course. No, not in here, Max.' He rescued the football and stowed it in an empty coal scuttle.

'It's getting dark already,' Euan said.

Robert moved to switch on the lamps, but Summer broke in, 'No, Euan promised.'

He looked quizzically at Euan.

'Oh, yes, I did,' said Euan. 'Robert, I wonder if you have a lantern. One with a candle, maybe.'

'Alexia might know,' he said. 'Or my mother.'

He left the room and returned shortly with both women, Alexia carrying a covered candle holder and a box of matches. 'We used this for that wonderful carol singing, remember?' she asked her husband.

Chantal drew the curtains so the room lay in semi-darkness. Euan lit the candle and took it over to the orrery, where he placed it in the centre of the sphere.

'Gather round, everyone,' he said in a melodramatic voice, and they all arranged themselves where they could see. Only Gran stayed in her chair, insisting she could see well enough from where she was.

'This candle is the sun. Stand here, Georgie, you'll see better. Now you can imagine the six planets – this is the orbit for Mercury here, this is Mars, Earth, Venus and Jupiter, Saturn –' he touched each wooden band of the orrery as he spoke – 'all going round the sun. You can see where the light falls on each one, and which part would be in darkness.'

Jude glanced round at everyone's faces, half lit by the flickering candle, all intent on what Euan was showing them. It was wonderful to see this group of people together – her family, gradually sorting themselves out after the revelation of so many secrets.

In a flash she'd been made to see her mother in an entirely different light. Not just as the selfish, rather worldly woman who found mothering a nerve-racking, puzzling business and abrogated responsibility first to one husband and now to another, but a rather more vulnerable figure who had never properly found herself after an early tragedy. Jude remembered how Valerie was brought low after Dad's death, when she and Claire had been forced to mother their own mother. The unexpected bereavement must have split open again the wound made by Marty's death. And the loss of the child, too, would have had long-term effects.

She watched Jon and Frank, who, if Jon's solicitousness of Summer and Claire was anything to go by, were quickly becoming family, too. Then there were her new friends at Starbrough

Hall. It was profoundly sad to her that this orrery and the other instruments and all the books would soon be packed up in boxes and dispatched to her office in London – sad, and yet the Wickhams were pleased with her. She'd done a professional job. She should be pleased with herself: this would be a successful sale for Beecham's – she felt it in her bones. It was no good being sentimental.

And now she peeped up at Euan, his face shadowed and gypsy-like in the candlelight, his eyes glittering midnight blue, with all the charisma of a magician, showing them the wonders of the universe with a flourish as of an invisible cape. She could hardly take her eyes off him, and then he looked back at her and his eyes crinkled in a smile that was like a secret between them. She narrowed her eyes in return and felt a prickle of energy pass through her whole body. Mark's face drifted into her mind, but it was mistier than before; she could hardly remember his features and she let the image float away. But the realization bothered her slightly. She didn't want to make the same mistake with Euan that she had with Caspar. Euan was very special. It wouldn't do to hurt him any more than he'd been hurt already. She was hardly listening to the lecture now, but instead quietly peeled away from the group and went to sit by Gran.

'It's been a very wonderful day,' Jessie told her, patting her hand. 'That boy, Frank's son, he's a good boy, I can see that. Do you think it's wrong to hope . . . for Claire, I mean?'

'Not wrong at all, Gran. But no one has ever been able to tell Claire what to do. Let's hope he can lure her.' Like a moth to a light, or tickling a trout, she thought, thinking they were the sort of metaphors Euan might use.

'And what made your mother come out with all that just now, I don't know. I always thought these things were best forgotten. You should get on with your life. Though . . . well, this business with Tamsin. I feel better about it now, you know. The thought of it was always like a hard knot here, inside me, but now it's easier. Perhaps Valerie will feel the same in time.'

Jude squeezed Gran's hand in agreement. Then she remembered something and said, 'Gran, did you ever have strange dreams when you were little? I mean about running through a forest?'

Gran shook her head. 'No.'

'Has anyone else in our family? I mean, going back in time. Your mother, for instance.'

'She never said anything that I can remember.'

'So I was the first.' Why? Why did Esther's story come out now, two centuries after her death, whenever that had been exactly?

It came to her later that night, as she lay in her bed upstairs, thinking about everything that had happened that momentous day. Tamsin's death. She'd died when Jude must have been five or six, and that's when the dreams had started. It seemed a ridiculous coincidence, but it was a hypothesis to work on. Running through the forest crying for her mother. Tamsin and Jessie had had to run from the soldiers. Summer had been lost, though not, she thought, unduly upset by the fact. Someone, a girl, had been there to protect her, to stop her from being frightened. Everyone assumed it was a real girl, but maybe it wasn't? Esther, Rowan, Tamsin, and other, unknown little girls who'd run through the forest, all shadows. She'd probably never know.

Chapter 35

She woke on Friday morning feeling dismal, all the joy of the previous day evaporating like the morning dew. Today the carrier was coming to take away the books and the instruments. Today she must say goodbye to everyone she loved here and return to London.

Robert was in business-like mode when she arrived downstairs at eight o'clock. Only his irritating tuneless whistle betrayed his nervousness. It wasn't every day he sold off the family heirlooms. Alexia had taken Max and Georgie off to a children's holiday club in the next village. Chantal came down for breakfast at eight-thirty, but went upstairs again with Miffy as soon as she'd eaten.

'She's upset,' Robert said. 'Understandable. I expect she'll keep to her room till the men have gone. I advised her to, anyway. What time d'you think the van will get here?' he asked.

'They thought about ten, but it depends what kind of run they have from London. Don't worry, they'll do all the packing themselves – they're expert at it. All we have to do is show them where everything is. Oh, and do you want them to use the front entrance or the back?'

'The front, I think. If we open both the doors they'll have plenty of room for manoeuvre. You're sure they won't be careless and damage anything?'

'I'm sure,' she said firmly.

The operation, as she might have predicted, went seamlessly, but it was so dreadfully sad to see the orrery and the globe muffled up in packing material, the books being wrapped up and put in boxes.

After the van had gone, she took a last look round the library and could have wept to see the ghostly shapes of the books left in the dust, the scuffs on the marble floor where the orrery had stood. 'I feel like a murderess,' she whispered to Miffy, who had wandered downstairs now the commotion was over. Chantal followed a little later, looking miserable and avoiding going near the library at all. Robert, however, looked more cheerful now that the deed was done. When Alexia returned with the twins at lunchtime, the atmosphere was almost normal.

After lunch it was time for Jude herself to leave for London. Robert took her case down and fitted it into the boot. She slipped her laptop and briefcase alongside, and turned to say goodbye to the Wickham family lined up by the steps.

'I can't thank you enough for having me,' she said, kissing Chantal and Alexia, hugging the twins in turn and shaking Robert's hand. 'I'll be in touch again very shortly, of course. We always like to consult clients on every aspect of the sale, so don't worry about that.'

'And it would be marvellous if you came to stay again soon,' Alexia said. 'You're a very easy guest. And thank you so much for that beautiful picture.'

'That's all right,' Jude said. 'I'd love to come again. Oh I'll miss you all.'

As she drove away she could see them all in her mirror, waving, before the vision grew misty with unshed tears.

When she reached the bottom of the drive she did what she suspected she would do all along. Instead of turning left towards the main road to London, she turned right. She'd just see if Euan was in. She didn't feel they'd said goodbye properly last night.

There was no car in the road, nor in the drive. She stopped the car anyway, walked up the path and rang the front doorbell of the cottage, waited, but no one came. As a last hope, she tramped round the back and into the field. The caravan was all shut up, as it had been when she had stopped the other day, after Summer had been found. Perhaps, now that his house was nearly finished, Euan hadn't slept there at all. She couldn't blame him, not after the trauma of the last week, knowing Summer had been the last to sleep there.

She trudged reluctantly back to the car, feeling disproportionately disappointed. He hadn't been warned she was coming; why had she expected him to be there, waiting in case she came? Perhaps he was still staying with his sister, she remembered.

She drove on rather than turning back, to pretend to the world that she'd meant to come this way all along. When she stopped at a T-junction she leaned against the wheel, dry-eyed but feeling a bit empty. She really had wanted to see Euan. It's all right, he said he'd call you, she told herself. She pulled out her map and plotted another route to the London road.

Chapter 36

'When you've got a minute, Jude, could we get together and talk about your piece? I went through it as soon as I saw it yesterday. It's very good.' Jude had hardly made it through Beecham's reception on Monday when she encountered Bridget on her way to some meeting.

'You are amazing, Bridget. I didn't mean you to look at it at a weekend.'

'I have to be amazing. Not much time left,' she said, patting her baby bump. 'Eleven all right? I'll come to you.' Her mobile started to ring and she fumbled to answer it. 'The photographs of the Hall are fabulous, by the way.'

Walking into Books and Manuscripts, Jude had barely time to greet Suri and Inigo before Klaus swept by. 'Morning, all of you. Jude, how are things? Meeting in my office in ten minutes?'

'OK,' she said, feeling dizzy at all the activity, out of kilter with the fast pace of office life.

'I'll bring you a coffee, if you like.' Suri stood up. She was wearing the lovely silver bangle Jude had posted to her, Jude noticed with pleasure.

'Oh you are wonderful,' She gave her some coins for the machine, and sank into her seat. For a moment the very thought of switching on her computer felt beyond her. Yet she knew from previous experience that by the end of the day she'd be swallowed up in the busy routine once more.

404 *Rachel Hore*

It had been horrible coming back to London on Friday, the car crawling through the London rush-hour traffic. Her little house didn't feel like a haven any more. It smelt musty and some mice had obviously been having a party; there were droppings all over the kitchen.

Most important was a sense of absence. It was Mark's absence. She'd never acknowledged it before, but now she did. He wasn't there any more. He was gone from her life, like a ghost in the house that she'd finally banished. And yet, strangely, she didn't feel lonely. She felt she was herself.

The post was mostly bills – oh, and a postcard from Caspar. It featured a medieval village perched impossibly above a gorge. The message was printed in small neat capitals, as though he were so used to computers he'd forgotten how to write properly.

Really wish you were here. Didn't make it till Thursday in the end. Back on the Saturday. If you change your mind, you know where I'll be. Ciao, C.

She thought about this as she lay in the bath. Caspar seemed a long time ago. She felt not the slightest impulse to change her mind about him. Instead she thought about Euan.

He rang her during the evening, just as she was working on her article, and she was so glad to hear his voice. After chatting for a bit she said, 'You'll think I'm daft, but I called by on my way home.'

'Did you?' he cried. 'What time was that?'

When she told him, he said, 'I'll tell you where I was. Up by the folly. I found out who our phantom gunslinger is. Remember the shots you ran from on that first day I met you?'

'How could I forget? Don't tell me, it's Farrell. The landowner.'

'Wrong. I don't think you'll guess. It's that odd-job man they employ at Starbrough Hall to look after the pheasants. George Fenton. I came across him out near the folly, carrying a rabbit he'd shot.'

'Oh. He was the one who blamed Barney and Liza for the thefts, wasn't he?'

'Yes. I've had a word with Robert. It sounds as though it's a case of gamekeeper turned poacher. Robert says Fenton was briefly employed by Farrell, but a couple of months ago Farrell let him go because of some dispute about money. And so he's resentful. I think he's just been wandering round shooting at things for the hell of it and committing petty vandalism. Robert thinks Fenton might even have fabricated the theft of the pheasants and taken them himself. Anyway, Robert's reported the whole matter to the police.'

'Well that's one thing sorted out. It wasn't fun feeling I was a target.'

'Absolutely not. I just wish the Farrells' plans were as easily dealt with.'

'Mmm.'

'Jude, I'm really sorry I didn't see you again before you went. It was . . . well, last week was pretty confusing, wasn't it?'

'To say the least.'

'I thought we both needed a break. But perhaps you'd like to come down again sometime soon. Shall we fix that? Once we've both got ourselves a bit straighter?'

'That would be lovely, Euan.'

She daydreamed about this on Monday as she waited for her computer to boot up.

'Here you are,' Suri said, making her jump, and she passed her a large cappuccino in a cardboard cup from the café next door. 'You looked like you needed the proper stuff.'

'Oh, Suri,' Jude said, coming to life, 'you are a darling.'

'How was your holiday?' Inigo asked stiffly from the next desk.

'Restoring in all senses,' Jude told him, 'if not exactly a holiday. And interesting. Fascinating, in fact. I'll tell you about Starbrough Hall, if you like. It's been quite an historical detective story.'

'Thanks, I'd like that,' he said, looking gloomy. She felt a rush of pity for him.

'Lunch today?' she asked, before she could think twice. He nodded. Damn. Now she'd have to put up with him moaning about Klaus for an hour. She really must learn not to pity people.

'Right,' Klaus said, showing Jude in before shutting his office door and fitting his gangly body behind the desk. 'The Starbrough sale. Scheduled for the first Tuesday in November, I see. Tell me all.'

Jude met his stern gaze. This was not a gentle chat, she decided. 'Well,' she started, 'we've got a story. I showed you a synopsis for my article, but now there's more and I finished a draft on Saturday.' She told him all about Anthony Wickham, his lost adopted daughter, Esther, about the discovery they had made. She told the story as Esther had written it, not mentioning Summer or her dreams, or any of their family's strange experiences – she didn't think it fair on them all.

'The seventh planet, eh? But Uranus did get found soon after, didn't it? William Herschel spotted it with one of his extraordinary telescopes.'

'Yes, he did, and I'm not trying to denigrate his achievement, but that's not the point. The point is surely that quite often one person in a scientific discovery or breakthrough usually gets the glory. But in many cases they are building on the work of other, less well-known people, or you'll find that there are a number of different people working in the same area, but one is lucky or gets the right hunch or makes the right links, then knows the right people to corroborate it. Like the discovery of penicillin. Alexander Fleming got most of the glory for that, but two colleagues shared the groundwork, and others knew about it before them. That's one thing I want to emphasize. Then there's the fact that Esther was a woman, working against the odds in what was seen then as a man's field of activity, as a man's assistant. And in the end, without him, sadly she was defeated. But that doesn't lessen her heroic role. And lastly, it's this wonderful, romantic story of a father and his adopted daughter, who devoted their lives to stargazing from a tower in a forest.'

'She vanished in the end, you say.'

Jude bit her lip. 'Yes. I wish we knew where she went. Or indeed where she came from originally.'

'I see. Quite a little mystery. So what now? We've announced the date of the sale, of course.'

'Bridget's already been through my article. And the books and the globes should be here somewhere.'

'They're booked in and safely stored next door, yes.'

'I'll continue cataloguing, then. And I've got someone to come and inspect the globes. So we go from there, really.'

'Excellent,' Klaus said.

When she returned to her desk she found an email from Cecelia. It offered some useful comments on her article.

Normal life, it seemed, was resuming.

The rest of the morning she spent dealing with correspondence that had arrived in her absence, catching up on the gossip, and having a long session with Bridget, a ruthless editor, who took her through the article like a dose of salts, pointing out awkward sentences, underlining ambiguities. Bridget left her with a list of queried dates, name spellings and references to check, with a deadline for the end of the week.

Bridget's final point was, 'Your article ends abruptly, you know, leaving the poor girl in the tower like that. Have you looked up local newspaper articles for around the date of Wickham's death? Surely there'd be something else you could discover about the whole matter.' It was a point that had been secretly bothering Jude, but she didn't know what to do about it. She could hardly use her dream as historical evidence. She sighed, called up the article on her screen to start tinkering with the earlier queries, stared at it tiredly and closed the file again. She thought for a bit. Perhaps research would mean another visit to Norfolk. A lovely warm feeling spread through her.

She and Inigo went to a pizzeria that was a favourite with the Beecham's staff, and there, indeed, Inigo did pour out a story of woe. Klaus had marked Inigo's card. Inigo didn't feel there was a future for him in the department. In addition his girlfriend had recently ended their relationship and really he wondered whether he should leave and find a job in academia.

'Oh, Inigo, don't be silly. You're good,' Jude said. 'This is a blip. You'll look back in a year or so and realize that.' Now she was seen to be doing rather well, she felt generous towards him. His job was his life really, whereas she'd come to see over the last few weeks that other things were important to her – her family, friends and maybe even settling down again with some-one. And he was skilled at his job; he'd brought in lots of work for the auction house and his careful, thorough work and his charming – if sometimes oleaginous – way with clients usually paid off. All right, she and Suri did privately laugh at him, and his dress sense *was* a century or so behind the times. But some people liked that old-fashioned dandy image from someone handling precious family heirlooms. Smarmy modern suits could look a little sharkish.

'Anyway,' he said, 'tell me about this Starbrough collection.' She explained all about Anthony and Esther and then, seeing he was genuinely interested in the story, and liking him a bit more now he'd confided in her, she decided to trust him, and she told him a little about Gran and Tamsin and Summer.

'It's as though I was meant to get this assignment,' she told him, and immediately felt a little guilty because she remembered it was Inigo that Robert Wickham had originally asked to speak to when he rang. No, she wouldn't mention that. 'It's given me the opportunity to sort out all manner of things. I'll show you the necklace, if you like, when we get back to the office. It's about to go off and be photographed.'

She'd left the box containing the necklace in the department safe. When they returned to the office she brought it out and, almost as a joke, draped it round her neck. She was wearing a low, round-necked top, and the necklace lay warm and light across her collar bones.

'What do you think?' she asked, turning to show him.

'Oh, it's really pretty,' said Suri. 'It goes with your skin tone.'

Jude was pleased. Summer's skin was like hers, so it would suit her, too.

Inigo's expression was puzzled.

'Is there something wrong?' Jude asked.

'No,' he said. 'I'm thinking. It looks vaguely familiar, that's all, but I can't think why. Can I see it?' He held out his hand and she let it coil down into his narrow palm. He lifted it up to the light, so it sparkled and shone, then returned it to her, shaking his head. 'No,' he said. 'I can't remember.'

She returned it to the safe and forgot about the matter.

Chapter 37

The next couple of days passed busily. The specialist in antique astronomical instruments visited from Oxford and promised a written report by the end of the week. Jude catalogued another batch of books from Starbrough Hall and tried to work on her article. She checked a number of references and sorted out the various queries, but was left with the nagging feeling that she needed to try harder to discover what had happened to Esther. A search for Norfolk newspaper archives on the internet initially suggested she'd need to visit Norwich again, but then she tracked down the most likely title, the *Norwich Mercury*, at the Colindale newspaper archive in north London. Their online catalogue indicated they had copies from the mid 1700s and so she arranged a visit.

On the Thursday afternoon, she took a Northern line train to Edgware, finding the archive to be housed in a high red-brick building that loomed over the line of huddled suburban houses opposite. Upstairs, she was shown the shelf she needed – one of hundreds of rows of shelves bearing great fat leather-bound files of yellowed print. She found the one that contained the *Norwich Mercury* for 1778 and 1779 and took it to a nearby desk.

Each paper was only a few pages long, so looking through it wasn't an onerous job. Starting on the day of Wickham's death, she carefully traced the columns of print announcing aristo-cratic social arrangements, the birthday balls and hunts, a man hanged for murder of his neighbour and the proceedings of the local courts, until she came to a mention of Starbrough Hall. It was the report of an inquest at the village of Starbrough.

An inquest was held yesterday evening in the village by the Coroner for the Hundred of Holt, on the body of Mr Titus Trotwood, who was found that morning dead on top of Starbrough Folly on the estate lands of Starbrough Hall, lately owned by Anthony Wickham Esq. until his death this past week. Mr Trotwood, Mr Wickham's Land Agent, it appeared, had gone missing the night before, his widow, Mrs Jane Trotwood, believing him to have gone to the folly to check a strange light seen there the previous night. Mrs Adolphus Pilkington, the late Mr Wickham's sister, and currently re-siding at the Hall, confirmed that she had despatched him thus, and mentioned that a young woman named Esther Wickham, said by some to be Mr Wickham's adopted daugh-ter, had disappeared, and was believed to be much disturbed in mind by her grief. Because of the recent heavy snowfall the attending physician, Dr Jonathan Brundall, had great trouble in determining the cause of death, but it is thought to be of a head injury, and it is possible that Mr Trotwood slipped and was hence the author of his own death. Esther Wickham's whereabouts remain a mystery, as does how Mr Trotwood became trapped on the roof of the tower, the trap door being closed, though not locked, against his escape. Mr Trotwood was noted for carrying out his duties as Land Agent faithfully and thoroughly. An open verdict was recorded.

Jude sat thinking hard. So Esther had escaped, as she'd dreamed, but Mr Trotwood had died. The Coroner's report questioned whether the two events were linked, and it certainly seemed likely. She was sure Mr Trotwood had denied locking Esther in the folly in the first place, and this sounded believable. Certainly to lock her in and wait three days and nights before visiting her there was a sneaking act that didn't seem to fit with her image of Trotwood, which was as someone direct, a man of action. Surely if he'd wanted Esther dead he would have dispatched her without delay, like he would a rabbit found in a snare or Anthony's poor decrepit greyhound. Why would he want her dead anyway? Unless Alicia had paid him to be rid of her unfortunate obstacle to the ownership of Starbrough Hall. The question remained then: who had locked the door to the folly?

She searched some of the subsequent issues of the *Norwich Mercury*, but nothing else of relevance caught her eye.

While she was waiting for a photocopy of the article, something else occurred to her. Esther had been found as a very small child in July 1765. It had been thought she was about three years old. There were two questions that she had asked herself, but never followed up. First, why did Anthony Wickham not try to find out who this child was and to whom she belonged? In Esther's journal he'd claimed not to want to. Perhaps he'd felt fond of her at first sight. Second, had anyone been searching for a lost child, especially one in rags of silk?

She returned to the shelves and found the volume containing issues for the *Norwich Mercury* for 1765. It would seem sensible to start looking in July – 21 July had been given as her 'birthday', but it was quite possible that Esther had been missed by her family earlier than that. She therefore began reading papers from the middle of June.

She read and read but there was nothing about lost children, and practically nothing about Starbrough and the vicinity that seemed even remotely relevant. A jealous footman had murdered a maid at a country house near the coast. Two small girls had been left orphaned by the death of a wealthy merchant at Great Yarmouth, but they were older, nine and seven. She trawled through all of July, but the only event deemed interesting to the *Norwich Mercury* for the area near Starbrough was the grisly discovery of a woman's body in woodland near Holt. She was some weeks' dead, the physician who attended the inquest testified, and killed by a single shot in the chest that had entered her heart. Her identity was shrouded in mystery, though her hair and clothing suggested she was not of working stock. She still wore a plain gold wedding band, which might indicate robbery not to have been the motive, but the fact that the body had been stripped of any evidence of her identity clearly puzzled the coroner. Jude turned the pages of the next few weeks' papers, hoping for some further mention of this, but there was none. Still, it troubled her. She returned to the office with photocopies of both articles.

It was while she was putting the finishing touches to her magazine article that Inigo, who'd been sitting quietly working at his computer, said, 'I've remembered where I've seen that necklace before.'

Chapter 38

Madingsfield Hall, Lincolnshire, is the seat of the Earls of Madingsfield, a line unbroken since Sir Thomas Madingsfield entertained Elizabeth I with such munificence that she almost bankrupted him. She bestowed in recompense the welcome prize of a peerage and the office of Gentleman Usher to the Royal Court.

Jude was reading the guidebook Inigo had lent her.

'James is the fifteenth Lord M.' Inigo kept turning to brief her as he drove them down to the Hall. He was not a good driver, hunched up on his cushion, too close to the wheel of his tiny black car, zigzagging between other cars down the motorway as though on a dodgem park. 'He was the younger son, actually. Smart bloke. Eton, double first in Modern History at Oxford, the City – Barings in fact, before they went under. Made an absolute killing in the eighties, then, when his elder brother fell off a horse one Boxing Day, he inherited the Hall. The finances were in a terrible mess. Turning it into a tourist attraction and arts festival venue has been the best thing for it.'

Lord Madingsfield was also famed as a collector and a canny dealer in arts and antiques, and, despite Inigo's recent disappointment, continued to be a figure that Beecham's courted, albeit a slippery one. Madingsfield, in turn, needed Beecham's.

So when Inigo rang him and asked if he could bring a colleague up to see some of the paintings for reasons of research, he was affability itself, and suggested an afternoon early the following week.

So here they were, parking in the huge tourist car park, but instead of joining the queue at the kiosk for tickets they walked through one stable yard and then another, round to a door marked 'Private' – the estate offices of Madingsfield. There the receptionist led them down a corridor and up a staircase to the large, elegant reception room that Lord Madingsfield used as his office. Madingsfield, a short, dapper man in a milky brown suit, with a hooked nose and a clever, mobile face, was sitting behind his desk, but when they were shown in he stood immediately to shake their hands. It was a cliché, Jude thought, as she felt the grip of his fingers, but the man really did exude power and a sort of mercurial energy.

She brought out the star necklace and laid it on the desk, then briefly told her story.

He studied it, then looked up at her and gave a very broad smile indeed. 'I think you've just solved a great family mystery,' he said warmly. 'How clever of you to come.'

'Who was she?' Jude asked.

They were standing beneath a painting, a portrait that hung in a chronological line of other family likenesses, in a mahogany-panelled library that stretched the whole width of the house. It was a full-length picture of a young woman in eighteenth-century dress. She was pretty this one, very pretty, with fair flowing hair, a pink and white complexion and huge, soft, emotional brown eyes. Her bodice was low-cut, and round her slender neck she wore a necklace of stars. The very same necklace Jude held in her hand.

' "The Lady with the Star Necklace". Her name was Lucille. Lucille de Fougeres,' Lord Madingsfield said. 'But the family always refer to her as La Fugitive – French for the Bolter. You'll appreciate the joke.'

Inigo smiled politely but Jude stared at her, unable to speak, a great line of connections falling into place in her mind.

'I take it she was French?' Inigo asked.

'*Très française*, I gather. Viscount St John, later the ninth earl, met her on a Grand Tour sometime in the 1750s, I forget the precise date. It was he who commissioned the necklace and made a present of it to her on their betrothal. They married in 1759, but in 1765, a few years after this portrait was painted, she vanished with their two infant daughters. The story went about that she'd had a lover before she married, and the pair were still passionate about each other and eloped. Of course, the family searched for her; though I wonder how hard – the scandal would have been dreadful. But there was never any trace of them found again. When seven years passed the courts declared her dead and St John, now raised to the earldom, married his secret mistress, one Hester Symmonds. Look, here she is, in masquerade dress. Quite the little flirt, I always thought. What a nest of singing birds, they all were.' Lord Madingsfield's expression was rather indulgent of them, Jude thought, but her mind was running free.

How curious. Two infant daughters. Not one. If one of them had indeed been Esther – and if so how did she end up on a muddy road in the middle of Norfolk – what had happened to the other? Had Lucille escaped with her, and where on earth had they gone? Back to France, perhaps. And how had the child who was Esther become lost? Too many unanswered questions. The only thing she could say with certainty was that now they had a strong idea, at least, of whose child Esther might have been.

'Why would Lucille have gone to north Norfolk?' she asked. She remembered suddenly the unidentified dead woman. Who was she? Another piece in the jigsaw maybe.

'On her way to a port, I suppose. Great Yarmouth, perhaps?'

'Would that really have been the most direct route to France?'

'We've no information about who the lover was or where they intended to go. We can't assume it was France; the Low Countries, perhaps. If you're interested, I have copies of one or two letters from that period that I consulted for our catalogue of paintings – people often ask about Lucille; they find her a romantic figure – but I fear there is little in them you'll find relevant.'

'I feel I ought to look at them anyway,' Jude decided, 'to be thorough.'

'And maybe while you're doing that I could show Inigo here something that might just interest him.' An amused smile played about Lord Madingsfield's lips.

'Of course,' Inigo said, perking up suddenly.

Oh Lord, Jude thought, I hope the wily old fox isn't going to wind Inigo up all over again. As they went downstairs she mouthed, 'Watch out,' at Inigo and he signalled his understanding with a nod.

The letters Lord Madingsfield mentioned were in a file of correspondence from the period. Jude sat in the air-conditioned archive room in the basement where the Earl kept any paperwork to do with the estate, though most of the Madingsfield papers were in archives in Cambridge now, he'd explained. She turned the plastic pockets in the file until she came to them. They were both dated 1764 and were from the Countess of Madingsfield, Lucille's mother-in-law, to her son the Viscount, who was clearly in London on business. It took some effort to get used to the handwriting, which was more florid than

Esther's. The first letter was mostly about the old Earl's weakening health, social events and estate business, until the bottom of the second page:

> I have conveyed to Lucille our decision that she may not leave the house on any pretext whatsoever. She received the message quietly and indeed has spent most of the week in her apartments, only walking in the gardens in the afternoons, when the weather allows.

The second letter was dated a month later and made reference to some 'new medication' prescribed for Lucille which 'seems to have beneficial effect. She is calmer and more manageable.'

As though she were a horse, it occurred to Jude, indignant. If there had been correspondence about Lucille's disappearance a year later, it must be lost or in Cambridge, for there were no more letters for the period in the file.

She sat back in her chair, tapping the end of her pen against her lips, thinking. Lucille must have been very unhappy, confined to this huge palace prison, having goodness-knows-what administered to her. There had been no mention of the little daughters. She should ask about a family tree in case it gave their names. She rang the bell on the offices' reception desk, where she and Inigo had come in, and a woman let her into another file room where there was a huge framed chart on the wall. Together they located the ninth earl and his wives, Lucille, and Hester, the mother of sons, but the line of descent from Lucille only said 'two daughters, died in infancy'.

'Oh, they don't even have names,' Jude said, rather shocked to see the assumption that they'd died. It was as though they'd been tidied out of history.

'They were called Amelie and Genevieve,' came the voice of the Earl behind her, making her jump. 'My researcher scoured the parish records and discovered the entries for their baptisms.'

'He must have loved her enough to let her call them by French names,' Jude said. She explained what she'd found in the letters.

'Ah yes,' said the Earl, 'but they were only daughters. I shouldn't think he was much bothered.' Behind him, Inigo gave a neighing laugh.

'I'm going to work on the hypothesis that Esther was Lucille's elder daughter, Amelie,' Jude told Inigo on the way home. 'Three when she was found. But how she ended up lost in the Norfolk countryside, and what happened to Lucille and the other girl, I haven't a clue.'

'What about that dead woman?'

'Inigo, we're getting a bit close to that lorry. Ooh. You mean—?'

'You said you read in the Colindale library about some local murder of an unknown woman.'

'Yes. She was thought to be well-born. But that would be pure conjecture.'

'It could be another good hypothesis to start with.'

'I suppose so. How did you get on with His Lordship?'

She watched a slow smile spread across Inigo's face. 'Old Madingsfield? Eating out of my hand.'

'Inigo, you've got to watch him.'

'I know what you're going to say, Jude,' he said, swerving into the fast lane and sailing past a sports car that must itself be breaking the speed limit, 'but life is full of risk. He has a collection of Elizabethan explorers' maps he wants us to sell and he thinks we'd do better with them than Sotheby's. I think he's quarrelled with his cousin there about something.'

'Klaus will be pleased. Well done. But watch the old fox, Inigo.'

'I intend to,' Inigo said, coasting across two lanes to join the North Circular. 'Like a hawk.'

Any faster round this bend and he'll be on two wheels, Jude thought, closing her eyes.

A text pinged into her phone. She opened her eyes and saw it was from Euan.

'Any chance 2C you this w/e?' it said. 'Found a clue. Also, moth hunt on Friday.'

Happiness bubbled up. She'd ring him as soon as she got home – there was so much to tell him about! To tell everyone!

Chapter 39

It was a perfect night for moths and stars, Jude mused, as she took the road out of Starbrough. This time she drove straight past Starbrough Hall, only glancing up quickly at its graceful lines, her attention really elsewhere. Ahead of her, above the hill, the sinking sun glowed amber in a sky of lambent gold, and when she parked the car in the lay-by outside Gamekeeper's Cottage and got out, she paused for a moment, listening to the forest settle into its evening routines around her, the air light and still and filled with the chattering of birds. Above her head swifts darted and dived and something in her responded, flying with them, exhilarated and free.

'Jude.'

She turned. And there was Euan, hurrying to meet her, real and warm and everything she hoped for. Reaching her side, he hesitated for the briefest of moments and she was nearly undone. There were things between them still, things unsaid. They hugged one another; she caught a delicious scent of soap and new-mown hay, and her skin tingled as his cheek brushed hers. They stood together, studying one another. His face was browner than ever, she saw, and the colour of his eyes made deeper by the soft blue and cream shirt, worn casually over a grey T-shirt and the usual jeans. He said, 'Aren't you coming in?' He hefted her bag out of the boot and she followed him up to the house.

*   *   *

'So this clue you wouldn't tell me about on the phone . . .' she reminded him. She'd told him all about Lucille, but he'd insisted on waiting to tell her his news. They were sitting out on garden chairs by the caravan with glasses of ice-cold wine and Euan was coaxing the barbecue into life. The meadow needed mowing again, she noted, drawing her bare knees up out of the itchy grass.

'Yes. Your grandmother came over on Tuesday,' Euan replied, adding more charcoal to the hungry flames.

'She came here? Really? I got the impression she didn't want to see how the house had changed.'

'I think finding out about Tamsin has made a difference. She wheedled my phone number out of Claire. Asked me if I'd mind fetching her. So I brought her over to tea.'

'That's very good of you.'

'No, not at all. It was rather fascinating. She showed me round my own house, told me how everything had been when she was a child. She's got some great stories, and when I took her home we looked at some more of her photographs from that box we got down from the loft. And she showed me something else, too. This is the clue. Did you ever see your old family Bible?'

'Yes, ages ago, though.' Gran kept it in the cupboard with her phone directories and some old sailing manuals of Grandad's. Its end papers and fly leaves had been used, as was common in many families, to record Bennett deaths and marriages back through the generations.

'It's a fascinating document. We looked through it together. It seems it wasn't only her father who was gamekeeper here, but his father before that. He, your great-great-grandfather, William Bennett, that is, was born in 1870. I don't know what his parents did, or where they lived, but, and this is the really interesting part, two or three generations before him I found a James Bennett who married a doctor's daughter. Hugh Brundall, this doctor was called. You recognize that name, don't you?'

'Brundall was the name of . . . Anthony Wickham's doctor.' Jude's eyes were wide with surprise. 'But he wasn't a Hugh, he was something else. Jonathan, I think. Wait, there was a Hugh. Esther went to the village school with him. Are you saying that he was my ever so many times great-grandfather?'

'I was wondering that. But stay with me, it also gave the name of the girl's mother, Hugh Brundall's wife. It was "Stella".'

Jude looked into Euan's eyes, shocked into silence as she worked it out. 'Stella means star, doesn't it? Like Esther. Oh, Euan. It's got to be only a coincidence.'

'It might be. Or it might not. I went down to Starbrough church on Wednesday, and took a look at the graves. And, indeed, there was a Hugh Brundall there, whose wife, Stella, died in 1815.'

'Of course! I think I saw that, when I walked round the grave-yard,' she said, trying to remember. 'I suppose the surname might have been Brundall, but I remember Stella because I was looking for "Esther". Oh, Euan, do you think that's what happened to her? She married the doctor's son?'

'It could be a complete coincidence, of course, but it might be worth following up. We've no other clues.'

'The parish records might have more information,' she whispered. 'Megan at the museum said they'd probably be in the County Records Office – 1815 is too early for the births, deaths and marriages registry. Goodness, if Esther died in 1815, she'd have been fifty-three, not all that old.'

'That's true. The Starbrough parish records are indeed in the county archive. I checked with one of the churchwardens. You can go tomorrow, can't you? I'll come with you, if you like.'

'Oh Euan, that would be marvellous, thank you. But . . . what you said, that Stella was in our family Bible. It would mean that the Bennetts were her descendants, that Esther was my ancestor.'

'Looks like it, doesn't it?'

Jude was silent for some time, trying to come to terms with that idea. 'And that would mean – oh God – I'd be distantly related to Lord Madingsfield! What a dreadful idea!'

'I thought that would amuse you! Now, the charcoal has heated up nicely. If you wouldn't mind helping me bring out the food, we'll get this show on the road.'

They busied themselves cooking then eating a delicious meal of steaks and sausages and salads, as the world around them sank into twilight and bats began to flit about. Jude didn't say much. She was still thinking about what Euan had discovered. After all this effort, it wasn't a Wickham ancestor she'd discovered in Esther, but her own. She just couldn't believe it.

'Euan, why has all this happened?' she asked. 'The whole story, I'm talking about – the dreams and Esther and Tamsin and . . . everything really. What is it all *for*? What does it mean? It's almost as though we got caught up in some whirlwind.'

He laughed. 'Now why on earth do you expect me to know the answer to that? I'm just a simple man, your honour.'

'Still, if you take the story back and back it goes back to Esther being frightened and lost in the forest.'

'Or before that, to Lucille being taken from her family in France. Maybe you can go back further than that. I don't think there's a simple answer, Jude. You'll go blind thinking about it.'

'I suppose so,' she said, and held out her glass.

'Mmm, simply delicious,' she said finally at nine o'clock, finishing a bowl of raspberries and cream. 'Now what about these moths?'

'You're sure you'd like to? I've got everything ready.'

'Oh yes. I haven't come all this way to miss the moths. Where are we going to hunt them?'

'Up by the folly. It's quite sheltered up there, and I'm trying to keep a regular tally.'

'How many do you think we'll see?' Jude asked, getting up, stretching.

'Oh, hundreds, I should think.'

'Hundreds? Really.' She'd expected him to say a dozen.

'You'll see. Now, I haven't asked you yet – would you mind being note-taker?'

'Your amanuensis?' she said, folding her arms in mock outrage, and he laughed.

'Never. We're equals, you and I,' he said softly.

If it hadn't been getting dark she might have been seen the tender look in his eyes. For now, with the gathering night, their mood was changing. The air felt as thick as treacle between them and they moved like dreamers as they put away the food and prepared to go out.

She helped Euan haul several bulky hold-alls of equipment into the boot of his car and they drove in silence the short distance up the hill, and right along Foxhole Lane to park near the folly. When they got out, it was to breathe air that was fresh and cool under the trees, the scents of earth and foliage strong, but there was no hint of rain.

'It'll be a good flying night,' Euan remarked, handing her the smallest bag to carry, his hand briefly touching hers so she felt again that tingling feeling. 'Are you sure you're all right with that? Moths are fussy – they don't like wet or wind or cold. There's not much of a moon, either, to compete with our light.'

Together, they passed through woods gleaming elegant black and gold in the dying light. When they emerged into the clearing the looming folly surprised Jude anew with its stark strangeness. It was theirs again tonight, the place they'd first met, the place where so many other important events had happened.

'We need to set up here, near the trees,' Euan said, lowering the bags he was carrying. Unzipping one, he lifted out what looked like a heavy car battery. 'Moths don't like it in the open. Here, grab the other end of this.' She helped him spread a white sheet on the ground then watched as he unfolded a large box with no lid, placed it on the sheet and fitted a strip of wood bearing a large light bulb across the top. Then he crouched down and she watched in puzzlement as he spread three or four strips of egg carton against the inside walls of the box.

'And those are for what?' she asked.

'The moths will circle the light for a while, and then they like to hide in the shadows near it but not touching – egg cartons are perfect. Perhaps moths are like people,' he said. 'They're frightened of being burned.'

'I understand,' she said softly.

He smiled up at her. 'I know you do.' Then he said, 'Can you find two sheets of Perspex in that bag there?' She foraged, then passed them to him, and he slotted them onto the box on either side of the bulb, to act as a lid, leaving a gap for the moths to go down into the box.

'This is a mercury vapour light, very very bright. Too much for our eyes to stand. Moths like the blue end of the light spectrum. We don't know for certain why they're attracted to light, but we think it's because they navigate by the moon and stars. Here we go.' When he plugged the flex from the light into the battery and switched it on, the bulb glowed pink, then so blue-white she had to turn away.

'Now all we have to do is hang about and wait for the moths.' He came to stand beside her, lantern in hand. 'Shall we walk a bit? It's lovely in the woods at night.'

It was now starting to get properly dark. Eerie, she thought, in this strange white light, to see the silhouettes of the trees all around. He gave her his hand and it seemed natural to take it.

'Can we go up the tower?' she asked, some instinct compelling her.

'If you like,' he replied, surprised.

They walked up the stairs and into the little room. She hadn't been up here since that day they'd lost Summer. It was back as it had been when she'd first seen it, Euan's papers spread across the small table. It felt tranquil, at peace.

'Can we go up on the roof?' Jude asked.

'Sure,' he said. He climbed the ladder and pushed open the trapdoor, and was there to help her when she followed him. When she was safely up, he switched the lantern off so their eyes could get used to the darkness.

She stood next to him without leaning on him, no longer afraid of being so high, gazing out over the darkening forest. She could just glimpse the upper half of Starbrough Hall, the odd light on here and there. The soft nightlight – that was the children's room, she told herself. The shadow moving at the window, she imagined to be Alexia, tucking the children into bed, or tidying their toys and clothes. Above, a few solitary stars were beginning to burn through the navy sky, between little wisps of cloud.

And all the time she was aware of Euan, waiting quietly beside her. 'I needed to come up here,' she said. 'To find out what it's like now.'

'And what is it like?' She could not see the expression in his eyes, but heard by his tone that the question meant more than the obvious.

'It feels peaceful now. I can't put my finger on it.'

'You've had no more dreams?' he asked lightly.

'No. Claire says Summer hasn't had any either.'

'That's good.' But the mention of Claire was between them.

'You know it was never Claire for me,' he said in a low voice.

'I know that now,' she replied.

'Would she mind if . . .' he said. 'I can't tell . . .'

'Are you asking whether I'm standing back, in case it hurts her feelings? Is that what you mean?'

'You've always been so caring of her feelings.'

She was surprised that he hadn't noticed how her thoughts about Claire had changed in the last couple of weeks. But if you haven't told him, how would he know, you idiot, she berated herself. And, anyway, now there was Jon.

'I thought about what you said. About me pitying her.' So much had happened since that conversation. 'I feel so differently about her now. I don't feel sorry for her any more. You were right. We must each live our own lives, make our own choices. What I feel about things is different to Claire.'

He was silent for a moment. Finally, he said, and his voice had a tender little catch to it, 'And what do you feel about . . . things?'

She reached up and touched his face in the darkness. He stepped forward and now he was holding her close and their faces were a breath apart. And then he drew her to him and his lips moved across her face in little moth kisses and then met her mouth and they both clung together, Jude finding her body fitted snuggly against the contours of his, and they stood pressed together a moment, feeling the beat of one another's hearts. 'Since you ask, I feel . . .' she whispered, 'amazingly happy.' She staggered slightly, as if from a surfeit of happiness, and he steadied her.

'So do I,' he replied, kissing her again. Finally he said, 'Come on. We'd better go down before we swoon and fall over the side.' She giggled.

At the foot of the ladder they stopped to embrace again, then he led her down the stairs, and at the bottom he set down the lantern and in a swift, impulsive movement, lifted her down the last few steps and pressed her against the wall, kissing her again very satisfyingly until she complained of lumpy brick digging into her back.

Then he laughed, and brushed moss from her hair and they went out into the night.

'Look!' he said and she cried out in surprise.

In the bright light on the far side of the clearing, a huge swarm of moths was swirling. 'Come on.' Hand in hand, they hurried over to the trap.

'There are hundreds of them,' she cried, turning all around to see.

'I told you there would be. Now, where's that notebook? Here, hold this, and here's a pencil and a torch, and now we'll have a look.' He knelt down, business-like, amid the swirl of insects and slid out one of the Perspex covers. Dozens of moths had settled on the egg boxes beneath, spreading their beautiful wings like ladies in crinolines.

'Look at that, what on earth's that great thing?' Jude cried, seeing a big furry golden moth.

'That's a drinker. It's named for its thirsty caterpillar,' he told her. 'Go on, write down drinker.'

She did so obediently. 'And this one is a common emerald.' A small bright green moth. She wrote that down, too. 'Two peppered moth, three satin whites.'

'Oh, they're gorgeous,' she breathed. 'I love those best.'

'Another two here. And look at this one coming. An elephant hawk moth.'

'Oh, it's marvellous.' She stared at the large, furry pink and brown creature that whirred around frantically before landing on the Perspex.

He put down one egg carton and picked up another. 'These tiny ones are more primitive. They're known as micro moths, as opposed to the more evolutionarily advanced macro ones. Ah.'

He scrabbled in a bag of plastic specimen pots and, taking one out, neatly potted what Jude took to be a tiny, nondescript insect. 'I'm glad I've seen one of these. A pinella. It proves my point about migration. This little guy must have flown some distance. There aren't any pine trees round here – not till you get near the village.'

'How will it get home?'

'It won't, I'm afraid. Adult moths don't live very long. They breed quite quickly after emerging from their pupas, and then their job is done.'

'All that effort to become moths, just to breed and die? That's awful!'

'Is it?' he said, pretending to study the pine moth. 'Mmm, I rather like the idea.'

She laughed, then broke off. 'Oh look!' It was now jet black beyond the circle of the lamp, and more and more moths were crowding in, dropping on the sheet outside the box, or circling madly above the light. Many plunged into the box and fluttered about before crawling into an egg compartment, ready and waiting to be identified. Euan called out name after name, and Jude scribbled them down, writing the foreign words phonetically if she didn't know how to spell them.

By eleven o'clock she'd written down 56 species. By midnight they had 110.

'That's incredible,' she said, when they'd counted them up.

'And there are different ones at different times of year,' he told her. 'Since I arrived here I've found nearly five hundred species just in these woods.'

'I'd no idea there were so many.'

'There are 2700 species in the UK,' he told her. 'And only sixty-four kinds of butterfly. We are losing one or two to climate change or whatever, but then we get sightings of new ones.'

'Do you log all these results, then?'

'Oh yes. There's quite a moth fan club in the area and we pool our knowledge. Now, I think we've seen enough, don't you? If you've got that lantern ready I'll switch off the light and we'll put everything away.'

She held the lantern and watched him dismantle the trap with deft fingers, shaking out the moths that refused stubbornly to leave egg box or sheet. There were moths in their hair and their clothes and they brushed them off one another, laughing, before gathering everything together, ready to take back to the car.

Overhead, the last shreds of cloud cover were blowing away.

'Look at the stars,' Jude cried. 'Oh, look at the stars!'

They stood together with their arms round each other, gazing at the light show above their heads. 'There are so many tonight.' And there were. Hundreds and hundreds. They felt dizzy just looking.

'Here.' Euan found the sheet they'd used for the moths, shook it out again and spread it out on the ground. They lay on it together, holding hands and staring up at the sky.

'An ocean of stars,' Euan whispered.

'I'm sure they're moving. The whole sky is moving,' Jude cried.

He laughed and squeezed her hand. 'Not the sky, Jude, the earth. The earth is turning.'

'Yes, of course.'

'*Rolling onwards into light*. That's from a hymn, I think.'

'I saw something. What was that?'

'A shooting star. It's the Pleiades. A meteor shower. Oh, there's another.'

And now she was looking for shooting stars, they were everywhere, sudden little trails of light, like sparks from fireworks, that shone briefly then vanished.

'It's an odd feeling, as though they're performing just for us,' she whispered.

'They are,' he said firmly.

They lay in silence, each thinking their own thoughts. And there came into Jude's mind another time where she'd stared up at the stars and felt supreme happiness. It had been after the school dance, with Mark, when he had promised on a star always to be friends. It had been one of the most important moments of her life. And now she had to accept that it was gone. Long gone. Into the past, like Mark had gone into the past. She tried to recapture the happiness she'd felt then, and the two moments, then and now, briefly merged with an intensity that made the tears start. Mark had gone, passed into the care of the Keeper of the Stars, but the stars were still there. And now, now there was Euan close beside her, waiting.

She rolled over to lie in the crook of his arm and soon he began to kiss her again. They loved each other as the earth turned under the ancient stars.

She stayed at Euan's that night, not that they slept much.

In the morning they drove to the Archive Centre in Norwich to find out what had happened to Amelie Madingsfield, who'd become Esther Wickham, and, finally ... there it was on the microfiche. Stella Brundall, née Esther Wickham, who had been buried in Starbrough churchyard on 10 March 1815. There was just the name, nothing further.

'Do you know what I've remembered?' Jude asked Euan later, as they shared supper at the table in the new kitchen. 'That Atlas of the Heavens in the Starbrough collection – you might not remember seeing it, but it's full of the zodiac pictures that inspired the ceiling painting in the Starbrough Hall library.'

'I don't remember, but you told me it was the origin of the painting.'

'There's something I puzzled over.'

'Only one thing? It seems as though we've had to solve a lot of puzzles.'

'We have, haven't we?' She leaned forward and ruffled his hair, and he pulled her to him and kissed her. When she'd recovered her breath she went on. 'Well, this puzzle is a hand-written dedication in the front of the book. It said "AW from SB". I thought the AW was Anthony Wickham. But suppose it was Augustus Wickham – Chantal said that Augustus changed his name to Wickham – and SB was Stella Brundall?'

'What, you mean that they became friends after everything that had happened?'

'I know we can't prove it, it's a whimsy.'

'Castles in the air.'

'A mere folly . . .'

'But it's a good hypothesis.'

That night, as she lay in that enchanted country between waking and sleep, she tried to imagine how it might have happened.

They met again one day, as she always knew they would.

At first after her marriage she kept herself to herself in their cottage in Felbarton, away from prying eyes, but as the years passed and her fear of discovery faded, there were occasions when some errand or a social invitation took her near the Hall. Once she was driven past it in a carriage, leaning forward in her seat to scan the beautiful lines of the building, curiously, as one seeking to rouse feelings long buried by examining the face of an old lover. She hoped for signs of its occupants – Susan shaking a duster from a window maybe, or Sam tending the grass – but in vain. They rolled past and she felt desolate.

Then, one Whitsun, nearly nine and a half years after Anthony's death, returning home after a night with Hugh's father, they passed Starbrough church, and the trap was forced to slow because the service had ended and people were spilling out into the road. Hugh nudged her arm and pointed out a solemn-eyed young lady in a cape of sky blue, dark curls escaping from her bonnet, shepherding two tussling small boys towards a waiting carriage. 'That's Mistress Wickham,' he whispered. And then, emerging from the crowd to join his wife, came Augustus. She knew him at once, though he was no longer the shy skinny boy she remembered but a thin, awkward man with a dazed expression. The trap bowled on and the scene dwindled. But troubled images began once more to haunt her sleep.

Another year passed and there came a glorious summer's afternoon when she walked across the fields with her two little daughters and their nursemaid, Molly, to visit Hugh's married sister at Holt. Where the footpath skirted the woods she saw a man approaching, a man walking with bent head and a dreamy pace, and as he drew closer she saw he was reading a book. They nearly passed without acknowledgement, so deep was he in his text, but then she recognized him. She almost let the moment go, but at the last could not bear to.

'Augustus,' she cried.

He stiffened and looked up, then stopped, staring at her as though she were some chimera, come to life from his book. 'Esther?' he whispered.

'I'm Stella now,' she replied, cursing Molly's curiosity. The little girls, however, deciding him to be of no interest, started prodding a butterfly that lay spread exhausted on the muddy track.

'Stella,' he repeated. 'Still a star.' His smile was feeble.

'Molly,' she said in a bright voice, 'will you walk ahead with the children? Mr Wickham and I are old friends and wish to speak with one another.'

She watched the girls dance away, the elder bearing the dying butterfly aloft on a stick like a captured pennant.

'What happened to you?' Augustus asked, his tone urgent, almost desperate. 'I thought . . . I was afraid you were dead. And that it was all my fault.'

'Your fault? How could that be? We were children, Gussie. We were powerless. Your mother—'

'You know my mother is dead?'

'No, I'm . . .' But no, she couldn't say she was sorry, not when she felt such a rush of relief. 'When?'

'Three, no four summers ago. Of a disease of the throat. In her last few weeks she could not speak.'

That must have been wonderful, Esther thought, but of course did not say. 'And your father?'

'Still lives, but he does not leave Lincolnshire. Esther . . . Stella . . . Why Stella, for God's sake?'

'I had to change my name. I did not kill Trotwood, Augustus, but Dr Brundall advised caution. I married his son, Hugh. We live very quietly. I wish to cause no trouble to anyone. Least of all to you and your family.'

He cried, 'Yet, though unwitting, you have caused me trouble enough for a whole lifetime.'

'How so?' she cried in horror, then, remembering those terrible events of ten years before, she was filled with cold anger. It was she who had endured trouble. Homeless, an outlaw, she had wandered with the gypsies for many months, frequently hungry, always shivering with cold, often ill with exhaustion. She gave them the necklace in payment for sheltering her – such a pity she'd lost one of the charms – so then she had nothing. And she saw a mystery: Rowan was not one of them at all, they'd disguised her as Romany by painting her hair. Whether she'd been a foundling like herself, or a changeling stolen from some rich family's ancestral cradle, they did not tell and she knew it was no good to ask.

Finally, after her pleadings, they delivered Esther to the door of the only person in the world she thought would help her: Jonathan Brundall. And he had looked after her for the sake of his old friend Anthony, and been generous when Hugh fell in love with her, when many another father might have forbidden the union. Hugh, after years of study, established a practice in a neighbouring parish and it was there that eventually they were quietly married.

'How have *I* caused *you* trouble, Gussie?' she asked again, her voice low, passionate. 'It was *you* who took my inheritance, *your* family who made me homeless, nameless. If I caused you trouble, it must have been by my very existence, and I can hardly apologize for that.'

He could not meet her eye. She was right when she blamed the influence of his mother. It was greater than Esther ever knew and the shame would always be with him.

It pleased him, now that he'd found her, that they should meet again. An invitation arrived to dine at the Hall and Hugh judged it wise that they accept. After dinner, Augustus took her to her father's library and made it known she might visit it as often as she wished. And sometimes she did. He'd kept it exactly as she remembered and it comforted her to sit there and think of her father. There was no other place she could do that. Augustus sometimes went to view the stars, but never again, all her life long, would she agree to visit the folly. To her it had become a place of violence and terror.

However, as a peace offering and in memory of her father she gave Augustus a book for the library, a new printing of the *Atlas Coelestis*, which delighted him, but he never found the courage to tell her his secret . . . the secret of what nearly cost Esther her life. Instead, after her death of influenza, he commissioned the wonderful painted ceiling, the library's crowning glory. And among her papers Hugh found a thick envelope addressed: 'To be stored in the Library at Starbrough Hall'. He opened it and read, 'An Account of Esther Wickham'. He took it to Augustus in person. And after he read it, Augustus, shaken, confessed to Hugh what he had done.

Through the half-open door, Augustus had glimpsed her stuff Bellingham's letter into the writing desk and was intrigued. Later in the day he found it there and read it, not understanding more of its contents than that his rival for the prize of Starbrough Hall was plotting something secret, something that could upset his mother's plans.

All the rest of that day he watched Esther, saw her secret preparations, and when she crept out to visit the folly that night he followed her. Once she disappeared up the stairs of the tower with the last bit of telescope, and the trolley stood empty, it was as though he heard his mother's voice in his ear: '*You know what to do, boy.*'

The question was whether to leave the little cart outside, where it might alert anyone passing, or whether to risk her hearing it and apprehending him in his mission. If he were quick, he decided . . . He rolled the cart inside the tower, slammed and locked the door, then darted back into the cover of the trees.

For two nights, afraid of what he'd done, he kept his deed a secret. Matters were overtaking him. Esther's disappearance was interpreted as running away, an admission of defeat, and Alicia announced it as such to the household. Lawyers visited, new documents were drawn up, argued over, signed. The dispute would drag on, with Anthony's lawyer dogged in his loyalty, but Esther's vanishment sapped energy from his case.

On the third night, a light was seen in the folly and finally he broke down and confessed to his mother what he had done. At first she was startled. Who would have thought that her weak sap of an infant could have taken such a decisive action? But then a look of cunning came over her face and he was struck by cold dread. When Alicia summoned Mr Trotwood and gave him his mission, Gussie took to his room. He'd never in his worst nightmares believed that his action would have such dreadful consequences. And, though relieved that she'd escaped, he was haunted by his deed all his life until that afternoon on the footpath when he set eyes on Esther once more.

Chapter 40

It was the week before Easter, the time when Lord Madingsfield always threw open the doors of his stately home for the start of the summer season. Every year he would mount a different exhibition from his archives and collections, one that showcased some aspect of the history of the house and the family. The thirteenth earl, an Arctic explorer, had inspired the previous year's 'White-Out' exhibition. The year before that had seen a celebration of the tenth earl's contribution to the eighteenth-century Agricultural Revolution. And this year, 2009, the International Year of Astronomy, offered the perfect occasion to tell the story of Esther Wickham, the lost daughter of Lucille, 'The Lady with the Star Necklace'.

It was this portrait that Jude saw first as she walked into the lovely panelled morning room for the private preview of the exhibition. Smiling and beautiful, offering no hint of the troubles shortly to beset her, Lucille looked down on the proceedings from her new home over the carved wooden fireplace.

'Euan, this is Lucille,' Jude said, and turned to see where he'd gone. Ah, he'd spotted Cecelia, and was bringing her over.

'I didn't see you arrive,' said Cecelia, kissing Jude. 'Hey, what a gorgeous dress! Come on, I'll show you both round before the crowds get here. And then there's champagne and canapés.'

'There's so much that's familiar, of course,' Jude said, glancing round again and noticing the orrery and Anthony Wickham's big telescope. She had assisted Cecelia in the early stages of preparation for the exhibition, but it was wonderful to see it in its final form. 'Oh, and there's Anthony's portrait from Starbrough Hall. It's such a shame there's no picture of Esther.'

'There's plenty about her, though. Why don't we start at the beginning?' Cecelia said, guiding Jude over to the first exhibit. Jude was transfixed. It was the necklace, cleaned and mended, lying on green velvet in an alarmed case, the diamonds sparkling like tiny fires in the light from the chandeliers. 'It looks . . . extraordinary,' she breathed.

'As fresh as when it was created, I imagine,' Euan agreed. 'I somehow can't believe that Summer will be allowed to keep it in her bedroom!'

'Still, it's a fabulous heirloom to have,' Cecelia said. 'Now, you start here and follow the exhibition round. You've seen some of it already, I know.'

'Well I haven't,' said Euan, his eyes crinkling into a smile. 'And don't rush me. I want to make sure I read everything properly.'

Cecelia and Jude smiled fondly at one another. The exhibition had been Lord Madingsfield's idea. Ever since November, when he'd appeared at the auction of the Starbrough collection and bought up so many of the lots, he'd pursued various different ideas with his trademark energy to make Esther's story known to the public.

His press release soon after the sale had set the tone.

Lord Madingsfield is delighted to announce that he has acquired the prestigious Starbrough collection of books, manuscripts and astronomical instruments. The observation journals and autobiographical material concerning Anthony Wickham and his adoptive daughter, Esther, of Starbrough Hall, Norfolk, offer a solution to a fascinating Madingsfield family mystery as well as representing a magnificent contribution to our knowledge of eighteenth-century astronomical discovery.

The auction itself had attracted a great deal of interest. Jude's article in Beecham's magazine stimulated features in weekly magazines and daily newspapers, and she was invited onto both television and radio to talk about Esther. Despite the unfavourable economic conditions, many collectors turned up to bid on the day. Competition was brisk for some of the items – the rare Sir Isaac Newton volumes, the *Atlas Coelestis*, the orrery – but in most cases Lord Madingsfield won out.

At a drinks reception in the evening after the auction, Jude introduced him to Robert Wickham – the only member of the family who had the heart to come to the sale – and to Cecelia, who bewitched him, and after that, everything had quickly gathered pace. A week later he contacted Cecelia to ask her to curate a very special exhibition at Madingsfield, where all the items he'd bought at the auction would be displayed, and Esther's story told at last.

Making money would always be a motive for Geoffrey Madingsfield, as well as high culture, Jude warned Cecelia. Yet in the case of the Starbrough collection these two interests became entwined with a third, something even more deep-seated and powerful: a passion for the family name. He'd taken a life-long interest in the Madingsfield mystery – what had happened to Lucille, the Lady with the Star Necklace, and her daughters – and the Starbrough collection had offered a solution. This three-fold motivation proved very creative and effective. Not least because Lord Madingsfield quickly established bonds with the current generations of the Wickham family. His visit to Starbrough Hall just before Christmas caused great excitement in the locality. He pronounced himself 'quite fascinated' by the library. With John Farrell's delighted permission, he was driven up to the folly in his classic Bentley to examine the place where Anthony and Esther had viewed the stars; soon afterwards he revealed an infrequently glimpsed generosity, offering Farrell a dazzling sum of money towards the restoration of the folly.

This in turn had an almost magical effect on the Farrell plans. The first outlines for the development of Starbrough Woods had, as predicted by the parish council, been turned down by the planning authorities in September, as were subsequent modified ones. When Farrell finally submitted a much more modest proposal for two eco-friendly holiday cottages on Foxhole Lane, offering to make a virtue of the folly by restoring it with Madingsfield's money and opening it to the public, the council seemed prepared at least to listen. And Robert and Alexia chose this point to announce their own plans to improve their income – to turn over some of the Hall's unused bedrooms for paying guests and for Robert to do what he'd always dreamed: to open his own specialist wine merchant's on the premises. Jude was interested to know what Chantal's place was in all this.

'Robert and Alexia say there will always be a home for me with them,' she told Jude one chilly January afternoon, when Jude called round for tea. They sat in the drawing room, for Chantal could not bear to use the empty library. 'And I would be very happy here, maybe helping Alexia with her work and the children. But first I will be taking what these silly modern magazines call "me time". In May I am going to stay with my late brother's wife near Toulouse and will meet all the family there. In June I visit my old school friend, Audrie, in Paris. Then I have booked a cruise. What do you think of that?'

'A cruise, Chantal, how wonderful! Where are you going?'

'I embark at Nice and we travel all round the Mediterranean, in a modest, elegant ship, not one of these huge ones. There are all these places I meant to visit when William was alive, but William, he only loved Norfolk. So now I am alone I must take my opportunity.'

The new sparkle in her eyes at the exciting thought of the trip, made Jude wonder privately whether Chantal would always be alone. She was so beautiful and graceful, and such a lovely person, it was very likely that she would draw people to her, new friends and, perhaps, suitors.

'That sounds a brilliant idea,' she cried, 'but, well, Euan and I hope you'll be home for our wedding in June.'

'You're getting married! Why am I surprised? Oh Jude!' Her hug told Jude how happy she was and they talked eagerly of how Chantal could fly back from France for the wedding in Starbrough church before joining her ship in July.

Chantal was also mollified by the idea of the exhibition and the restoration of the folly. 'Happy things can come out of sad ones, Jude, we must always remember that.'

She'd been looking forward to the opening of the exhibition today for ages.

'Oh, they're here,' Jude exclaimed now, waving. 'Wow, the whole family's come!'

There was Robert in the doorway, and Chantal following, holding little Georgie's hand. Just behind were Alexia and Max, no, they'd stopped to gather up Max's suitcase of wooden trains, which had spilt open. The grown-ups all greeted one another, shaking hands, kissing and hugging, then Cecelia took Chantal, Georgie and Alexia to see the necklace, leaving Robert

to manage Max and Thomas the Tank Engine and to butter up
Lord Madingsfield, who had just glided into the room beaming
with triumphant pleasure.

Jude and Euan took the chance to walk round by themselves,
starting with the first storyboard. Cecelia's story of Esther, like
all really satisfying stories, began at the beginning, if we can
ever say that there was a beginning, for Lucille, the young,
unhappy French wife, had her own story before she arrived at
Madingsfield, and maybe it was only possible to guess at how
she'd been torn away from family and homeland and, crucially,
from an unknown man who'd won her heart, to make a handsome match to a wealthy English aristocrat.

The storyboard showed a portrait of a sensual, but unsmil-
ing young blade, with a twist of cruelty about his mouth. This
was Lucille's new husband, the Viscount, heir to the Earldom
of Madingsfield, darling of his mother's eye, to whom no one
in life had ever said 'no'. Cecelia had obviously had marvellous fun digging around in the Madingsfield archives and
elsewhere to build up this description of him. But she'd been
scholarly as well and careful to separate evidenced information
from mere suggestion and rumour.

Jude had helped by researching everything to do with the
dead woman found in north Norfolk woodland in 1765 – largely
newspaper reports of the time, for the coroner's papers had not
survived. Although it wasn't possible to say definitively that
the woman had been the runaway Lucille, there were several
details that pointed towards it: her clothes, her physique and
the fact that her skin and hands were fine, that the coroner's
report had described her 'possible foreign appearance'. She'd
been shot at close range, the motive apparently not robbery, for
a gold ring adorned her wedding finger and some coins were
found scattered on the ground. No one knew who she was or

where she'd come from, and though it was posited that she'd borne at least one child, no report mentioned the discovery of two little girls.

One of whom was Esther.

The next storyboard featured a painting of Starbrough Hall and quoted what Esther reported Anthony had told her about finding her in the road as a baby, clutching Lucille's star necklace. There was a certain amount of careful conjecture about what might have happened to the other little girl. Jude saw Euan frown.

'Did Cecelia not think that the gypsy girl might be Esther's sister?' he asked.

'I wondered that. There just isn't enough evidence, Euan.'

'But Summer thinks she was. I suppose we can't use dreams as evidence though.'

Jude shook her head at him fondly. 'Not really.'

The third storyboard described Anthony's stargazing hobby. Two of the observation journals lay open in a case, together with labels offering Jude's transcript. There was a video, too, with a voiceover, taking the viewer up the folly, where Cecelia's team had reconstructed the telescope now on display.

The exhibition then moved on to explain carefully the importance of the Starbrough discoveries. Another video traced the story of Herschel's identification of the seventh planet, Uranus, and in another case could be seen the entries in Esther's handwriting that showed that she had seen it first. One of Josiah Bellingham's letters and its transcription lay next to the journal in the case.

Finally, in another video, Jude knew she would come face to face with herself, dressed in eighteenth-century costume and relating the story of what finally happened to Esther and why she was important. But there was someone already looking at the video. It was Claire!

'Hello, stranger, have you just arrived?' Jude said, coming up and touching her arm.

'Oh, sorry,' Claire said turning round with a smile. 'I was just coming across to say hello and saw this. It's so funny.'

'Funny?' Claire was still capable of saying the wrong thing.

'Oh, not funny ha ha,' she mumbled, seeing Jude's face. 'I meant it's kind of weird . . .'

'I suppose it is.'

'Summer will love it. Here she is now. Summer, come and look at Auntie Jude in fancy dress.'

Jude swung round to see Summer marching in imperiously, little Georgie immediately leaving her mother's side to pad adoringly behind. Then came Jon, his face as open as a spring day, carrying Summer's rucksack, for he'd become her humble page. Jude watched him and Euan shake hands enthusiastically before she found herself in his bear-like embrace.

'Great pile this!' Jon said, meaning the house and grounds of Madingsfield. 'A good place for a rock festival.'

'I think Mozart is more Madingsfield's thing,' Euan said. 'But I agree with you. How you run a place like this as a business, I don't know.' And they went off chatting to look round the exhibition, leaving Claire and Jude and the little girls together.

'Ooh, while I remember,' Claire said, pulling an envelope and a package out of her handbag. 'Happy Birthday two days ago. I forgot to put these in the post. It's been so busy.'

Jude opened the card first. 'Happy Birthday to a real star!' it said on the front.

'Summer chose that,' Claire said, then as Jude started to open the package she continued, 'I hope you like what's in there. I'd have done it before, but I thought you didn't believe in it. I was worried you'd laugh. But now, well, I wanted to do it.'

Jude pulled out the pretty presentation box, all covered in

gold stars, and opened it, her heart flooding with joy. It was a star, her very own star. 'Judith' it was called.

Claire looked surprised at the strength of the hug Jude gave her. 'Are you crying?' she said, disbelieving.

'Oh, I'm just being silly. Thank you, Claire.'

'And me,' Summer said.

'Of course, Summer, and you. How are you, darling?'

'I'm fine, thank you.' She turned to Georgie. 'I'm going to be Auntie Jude's bridesmaid.'

Georgie looked amazed and immediately said, 'I'm going to be her bridesmaid, too.'

Euan was drifting past and heard. Jude shot him an anxious, querying glance and he mouthed, 'Go on!' so she said to Georgie, 'Would you like to be a bridesmaid? Summer will help you.' And Georgie, almost bursting with the news, ran to tell her mother.

'They'll be very sweet together,' Claire said.

'How about Max as page boy?' Euan asked.

'We can but ask him,' Jude replied. The Wickhams had kindly offered the Hall for the reception, so it seemed an obvious thing to include the children in the ceremony.

'So have you worked out where you're going to live?' Claire asked, ever practical.

Jude and Euan, who were looking at Claire's gift, smiled at one another.

'It depends if a job offer works out,' Jude said. The acquaintance at the auction house in Norwich she'd consulted about valuing the necklace, had slipped her the news they were recruiting. She'd applied for the job and the final interview was next week.

'You can't persuade Euan to move to London, then?' Jon asked, his eyes twinkling with humour.

'We would work something out, I'm sure,' Euan said. 'But it would be great for Jude to get this job.'

'It would be a step up. More responsibility,' Jude told Claire.

Beecham's had been an even more difficult place to work over the past months. The Starbrough auction had been a big success, if not at the level her boss, Klaus, had predicted to senior management. But the recession was biting and there had been staff cuts in other departments. In addition, Klaus had put paid to recent speculation by announcing that he wouldn't be retiring at all in the near future. Hence a job like the one she'd applied for was a real opportunity. It was strange how circumstances continued to rearrange themselves to persuade Jude finally to put her little house in Greenwich up for sale and to move towards a new life with Euan. If this new job didn't work out, she had a strange feeling that something else would. And at some point in her life she thought she wanted to turn to research and writing, and that was certainly something she could do in the country.

And now the exhibition room was filling up. Jude waved at Inigo, who was talking animatedly to one of Madingsfield's protégées, an earnest-looking young woman who was hard at work, she knew, on writing a history of Madingsfield, and who seemed to share Inigo's taste in dress. Jude had a sudden wicked thought about their two very similar work suits going together to the dry cleaner's.

'What are you smiling at?' Euan said.

'Oh, nothing, just thinking what a lovely occasion this is.'

'Jude, Euan, come and have a drink,' Lord Madingsfield said, walking over waving his arm like a traffic policeman. 'What do you think of it all?'

'Really fabulous,' Jude replied. 'It's wonderful to think of Esther taking her place in history now.'

'And to find we're all family,' he said, with his slow vulpine smile.

'Oh, the Bennetts are a very minor branch,' Jude replied hastily. It would never do to assume a grand manner with the great Lord M. 'There's only one thing that troubles us,' she told him. 'And that's what happened to Esther's little sister. It's a shame that there's so little evidence.'

'You haven't seen the showcase with the astrological chart, then?'

'No! I lent that to Cecelia some time ago. Where is it?'

'Over here.' He took her over to a display near the end of the exhibition, and there it was, the small piece of parchment that she and Claire had pored over.

'Cecelia showed it to some expert, who says it was cast in the autumn of 1763. Not a significant date for Amelie/Esther, who was born in the spring of 1762, but it was for her little sister Genevieve, born the year after.'

'But how did it get into the hiding place in the folly?'

'That, of course, we cannot say.'

Jude turned and called to Claire, who came across with Summer.

'Claire, look. Lord Madingsfield says this chart I found must belong to Esther's little sister.'

'It's been mended,' Claire said, staring at the document.

'Can I see? Let me see.'

Summer stretched on tiptoe, her breath misting the glass of the case. After a moment she said, 'Oh, that's Rowan's. She hid it in the folly once.'

And the grown-ups all stared at one another, speechless, as a little girl once more stole the show.

Above them all, smiling out across the room, Lucille kept her secrets still.

July 1765

She thought about leaving them behind. They'd be safe, she knew, looked after by a triad of nursemaids, trained up in that narrow way deemed suitable for daughters of an English earl. She was hardly allowed near them as it was. 'In case it tires you, my dear', was always her mother-in-law's excuse, and indeed, on those days they made her take the medicine she saw the world as though from under the sea, wishing only to lie down and sink to the bottom. 'Hysterical', she'd heard the doctor once describe her. 'These foreign women often are. It's in the blood, don't you know.' 'St John should never have married her,' the Countess snarled back. 'A plot by the girl's parents, we knew nothing of it.'

Hysterical.

Lucille felt warm tears surge down her cheeks. What seventeen-year-old would not be 'hysterical' after being ripped from her childhood home and the arms of a handsome young lover and forcibly married to a passing stranger, a man who could blow from hot passion to cold heartlessness in an instant, who dragged her off to a foreign land where the countryside rolled grey and featureless and the damp seeped into her bones? Two children were born of his cruel acts in the bedchamber that could never be called love-making, before his obsession with her beauty turned to indifference and he took a mistress. Then, like a flare of light, came a letter from her dear Guillaume, smuggled in by her little maid, Suzette. He was lately come into his inheritance, it told her. She was to meet him at the White Horse Inn in Great Yarmouth and they'd sail together for freedom.

She would go or she must die.

But she could not leave her daughters. Suzette would help her, fluffy little Suzette. She did.

Carefully they made their preparations. The plainest of clothes, her valuables in a pouch under her cloak, a small valise containing clothes and essentials, a wallet of food and drink. It was a dark night with no moon when they slipped out of the dining-room window, she and Suzette, stumbling across the park, each with a bag and a sleeping child, to a door in the wall and the carriage Guillaume had sent her, driving away into the night.

How did her husband find her? The inn at Lynn, she reckoned, where they stopped to change the horses. The landlord had stared at her curiously and muttered something to his wife. Yes, they'd remember a fine-featured foreign girl with a pert maid, two pretty babies and a wild expression, travelling without escort. And they'd have told Viscount St John where she'd gone, too. There were spies everywhere these days, the revenue men on the look-out for smugglers, the militia hunting down highway robbers. She urged the coachman to take a less known route.

At Fakenham, Suzette simply vanished. Lucille gave her money to buy sleeping draughts for the children, but she never came back. Whether she'd run away or been murdered or kidnapped, it was impossible to tell. All she knew was she must hurry onwards or miss the assignation.

It was on the road south of Holt that St John outrode the carriage, his pistols flashing silver in the twilight. 'Hold you

fast,' he cried. 'You have my wife.' The coachman was terrified,
the horses reared in panic. But while her husband dismounted
and started to force the carriage round, she opened the door
and out she tumbled with her daughters, then dragged them
trembling and wailing towards the trees.

She would not go back to Madingsfield, her prison.

St John let go of the coach horses' bridles and started in hot
pursuit. His mistake.

Taking his chance, the coachman whipped up his team and
the carriage leaped forwards, rattling onwards and empty
towards Yarmouth. Mustn't look back. Not his business. He'd
tell the gentleman his lovebird had changed her mind.

At the fringe of the forest, Lucille caught her dainty foot
in a rabbit hole, turned her ankle and lurched to the ground.
'Run, *mes petites*,' she cried, her eyes misting with pain. 'Hide
yourselves.' She pulled out the pouch containing her jewels – a
premonition, perhaps – and thrust it into Amelie's hand. 'Take
this and run. I'll . . . I'll find you. Now *run*.'

Sobbing but obedient, Amelie seized Genevieve's tiny hand
and they tottered off into the trees. 'Come, Genna, it's hide and
seek,' she soothed Genevieve, as she helped her crawl into a
tunnel in the undergrowth.

They heard the shot but they didn't know what it meant.

They never saw their mother's body, and for that she would
have blessed sweet Mary and all the saints.

They heard the man called Father crashing about shouting their names. But they were too frightened to come out.
When a long, long time had passed, they didn't hear him
any more.

It was getting dark, very dark in the forest. Amelie and
Genevieve rolled up together in their hiding place for comfort
and warmth. By and by they fell asleep.

Amelie woke in the middle of the night, shivering, and cried out, '*Maman!*' But there was no answer. She lay whimpering for a while before drifting back into troubled sleep.

When dawn's cold light began to filter through the trees she woke once more. Needing to pee, she distangled herself from her still-sleeping sister and crawled out onto the path. '*Maman,*' she called. '*Maman!*' She clutched the pouch her mother gave her. Whatever happened she mustn't lose that.

She managed herself as best she could, then walked up the path a bit, calling for her mother. She didn't come, though she'd promised she would, and it was very frightening. Was it this way they'd last seen her? Amelie stumbled on, hopeful, round the next corner and the next, but there was no *Maman*. She saw a bush with bright red berries on it, and she picked one and put it in her mouth. It tasted horrid. She spat it out. But she was very hungry so she took another and another, and swallowed them down.

She heard a cry and remembered Genevieve, so she turned to go back, running along the path looking to left and right for their hiding place, but not finding it, and then the path became two paths and she wasn't sure where to go. Another cry. It must be Genevieve, waking up wet and hungry and alone. She followed the sound but could never catch up with it. Perhaps it was a bird. And she couldn't find that tunnel in the undergrowth where they'd slept. Soon, tired and terrified, her belly aching from the berries, she threw herself down on the path and gave way to hopeless, racking sobs.

The day passed in an endless torment of fitful sleep and cruel awakening. Once, as she lay curled up by the path a fox trotted too close and sniffed at her. It drew back when she screamed. Another time her skin prickled as a snake swished passed, but it vanished under the leaves. Often she called out '*Maman*' or '*Genna*', but as the hours passed and the shafts of sunshine moved slowly across the forest canopy this was uttered as a comforting mantra rather than with any hope of response. By the time the daylight dwindled, '*Maman*' was the only word she could remember and when, half conscious, she staggered down a grassy bank and fell into a muddy lane, that too was forgotten.

As if in a dream come the vibration of thudding hooves, the lively clink of harnesses and a man's cry. Then strong arms sweep her up, the man says, 'What have we here?' and another life begins.

Author's Note

The village of Starbrough, the Hall and its folly are products of my imagination, but they have grown out of the north Norfolk landscape. The area around the lovely Georgian town of Holt in particular has been an inspiration, as has the poor ruined folly at Wickham, near Worsted, whose origins, strangely enough, lie in a tale of two jealous sisters. I have taken a small liberty with the geography and the coaching route in the final scene.

It was while I was developing my story about a stargazer and his adoptive daughter that I read about William Herschel and his sister Caroline in Richard Holmes's marvellous history of eighteenth-century scientific endeavour, *The Age of Wonder*. Herschel discovered Uranus, the seventh planet, in 1781, and I was interested not only by Caroline's huge contribution to her brother's work but in the fact that at least one other astronomer before him had seen the bright object near Gemini but had not known what it might be. Suppose others had, too, and suppose one of those others had been a woman, what is more a woman of no name, whose origins were mysterious. This is Esther's story.

I would like to thank a number of people who helped during the writing of this book, though any mistakes are my own. Dr Hilary Johnson for her suggestions and support, Dave Balcombe, astronomer, for his excellent advice, Jaqi Clayton, who knows all about naming stars, staff at Bonham's auctioneers, particularly Simon Roberts for information about procedure, staff at Sculthorpe Moor Community Reserve for information about moths, Cindy Hurn for visualization techniques. Great thanks are due as ever to my agent, Sheila Crowley, and her colleagues at Curtis Brown, all at Simon & Schuster, UK, but especially Suzanne Baboneau, Libby Yevtushenko, Sue Stephens and Jeff Jamieson, and my copyeditor, Clare Parkinson. Thank you to David, and also to Felix, Benjy and Leo, who, like little Max Wickham, will insist on playing with their football indoors!